D1058357

the night of the tiger

the night of the tiger

by Al Dewlen

New York Toronto London

McGraw-Hill Book Company, Inc.

Published by the McGraw-Hill Book Company, Inc.

Printed in the United States of America

To JEAN . . .

Of whom nothing

written, said, or sung

can be worthy

the night of the tiger

Prologue

AT the far side of Texas, in an almost no-place country joining land which is fertile to the remainder which is desert, the shriveled goating town of Coldiron, Cold County, was built and still is. It amounts to a shabby puckering of exhausted buildings on a tired-out landscape, a place peculiarly trapped and nowise resisting, but rather, compatible with the blood-red soil and the stumpy red hills and the nude black thickets which fence the town in and stir as if to strangle it at each cruel whimsy of the winds.

Whatever man's view of the matter, this stillborn ground was most certainly made by God, and most certainly blessed with His purpose. For, had He not stomped the dust from His feet just here, packing down enough plain for the townsite, and spat just there to create poor little Dirty Creek, and scraped out His fingernails heedlessly, so as to mound up the scattering of raw-flanked hills, would there not have been a Jumping-Off Place to His earth? Mightn't there have been a ghastly tattered edge where the fertile land ends, and a ragged edge where His romantic desert begins, and only a terrible pit, deep as Hell, in between?

In any case, there lies the land, red and blowing, and huddled on it, Coldiron.

The town sizzles and worries away its summers, suffers out the icy gales of winter, blinks sore eyes against the gritty gusts of spring and autumn, and endures. It endures quite well. Hardly anyone actually hears the sing and moan of the wind playing the tight wire fences, and not a fool you could name goes gutting himself in the old-time wars against thistle and mesquite. Not any more.

Take vitality, importance, hope, cordial climate. These Coldiron, Cold County, does without. In lieu of them the town has its tender and violent memory of the Reprisals.

The recollection is one time has tamed. Seventy-some years of telling, of sympathetic hindsight, seem to have chipped away the barbed edges of the fact and shaped the leavings into sort of a legend. Coldiron has come to date many things from that spot in its history. New preachers come and go, oldsters die, dogs are snakebit, or a boy splits through his blue jeans in a time measure of "since the Reprisals."

The date was August 16, 1884. A hot Saturday evening. The Mexicans, who in quiet good grace continue to bake alive in their tin-roofed shacks near Dirty Creek, recall it as *la noche del tigre*—the night of the tiger; as they say, gently, a night of souls sent to final torture, and perhaps of a soul or two snatched back. If the fact were stated, that particular evening didn't produce Coldiron's only glory or its only disgrace. But somehow the happenings of that night and that terrible August laid the stamp of worthiness on a worthless land, so that now this desolate country can never be entirely forsaken.

The legend, if it be that, is sensed quickly by the stranger who loiters on Crowder Street. It is carried by the sand flinging against his face, by the heat that weeps his armpits; its weight seems to be putting yet more sag in the rooftops, as if the story were some great dirty fist holding down a community and a land which, otherwise, might drift skyward and merge with the dust devils and go spinning away.

Such a stranger, upset by such an awareness, was the Federal census taker for 1950.

Mr. Delahay, his name was. An eager, large-nosed young man with two pairs of spectacles, one pair for reading, another for finding his way about. This is important, for without eagerness and well-assisted vision, he might have missed the weed-clogged turn off the highway, might have failed to discover the narrow, wind-eroded side road trailing off west through the brush.

Actually, he might have overlooked Coldiron by seven bumpy miles, as did his predecessor ten years before. But Mr. Delahay was alert, and he arrived. His count was 431.

Not long after the census, a fresh sign went up on an elderly *bois d'arc* post at the one surviving entry into town, and it read: "COLDIRON, TEXAS. SITE OF THE REPRISALS. POPULATION, 500."

The jacked-up figure was painted there by direction of a wool buyer who served also as mayor, and no one objected. As the mayor explained, Coldiron had numerous pregnancies, some confirmed, others suspected, that the young census taker had neglected to investigate, and hardly anyone you could notice had died.

It was true, Mr. Delahay may have finished his work too hurriedly. For during his stay he had unnerved himself, chiefly over his own nonobjective behavior. He found that his tally counted in the battered giant, Julius Rupp, and the beautiful Jessie Rupp, and Brooks Durham. He had counted in, besides, the homeless dark girl, Maria Quintero, and Elwood Coates, and even the wisp named Johnsy Hood. These were the legend people, all of them long dead. But however hard he tried, Mr. Delahay could not cut them from his lists.

Coldiron had dangled bits of its legend before him, then fed it to him piecemeal, and at last had rubbed his nose in it. The young census taker was annoyed, then interested. Finally, he was enchanted.

His first day in town, he found the Christian name of "Reprisal" seventeen times. It belonged to suckling little ones, to unscoured schoolboys nicknamed "Rep," even to a housewife or two, and to many of the very old. He found, affixed to a doorstep which was actually a rotting cottonwood stump, the blind old Mexican named Raol y Reprisal Menavedes, whose birth moment coincided exactly with the last blast and fury of that August night, and he listened to the old man's words.

"At the sight of Julius Rupp, the Tiger, in the street, my mother went running, and peace be her rest, she hung her foot in an idle keg, and she fell, there in the alley next to Tate's, wounding herself tragically—it was a pity. No one had an ear for her cries, not on that night. They say my birth was very quick, in the sand of the alley while Julius Rupp finished his killing around the front. Now mark me, Young One, the first sound upon my ears was surely the sound of the Tiger's gun! Oh, no one believes this is true. Yet it is, I know. You see, I well remember it!"

Mr. Delahay passed this off in his serious, well-bred way, for, at the time, he hadn't encountered the legend's landmarks. But he did encounter them.

There was the old Rusk House hotel, where the sweet-eyed Maria lived and dreamed of a finger ring with green lights deep inside, where also the pretty Johnsy Hood powdered and perfumed and primped himself and almost got rich before he died. There, at the far end of Crowder Street, was the weedy lot where stood the old mansion that first was Miss Gussie Larkin's, the house the beautiful Jessie toothed and nailed to hold on to. Over that way stood the bank where Brooks Durham nearly won his sanctuary; yonder, once, was Tate's barroom, where the lost Elwood Coates sat in his lonely stupors and talked without end to the friend he called the Little Whisky Man. And here, young fellow, about where we stand, is the very spot where the grand and terrible Julius Rupp waited and smoked and mused of two women and of the punishment of his enemies.

The census taker looked where they pointed, sweated powerfully with his listening. His young mind, though green, cautioned him that to include these legend people in his count would be, at the least, a sin against accuracy. Yet to omit them, his soul warned, would buy him a restless memory, as though he himself had done a multiple murder. It never occurred to him that those who look back have neither present nor future, that what is past is damn well gone.

So, Mr. Delahay's report went in.

The current rolls of the United States Bureau of the Census declare Julius and Jessie Rupp, Brooks Durham, Maria Quintero —all of them—to be among the living citizenry of Cold County, Texas. Which gives Coldiron, it seems, an eternal grip on its aging August sadnesses. For, in the face of such official evidence, who will try to rob the town of its cherished splash of blood?

Certainly not I.

Chapter One

INDECENT, that's what the day had been, each hour smoking its way past as if spewed from hell, directly at Texas, with warmest regards. But now, with the sun sagged to rest and its sorriest done, the trail to Coldiron was less of a pain. On either side, the sawed-off clay hills had cooled to a less fiery orange, and their shaggy tops of hissing dry grass had hushed, resembling in their silence only unruly yellow heads of bristling, short-cropped hair. Under the dusty gray light dividing late afternoon from the whelping evening, the hills seemed to snuggle much nearer the packed dual ruts and to watch, almost with friendliness, the man who rode there so slow and alone.

He was a high man and wide, sitting tiredly on a tuckered dun mount of plentiful rib and frothy nose—a coyote dun, people called the kind, with a rise of black hair that marked the ridge and crease of its back. Now and then the animal nuzzled at the dust. The horseman wore a paled-out shirt, once blue, and denims slickened white where they hugged his heavy thighs. His hat, pushed far back now that the sun had about used up its wick, had a flat dirt-caked crown; the sides were scalloped all around by sweat patterns, new and old, and its wide brim stood out board-stiff under its yet greater crust of trail grime. In front of the man the unscarred stock of a new Winchester carbine jutted up from a dried saddle boot, and behind were glutted old saddlebags, riding with a weight clearly remindful to both horse and rider.

The man lifted his head and squinted bloodshot eyes at the sunset. His face was large, the forehead leathery and grooved, part of it hidden by the coarse brown strays from a thick mess of hair, and beginning at the curveless cheeks was wiry proof of a long ride between shaves. If scissored, particularly, the dirty chinpiece might have become the respectable beard of some fashionable eastern lawyer. But this was no easterner, and no lawyer. Julius Rupp, his name was: buffalo hunter and freighter, lately finished; presently a traveler juiced out by the sun, uncertain and impatient, and now that he moved toward her instead of away, pleased to be gut-lonesome for his wife.

He grunted his estimate of the sun and reined the horse and slowly climbed down. He swore deeply at the saddle stiffness of his legs, walked with a scant limp to the dun's right forefoot, had a look at the loose shoe, straightened and spat the grit off his teeth, moved to the trail's edge, spraddled, began to relieve himself. His free hand clawed thoughtfully through the beard. The unhandsome mix of brown and red crackled like small gunfire as its tangles yielded. Then, rested, he walked back to the drowsing animal. He leaned into one of the hollow tan flanks to make a cigaret.

An upstart wind gust, dragging a whirlpool of dust behind it, snatched away the first measure of tobacco. When the flurry passed, he kicked a stunted tumbleweed away from his feet, straightened the paper, and began again. It was, Rupp thought, a dirty country. Sometimes the wind let off of an evening, leaving only the ground heat to worry a man. Other times the wind howled on through the night, scooping up dust, if dust lay anywhere about, and choking you with it. Or, it dealt up sand that cut your hide and made you lock shut your mouth and eyes. It wasn't much of a country to come back to. But he grinned. It wasn't this land that drew him.

He licked the cigaret and lighted it, leaning against the horse more heavily. He looked at the nearest stubby hill and the thin smoke which pillowed up from beyond it and hung together despite the occasional gasps of the coming nightfall wind. He studied the smoke, and the land.

After eleven years gone, you'd think a man might see his home country as though for the first time. Yet this rocky slope in the trail, the flat-roofed hill he faced, were set in his recollection as though he'd gone clumsying barefoot across them only the day before. The hill was small with steep sides, redly naked, and jutted with white rock; its edges seemed to have been trimmed off with an ax and left to bleed. On the yonder side, he recalled with a curious shiver, ran Dirty Creek.

They'd named the staggering little stream in a time long past, when buffalo grazed these breaks and in their filth and stupidity fouled the water even while they drank of it, so that thirsty men and horses had to shy away. But during Rupp's lifetime it had been a good creek, cool to wade and clean to drink from when he was a boy, and sometimes generous with its crawdads and black bass. As always, when Rupp thought back to those days, he had to think on, until somewhere he fitted in Jessie.

It had been on Dirty Creek's sandy apron that, one day of a velvet spring, he picnicked with Jessie Larkin on the surprising good things she brought from her big house: the fat, browned legs off a dominecker chicken, one apiece; golden, tangy cider from a fruit jar, cooled in the water; little black cakes in the shape of triangles, with raisins pressed into the top, and after these, *peloncillos*, those small cones of sugar that Mexicans made and sold, and fine to taste, if very nearly too sweet on the tooth. All were things that Julius had scarcely known. Just as suddenly he scarcely knew Jessie for the solemn way she followed him to explore the plum bushes, the mincy way she waded behind him along the stream, the awkwardness with which she toweled off her feet with her hands, so that without help for it he glimpsed the frailty of her smallclothes, and reddened with it, as he reddened, also, from the new turns and fills of her dress, turns and fills that only the past winter could have put there.

The one greenness of the year was lying soft on the land, that day, and Rupp's boy blood grew oddly rich over her ruffles and ribbons, the smoothed-out quiet of her voice. Once he was shamed at a quick imagination he had, of what a shanky whiteness she must be, underneath.

Oh, he had seen the girl Jessie Larkin, often—plenty of times, floating in, floating out of Coldiron's shops, peeking out between the tasseled curtains of her Aunt Gussie's sway-topped old surrey. Those times he'd told himself, "Now there, by God, there goes a pretty one; call her skinny if you will." But then he'd spoken only as other boys spoke, and he'd not measured her as she was here by the Little Dirty. It had never occurred to him she would have breasts, or even (he was certain of a sudden) a navel, if you got down to it. It upset him that before this he must have thought so pretty a face would grow only at the high end of a stem.

After they had eaten they sat on the sand, speaking little. Then their eyes met and struggled, and he angered. He cocked himself to toss a stone which would splash water on her, opened his mouth to speak his mind about rich town girls who bring triangle cakes to ragged farm boys and eat with them beside a creek so they can call it a picnic, and he did neither. Instead he leaned, meaning wildly to kiss her, but only brushing her red foretop of hair, and then he was up running, hard, back the way he had come. He knew he was leaving his fish line behind, but he sensed he would not come here fishing any more, at least, not with his feet bare. And he understood he wanted to marry Jessie Larkin, and must, if it took all his years.

It nowise did. The ceremony took place on a Sunday in May, in just the next year, and it was a good wedding, all things taken into account. He liked to recall how Jessie's eyes had shown through the veil. And God, he should never have left her.

Now the remembering had wrung the ease out of Rupp's body, and he sucked strong on the stub of his cigaret, and climbed the horse. He pulled the prideless dun head around, kneed hard, moving the animal toward the hill and the smoke.

"We'll not make Coldiron for the night," he told the loose dun ears. "Oughtn't to let Jessie see me all whiskered and smelly, anyhow." The fact of his homecoming after eleven years would deal his wife shock enough.

The horse climbed unwillingly up from the trail, its muly black nose bobbing low, just clearing the spike-bladed soapweed clumps and flushing a sage hen ahead.

Beyond the red hill, Rupp recalled, lay a smear of tough grass, then the flair of sand and flat white rocks rimming the stream. That's where the smoke began and where the camper would be, there on the creek bank. Might happen, Rupp thought, that the man would be free with his food and fire, perhaps owning a sharp razor as well, and content to lend it. He felt his teeth tighten down on the falsity of his thought. It wasn't food or a razor he hunted. He wanted a camp partner on this final night before Coldiron. During these last few homeward days, he had come to dread meeting the moon hours alone.

The nights he'd spent along the trail he'd thought mostly of turning back, of quitting his goal before chancing that it wasn't even there. But then he would remind himself, at odd times aloud, that if his long hard-case years among freighters and oxen and half-breed hide skinners and rotting buffalo carcasses were to end in sense, he must ride on into Coldiron.

He would, in the morning.

New clothes, first off, and a haircut and a tub bath. A big whisky, just one, and something sweet and pleasing to pat on his face. Then, provided his mind hadn't weighed and balanced the matter too thoroughly, he'd hunt up Jessie and cool his blistered eyes on that freak, cloud-gray streak which raced back, fence straight, through the bronze of her hair—or did, at least, the day he fought her and left her.

Abruptly the horse sank under him, stumbling, and Rupp yanked up the dun head. "Damn you, hoss," he grumbled gently, "don't go sticking your feet in them holes."

Many times Rupp had planned his way through the reunion with his wife, trying to calculate it down to the last small word and motion. He mustn't hangdog it, or fritter off time at gawking—at least, none of the critical time at the outset. Instead, he would pass her the burdened saddlebags, being quick about it, and he'd say something like "I made it, Jessie—seventeen thousand cash money, earned honest, and I'm sorry it taken longer than I figured." Seventeen thousand; that was money, and it could testify to a woman for itself, or for the man that had it, for that matter. As she took it, he would grin, and if he grinned big enough, his wife might not notice the button-sized chunk blown out of his right ear, or the little limp he had from the frostbite that got a few of his toes. After that, it would rest with Jessie.

On this he had speculated with fear. He must make sure she understood that seventeen thousand was wealth, that her husband was no common hoe hand on a red-dirt farm. She might then cry out and reach for him, or do some other tender, female thing, and he would hold her. Or she might break all apart, pelting him with the years' bitternesses, if the years had been so, and then he would have to speak softly and very, very right. But since taking the trail, Rupp had thought mostly how Jessie might scream and rail and hie him straight on to the devil.

He licked his broken lips. Well, at least, tomorrow he would know. And if it came off cold? He could not plan that far; to do so, it seemed, was to curse his chances. Yet perhaps a man with seventeen thousand hard cash could buy his forgetting, easy as buying a place for nesting in.

The dun wheezed in a last sore-footed lunge to the hilltop, and halted. Up here he felt more wind, and it spanked his face with glassy sand. Rupp stood in the stirrups, shielding his eyes with his hand, and he gazed down a bald red slope falling off to a matted yellow flat and the bleached gyprock banks of the Dirty. It was somewhere here—yes, over near those willows, that he'd eaten cakes with Jessie. The spot looked less green now, the trees not so tall, the sand less clean, though he knew it could not have changed. Seeing it numbed him, so that he only partly heard the hoofs, barely glimpsed the blue roan and rider scudding over a hummock beyond the creek.

Rupp rubbed the dun's neck, scooping up the lather of the climb and slinging it from his hand. "Guess our man smelt us coming," he said. "Must of thought he was fixing to get trampled by a herd of goats."

He eased back in the saddle, until the sound of the fleeing roan stopped, and he breathed the smell of stout coffee coming up the slope to meet him, as if in a welcome of its own.

"Hello, the camp!" Rupp yelled.

He sat a while longer, waiting a reply. When it didn't come he shrugged and spurred lightly on toward the sand flat and the fire.

It burned, he saw, on the sand a few paces back from the stream, tindered big, too high for reasonable cooking, and fueled with everything handy. Chips, dry sunflower stalks, and he could make out green mesquite cuttings worming at the center, newly put in. A dented coffeepot steamed on raked-out coals at the near edge.

Rupp reined in short of the fire. He hailed again, and watched the brush across the creek. After a moment he said, "Well, hell," and dismounted, though unanswered and unasked. The movement made him careful of the sweat chaffing which smarted his crotch, aware of the dry scrape of his hardened clothes. Briefly he eyed the motion of the stream, its water now black and lazy in the evening dim and the tinge of fireglow, and he smiled at it. Before riding tomorrow, he'd peel and get in there, try to soak out some of the hide-hunter stink that no breeze, here or in Kansas, could air away. He would, if the camper had soap, and didn't mind.

Rupp stepped well away from the horse and rifle. He used both hands to push back his hat, showing it plain he was unarmed. The rider of the roan would be watching from out there someplace, which was the cautious way of this country. The man would be deciding whether to let him stay or to drive him off, maybe pointing a gun while he considered. Rupp listened and moved nearer the fire, until his toe overturned a tin cup in the sand. Slowly he bent to the cup and the piece of gunny sack beside it.

"If you're a mind, I'll help myself to some coffee," he called out. He heard nothing.

He squatted, folded the sack around the handle of the pot, and paused, giving the owner a moment to shout or shoot. Then he poured the cup full. As he turned his head to hack and spit out his throat's dust, he saw the calf.

The animal lay bunched in a three-footed tie, its red leanness almost hidden by a tangle of broken cattails, its upside flank billowing in terror.

Rupp saw the cup wobble itself in his hand. He steadied, and stared at the fire that was no cooking fire. Back of his teeth he cursed himself; this was a branding camp, and the day was August 13, late for branding.

He knew there were cowmen who branded wild cattle the year around, men who maintained their ranch headquarters under their hats. But these fooled little with calves; a calf would follow its mother, and it was the mothers they marked.

A slosh of coffee spilled out on Rupp's thumb, and quickly he swore aloud, making a good friendly show, and he called toward the brush, "Man, this is coffee; fit to drink!" though he'd not tasted it; and through the fast-dropping dark he stared on at the fire, straining, until at the creek side of it he found the iron. It was no more than a cinch ring wired to a green willow rod: a contraption Rupp knew as one kind of running iron, and he felt his body breaking a new sweat, and he steamed in it. Still squatting, he turned his gaze carefully west across the Dirty, toward the rise where the roan had vanished. Now he could imagine a frightened rifle beaded on him, helped well by the fireglow.

In the instant fear had him. He clamped both hands around the hot tin cup, not feeling the sting. He condemned himself. While at play with the old thoughts of Jessie, he had blundered in on a cow thief. And with the man watching out there, he couldn't well stay, nor could he ride out.

Then the fear left him. He blew across the scalding rim of the cup. He was bound and certain to see Jessie tomorrow. Whatever his guilts, it was meant he should make it back.

Through the years it had been the spine of him, if a wavering one, the clung-to belief that he'd have his homecoming and a new chance with Jessie. Even the sourest of his luck could be read as sort of a backwards proof of it. The day his Sharps Big 50 blew up in his face, tearing away only a bit of ear. The screaming Kansas blizzard that caught him on the open shooting grounds, slashing at his life with all its sleety claws, yet howling off beaten with no better trophy than his toes. That stupid, murdering stampede along the Arkansas, set off by a sickly English sportsman with a yellow feather sprung out of his cap, when the buffalo rumbled so close he gagged on their stench, yet he had walked away, stepping around the muddied rags and the strings of blue entrails which marked where John Tom Whitebird, his Pawnee skinner, had lain. And later, at the mourning of old Whitebird in Dodge, on a night bleak with a little grief and much whisky, when the mad-dog Texan, Clay Allison, gunned at him, and missed once and twice misfired.

These things, mounting up one on the other, had given Rupp whatever it was he believed in. He could not name it. Sometimes he wondered if it wasn't the fate business that piano men sang so loud and so often of in saloons, a hundred verses at a time. Whatever it was, wasn't he meant to end out with Jessie, in a clean shared bed?

He let his gaze wander toward the good sound of the water, and he settled lower on his haunches, and was comfortable.

At once he understood that tonight he'd not be troubled by notions of turning back. He had his pile, and come morning, he would again have Jessie.

The voice went off behind him. "If he wiggles," it bellowed, "I'll be blowing his shaggy damned head off, smack into the crick!"

Chapter Two

THE shout went through the early dark like the double load of a shotgun, slamming off Rupp's back and off the sand and rock, spending itself away along the sudden gashing bends of the Little Dirty, hardening Rupp as he was, his seat on his heels, the coffee cup level with his beard.

"Got him cold, by God!" the buckshot voice exploded.

As it echoed, powerfully, Rupp's thighs cramped and his stomach pinched up in emptiness and doubt, and he set his hunter's ears hard on the sound of movement behind him. Two men, or three, he made it, none of them the hidden brand runner he had feared. These, rather, had stalked him up from the trail side, the east, and he swore to his eyes he'd gut and tan out the dun horse for having not so much as sighed to warn him.

Again the big voice fired off, thundering how he should rise and turn and stand almighty easy, else be gunned butt over appetite into the fire for the thieving tramp he was. Rupp thought of the fortune in his saddlebags, his passage money back to Jessie, and of the good new rifle in its boot, now too far away. Then he slacked a little. These men likely weren't thieves, for thief was a hard word, and road agents themselves wouldn't bandy it around.

"Move, you!"

Rupp lowered the fragrant cup. He was pained, almost forlorn, at having not yet drunk from it. He hauled himself up straight and turned. There were three of them, fanned wide, as if to herd him into Dirty Creek.

"You're kind of crossed up," he said.

"Look at him!" the same thunder voice yelled, "He's a stud, ain't he?"

It came from the man in the middle, beginning deep in the squat, hogshead shape of him and rumbling out of a face pocked and wind-burnt, a face ugly for the way it caved in at the last moment around the close green eyes. The eyes, Rupp saw, had smears of brown somehow hard to look at, and an edging of that flame which means hard liquor, used raw and used frequent. The man had a cowman's warped legs gnarled into leather britches that were once soft and yellow but now black and slick with age. His stubby weather-cut hands were in front of him, one holding a revolver hip high, its hammer locked back.

Rupp's belly growled, and he recalled he was hungry. He said, "I was just passing—"

"Oh, hell!"

It spilled hotly, pitched high, from the man at Rupp's left. Rupp looked at him.

First impression, in the firelight, was as of a boy standing uncertainly on small feet now planted bravely apart, a boy extending a tiny nickeled pistol, handled in ivory, holding it eye-level, far and away, like a fevered target shooter on his first trip out. The youth was joltingly handsome, close to womanish, even, with a girly plumpness curving out the fine brown suit and natural kid vest. The face above a flag-red scarf was cubby fresh, blue-eyed, long-lashed, the cheeks a baby-butt white, maybe even powdered, the nose was slim and straight, the lips full. All the parts belonged remarkably to each other. On the dark head sat a cocked-over English derby, clean and hard as a new tin bucket. During Rupp's inspection, the small gun shook.

Rupp turned back to the cowman. "I aimed to say, I rode up not five minutes past. Wanted me a hot-water shave and I—"

"That's a Chester calf you got your piggin' string on," the squat cowman cut him off.

"It's no string of mine."

Rupp watched the green-eyed man advance on him with steps that were a succession of good fortune, since he did not fall, though on any one he might have, and he sensed, then saw, that the pretty man was likewise working in. He grew cold. He stood beside a rustler's fire, and yonder lay a calf, and behind him was the cinch-ring iron. Then he eased; the men could know nothing of his saddlebags.

They came on. Rupp wondered if he might hit for the creek, get across it.

"Whoa up, you two."

The order spoke calmly from the still man, off to Rupp's left, and was at once heeded. Rupp had forgotten this third man. Now he looked at him.

The man showed no weapon. He lounged on one solid post of a leg, seeming cooler and cleaner than was expectable, and his frame spread big in all directions, big the way Rupp judged a man ought to be. He was town-dressed in a stiff, standing collar spun for indoors, flap-pocketed pants, heelless Wellington boots nicely tallowed. The unhatted blond hair looked like dry straw restacking itself in the wind. The square face, Rupp decided, carried some man to it. Something like a storekeeper, maybe, one who'd bought his full share of gristle while getting whatever he had got. One of the kept hands was tricking around with a large gold piece chained to the open vest as a watch fob.

Rupp nodded, feeling better. "If it's a thief you're huntin', you ain't found him. I seen a roan take off."

"Make him shut up, Coates!" the pretty man blurted, excitement a strange heat trembling in his voice.

"Hell yes, shut up!" the drunken cowman said.

The last light had gone, quickly, as if by the death of a candle, and through the pale flush of the fire Rupp scowled to make out the boy's small gun, held lower now, and the soft white finger crooking around the nickeled trigger, and he said nothing. He noticed how the wind had slowed.

"What's that awful stink?" the boy yelped.

"Buffler," the cowman answered.

"What?"

"Buffler, damn it. This one's a hunter. Buffler hunters all stink that way. Smell like old guts all the time."

"Go to hell," Rupp said. "All right if I drink some of that coffee?"

It drew no reply, and Rupp waited, suddenly thinking of tomorrow and the money and Jessie. He could see the big straw-haired man moving away from them, strolling toward the thrashing cow brute, appearing to pick a path that would keep the good Wellingtons safe from the cow piles.

The cowman called after him. "It's a JC cow, ain't it, Brooks?"

"It is."

"Haw, square in the act we got him! I can see the iron from here."

"So?" said the straw-haired man.

"So, hell, what do we do with him, huh?"

Rupp folded his arms; things ought to cool a bit now, for time was passing and they were talking, and mostly when men talked, they came to reason. He watched the shadow of the man called Brooks as it bent over the calf, heard him grunt "ho" as the animal fought, saw the hands picking at the tie rope, heard the shadow say quietly, "There's a Ranger company putting up at Hudlow. Guess you could ride him over there."

"Haw!" the cowman spat. "That's a Chester calf, ain't I right? Me, I'm the goddam foreman, ain't I? I'd reason I got the say-so here."

"You bet, Coates, you call the shots!" the pretty boy cut in. He had edged close, so that Rupp caught the odd garlic-tainted spasms of his breath.

"No harm in coffee," Rupp said. But he did not reach for it. Behind him, at the creek, a bullfrog sounded off, reminding him the day had been long and he was tired. He kept looking at the man Brooks, now straightening up, flicking the freed piggin' string at the panicky calf, shutting off the bawl it began, helping it settle on which direction it would run. He was unrushed, this man. He pounded the dust off his trousers and came toward them.

He said, "Might be there's a say-so for Coates. But there's none for you, Johnsy Boy. You got no stake in this."

"I wasn't saying—"

"Just don't go getting het up, Johnsy."

Rupp sighed. "Smoke," he said, so that his hands poking at his pockets wouldn't call a bullet, and he found the tobacco. In front of him the drunken Coates and the pretty Johnsy had their heads together. The squat man muttered, the boy whispered back.

Starting the cigaret, Rupp frowned at the stiffness of his fingers, and he blamed it on his anger. Once they finished their messing, he thought, he'd tell them what was, and then he would eat and wash and rest, and tomorrow he would buy this Brooks the tallest jug in Coldiron, and if it wouldn't embarrass Jessie, he might sneeze a little hard on the other two.

When he looked up, they were studying him.

"Mister Brooks, I been tryin' to tell. . . ."

"Name's Durham," the straw-haired man corrected sharply. "Brooks Durham."

"Well, I came off the trail—"

Johnsy stopped him, jumping up close, his tight garlic voice rattling, "You, you're one filthy son of a bitch, ain't you!"

Rupp seized at the red-scarfed throat. Then he knew it was wrong; it had been counted on. The boy's fancy pistol glinted as it came, high, hard on Rupp's good ear. He felt the blood explode over his cheek. Next his body was pivoting, pitifully slow, meaning to miss the fire as he fell, and it seemed a hopeless effort, yet he did miss it and was down. He heard Coates's happy bellow, like a drunk shooting the doorknobs off a bawdy house. Behind it was the flat sound of Brooks Durham saying "Johnsy Boy, you make me sick!"

Rupp groaned, turning his body on the burs in the sand. He thought of Jessie, of putting his big cash money in her hand while grasping a warm firm hold of the other. Pain, a wicked heartbeat of it, jarred his head. He was blood mad.

He gasped at coming to his knees. Three feet off, and looking showy despite the tiring light, he saw Johnsy's boots with their spotted hair-on tops. Rupp's breath steadied. He felt proud to the ground, then, of every eighty-pound buffalo greenhide he had ever pitched head-high onto a freight wagon. He put them all into the blow he drove at Johnsy's vest.

The pretty man spewed; Rupp felt him crack and fold.

"I'm damned sick being put on as a thief! A man don't grab some four-dollar calf when he's got money."

Rupp was still pulling to rise from his knees when the boot broke his forehead. He heard the impact, as of an ax biting timber in some low valley where the hills caused a brittle ring to linger on afterwards, and in the last moment, he thought how he'd hate it, Jessie seeing the bruise.

Far off and high, a panther wailed like a woman mourning, and the sound crossed Rupp's mind with the thought that the bounty on cats was ten dollars. Then he remembered. He was lying on his front, aching with a deep cussedness that meant he'd been stomped, and it seemed his flesh was cooking from the fire, as though the coals had been stoked up. Immediate rage tightened his jaw. The skin had a stretchy feel from its scab of sand and spoiled blood. Not to swear out, he swallowed. While his eyes began learning their way in the firelight, he sucked in flint doses of the smoky air. Soon he could see the handsome one, the youth called Johnsy Boy.

The boy was bending beside Dirty Creek, his ladyish turns looking less round. As Rupp watched, Johnsy retched, choked, strangled out an oath, and vomited as gracelessly as any ordinary man. In a moan the boy slumped to his knees and cupped up water from the stream, splashing it over his face.

"Sick, old stud?" boomed Coates's big voice, laughing.

Rupp dizzied and closed his eyes, dueling with the void that reached for him. After a while he heard their voices, the drunken Coates and the straw-haired Mr. Durham, and he held himself still. If they talked enough, the violence would drain out of them. He caught all the words he could, laying each to record in his head. Shortly, he had the names. Johnsy Boy Hood, Elwood Coates, Brooks Durham. Three men somehow wrong together.

As he listened, he realized it was Durham he cursed the most. Durham was the strong one, if unarmed; Rupp had recognized this from the start, the same way he could in an instant point out the lead bull among a thousand buffalo, and be certain he was right without knowing how he'd done it.

Johnsy's body snapped like a whip. He was vomiting dry. Coates's laughter cannoned out, covering the swish of the creek.

Durham's even voice said, "I don't mean to sit here swatting skeeters all night. Let's settle on something."

"Hell, Durham, whyn't you tail it on back to town? Me and Johnsy, we can take care of him, to a fair."

"You're drunk."

"Sure, stud, that sets me at my best, don't it?"

"I expect so. That's why I'm staying."

"Now, Durham, what you mean by that?"

"I mean you aren't hanging that man for stealing one half-starved stray."

Rupp heard a stir as the two men rose, fast. He felt the blood speed through him, flooding away the numbness and leaving the pain, and he warned himself, wait, they're talking. God, let them talk!

Coates's voice tapered down. "Lookee, Durham, ain't any use of us havin' such a howlin' tit-to-tit over this."

"Tête-à-tête," Johnsy called, choking, from the creek.

"Maybe it's more'n one calf," Coates went on. "The JC is missing a heap more, Old Man Chester says so, and I'm his goddam foreman, ain't I? It's two days ride to them Rangers, so we just string him and—"

"No."

The night at once quieted; Rupp could hear their breathing. He glanced again at Johnsy. The boy sat near the water, holding a dripping handkerchief to his brow. Beyond, a horse snorted, and Rupp peered toward the sound. He distinguished four animals, untethered and nosing at sparse clumps around the willows. He made out the old dun by the gaunt hip points, the Winchester stock ramming up from the saddle, and he calculated.

Two, maybe three seconds, he decided; that would get him over there, and in between, he'd have to run down Johnsy Boy. A couple seconds more, provided the dun didn't bolt, and he'd lay his hands on the carbine. Then, by God. . . .

Only, wait. Let them talk.

Coates's tongue slowed, seemingly in its liquor, and now he did not yell. "Durham, you ain't in town, and you ain't the big bossin' muck out here. And you ain't got a gun. That makes your pole a little too short, don't it?"

"Don't bank on it."

"Aw, how come all the hassle? I ketch me a thief, I aim to bring him to his milk. I'm the foreman, and you—"

"I bargained to ride out for poker, Coates. Nothing else. I don't say you ought to turn the man loose. But hear me, damn you. There's a rifle on that dun horse. If you mean to have a hanging, you better kill me before I get to it!"

Talk, talk. Rupp looked at the horses; he must not wait too long. But not yet, just, not until his sight quit dimming in and out. The cold echoes still clattered in his skull; he had thought it Durham who kicked him. Now he wasn't sure, this Durham, Durham, Durham. . . .

Again it was sound he awoke to. Durham's voice, saying, "All right, but it'd be damned savage."

"That ain't savage!" Coates blew off. "Not like Kiowas, or such. Trouble is, you ain't old enough. I mean, you wasn't in the war. Why, hell, it was a regular custom in the army. Man stole something, you caught him and laid a T on him. When that big buffler-stink comes alive, we'll—"

Rupp lunged. Only he didn't come up running. He sprawled on his face, hard, suddenly sick. His wrists had been bound behind him, the thong threaded through his belt, and his ankles were hobbled, and he was got, and he hadn't felt the bonds at all. He held up his head while his big notion hung on a moment more. Then he could not see the horse, and hope died hard. He lay sick.

Coates stood over him. "Well, big stud!"

Rupp recalled how he had stood by once at a man-branding where they'd first tried the iron on a buffalo robe to get the design right, and it amazed him that then, back in that winter hunting camp, he'd thought almost nothing of it.

Hands wrenched him over until his bound fists gouged into his back. Coates stunk of sour clothes and stale whisky as he bent close, stripping Rupp's shirt open to the belt. Rupp tried to sit up. "Listen to me!"

"Johnsy Boy!" Coates shouted. "You, now, you can do the honors! Ain't that what they say, do the honors?"

Rupp twisted his head, staring as the pretty youth came off the grass and ran to the fire. He felt the cords swelling outward on his neck, heard the dry rasp of his own breath.

"What you aim doing?" He choked, and instantly damned himself for the weakness of it. God, he was begging them!

Now Johnsy stood tight beside Coates, hunching a trifle to the fore, one arm cradling his chest. The round baby face had been vomited away, or rinsed or raged away, so that Johnsy was no longer handsome. In his right hand was the running iron, the circle of it a flaky red and quivering a little on the willow stem.

They've talked, talked, and talked, Rupp thought, all evening they've talked. Still they're going to do it!

Coates leaned, spat a spray on the iron, and the metal spat back. Johnsy was stooping and the firelight broke over his face. His eyes bugged white, the dark centers ablaze with an awful happiness, and he was babbling.

". . . bust a man's ribs . . . roll a twenty-dollar suit in cow dung . . . filthy goddammed tramp!"

Rupp's knees jerked up. "God's sakes, that rustler lit out before I got here! I swear it! You, Brooks Durham—"

Coates tromped a boot on Rupp's throat, flattening him to the sand, digging the spur into his shoulder, and Rupp watched the iron drive to his chest.

He heard Durham's voice complain, from far off, "You're scaring off the horses!" and he looked, and he saw the big straw-haired man chasing off after them. Rupp thought of the gun, and the saddlebags, out there and undefended, and he thrashed under the boot, bursting to shout. Then he heard a crackle, smelled the singe. There was a daylight moment before the fire and agony took, and in it waited Jessie, motionless in a dress red as wine, the skirt flared wide, the waist set close with not a wrinkle, her shoulders thin and bare above the red, all as it had been at their wedding party, and that, too, had been on a Wednesday. No, no, the wedding was a Sunday. . . .

The iron was cutting a rut across his chest, dragging like a braked wheel. He knew when it lifted and butted down again. He wondered if he had screamed, or if he would. A long time he fought it. Then he felt his body convulsing.

"My God, that's enough!"

It was Durham's voice. Durham back with a rifle.

"Stop it, damn you! Or I'll kill you both!"

Chapter Three

OLD Dub Stokes, who in truth wasn't Dub Stokes at all, but was August Stokes Weinbergen, who'd had to bob off his name years back, since hardly another man could correctly spell or say it, raised a tough old hand and slid it inside his flannel shirt and rubbed gently at the rheumatism which throbbed there, next to the bone, and which now and then stung him like the bedevilment of a million red ants. The Wednesday evening heat snugged up to his heavy old shape, the way it snugged close to all of Coldiron, now that the wind and sand had stopped, and it called out of him a sweat he couldn't much spare.

For the rheumatism, people said, the summer heat fell as a merciful blessing. It helped a man store up for his winter agonies. But as Old Dub settled himself on the bale of scrubby wild hay neglected just outside the broad doors of his livery barn, he had strong doubt of this. During this summer, the awful squeeze of his shoulders had continued unbroken. A sign, maybe, that he'd not make through the long blizzard months ahead. Offhand, he couldn't vow he very much cared.

Grunting, he scooted back on the hay, so that his back might rest against the stable's tall, board-and-batten wall. He supposed he ought to be up mixing a dose of calomel, or directing that no-good nigger hired man at the evening feeding. But he did not rise. Instead, he pulled out his lower lip, filled the space in front of his teeth with snuff and sat and blinked at the pleasant nip that resulted.

Dub was crowding seventy and giving thought to it. When a man is draining down, with a good sound business on his hands, what he most needs is a son to do his pushing for him. Dub reflected on how he might easy have had such a son, indeed, would have had, except for accident. And what man, wise or foolish, can deal with accident?

He turned his eyes toward Crowder Street, where in one easy sweep he could see most of the town. Coldiron, now. Like so much else in his life, this town was itself only an accident. It hadn't been built, it had happened; nor had it been named, but merely labeled.

The Mexicans, he remembered, had wanted to call the place San Pedro; the whites, who referred to it first as "Dutch Settlement," wanted it named Coldtown, and the Post Office thinkers, while leaning toward the whites, turned it into Coldiron, since already, someplace, there was a Coaltown which might be confused. So Coldiron it became, and they named the main street "Crowder" for an honest mule who died bravely there, and as a sop to the Mexicans, let them call the only cross street "Pedro." Thus there stood here a town that never should have been. A windy, unhappy place dedicated to a saint and a mule.

Oh, Coldiron had risen on land free for the taking, and had Dirty Creek's trustless water to dip from, and game of a sort roamed the red-ribbed breaks where wild plum bushes and mesquite squabbled with each other. But this, back in 1854, would have attracted scarcely anyone.

For one thing, the soil. This shiftless earth moved all the time, and was bloodshot to look at, and mostly scalped of grass by winds eternally slashing like God's own angry cat-o'-nine, besides the white rocks strung about, bedded deep, as if set on purpose to fend off plows. All this, without mention of cold that was the coldest and heat the burning hottest. Coldiron had begun not on promise, but as a refuge. Dub and the others who built it had been chased here.

Sometimes in the evening, when someone stopped to sit with him on the hay, Old Dub took his snuff stick from the groove it had long since made in his lips and explained these points, and proved them. Telling of the old times pleasured him, and it helped wear out the hours before he need climb to his bed in the back corner of the barn loft, a bed still womanless after all these years.

Carefully now, Dub fixed his mouth to spit. He estimated the distance and let go. "Holy damn," he said, and stared down at the brown splash on his shoe. It was one more accident, and he sighed, as, when in a mood, he could sigh over this town.

As he recalled, there had been thirty-nine wagons in that first train of thirty years ago, the people mostly of Pennsylvania German stock, the same as himself, their habits mostly unaffected by a generation's misplacement in Missouri. Ah, how these, the real Germans, had loved their five meals a day, and pink shades for their windows; and this much they expected from the West, whatever else. They had been moving from Missouri's black bog holes, and from the black-skinned men who somehow laid hold of liquor during or after the abolitionist speeches, and from the railroad land greeds as well. Most had an eye out for a likely land for corn; a few wondered, timidly, if much remained of California's gold.

It was a train worthy to look at, as it began. The trim new wagons, hooped and tarped, with bright blue beds and running gear of sunset red, drawn by mules with bells on their hames; behind these, the great creaking Murphys with their seven-foot wheels and iron tires and ox teams of ten to handle the five-ton loads, and all of it trailed close by a swarm of shrill children, a few hippy milch cows, and the solid unpretty women who swished through the grass in sturdy, competent strides. Dub had not forgotten how lordly he had felt when, well mounted, he took his turn as outrider, watching the noisy whole of it cutting trail to the crack of bull whips and the prod of the long *carajo* poles jabbed incessantly at the oxen. There seemed to be a godliness, too, about keeping a pace laid by the space between suns and water holes.

They had passed, or meant to pass, across the vast grass table of the Llano Estacado. But, as Dub later told Sam Heidel, "we traveled the wrong season, and we were German, and farmers."

This last, Old Dub had decided since, was why not a man jack of them owned the feel for new country, that saving feel which seemed to rear up when wanted in the Kentuckian who drifted west, or in the wandering man of Tennessee. So in that spiz of a February, nobody paid mind to the big star that began blinking too close to the moon, or to the way the wolves howled from high ground instead of the bottoms; they hardly noticed, even, the first cold blue fingers of sky which meant a High Plains blizzard in the making. When the snowy heller hit, they reacted as sheep.

The big-knuckled men rounded up and counted the children, hustled them into the wagons along with the silent, stark-faced women, and let the train run.

Southward it jolted, ahead of knifing ice and a north wind that groaned of death each time a team slowed. Sleet herded them to the last edge of the grass tableland, drove them recklessly off it, down the steps of the cap rock, into the pin oaks and gravel breaks where they could no longer hold a tail end to the storm. There wagons upset, animals escaped, and order panicked away in the stinging white blindness.

Even now, so long afterward, and amid the sincerest of summers, Old Dub could take chill from remembering that ride.

It was on a sandy, hill-guarded flat on the second day that the teams balked finally, or died between the trace chains, except for Helmet Berends's cast-eyed gray mule, old Crowder, who had to be shot dead before he'd cease his infernal hauling. Here the twenty-three wagons that remained and the exhausted, frost-bitten people to whom it no longer mattered if the wheels rolled, created Coldiron. Providence? No, devilishly accidental. Dub was satisfied of it. And the flu outbreak made the place stick. Old Dub nodded to himself. More accident.

Most everyone came down in rigors. Little ones cried, and coughed, and strangled, and died quickly. Grown folks went in less hurry, with louder complaints. When it was past, no family was left whole. Those who stayed out of their graves cursed this cold barren country as if such sounds might thaw the air, and some accused the Lord for not minding His job. All laid plans to repair up and get out, and they might have—except that the Mexicans arrived.

These, the *Tejanos,* they called themselves, dragged on to the flat the first sunny day after the storm, riding unsaddled asses and huge slab-wheeled oxcarts held together by pegs and greased with prickly-pear juice, so that the axles wailed only deafeningly.

The oxen were yoked by the horns, so that every jar of the road must have addled the poor brute brains; sheep bleated, the men looked cold and ragged, the women slatternly with their dirty shawls flagging—people in "reduced circumstances," so the Germans termed it, and enforced it, ever after.

No one welcomed them. But it was Dub who, with his good Fox shotgun across his arm, heard out their tale of flight from the *brasada,* the south Texas roughlands, and the savages warring there. It was the Mexicans, Old Dub remembered, who, while being softly grateful in their round-tongued Chihuahuan Spanish for a watered place to rest in, first supposed a living might be bled from this naked red country; and it was they who, by saying rosaries for the few dead they buried, reminded the farmers that they could never in Heaven's decency abandon so many, many German graves.

The mounds had been laid out in close rows at the south fringe of the little plain. Old Dub himself had picked the site after the first helter-skelter of the early buryings, and he had used his almanac, and gotten up at two o'clock in the morning to align the first grave with a star, making sure the dead would rest square with the world. And with others, he made positive the Mexican graves were dug rods away, so that brown Catholic dust might never mingle with the good German white.

Two of the headboards, cut from wagon sideboards, were marked Rupp. They were carved, "Dennis Rupp, asleep with Jesus," and "Juliana Belle Rupp, true wife, Godly woman, tragically dead of the flu on the date of her firstborn son."

Partly, the epitaphs were accurate. Juliana Rupp had died, truly, on the birth date of her first son, the first child born in the mourning camp. But it wasn't of the flu.

Dub had seen the terrible look on that fair, wide-shouldered woman as she rode through the blizzard in labor, and the same look lingering when later, on the flat, he helped Dennis Rupp chip a shallow dugout in the frozen ground, with axes, and they roofed it with a wagon sheet. It was almost as they finished that Juliana Rupp bore her fat loud son and, refusing to look at or feed him, began to die.

The passing was not in peace. While Dub stood in the dugout doorway and Enrich Kampmann worked just beyond with a blanket, trying to fan inward the heat from a fire outside, Juliana screamed and prayed doom on her man. Dennis Rupp stood silent beside the pallet he'd lain for his wife, his head bent as she cursed the groin and desires of him which, *Mein Gott,* couldn't he see was stealing her life?

Dennis Rupp grieved his woman, grieved his young beard wet as he bathed her body in icy water from the Little Dirty and dressed her in her wedding clothes and put her outdoors to freeze, so that she might keep until he built a coffin. Only, there wasn't wood enough. Dub lent his hand to fashion a shroud from a buffalo robe. Then they read quietly from the Book, and buried Juliana as deep as they could dig, setting big white rocks directly over her to turn back the wolves.

After that Dennis Rupp lay down with an ague that got to be the flu. He named his son Julius, in memory of his wife, and Dub always thought his friend didn't make much of a fight of it before he, also, was dead.

Enrich shook his head over the child. "Here is one born to trouble, if ever one was," he said.

"No," Dub said. "There's Helena."

And there was Helena, Dub's own good woman, her small girl child newly buried from the storm, her immense jouncing bosom aching with loneliness and the weight of its milk. Gentleness padded her soul, abundantly, much as the soft flesh cushioned her great body, and hungrily she folded her round arms into a warm cradle for the infant.

Dub moved them out from camp, into a sod-roofed dugout he built against a hill. He put a plow into the red dirt and planted Jerusalem corn, and later, gooseneck maize, and a trial patch of redtop sorghum. Nothing did well. But Dub kept trying, as befitted a man who had a son. Except mostly, the boy belonged to Helena.

She began trading her baking for sweet potatoes the Mexicans somehow managed to raise, cooked them soft, and spooned them down the baby.

"To make his stomach strong," she told Dub, and he laughed at her.

"Injuns, they stuff their younguns with buffalo blood and guts, for that exact same reason," he argued. "You want I should get out and kill us some guts?" Helena did not laugh.

Nights when Julius yelled over the cramp-colic, Helena sat

up rocking him, one big hand gentled over his belly, her voice coaxing him quiet and whispering what a fine important man he'd grow to be. There was a thing in this Dub disliked, for if ever she told the child, "a fine man like your second father," Dub never heard it. And something else, too, that caused Dub to halfway pay court to Helena the next day, as if they were young, and they were not.

As the boy grew older, it seemed to Dub, Helena tried to sort of keep her hand on his belly. She sent him to gather sticks for the wash-pot fire while she made lye soap; she let him crank the grinder when she put up souse or hogshead cheese, and afterwards made him pull-taffy in reward. She taught him to trap jack rabbits, so that at hog-killing time, she might grind them into the sausage, making it go farther.

During summers, she baked tiny ginger cakes and packed them in a box with an oilcloth lining, sending Julius into Coldiron with them to peddle them on the streets.

"They are a nickel each," Helena told him, "and a bargain at the price. Hear me—do not beg anyone to buy. Do not beg, ever. And half the nickels will be your own."

Dub needed the boy in the fields.

"Why send him at all?" he asked his wife. "Hell, he's of a size where I could use him."

"Julius speaks too little," she said. "If he must sell cakes, won't he find his tongue to sell them with?"

She made shirts for the boy from store goods, while Dub argued, and uselessly, that flour sacks would do quite as well; for what else did other children wear, in this country where money was so short? One autumn she troubled through the raising of a flock of tame turkeys, dressing them, salting them down in rented hogsheads, and shipping them east. With the money Dub thought to spend on a more fertile seed, she bought a McGuffy reader and a Webster's Blueback speller for Julius, besides shoes and two featherbeds—the child needed featherbeds to sleep between, she said, for hadn't a fierce chill been born into his bones?

Helena saw to it Julius had sugared mush for breakfast, not sowbelly, because mush pleased him better. Sundays she took him to meeting in the cottonwood arbor, so he would be touched with "the Word," even if mostly it was preached about Old

Demon Whisky, and how Coldiron's good people must take care as long as the Mexicans stayed unsaved from the Old Pope of Rome and his pagan ways.

Always Dub's wife took pains to put down May butter, churning it in the spring when the cow was fresh and burying it in a crock jar in the dugout floor, so that at Thanksgiving and Christmas, Julius might have hot bread thickly buttered. Once when she punished him for getting into the crock too early, it was only with the mush stick, and lightly, and afterwards she hugged him and cried. It was in the same week that Dub came in from the withering corn and saw the boy in the lot, squatted beneath the cow, taking his milk directly, the heathen way that wild spic ragamuffins fed from their goats.

"Damn it!" Dub yelled, and he caught up a loose barrel stave. Julius only grunted under the whaling, refusing to squall, and Dub threshed him all the way to the gate. Helena met them there, screaming. Until Julius's bruises dissolved, she kept Dub from her bed, and for months Dub couldn't stir much of a feeling for his son.

But, giving credit, the older Julius got, the more he was a lad of his own. He demanded nothing, whatever Helena sought for him. Occasions, even, he outright fought her, as when she planned him a blue velvet suit, or aimed him to gag down a gum of figs and senna leaves as a physic, or evenings when she tried setting him down to his speller. Dub knew it before Helena did, that this was a sprout who'd not be leashed too close.

Julius stole off to look in on cow camps, or to watch the freight wagons pass on the trail; he went off to Coldiron to crowd in at the Mexican chicken fights, or to peek in the windows of the new pesthouse where sick *Tejanos,* and some unsick ones that the whites needed put away, were locked in and guarded. One particular day the boy went to see a man who made a show of baiting rattlesnakes with his wooden leg, merely to hooraw about the shock you could see in their devil's eyes as their fangs blunted on the hickory.

Neighbors who saw Julius in the corn patch remarked how tall he stood for his age, and called him a farmer, natural born, and they laughed to Dub at having heard the boy swear out, "*Sangre de Cristo!*" on a dirty hot afternoon when his hoe kept dulling on mesquite grubs.

Dub laughed with them about the oath. But about the grubs he could not smile.

"Now, woman," he told Helena, "I didn't put them grubs in this sorry orange ground, and I ain't taking them out, that's a fact," he said.

"Well—"

"When I am big," the boy put in, "I will dig out them goddam grubs and make us more corn."

If Helena had not seen Julius to bed supperless, Dub himself would have done so. Nevertheless, it burred Dub's neck, for he knew Helena punished the boy for his language, not for having sassed up to his parents or for being so goddam kid ignorant about mesquite grubs. Sometimes Dub wished he wasn't so stuck on his wife, too stuck to brace up and rowdy with her.

But he softened to Helena when later she told the boy, "When it comes to them grubs, son, your father is the wiser."

Ten years they were a family, until on one smoking summer forenoon Helena swooned under from the sun while pounding clothes in Dirty Creek, and chilled after that, and died on the sand with the boy catching grasshoppers close by. When Dub fished the lost washing from the stream, he found each piece belonged to the boy. There wasn't even a sock of his own. From that moment Dub Stokes had no son.

At every sight of Julius, Dub's throat gorged over how poorly he had swapped off his wife. To show for her, he had but a stubborn whip of a boy, one who in the end had done for both his mothers. It grew hard for Dub to put down what flared in his heart. Someway, people sensed this.

"Name of heaven," said Sam Heidel's wife, "can't you see that boy is grieving, every whit as much as you?"

The circuit preacher rode out, mainly to say it was a black sin to hate a child, them being so fresh spanking clean from God, and the preacher sank to pray on his knees in the feed lot with Dub standing over him, near to busting at being meddled with.

What people say never fixed a man's feelings.

Dub went on calling the boy son, saying "son" as he sent him to hoe the runty corn shoots that yellowed almost as they speared out of the red earth, or sent him to tend stock, or to ply a scythe to the thistles. Soon the boy wore flour-sack shirts, unhemmed, and ate sowbelly for breakfast, without mush. He spoke very little, and mostly he obeyed, seldom giving excuse for a stropping. There were times, like when the boy finally agreed about the grubs after having dug out a few and having seen that the corn did no better, that Dub almost forgave him.

At twelve Julius stood big; his hoe could span five rows in one reach, and he could see after the place by his lonesome, although now Dub knew the dirty dry claim was hardly worth living out. That year Dub took to riding.

He stayed away days and weeks at the trip, driving along a few head of horses to swap, or Merino sheep got off the Mexicans and which he could drop in cow camps where men got so sick of beef. Dub meant to get hold of something in the shape of money, leading to a business, maybe, where he could eke out a living more respectful and less lean.

But on the several seasons that he rode as far as San Antonio, and there sat in the paper-lanterned German beer gardens having his schooner and pretzel and weinerwurst while he looked at the women, he understood his search was partly for a stake and partly to fill his empty bed, and he hunched that the boy Julius knew this, much as well as he knew it himself, and he felt, always, the press of how the boy inwardly condemned him for it.

For this, it seemed reasonable, the preacher was to blame, for one time in Julius's hearing, the Reverend had argued loudly how one woman such as the sanctified Helena was sufficient to any man's lifetime, and ought to remain sufficient, even when only her ghost lingered. Dub had angered, and riled yet worse when he saw agreement in Julius's eyes. Still, he tried to serve the boy well.

Dub never left him to shift entirely for himself; this he could swear, whatever people said. Always before he left, Dub spoke to the neighbors. But the boy bowed up and tautened and turned off the meals they offered, making do with the game he shot, or a once-in-a-while nest of quail eggs found in the brush, until the neighbors quit bothering and quit worrying.

Julius hunted the breaks, trading skunk and rabbit pelts for shells and flour, and just about every whipstitch, while in town, tried his fists on the Coldiron boys. Sometimes, Dub knew, Julius spent whole days at Dirty Creek, gaming with the bass when he ought to have been bending his back over the crops. Dub had always wondered, too, if the creek hadn't been a place for meeting Jessie Larkin.

This occurred to Dub afresh now, for his eyes still idled over Crowder Street. Through the dusk he could see Jessie, sound figure of a woman that she was, locking her shop door and making ready to commence her walk home.

Jessie used often to come and sit with him, but it was seldom any more. The tie had never really fastened between them. A father-in-law wasn't in fact much kin, Dub guessed, and the sort of second-pick, father-in-law-by-accident he himself was amounted to no kin at all. Besides, Julius Rupp had been gone a long, long time.

Old Dub had another rub at the rheumy shoulder. He kneaded his bottom on the hay until it rested more comfortably.

"High time," he grunted as he heard a song starting back inside the barn.

The singing meant that no-good nigger was finally forking out the evening feed.

"High time," Dub said again.

"Get off here, Henry?" said Miss Gussie Larkin.

She sat dirty and wind-scalded in the first stage that stampeded into Coldiron. It came early in that sandy hell of a spring, just following the war, and Miss Gussie frowned out the canvas-curtained window at the wild whooping crowd that gathered and tried to show itself not disappointed at how plain and run-down and springless the coach was, and she used a soiled handkerchief to pad her nose against the dust through which the town people grinned. She shook no leg about climbing out.

"Yes," her brother said. "This ought to be far enough."

Major Henry Larkin stepped past her and down to the street, a meatless and flat-jowled poker, dressed a gentleman and likely of less age than his pile of white hair claimed for him. As Coldiron learned shortly, he was a man "held-in" to a caution, if not a frazzle locoed in his ways.

Miss Gussie got out unhelped. She was herself a not unpretty dump of a woman, though many a wrinkle past her youth, and her hands had a dainty strength when they brought the child out of the coach after her.

"My niece," she said. "Jessie Larkin."

This girl of ten was redhaired and very white, her thinness seemingly held together by satin ribbons—ribbons on her shoes, at her waist, her throat, besides a gray bow on her bonnet. Already the child had been put into bustles, but if there was to be shape to her, it lay well ahead, and in the crowd a Mrs. Lavender was heard to whisper, "My Lord, she's a gawky little slip, ain't she?"

Major Larkin touched his hat to the watchers and the three of them went direct to the Rusk House, without even a glance into the new Butterfield depot.

"Won't there be savages about, Henry?"

The major did not smile at his sister. "We'll find savages anyplace," he said.

Coldiron caught its garters up, impressed, for the Larkins took the three spankingest rooms in the Rusk, requiring that heating stoves and mirrors be provided in each, although with but three of them in the party, people thought, one room should have served tolerably well. Major Larkin paid down six months rent in advance, and paid it in gold. There was the feeling that dignity, or blue-bloodedness, or something much as rare, had arrived in Coldiron.

The next day Henry Larkin used gold to buy three town lots from Enrich Kampmann. He handed more gold to a Mexican named Jesus Trespalacios, a sheepman, and Jesus was tickled enough to pitch a fandango greased with ample mescal, since he only pretended to dispute the ownership of the Kampmann property as a manner of claiming, publicly, that there was in spite of everything some salt and hard spine among his people. The three lots lay between Pedro Street and the cemetery of the whites, fronting north and on Pedro, with Crowder Street running up to them like a private path.

Then the Larkin wagons began to clatter in.

The first ones, hired out of Kansas City, brought mortar and tar, kegs of nails, paint, and thousands of feet of good lumber, cured and planed—a fortune's worth, so that some who helped unload stole off sufficient to put floors in their own tents and soddies, with confidence it would never be missed. Afterwards came a stageload of carpenters who first of all built a picket fence around the lots. It was in piecemeal, from the carpenters, that the town learned about the Larkins.

They were Georgians, it was said, building in Coldiron on what the major had been alert enough to save from his war-shot family holdings, and, if the winks of the carpenters could be interpreted rightly, on whatever he'd managed to steal. And Miss Gussie, it was gathered, had never as much as fringed on marrying; if any man, even a Union soldier, had once lifted an impassioned hand to her, the incident wasn't known. Then, the child Jessie, whose fire hair looked as if it was going to have a gray streak in it early: she was the daughter of Henry's and Miss Gussie's tight-strung younger brother, who starved himself to death in a Northern prison after hearing how his wife disappeared from home in the same hour that a handsome Yankee officer deserted.

Henry Larkin spent every day on the job, seeing each timber and stud crotched into place, and quickly it was plain that the house was building from a pattern held deep in his memory, to where it drew a pain to his pale eyes as he roused it out. "The mansion," people called it, well before it was finished. Its size and the slight rise of ground it covered gave it a sort of starchy command over Coldiron, not mentioning the awesomeness of the vast, high-ceilinged rooms with their black mahogany and shining walnut, or the bright wrought-iron lightning rods bolted to the roof. Broad galleries wrapped across the front at both levels; slim columns spiked up in the fine Mississippi style. White paint which, in the sun, had to be squinted at, dazzled on the siding. It was a sight to see. Cowboys and herdsmen and hunters put in from fifty miles around to see if it was true, and stayed a spell to drink over it.

"Such a house, out here in nowheres," Si Tate said, on the day furniture and tapestries and do-dads commenced to arrive. "I'd lay my wife agin your's that this major is holing in from a firing squad."

By bits the town got the notion Henry Larkin was fixing a nursery room upstairs. It was small, low-ceilinged, painted to the color of dove. It seemed too much a baby room for the niece, and folks watched it, and suspiciously watched Miss Gussie, until one day partitions shut off the view. But they noticed that some of the furniture that was carried upstairs was built half size. Nobody was ready for it when, as the house was finished, Major Larkin moved into this baby room himself, shut himself in, and fell busy at drinking himself to perdition.

"Touched, that man," Texas Wells said, and people had to let it go at that.

Miss Gussie was different.

She asked Coldiron's white ladies to come for tea, and they hurried up, making dresses they couldn't afford, and went. In a parlor big as the Rusk House lobby, Miss Gussie organized a temperance society, just as though her brother were cold sober upstairs, and she announced that the town must at once fetch itself a full-time preacher. Between the pills she kept swallowing for her stomach's sake, Miss Gussie pledged the left-over materials from "the mansion" to help raise a churchhouse, where also, she said, a school must be conducted every week-day for children such as Jessie.

"We women must civilize things," she said. "We'll have to work, *to who laid the chunk.*"

She bought an old surrey, the best that could be had, and behind a fat pretty team set about the civilizing. Boys playing their games of foot-and-a-half in the street learned to skitter out of the way when the surrey came tearing, and always they watched it pass, to see if the redhaired girl was riding with Miss Gussie, and whether she happened to look out at them. Several such times Julius Rupp saw Jessie. He wondered if she understood the game they played, and that he had won, or leastways would win, damn sure, before it was through.

But he had grown well out of the street games before he heard her speak.

Julius was in the hot strip of alley alongside of Tate's, sitting astride of Turner Wallace, for Turner had made mimic of his bare clodbuster feet, when he looked up and saw her. She stood at the alley's Crowder Street mouth, holding a two-handled basket in front of her, staring at the blood on Turner's face.

"You . . . you have hurt that boy," she said.

Julius got up, letting his enemy flounder up and run. "Likely I did," he said.

"Your mama, she'd not like it, if you act a bully," Jessie said.

"No skin of yours."

"I might tell her, sir, I might!" Her basket raised, as if she might choose whacking him with it.

"You couldn't," he said. "She's dead."

"Oh," the girl said. "I . . . I hate to hear tell of it." The basket let down. "Are you fifteen?"

"Sixteen," Julius lied, because she had guessed him right. He wondered if he'd known before that her eyes were a calf-brown color, and he thought she was as pretty, every bit, as the dun-haired lady you could see at the Two Bulls saloon any evening, the one they called Little Dot.

"Who watches out for you?" Jessie said.

"Me."

"Oh." She reddened, then smiled. "I'm that way, too. My mama and papa . . . I'm a tragedy, my Aunt Gussie says."

"You got a big house."

"Yes. Except it don't get warm in the winter. Where do you live?"

"Dugout," he said. "North a ways."

"Oh."

"What's that you're totin'?"

"Food to eat."

"What kind, huh?"

"Oh, it's things."

"You aim peddlin' it?"

"Of course not. It's a nice day, outside of the dirt, and my Aunt Gussie has ladies in, and she says I can have an eat-out, if I watch about going too far."

"Well," Julius said.

Her hands took a hitch-up on the basket. "I'll go to the creek, I guess."

He said, "well" again, and they stood while a burst of sand and a loose hat, with nobody chasing it, blew past them. Then she started down the alley, past him.

"Hold on," he said. "That ain't the way."

"I know whereabouts the creek is, sir."

"Well, that way you got to go through Mex town. All them pepper-bellies—"

"I don't care."

"I mean, it ain't much to the creek, that way. Them Mexicans, they've cut ditches off it so as to water beans and stuff. If you head out the trail, north, and cut off west, they's willows and grass, and sand to set on."

She stopped, hugged up the basket, and of a sudden, smiled at him. "I . . . I don't guess I know how to get there," she said.

He walked to her and quick, while he could, he said, "I'll pack the basket."

They went up Crowder Street, the wind shoving them, saying nothing until they reached the north end.

"Yonder, that's the pesthouse," he pointed. "I might just look in." He turned from the street, feeling that she followed, and proud of it, until it settled on his mind that she was merely keeping an eye on her food, and no more.

The pesthouse was of raw planking, and this a sad waste, some still said, since adobe would have done as well, while making the subscriptions for it easier to bear. Together Julius and Jessie crept to an iron-barred window. They looked into a stink-rot room where Mexicans lay spread about in a straw wallow on the floor, boiling over each other, as somebody once said it, like maggots in a sore.

"Oh," Jessie said, and coughed, and put her hand over her nose, as Julius had done already.

As they looked, an old man who had no shirt moaned, put both hands under his head, raised it, and stared back at them.

"Why are they here?" Jessie whispered.

"Cripes, it's smallpox in there."

"That old man—?"

"Him, he is Jesus Trespalacios," Julius said. "Mr. Kampmann had him stuck in."

"You . . . you mean he doesn't have the pox?"

"I reckon by now he's caught it," Julius said.

Jessie pulled away from the window. "It's—awful," she said.

He led her back to Crowder, then on to the burning red trail and along it, and he liked her, up and down, for how she kept tagging back, always a pace or so behind.

Without intending it, he said, "I was in town one night when they was a slew of cowboys got rippin' drunk. One was on his horse, and he throwed his rope over a toilet house and towed it a ways. They was a woman in there."

Jessie blushed, but she smiled, and he grinned with her. They dogged the trail into the red hills, and when the sandburs gigged into his feet, he didn't bend to pick them out; instead, he dragged his foot soles a little, until the stickers raked out or broke off.

"The woman in that privy was named Mrs. Lavender," he said.

"It's very hot," Jessie said, in a rush, as though she didn't thoroughly care about what sights he had seen.

He turned her off the trail, guiding her clear of a prairie sinkhole where an acre of ground had cracked all around and fallen ten feet, and he stomped out a path for her to the flat top of a hill. There they could see the Little Dirty and its willows, and beyond it the breaks tangled with mesquite and cottonwoods, plum bush, and a few chinaberry and hackberry trees, all footed underneath with dry red earth and white rock and patches of runty water grass.

"That bluff," he pointed. "If you watch close, you can see the bees hoppin' in and out of it, and you can tell which holes they're hidin' their honey in."

Jessie wiped her forehead, waiting for him to take her down. She kept looking up to his face, and she said, "What's in my basket is mainly fried pies."

That July they brought Major Larkin down from his nursery room, dead, and for a long while after the services, a big fluff of black crepe hung on the door of the mansion. Jessie wore a plain dress, solid black, the rest of the summer, but she kept coming to the creek, and Julius was pleased when, shortly, she found out that for eating there, meat suited better than fried pies. During the second summer she came often, since Miss Gussie opened up a ladies' emporium on Crowder Street, "to busy my idle hands," leaving Jessie with looser strings when it came to passing off her own time.

Julius knew she frighted off fish he might otherwise have caught, and sometimes he chewed at her, about this and about wagging out food for him as if, by damn, he couldn't shoot better vittles for himself. Jessie fussed back, about his shoulders being weighted down with chips, and about how much food had spoiled the days he was supposed to show at the creek and didn't. Then came the spring when she brought the black triangle cakes with raisin tops, the chicken legs, the *peloncillos*, when it struck him she lived now in a corset, all at once a woman, as much so as any, even Little Dot.

He regretted the change, regretted that he'd tried to kiss her and afterwards had run. He hated the dugout and pens when he got back to them, hated the sorry homestead which wasn't even his own, but Old Dub's. He fell to new habits, getting regular at shaving off the soft beard his chin grew. He wore his good boots steadily, no longer saving them, and every day he tallowed the leather in case he might see her.

The year he was nineteen, and Jessie two years shy of that, was Coldiron's worst. The drought cut down the corn, fed the grass to fires, baked Dirty Creek down to a sour-smelling trickle. By September the sun and wind, like a forge and bellows, had blistered off the country, leaving little besides misery, and the people. In the hill above the dugout, the spring ran dry, and only a hot draft came out between the rocks. Julius went to hauling water from the Little Dirty.

He had two wooden barrels on a borrowed wagon. He drove into the creek on water days, and took all afternoon dipping the barrels full, using dried hollow gourds. On an afternoon when his sweat dripped into the stream each time he bent over it, Jessie came over the hill. She brought no basket.

For a time she sat on a rock, watching him. He did not stop until the barrels were leveled off, if partly with sandy mud. Then he turned down his pants legs and got into his boots and sat on the bank, a good distance away from her.

Finally she said, "I nearly died, walking out here."

"Why do you come?"

"It's . . . well, it's some place to go."

Julius chunked a stone into the water. "Maybe if you'd stick home, some of them town boys would . . . maybe they'd drop by to see you."

She put her chin on her knees, staring down at the lines she cut in the sand with a stick. "They would," she said, "and . . . they do. Only, I don't want them to."

"Well," he said, and threw again at the shrunken stream, feeling good, even if he was sapped out and tired.

"Julius, why won't you ever call at the house? Come to visit, I mean. Just come up and talk."

The good feeling went; he had churned up his own bog.

"I'll come to that place when I get ready," he said, "and right yet, I ain't."

"If you don't, I can't come out here any more."

In his first notion he blamed the drought; if it had taken all else worth having, it would naturally take Jessie too. "It's your puddin'," he shot at her. "Mix it anyways you like."

"Oh, that's not what I mean. Aunt Gussie . . . she says I'm not to come; that if a boy or anyone cares to sit with me, he can come to the house and make it proper. She says she means to meet anybody who—"

"In town at school, that's where they raise 'em pious and proper."

She stood up. "I hate you, Julius Rupp." She whirled, her skirt tent turning slower than she, and she sobbed herself up and over the hill.

Julius lay on his one-legged bed in the corner of the dugout that evening, staring around at the rusted stove, the pole table and chairs, the crumbling shelves sculped into dirt walls, the cracked dirt floor that was bare, except for a straw mat in the middle. He was grateful for nothing he had, except that Old Dub was away again, this time with sheep to swap, leaving him to himself in the cave. He looked up at the stringing, yellow roots of sod dangling down between the rotting roof poles, then caught sight of a two-inch scorpion climbing slowly upward on the farthest wall.

"I wish a scorpion would latch onto her," he thought. "I'd grab her, and kill the thing, and split her skin open with my Barlow knife, and put my mouth on it and suck the blood clean."

If he did, she'd be beholden to him. He herded the idea no further. He got up, threw Dub's work shoes at the scorpion, washed, shaved, gouged his fingernails clean, then dressed in his best clothes, swearing bitterly at how much too tight they'd drawn during his growing, and he rode Dub's youngest and raunchiest mule into Coldiron. He kicked the beast straight to the mansion. He walked through the gate, under an arbor and along the red and white stones to the gallery, across it, and to the high white door. He glanced up at the half-moon of glass above it, real glass, set where orange lamplight showered out, but where he couldn't see in. He knocked—hard.

Jessie came quickly. "Oh," she said. "Julius!" She stepped out into the gallery shadows, shutting the door behind her.

"All right," he said, "I'm callin' at your house."

With Aunt Gussie it set poorly when Jessie told her, quietly, that she meant to be married. Miss Gussie's insides stirred, putting a terrible turmoil in her system, and she had to double up on her medicines and make a trip to the doctor to be bled.

Miss Gussie knew hardly anything of the Rupp boy, only that he was a foot taller than any man she could call to mind, and a dutchy, and strapping, and quite penniless, and without kin, unless you counted that Dub Stokes, or Dub August Wine-something, whichever his name was.

"Jessie dear, my God!" Miss Gussie said. "Even that name—Rupp. It sounds like an upset stomach!"

"Don't say that, please. I love him."

"Child, how could you? Move into that . . . that wolf's den he lives in, eat the lick-molasses and biscuit, or whatever he uses to hold body and soul together!"

Jessie kissed her cheek and tried to laugh it away. "Auntie, Julius says that when your head bobs that way, it makes him think of a hen pecking grain out of cow piles."

"See!" Miss Gussie screamed. "That's it! That's how he talks! Oh, that overgrown ragamuffin!"

"Stop it!" Jessie lost the smile she had for her aunt. "I will marry him. I will!"

Julius felt the war Miss Gussie began against him and, although he understood her why of it, sometimes spoke to her in less peace than he might have. He knew that because of it, Jessie wept a lot. Miss Gussie would meet him at the mansion door, seeing to it that like a small boy he stamped off his feet. In the parlor her questions kept him from getting his back against the chair. What was it he planned doing with himself, she cared to know; didn't he ever make it to church, and if it should rain, mightn't the dugout become a place to drown in?

But Miss Gussie put on her Georgia manners for him, passing him half-cups of tea with grand Georgia flourishes, breeding an extreme courtesy into her voice. In it, he knew, he must appear less graced, even, than he was. Yet he bore it—for Jessie—and because of a hardening thought he had, that Miss Gussie had fair cause.

Then came a sandy night in early May when Julius stalked the mansion as if to kill it. He galled to fight; his day had flinted him for just that. Near noon the cow had grazed up onto the dugout roof, so that the roof fell in, bringing a wall with it. It was angry work hauling the cow out and burrowing under dirt and roots and wood for the things which could only be piled on the hillside. Behind such a day, by God, he'd not be challenged to stomp off his feet on the porch of the mansion.

But Miss Gussie had changed.

Her powdered face seemed to have shrunken overnight, its round lines sagged straight, and her eyes looked dull and wide. She welcomed him inside as if desperate to have him, if not warm about it. At once he saw how Jessie, also, looked ill. He started to ask; some hawker had sold tinged meat from a handcart, it was thought, and a poison sickness was going around, so that if talk was listened to, at least one Mexican peddler was a certainty for the pesthouse. Before he could speak, Miss Gussie got him into the parlor. She sat him on the big, needlepoint settee, next to Jessie. "Now," Miss Gussie sighed, "the wedding. We ought to get on with it."

It shook him; Jessie would be his wife! A man could swallow back anger, the shame of a caved-in dugout, at such a time.

They were married in a wild-flowered and shined-shoe ceremony at the new Coldiron Union Church, and though Jessie angled here and there with her youth, she stood at the altar a woman, nonetheless. No amount of coppery dust—and wads of it raised to whine on their wedding day—could blind him to her woman's turn of figure, despite moves and poses still coltish. She had a woman's soft full mouth behind her veil, and a woman's strangeness woven into the streak of gray which tapered back from her forehead and crisscrossed at last in a tight bun she wore at the nape of her neck.

Miss Gussie, too, was admired. She worked fiercely, getting everything ready in one scant week, and in style, just as if Jessie were marrying into the Davis family, or the Montmorencys, or Lees. "Like a Christian," people said, Miss Gussie "looked to the bright side of it." Dimly Miss Gussie could see that there was such a side.

For one thing, her niece would elude the trials of spinsterhood, such as the latest one plaguing Gussie, which concerned the horrid discomfort of an electric-magnetic belt she had to wear under everything else, constantly, to relieve female disorders that with marriage might never have been. For another, there was the race and heat and rare excitement of a church wedding to be contended with.

Mr. Stokes (or was it Mr. August?) put almost nothing into the affair. He did show up, and he yielded five silver dollars as a wedding gift. But this he handed to Jessie rather than to Julius, the day before the service, which galled the boy thoroughly. It was Jessie and her aunt who spent the money on new trousers and a pair of glossy shoes that the rube of a boy could scarcely walk in. The other expenses fell to Miss Gussie.

She made a small to-do of this, and a large to-do of sending her shop patrons to the ceremony. The upshot was that Julius could call the names of few who grinned and stared during his vows.

An hour afterward, Julius went alone in Miss Gussie's old surrey to Dub's homestead. He packed what he had saved of his own from the wrecked dugout: a worn sugan, the books Helena had bought for him, the Spencer rifle, the discarded cavalry saddle he'd repaired, his clothes. He pointed his thoughts to Jessie, and to no one else, as he drove back and along Crowder Street to the mansion of the Larkins.

He and Jessie took three rooms upstairs, "rent-free," Miss Gussie made clear, though it put him on edge, for Jessie didn't object, and he himself could not. But in the outset there were offsetting things, rich and tender.

The first morning he awoke before dawn, feeling light of head and singy of heart. Barefoot, he braved his way downstairs and found the kitchen and later roused the incredible creature he'd slept with by whiffing fresh coffee steam toward her nose.

She stirred quickly, almost hitting her head on the cup. She smiled. "Put the cup aside, Julius."

When he turned back, she hugged her bare arms around his neck, pulling him down to her. "Husband, husband, husband!" she whispered, and her lips moved against his neck. Before they tried the coffee, it was cold.

In after days the coffee was their ritual. Some few mornings Rupp stirred to a mug of the hot good smell held near his own face. Behind it would be Jessie, laughing like mandolins, her bronze hair tumbled vine wild, and she'd tease how this time she had won their game. On such mornings his chest would roar with what he felt for her, and his tongue was apt to outrun itself, relating with strong promise how, very soon, they'd live in their own house, wear their own finery, and take Sunday drives in their own tallyho, all paid for by a business of his own, built for her, and where the whole county would favor to trade.

"You'll be very busy," she said. "We have to . . . well, this house, it has a baby room to fill."

Rupp had no hard and fast notion what his business would be, or how he'd come by the money to commence it. But he handled animals better than most and had a sure hand with tools. He offered these skills to Coldiron.

He talked first to Old Sam Heidel, at the mercantile.

"Guess I could use a boy," Sam said. "Part-time, you understand. Be worth about eight dollars the month to me, I'd say, to have the store cleaned out of a morning."

Rupp hit up Silver Drake, boss at the freight station. He looked in at the blacksmith shop, the wagon yard, the new tin shop going up. Once he hired out for three days to a stranger who had a born-in gift and used a divining rod to settle on likely places to dig wells, but the man got off without paying. Before long Rupp got down to trying Si and Lacy Tate, the brothers who could use, at best, only barkeeps and card dealers, besides a once-in-a-while drunk for swamping. At each turn it came down to nothing, or to boy's work at boy's wages.

Some sent him smarting away.

"Ain't you Old Dub Stokes's boy, the kid that married Miss Gussie's little niece? Well, if you crave a job of work, you could maybe give a hand with chores, off and on. But hell, how come? Miss Gussie ain't asking you to, is she? Boy, they say she's got a plenty. Fixed. You learnt how much, yet? You might be rich as old Jay Gould hisself, son. Now, was it me in your boots . . ."

It had clogged up in him when on a summer Saturday he talked to Texas Wells at the stock pens. Texas prodded it at him again, and Rupp let out his mouth, and let it out good. As he finished and turned away, Texas slapped him to his knees. Which mattered, itself. A man gets a fist; boys get slapped. That Rupp was close to twice Texas Wells's size was of no account; the hurt was Coldiron refusing to reckon him a man. Maybe to do so it would have to concede, a bit, that its own good day and time were passing.

Rupp walked from the stock pens around the east side of town, to hold clear of Crowder, to enter Miss Gussie's big pot-bellied house the back way. He stared at the pink dust his feet stirred, at the heat shimmer that put a writhe to the flat horizon. The shock of Texas's hand tingled on his jaw, and he knew he'd ask nothing of Coldiron, ever again. The day had cut the last of his strings.

When he was small, he could remember, he had wandered into an arroyo where two men swore and sweated at branding and holding together a little herd of wild cattle they meant to drive north. One hook-horned old steer, though branded, kept breaking away, drilling back into the brush and his hidden bedding place. They roped and threw the brute, and while one man sat on its head, the other took needle and thread and sewed the eyes shut. After that, the animal carried his head low, and stayed with the herd, making no sound.

"By God," Rupp thought, "they'll not stitch my eyes shut."

He had to carry Jessie to Berends's outdoor party that night. Jessie looked a beauty in a bluish dress which took a low dip in front yet had a stiff collar standing high against her neck in back, and she danced excitingly close to him, her hair bouncing to "Run, Nigger, Run" and "Little Sally Waters," which seemed to be the only tunes the fiddler could play. Texas Wells was there. Rupp could hardly smile back at his wife. His mind kept gnawing at the town, at the meaning it had hung onto his marriage: up the ladder. Over and over his thoughts damned them all.

By midnight they were back at the Larkin house, sitting out in air almost clean and breezed with moon and the whir of locusts as it passed them and their wicker chairs on the upper gallery.

"Julius," Jessie said, "what's . . . what's wrong? You've been a bear tonight."

"I decided," he said. "We're moving out of here."

She took her hand off his. "Moving? My, whatever for?"

"North, maybe even west," he went on. "Somewheres that we can make it or bust in a furrow of our own choosing."

She leaned a little back from him, so that he couldn't see her face for the shadows. "Isn't it . . . isn't it nice enough here?"

"My mind's set."

"Is it?" she said. "Shouldn't we have talked it over?"

"That's what we're doing. Kansas, I guess that's where we'll go. They's men there who'll stake you to an outfit, and you kill buffalo and fetch in the hides, and you split. I shoot good, Jessie."

"Oh, I know you do. But those terrible hunting camps. How could we—?"

"You can get a room at Dodge, and I'll see you whenever I come in with a load."

Her voice smalled down. "You . . . you aren't letting me discuss it with you!"

"I decided," he said. "We'll get, soon as I can lay aholt of what we'll need."

He'd not considered that Jessie might not go. Though he wouldn't spit on the days he'd had in Coldiron since his wedding, he had gotten a kind of sureness from the nights, a feeling when he made love to her that she would go anywhere, do anything, if only it was with him.

He hadn't meant to speak of Texas Wells. But now he told her.

"Oh, Mr. Wells," she said, "*he* isn't anybody. We don't have to go packing off like beggars, just because things are . . . well, unsteady right now. There's time, so much of it!"

"I ain't waiting," he said, his voice hobbled low, but only so Miss Gussie wouldn't hear. "Dub Stokes says a man will wear out or rust out. It ain't my bend to rust."

"Isn't, you mean to say."

"Goddam! I said what I meant!"

They sat tightly quiet, hearing the locusts and the shrill whinny of the night girls at work in the Two Bulls. Then she reached her hand to his.

"Oh, Julius, it's Aunt Gussie, don't you see? She's not well; you know it. And she's been heartbroken so many times, and—I suppose we have to talk about it—she's hurt now, about us. We can wait, Julius. We have to!"

He stared at the street as she talked on with a husky finality, of how Aunt Gussie could count the breaths left to her, and likely count them exactly right, of how poor a bet it seemed to lay a sure present time against some risky thing ahead. Had Jessie swelled up in rage, he knew, he'd have been ready to fight her down. But she didn't anger. She reasoned with him—in simple ways—as though, by God, he were a foolish, ruffled child!

Whether child or man, he knew he didn't particularly care about Aunt Gussie. He had grown gut full of her fluttery mothering of Jessie, and gut full of all her selfish demandings for herself. He was tired of Aunt Gussie's pills and purgatives, her swigging of Congress Water and Hale's Honey of Horehound and Tar, and most of all, he'd had enough of that phrase she applied to everything.

To Aunt Gussie the wind blew *to who laid the chunk*, and the sun scalded the same way, and her dyspepsia troubled her *to who laid the chunk*, and if she was determined and bound to die, Rupp thought, then her marker should read, "Here lies Gussie Larkin, to who laid the chunk, and the *chunk* CHUNK CHUNK!"

There was no saying of such things to Jessie. He'd been unable to say clearly, even, that what he wanted from living was to win something and hand it to her, that she must step down from the Larkin house to where he was, so they could climb back up together.

During the next weeks they talked the move, over and again. Each time, it seemed to Rupp, fewer of the gentle married words, less of their upstairs world, lay between them. Soon they could talk only of leaving or not leaving, and he found he could go to bed with Jessie and want only to sleep.

"Jessie, a red dirt hole ain't any place to live in."

"Oh, Julius, please! We've settled all that."

"Aunt Gussie," he said.

"Oh, good Lord, Julius. Quit blaming her for what I think! She wasn't always this way. She's sick, and she . . . she doesn't understand about us, and I've had to lie to her."

"Aw, hell's bells!"

He stayed away from the mansion as many hours as he could each day, working in the boy's jobs wherever he could light on them, hoarding his earnings. He spent a week trying to trap a pair of wild horses he could saddle-break, but failed at it, and afterwards went to pricing whatever animals he saw. As his cash built, he began considering how he could squander off a token of it on Jessie. In the end he bought her a used sidesaddle that she would need for Kansas. She looked at him, and cried, and did not take the saddle from his hands.

It was the next day that their morning coffee play shut off. Rupp missed it, and he counted that Jessie did too, quite as much. But from then on, it seemed they dared each other to start the game again, so that neither of them could. He planned how he'd bring the tender mornings back, someplace with Coldiron shaken off and forgotten.

In early autumn, Rupp had gathered the least money that would serve. He set down his deadline.

"If you'll say what stuff you'll need for horseback," he told Jessie at supper, "I'll buy it, and we'll be ready."

She got up and left the table.

"It's a big house," he yelled after her, "but hear me, they's a heap bigger world outside!"

Then he heard Aunt Gussie calling from her room, "Jessie, what is it now?"

Rupp was sorry, and he told her so in bed that night. Then he tried to make himself clear. Others were leaving; it was the flat-broke year of 1873, when people, outside of the three in the mansion, licked their fingers carefully so as not to waste even one smear of grease. In the east, where the markets were shot through, they called it a "panic," according to Aunt Gussie's copies of *Harper's Weekly*. In Coldiron it was spoken of as "hard times," and barter was coming instead of buying. Besides, there was the Texas fever. Some called this the splenic, and some Spanish fever. Whichever it was, whole cattle herds went wall-eyed and died, and a good batch of young men and a smattering of the old ones were, like himself, sighting northward along the trail to Kansas.

It was not so fevered or galloping as a gold run, as Rupp had heard tell of gold, yet in some ways the same. The broad grassy plainslands to the north grazed buffalo to all get out. Kansans wanted this graze cleared for beef, and hunters were welcome. At the railroad in Dodge, a man could ask two dollars or better for a winter hide, a nickel a pound for choice buffalo meat, provided he cared to bother with butchering and curing it, and he could draw upwards of ten dollars a ton for bone. If he had wagons and a Sharps Big 50, and if God had given him a passable shooting eye, he might cut down forty to a hundred head in a day.

Telling Jessie about it was the longest speech Rupp had ever made. When he finished, Jessie said, "I love you, Julius," and went the rest of the way to sleep.

He lay bright awake the balance of the night, taut with his fury.

Rupp bought a pair of wind-broke Spanish ponies, still a fit pair, if ridden at a walk, and a sound, though blind, mare to carry his pack. Jessie he loved; he was sure she'd not let him leave alone.

The sky, the street, the big house were hued red by a hanging dust the morning he took his horses from their stakes near the graveyard and led them, saddled, around to the front gate. He went inside and upstairs, to their bedroom. Jessie stood beside the bed, her eyes browned deep with their dread, if dread it was. It stopped him that she still wore her nightdress, the soft white with the broad collar of gray which now matched too close the look in her face.

"You ain't dressed," he said, and he saw the bag he had spread open for her on the floor, yet empty.

"You're . . . you're going? Really going?"

"I ain't beggin' nobody to buy my ginger cakes," he said. "Now—"

"What, Julius?"

"Nothing. Let's bundle up your clothes."

She gripped a small hand on a bedpost taller than she. "Julius, for God's sakes. You know we can't go. Please, now, I've told you. Aunt Gussie—"

"Aunt Gussie, hell!" It seemed the second time he'd barked out at her. "Everything for Aunt Gussie!"

Before Jessie spoke he felt her rage slipping free, as his own had loosed itself already.

"Damn you, Julius Rupp."

He straightened from the feed sack he was filling, and he saw the quiver of her slim body under the spread and blossom of the gown.

"You . . . you don't see anything about my Aunt Gussie. You want to know what's wrong with her, what happened to her? Why she changed, and gave us a wedding? I'll tell you, Mr. Big, I'll scream it at you! It's because of what I did to her, oh, you Mr. Big! I told her we *had* to get married!"

Rupp let go the bag. He stared at her. It came on him like a slow creeping moss, this thing he should have guessed, or found out on that day Aunt Gussie began the wedding plans. But he'd been too drunk with Jessie, blind drunk. What was it Jessie now told him? That it had taken a foul, shotgun lie to grease his way into the mansion of the almighty Larkins!

"I could kill you," he whispered.

"Oh, Julius, see it as it was. I love you, I had to have you, and there wasn't another way. Oh, Aunt Gussie, she swore she'd certify you into that . . . that hideous pesthouse, unless I gave you up. It was awful, Julius, and I had to. I said that we . . . at the creek, I said . . . I had to lie! Can't you see?"

"Yes," he snapped. "Me and the spics, we know our place."

She shook her head, hard. "We have to stay, don't you see? I've almost killed Aunt Gussie and—no, I mean pretty soon she'll know it was a lie, and maybe then she'll like you better . . . oh, what is that you're doing?"

"Packing." He choked. "Are you coming?"

Jessie went around the bed, to the side away from him, and she sat down slowly. "I cannot," she whispered.

Often in the years after, Rupp pictured the fragments of that morning. Jessie sitting bent on the bed, unmoving. Aunt Gussie lying down in her room, weeping, sipping Brown's Iron Bitters for her heartburn, and belching *to who laid the damned chunk.* And himself, wordlessly in and out of the house, loading the horses.

Even when he had walked under the arbor, along the stone walk and out the gate, he knew he expected Jessie. She'd wait, and wait, and then come running.

As he mounted he glimpsed her face at their bedroom window, grayer yet, her eyes barren and dry. He prickled the old mare into a commotion on purpose to stretch out the time. But she didn't come.

Sweating, sick, he clucked the horses off along Crowder, north toward the trail, leading the better pony that wore the empty sidesaddle. His thoughts boiled madly. In a moment she would appear beside him, riding.

When he looked back, it seemed Jessie waved. He swore and kicked the crippled horses to a trot, and he cried as a boy might, and didn't wave back.

Chapter Four

"THIS here Jessie woman you keep moanin' about," a voice said, "she must of been one heap of gal; but me, I'd ruther figure they's as good a fish in the sea as ever was caught."

Julius Rupp turned, retreating from the sun's morning bead on his face, and from the hard press of how he'd lain, on his shoulder with his knees pulled high, as if these, the knees, might smother the flame on his chest. Working over onto his back, he discovered, as twice he had in the night, that he wasn't dead, but merely a man who'd been sent for and couldn't go.

"Hey, that was sort of a joke I made," the voice said.

Rupp's head was propped on a saddle, and in instinct he knew it was his own. He began hearing the grumble of the Little Dirty's sluggish flow; he felt coarse warm sand gritting against his naked back where his shirt had scooted out of his belt and he felt the hot swat and sting of a rising new wind, and he smelled the smoke of a chip fire. He saw first the black ash of last night's fire. Memory caught him up and he jerked to come off the ground, and heard himself groan.

"Easy does it, big hoss," the man's voice said.

Rupp squinted to locate the speaker. Instead he saw the wound on his chest.

The black-red ruin spanned jaggedly from armpit to armpit,

and downward along his middle to his waist, edged ragged, blooded raw, oozing a fluid the color of tequilla, the whole searing at each wisp of air. Along the brand hung shreds of dead yellow flesh, so that the T seemed to be rotting while it burned him alive.

"Must of laid that iron to you about a half-dozen times to leave a mess like that," the man said softly.

Rupp gritted and sighted along his toes at a small man who squatted beside a nubbin of a fire, busy with the contents of a warped black frying pan. The man stabbed a long knife into a chunk of beef, turned it, shook the knife-point free and lowered his cookery back onto the smoldering chips before he stood.

He was a reed, a dry stalk with iron-gray hair dropping stiff and dirty to his shoulders, blowing out from his wrinkled sliver of a neck, and his bony arms sagged away from him like dangling ropes. He wore a hickory shirt, and overalls fitting like a blanket flung over a bush to air, and the Congress gaiters some cowhands favored over boots. Rupp growled at his chest, and raised onto his elbows. They stared at each other.

"You been goin' on all night about this Jessie gal and cup cakes," the small man said. "I left that uncovered; didn't hardly know what else, not with a hellbender like that one. Figured it might go to healing if they was some air gettin' to it. You know, air is—"

"The damned air, that's what's killing me!"

"Sure, if you want a patch. . . ."

Rupp looked again at his chest. They'd burned in their T for thief, all right, those three bastards, dug it in deeper than any feeling man would treat a cow's rump, and now he saw, at intervals, the long clear blisters, cutting across the brand as though in some drunken afterthought they'd tried to cross it out.

He tasted blood and knew he'd been biting himself.

"I'd guess it was a runnin' iron," said the small man. "Sawed in so deep, the way I've seen a cinch ring do; looks like that, to me."

Rupp flattened his palms on the sand and pushed himself up to sitting. At the motion his skin seemed to stretch, crack, then pop apart, as though made of rotted denim. He heard it as much as he felt it. "God," he said, and looked at himself.

The little man echoed the word and walked toward him,

stopped, and stood doubtfully on one leg. "You poor cooked hoss," he said.

Then Rupp thought of the money.

He twisted around on his seat toward his saddle, and if the pain whimpered in his throat, he damned it. The old bags remained in place, lashed in back of the cantle. He slapped the one nearest. It did not collapse. He unlatched the buckles and yanked up the flap. The bag was packed with buffalo grass.

He grabbed for the other. More dirt and roots and crumbling grass. He swore, until he choked on it. Then the small man laid hands on his shoulders and was forcing him back down.

"You ought to stay easy, son. Stay easy."

Stay easy!

Rupp spied more gear scattered about on the ground. A gaped-open pack with one binder strap stiffened up straight by the wind, a blanket roll in poncho, a food sack. He pitched from the little man's grip, groaning at the hot burst and tug of his wound, and on hands and knees he went after it, plundering, slinging, hunting.

"Hey, ox, that there's mine! Hold on, you got into my stuff!"

Rupp couldn't stop.

The little man walked wide around him, slowly, and he whistled. "Hoss, if you don't know it, you ain't clearly in your senses."

Rupp's fingers had been clawing, as though he might yet strangle up the money from the sand, the way he'd squeezed and worked and bled it out of a wild country in wild years. But even before he quit, he knew it was a madness. His money and Jessie's, his measure of how far a man could scramble uphill from a dugout, was gone. Seventeen thousand dollars, grubbed out in eleven seasons of buffalo killing and fly-bitten butchering and close dealing and lonesome, freezing freight hauls, was taken from him.

He sat on the ground, still.

"Whatever you lost," the small man said, "you ain't doing that burn any good." Rupp watched him return to the fire and take up a stick with bread dough wrapped around it and hold it close over the fire.

A slow line of blood went hunting its way along the creases of his hand; Rupp looked at it, and seemed to remember scraping it over a buried rock.

"Making us some eats, hot bread and wohaw," the man said. "Eats help. In this bitching country, you got drinking water and eats, you got a right smart, I say."

Rupp scrubbed his palms over his face. Dirt and dead blood sloughed off in them, and the fire stirred on his chest and licked inward. He recalled suddenly how the seventeen thousand had looked. Paper money, bright new green and bundled, forked over to him that last day he had ever hoped to see Dodge. Tater Smith had met him in the middle of Front Street, and they'd stood against Rupp's wagons, talking first about the hunting, for Tater, like himself, was one of the die-hards.

The hunts had been forced south from the Arkansas in '74, on down into the North Concho country of Texas, and by '79 it was about all done for most men; the time of big kills was over. But Rupp had kept dogging the remnants of the big herds, wherever they went, because his pile wasn't yet enough, because hunting was what he knew. But that forenoon in Dodge he'd known he was through, and was glad of it.

"Could be I'm gettin' the fat end of this," Tater had said when he sized up the outfit. "They's eight six-yoke bull teams, and the mules, and seven five-ton Murphy's, I make it. With them Sharps rifles and the load of hides throwed in, it runs maybe a little heavy for the price."

"It does that," Rupp had agreed.

"It's no skin of mine," Tater said, "but to sell off a good outfit this cheap—hell, I'd like better to go partners with you. They's hides yet to be took, if a man's got the sand to cross that Rio Grande."

"No. I'm finished."

"Right now I'm looking at this bone trade, Rupp. We can load bones for a year, right where we been gatherin' hides. Stop at the crick just afore we make it in, and soak 'em down good for weight, and draw twelve dollars a ton."

"I got what I come for."

Tater Smith hunched his shoulders and sighed. "You're the driver," he said. "Guess I mainly hate seein' a good buffler man pullin' out; they's been such a hoppin' bunch of 'em not worth the powder it'd take to blow 'em to hell, or halfways. Truth is,

I always did aim to split some tanglefoot with you, sometime when us both got in with the cravin'."

"If you're satisfied of the price," Rupp said, "we can deal."

Smith nodded and passed it across. Fourteen thousand in snapping green cash to den up with the three thousand Rupp had stowed at the bank. As he scratched his name onto the bill of sale, Tater said, "Just what was it you did come for?"

Rupp did not answer; he couldn't talk of it. At least, he couldn't much say to a man as sun-cured and thorny as Tater Smith, "I only built this up on account of a redhaired girl and a mansion house and a two-bit dry-land town." Or could he explain that he'd sworn to price himself far upwards in the cockeyed, devil's market that men are bartered in. For then Tater would ask why he'd put it off so long, when often the hunts had strung him southward to within a day's ride of Coldiron, and he'd have to say he'd just now gotten his nerve, and gotten it, as best he could nail down the strange way it came, from seeing a smiling young woman walking along Front Street, her hand tucked into her husband's arm, her sharp little heels appearing to knock up bright happy sparks.

So Rupp had handed Tater Smith the signed bill of sale, and he had said "so long" to him, nodding to Tater's latest pimply-skinned squaw, and he muttered "go to hell" to Buck and Brindle, his lead bulls, and after pausing to pick a tick off Buck's ear, he had crossed the street to where the old dun horse stood hitched and dozing.

Now, almost back to Jessie, he had lost his handle on her. His mind pictured how Johnsy Boy Hood, the drunken Coates, and Brooks Durham had looked in the firelight.

Those three. They had killed him, after all.

A grease bubble rose and shot off in the little man's skillet. "Too damned fat, baby beef is," the man said. He lifted out the meat and put it on a tin plate. "Prefer me an old iron-sided steer anytime. Where it cooks out dry. Though I will say, even that ain't the best I ever et. Once I rode in on a party of Lipans, and they set me down to a fine hunk of meat, and I'd done got my fill before I knowed what it was. You know what it was? Turned out that was roast leg of Comanche." The man laughed heartily over his lie.

"Who're you?" Rupp said.

"Nobody much; name's Hanley. Happened I found you." He started the long knife sawing on the beef. "Who done that to you?"

"Three of them."

They had sat around, the three, and talked and argued as if holding lodge meeting, and still they'd gone ahead and done it. He had never believed they would.

"Know who they was?"

A wind gust flapped Rupp's open shirt across the brand, and it stuck. He trembled and peeled the shirt loose, slowly. A thin new blood began seeping. It clung to the burn in pallid brown tears. Rupp got up.

"I know 'em," he said. "By God, I do!"

Hanley delayed with the food to study him up and down. He grunted. "You look like bitter hell," he said.

"What day is it?"

"Thursday, I make it. About the fourteenth of the month." Hanley tore chunks of hot bread off the stick, flipped half the meat onto a second plate and stood, frowning, his eyes apprais-ing.

"I'd peg you as one of the kind," he said.

"What?"

"Thinking out loud." He offered one of the plates. "Eat?"

"No," Rupp said.

"Suit yourself," Hanley shrugged. "Only, a man ought to eat every chanst he gets."

He sank down on his spurless heels, letting the long gray hair fall forward almost to hide his face, and he began eating. As he chewed he made sounds, and his long underjaw seemed to close inches too far, as though he'd parted, and thoroughly, with his teeth.

Rupp turned toward the creek, his legs shimmying, near too limber for his weight. At the water's edge he knelt and leaned out over a gyprock crevice where a bit of the Little Dirty backed up into a still shallow pool. As he cupped his hands toward it, he saw himself mirrored.

The sore was a hideous fleshy ditch, sectioning off the rusty mat of chest hair now pasted down by gore. On the honest face of the water it had the look of hell's keyhole, and Rupp cursed aloud as no mortal should swear, spending all the foulnesses he'd ever gleaned from this harsh red country. Across the creek a feeding chaparral cock bobbed upright, gulped back its clatter, jumped, and struck out running.

Hanley's voice pushed its way around a mouthful of food. "Man, you ain't doing no good like that. No sense going to the bats; you'll heal up, or you'll die, and either one, what'll you be losing, noways?"

Rupp kept staring at the water. He had reached thirty last February, and he was old. Old, no, he was past it, he was dead but not laid out. He saw the puffed cherry bruise on his forehead, the beard clogged in grime and blood. Two shattered ears, now, and between them, the heartless gun-barrel eyes. This shot-away husk, was this what he'd thought to bring back to Jessie and the sweetness of her arms, as if handing her a gilded prize? The man she had waved to from her window had owned earnest gray eyes, a clean chin, a whole tall body. But this face on the water: maimed, grizzled. . . .

He rammed his fists into the image. Roughly he washed, stinging his cuts with the water, letting it drain off from his beard in a dozen pinkish streams.

"You," he yelled, "you got a razor?"

"Now hold on, feller. You ain't so bad off."

"Bring the razor!"

Hanley's voice deepened with the sham in it. "If you'd just as leave, I'm carrying a gun you could borry. Man could do it cleaner that way."

When Rupp turned, Hanley was grinning, confirming that he had used up his teeth.

"I can't do much shaving with a gun."

Hanley set aside his plate. "Got a good razor," he said. "Stole it off a barber. Say, you ain't no great hand for jokes, are you?"

Rupp went at it soapless and cold-water, indifferent to the pull and the quick red welts that blunted up behind each pass of the blade. As he shaved he realized that his mind was rooting for some old familiar ground, a known place from which to take up again. He was thinking of all the times he'd crawled to within a hundred yards of a feeding herd and set up the heavy Sharps on its shooting sticks and laid out his hand-loaded shells in rows beside his knee and put his cooling swabs to soak in the water bucket and let fly in the cold, Big Fifty thunder. Only now, the thoughts had nothing to do with buffalo.

He finished, washed the razor in the pool and dried the blade on his shirt front, trying decently to regret how he'd dulled it. His knees snapped as he got up. "Guess I'll try that meat," he said.

Hanley handed him the plate.

"You a buffalo man, ain't you? A hunter by trade, I mean?"

Here it was once more; anybody could tell a buffalo man. If you hunted, you weathered, and you got to smell like the rotting carcasses you deserted on the prairie, and your face took on the savage hunger of the wolves that gorged amid the rot. Riding home it had been the smell he had most worried about. They said it was a core-deep stink that had to wear off, like a scar, or the recollection of a woman you wanted and couldn't win or buy. But this concern was behind him now.

"I was," he said.

"Guess you been up in Kansas, then," Hanley said.

Rupp winced at the chewing; his jaw balked on swollen achy hinges in each moment before his teeth came together.

"Expect you been around Dodge, huh?" Hanley was saying. "Maybe you know some of them hustlin' women up there? Big Nose Kate, maybe?"

Johnsy Boy's fancy pistol, Rupp thought, that would account for the jaw, as it had accounted for his good ear. Johnsy Boy Hood.

"I've heard a heap about them Dodge women. I been told they'll rassle you blind and drink you blinder and slit your throat, all in one night for the same flat fee." Hanley talked on, laughing around a finger he'd stuck into his mouth. "Read a piece about Dodge in that Fort Worth paper oncet, said a man blowed another feller's head off in a pool hall and one of them women got down and patted her hands in the blood, and giggled like crazy. Always wondered if that was so, if them light ladies in Dodge was sure enough like that."

It was like that, in this country, Rupp thought. A thousand miles around you'd hear about the sluts, but take a decent woman and you'd not hear a word of her, not once in eleven years.

"Man told me you could go into that Big Nose Kate's and have her run 'em out, one at a time, where you could sort of check them over for chilblains and have your pick. Never been to Dodge, myself, but I've sprinkled a little joy amongst them chili queens at Laredo, in my time, and oncet I got to Dallas and bought me a ticket to that Black Crook—that's a naked-leg show, you know. There was one girl in it, she broke me up, that one. Full-blood Frenchman, she was, born in France, and she got mail that proved it."

Rupp quit the meat. He walked to the Dirty and washed his plate.

"You afoot, Hanley?"

"No. Got a pony staked to grass, past the rise yonder."

"Then you might as leave ride him."

The little man looked up, startled. "Figured if I could help I'd stick by. Got a shack up in them hills, run a few cows, but nothing's crowding me, so—"

"You can get."

Hanley got up and squared around, his hand sliding to his pocket, and Rupp supposed there was a gun there.

"Maybe if you wanted me to catch up your horse and saddle him for you. You ain't in no shape."

"I told you twice, already," Rupp said.

The small man's lips tucked back, making a gummy sucking noise. "Son, maybe you need you a round of physic," he said. "I don't see no cause for gettin' hard." But he turned and began wiping out the skillet and piling his cookery together.

Rupp sat down on his saddle, watching Hanley pack, wondering why he stung to drive the man away, and at once. Was it the wench talk, which could feed you up so fast and which, if listened to, even idly, could stick to your thoughts like an unhealing scab? Or was it that now he dast not feel owing to anybody?

His eyes lowered to his chest; perhaps he ought to see about washing the sand out of the wound. He shuddered, and knew he wouldn't try. When he looked up again, Hanley had his gear assembled around his feet, and was watching him and shaking the gray head.

"I knowed a man once, name of Charley Don Coffin; got hisself burnt in a grass fire, up on the Diamond Tails. Nothing as bad as you, either, but he festered up and mortification set in and he died in a hurry."

Hanley dangled one of the rope arms into his grub sack and

came out with an unlabeled tin bucket. He sent it rolling across the sand, toward Rupp, and nodded at it.

"They's lard in there," he said. "You can smear it on, though if you was to ask me, I'd say it's too damned late to do much good."

Rupp meant to say "thanks." It came out an oath.

Hanley picked up his pack and bedroll. "If the Lord made ary a mistake," he said, "it was how He always put the devil's temper into big men, so us sweet-souled ones has to put up with 'em." He walked to the creek, waded it thigh-deep, climbed the hummock beyond, and dropped from sight without a look back.

Rupp unstrapped his blanket roll from the saddle and spread it on the grassy stretch near the willows. He hauled out the coarse underwear he was inclined to wear only in winter, and out of the back he cut a square of cloth and punctured holes in each corner. He tore off long strips of hem and tied one through each hole. He greased the rag with a thick layer of Hanley's lard and plastered it over his chest. The brand seemed to cool.

Cautiously Rupp got his hands behind him and tied the strings, one pair around his neck, the other around his waist. It was in the tying that he noticed the swelling cuts on his wrists where the bonds had been. The piggin' string, he guessed.

His shirt was scorched and filthy, and the buttonholes stuck shut with dried blood. The buttons were gone. He pulled it together over the patch and pinned it with mesquite thorns. What remained of the underwear he put into the bedroll along with the lard can. He took out an oily canvas bag, and out of this he drew a long-barreled Colt revolver.

Taking time he swabbed out the bore and chambers, and he loaded it with five shells. He backed off his belt a notch, making room for the weapon in his waistband, and he flipped out the loading gate, so it might overhand the belt and hold the gun in place. He found his bridle swinging from a willow limb. For a half-hour, then, he walked and whistled against the wind, until he raised the dun a mile downstream where it nibbled from one dry wad of bear grass to the next. He led the animal back and groaned, there being no one to hear, at the way his chest bid to split as he lifted the saddle up.

When he was ready, Rupp paused with a hand on the saddle.

He looked across the dun's underswung neck at the heat and the red-dirt funnels twisting up around the hills.

"If I'm going to fester," he said aloud, "kindly hold it off a little spell."

It struck him the words came close to a prayer, but it wasn't one, and damn certain. If he'd not been plain on such things before, he was clear on them now, and if there was anybody he could pray to, it was, like Hanley said, just "nobody much"; it was the man holding this horse.

Rupp brushed down a spray of the scraggling black mane. "Ought to knock you awinding, letting them three creep in on me that way," he said to the horse, but he said it quietly, and he let the shivering black nose nuzzle him before he set his teeth against the pain and mounted.

He limped the dun over the hill back to the trail and turned south. In a lapse of the wind, he smelled the buffalo on himself, and he thought how, except for last night, he'd have soaked himself in the Little Dirty a good while before riding.

Chapter Five

RUPP reined the dun atop the last red hump of the trail before the meager incline and the widening, deeper rutting which, after a loafing S curve, turned the trail into Crowder Street. He sat staring down at Coldiron, bunched close below him in dusty heat and in a kind of native scabbiness: a tired blown clutter on the spare-looking flat which had been skinned, long since, of all its summer life, so that mostly there was only ugly earth to see.

Scanning it he felt a small threshing begin under his belt. It was as if a bullbat had snared itself there and wanted loose, and it was uncalled for. The flutter was not at the sight of the town, he could swear, but at his own awareness that down there somewhere was Jessie, looking pretty and being busy at whatever the day required of her, and down there, also, the three men who had blocked him from her. He rubbed a hand against his flank, and grunted, and kept looking while the rumpus beat on.

He could see Crowder's full length, sweeping down to butt into Pedro, and the great face of Miss Gussie's mansion. He made himself gaze past the big house, to where there was only the graveyard in which his mother and father lay, and where Helena Stokes lay, and where it seemed the three of them had always lain, as if they had never lived. The town had raised a fence around the cemetery, he saw, using cedar posts and the strange new "bob" wire, as though human spirits, like cow brutes, wore horns and might get away.

Rupp shook his feet free of the stirrups and stretched his legs while he waited for the belly flutter to simmer down, and he took notice of the killing sun, too close to this land and jabbing its angry seep through his greasy chest rag, multiplying the scald of the wound.

That pain, now. It would want to hold him, Julius Rupp, in his proper goddam place. Pain did that; it sort of dragged you down to your right size, let you know you didn't matter, not a flip. It did to you what a night alone on the Plains might do if you happened to look up and if you'd gotten used to standing under seven-foot ceilings where you could stand so importantly tall. Except a man couldn't afford paying mind to either one—not to pain, or the sky.

Rupp squinted.

Off to the right he could see the swing of Dirty Creek, fleeing out of the stumpy pink hills, snaking crookedly parallel with Crowder Street, sawing off Coldiron's west side, unevenly, and there, along its banks, the crouching flat-roofed *jacales* of the Mexican community—the *Pueblito Triste,* as a padre called it when he visited, because the fig trees died there within three days of their planting. The mess of mud-and-wattle huts was salted now with board shacks and a few tents, and more of the narrow water ditches hooking the Little Dirty into back-yard gardens, and there were new staggered rows of unplumb outhouses. The whole Mexican cluster, he concluded, had thickened, as had the rest of town. Coldiron had grown, God knew why.

Rupp twisted away from the southwest wind and brought out his tobacco. Starting to roll, his fingers frogged and went flimsy, and he muttered at them. Then, before he realized he was looking at the town again, his eyes had stopped on the house.

From where he sat the dun, the mansion appeared to rise square in the middle of Crowder, giving the red-powdered street and the trail a surprising finality. Under the fiery scrutiny of the sun, the white siding looked scaled, as though diseased, and it seemed to beg mercy and new paint. But, paint-thirsty or not, it was still the mansion. Despite the years, Coldiron's shops and saloons, its dwellings and barns and toilets, still spread out meekly from the Larkin grandeur. Rupp felt the climb of the old hate he'd learned for the place, and he wondered if he would have hated it still, had it become the Cold County courthouse, as once it might have.

Miss Gussie, as part of her "civilizing," had offered the house after Henry Larkin died, and it set people to talking of an election to organize the county and make Coldiron the county seat. But the election had never come off. Organization meant officers, and salaries to pay, and roads to build, and heaven knew what else, and such things shouted of taxes. The mossbacks shook their heads. The Mexicans couldn't pay, and the whites didn't care to. It was frugal and saving just to remain attached, and loosely, to the neighboring county to the east, for judicial purposes. That kept law a hundred miles away, and the county could make do with wagon trails and a touring judge who didn't tour much, and everybody could hold his tax money in his pocket. And as they told Miss Gussie, it was best, since thus she'd not be discommoded out of her fine, fine house.

The old dun stamped and switched its tail against an attack of heel flies, and Rupp steadied him. Then he was shading his eyes with his hand, picking out the particular window on the mansion's upper gallery. His face heated, as if someone were watching him and could tell his thoughts. Yet it was hard not to think of Jessie in that room, her bronze hair let down and tumbling over her face, and perhaps over his, its folds heavy with the fresh warm scent of her mail-ordered lily-of-the-valley perfume, and her low voice making a true fact out of an unreal tenderness, there in the dark.

In a sudden rush, Rupp pinched the fire off his cigaret and dropped it in the shuffling red dirt, and now the pulsing at his middle was shaking all of him. He kicked the horse, more sternly than it deserved, and bent the tan head away from the trail.

He rode westward at a walk, curving wide around the town's haphazard fringe of leaning buildings, toward the Little Dirty. Under scrub oaks barely left alive, despite the exposed roots that clutched to the very bank of the creek, he unsaddled and spread his blankets on the hot ground. Freeing the dun to shift for itself, he lay on his back, smoking, now and then wallowing wildly at a flare-up of his chest. Once he moved to a rock and sat with his back to the sun to break down, reclean, and oil the revolver. Twice he got up and walked to the water to drink from his hatbrim and to rinse the terrible heat out of his face.

At midafternoon he stirred a stunted fire of chips yet too fresh and he warmed stale coffee he carried in the spare canteen. With it he painfully ate a long twist of jerky. Returning to his blankets, he stretched himself against the total soreness of his body and covered his face with his hat. He slept, but poorly.

A thick scale had formed on his ear, and another in the center of the bruise on his forehead. Both still throbbed, and with his eyes shut, the fire at his chest outburnt the sun, and a fever sweated him until he was soaked and sticky and cursing while he dreamed of nobody he ever knew, enacting horrors he'd never seen.

When he aroused it was dusk. His fever seemed worse, but his body had dried, suddenly unable to sweat, and he panted at rolling his bed. He stuck the roll into a parched sage clump. Abruptly his tongue grew hair, and he wanted whisky, the furious way that he had sometimes wanted a woman. His body seemed to have locked itself at the joints with sting and heat. He cried out at saddling, and again at mounting, and he gritted his teeth at each jolt as the old horse ambled back to the trail.

The first false darkness was shading the town, putting a peace on Crowder Street that didn't fit. Lights were being lit, but a few Mexican boys remained out, calling *"leche!"* and leading the goats they'd milk on the spot if someone wished to buy. One boy was leading a burro and selling firewood off its back. Rupp rode in slowly, not craning. He kept his face straight ahead, taking in all the strangeness, but only with the travel of his eyes.

New buildings, less openness to the street. New names on signboards. New shops, some now with red-rock fronts; one, even, with a street-side facing of brick masking the old adobe. A new grocery with barrels of kerosene sitting out front, a land office, a woodyard with cordwood up for sale. The Rusk House, now painted red. A lean-to furniture store, added on to Belmeade's Funeral Parlor. A barbershop with a broad front window of real glass.

He missed the pesthouse, and cast around until he located the plot where it had stood. Only the blackened ruin was there; it had burned.

He rode past a huge livery barn at the north edge, on his

right. Glimpsing the sign above the door, he turned his head to look again. "Dub Stokes, Esq." it said. So the old beer crock had spared the time from his hussies to lay hold of a stake and at last had his business. Better, Rupp thought, if the old Dutch had gotten, instead, a whole-souled case of the yaws, or maybe a thorough beating with a barrel stave.

On the same side was the Coldiron Union Church, the place of his wedding and of Jessie in her veil. Its spire was still white and spiking high upward in the heat. That spire, it meant something in religion, Rupp had been told; must have been Jessie who explained it to him, but whatever it was, he had forgotten.

But he remembered the smells that came at him, of Texas Wells's stock pens off to his left, the horse-flesh smells, the odor of privy lime, and of grease scorching during the evening cooking.

"I could bend this horse around, and rake him, and ride him to death, back to Kansas," he thought.

But he wouldn't, God no; he had his pain, and the gun hung light in his belt.

Rupp had come even with the churchhouse when he saw Miss Gussie's shop. A light burned inside, and not reasoning, he kneed the dun left, sharp away from it, and crowded hard into the narrow alley between the Rusk House and Belmeade's. He was deep into it before he stopped. Stiffly he got down, and he walked back along the passageway to where it opened onto the street. Then he leaned against Belmeade's rough cracked wall, waiting for something he couldn't name and hearing the short pull and blow of his breath.

He watched a wagon rattle past, and another, and riders straggling in, hitching up, vanishing through swinging doors. Somewhere behind him, back in the east part among the houses of the whites and the steep German roofs, a woman yelled "supper!" to her younguns, and recited their names, and hollered it was panbread and sorghum, and no complaining. There was the sound of chickens squawking over their grain, and then, behind the funeral parlor wall on which he leaned, a man's voice, maybe Belmeade's, said, "Damn, but she was a scrubby old crow, weren't she?" and another man answered with laughter.

Rupp's eyes idled over the sign across the street, now fading rapidly in the dark. It read, "Jessie Rupp's ladies emporium," where before it had read only "Gussie's." He peered hard; it hadn't occurred to him that Aunt Gussie might be dead, that some of her ailments might have been actual. Then the air struck him as quickly cooler, less grimy. Jessie Rupp, it said. She still used his name, the name like a sick stomach, Aunt Gussie had said, and he swallowed, surprised that he must have feared his name had been put aside. Then he saw Jessie.

She came out onto the sidewalk, closed the shop door, started to lock it. Instead, she went back inside, and he saw her tight-waisted silhouette as she bent and blew out a fat-oil lamp she'd almost forgotten. In a moment she was again out front, locking the door. She shook it, making sure, and she glanced around the street before she dropped the key down the neck of her dress.

Rupp found his sweat now, it washed in a flood over his fever. He couldn't tell the color she wore, but he made out the pile of white lace which fluffed at her throat as if kissing its softness. She carried a parasol and in the other hand a flowered straw bonnet. As she set out south along the street, she swung the hat by a ribbon, like a small girl bound home from school. When she neared Tate's, the hat stopped, and her eyes kept very directly to the fore, and her back seemed to tense against Tate's brassy piano, as if it startled her with its loud preliminary assault on the night.

It was in the steady yellow light that spilled over and under Tate's doors that Rupp downright saw her. His teeth clicked. Jessie hadn't changed.

Her hair gleamed its old brilliance, and he thought the light silvered off the freak gray streak in it, the streak no wider than he remembered, and no whit less magic. The mixed girl-woman look of her was there; it flagged at him in each switch of her walk.

Eleven years! Yet she might have been, as before, seventeen.

Rupp stumbled out of the alley to keep her in view, and his eyes batted against the cloud troubling them. Tonight was one he might have spent with her—yes, even in that peacock of a house. He thought of the money he'd brought and lost, and cursed the losing; and he remembered the image of himself in the creek, and his lips locked down beyond any curse he knew. He stepped back, covering himself deeper in the shadow.

He watched her until she melted into the far dark, walking

rapidly, and when he could no longer see her, he listened for the sound of her heels.

For a moment he looked at nothing, then toward Tate's and the liquor he needed, numbing liquor to calm the pain and the fire. He stepped into the street. Suddenly he turned south, and was running—running after her.

Chapter Six

WALKING home, Jessie Rupp kept to the west side of the street, a departure from her habit and quite a rare one in the sense that her decision to do so had not been considerately made.

This way she must pass Tate's saloon, and farther on, the more girly and rowdier Two Bulls, thus twice risking the guttery language and ribaldry and debauched smells which charged out the yawning doors of these dens and scattered over the street much like—as the Reverend Gossett had stated it, repeatedly, from the Union pulpit—"the foul outpouring from a broken carbuncle."

Although Jessie did not see these places as corrupt to so great an extreme, she nevertheless crossed Crowder directly in front of her shop on most occasions when she worked late, then followed the east side all the way to the house. On the east, she need defy only one drinkery—Harlan Swift's and relatively sinless, as such places go—and she could also, in the second block, savor the fine warm breath of new bread being ovened in Mrs. Lavender's bakeshop and delicatessen.

But tonight she was on the loud west side and as she walked she grew curious as to why. It was unusual for her to decide and act without first conducting at least a small debate with herself.

She whipped up her step and thought pleasantly ahead to the

quiet, solitary nip of mild brandy awaiting her at home. It was a secret indulgence and an occasional one, reserved for the evenings that followed the severest or the loneliest of days. She smiled. If the ladies of the Ladies' League for Temperance and Law even suspected, Jessie knew, they'd take off a bit of time from the Honorable John P. St. John's prohibition campaign for President and use it to expel her, and afterwards she'd be gossipped about to a caution. The League would never digest the idea that a woman alone and carrying a man's burdens might, at odd times, require a man's props to shore up her spirit, or that she might need sometimes to vary the respectable brandy with mescal or the brown and smooth habañero. Or could they grasp how one must support a small hidden sin one can laugh at in privacy, thus to ease the weight of the greater irreparable sins behind.

And that, Jessie thought, came near to being a philosophy; she wished she had someone to tell it to.

She gave her bonnet a swing in her hand, and suddenly she knew why she was walking along the west side tonight. The knowledge put a brief stutter in her step. It was the same reason she had loitered against going home on time, the reason she had stayed late to clean the shop when Thursday wasn't regular cleaning day and the shop had scant need of it. It was Brooks Durham, of course.

She should have thought about Brooks a good deal today. She had not.

The Stockman's Security Bank stood on Crowder's east side, and Brooks Durham, as bank manager, had his sleeping room immediately above it. This one evening, she realized, she'd not wanted to pass beneath his window, in event he watched for her to pass, as often, he had told her, he did.

Now she was in front of Tate's, and she quickened her step to shorten the time of her plunge through the smoky span of saloon light that splashed across her as it fell out onto the sidewalk and the street. As she passed the piano flogged into "Sandy Land," and she heard her heels matching time with it and her voice humming.

Jessie hadn't become a prude, she was sure of it—at least, not an utter stick like so many of the League ladies, the stars be thanked for that. Perhaps it was because she had watched Aunt Gussie's spinsterhood, poor Aunt Gussie, and had remembered it.

But on the other hand, since that night not a week past, when the dark-haired man came floating out of Tate's, and gave a look, and came riding his liquor straight at her, his lips drawn in until his mouth seemed only a mishap with a razor. . . .

She shuddered, recalling the fetid garlic breath of him, the damp white hands on her shoulders, the outrageous drunken words spouting out of him. The filthy, filthy swine!

But as she walked past Heidel's pitch-dark mercantile store, she smiled to herself, confessing she had a small pride in what had happened that night. She'd been stronger than that man; she'd not needed to cry out or sink into a dainty female faint. She had simply managed for herself, and quite well. It seemed a part of the pride that, when later she discovered the pig's name, she did not mention it, or the incident, to Brooks Durham. Brooks would have scoured up the man and beaten or killed him, and there'd have been a useless uproar over a cheap little gambler, and she doubted this Johnsy Boy Hood was worth it.

Ahead Jessie could see the lights of the Two Bulls, there beyond the barbershop and the hardware and harness store. The Bulls' rattly piano was under punishment, as if to duel the one down the street, and edging the flouncy sound of it like a soiled lace were the guffaws of the men and the strained trills of the girls. Once more Jessie sped her steps. Two blocks more, then home, and the itchy luxury of breaking out of her stays and tasting the brandy, and perhaps resting a whole hour before beginning to dress for Brooks.

He'd wear his gray suit, the one he held aside for church and for her, and he'd look immense in it, and immensely stable, the way her house used to look stable, and she'd have to decide very soon how to answer him.

She came almost abreast of the Two Bulls, and she felt an unease. She changed her hat to her left hand, and with the right she squeezed hard on the handle of her parasol. She crossed through the patch of light, yet strangely she breathed no easier. On an impulse she turned and looked back.

He was there, she must have known it. A shaggy bull of a figure, charging her from the street, limping so that one foot dragged up dust. She stared, not believing. Oh, not this again! Then she knew she ought to be running.

The man slowed, then came on faster, his huge body bobbing

to the limp. It struck her he thought she had turned to wait, that she was a frump and inviting him!

"Stop!" she called, and she swept the parasol up over her head.

The man came on. Foolishly she yearned to dress down that do-nothing town council that paid no mind to Brooks about getting street lamps, or hiring some law, but preferred frittering through its meetings with talk on "the spic problem," or in chattering about Lacy Tate's old red hound dog that had found a spot on the flat where it could howl and get a perfect echo, and so sat there all night; an old dog howling and listening and howling and listening. The thoughts were wild; she hadn't her poise this time. She was madly afraid and she longed for light, any light, even the tainted glow from the Two Bulls. But she stood in the dark, and it seemed she had frozen, for she could not run.

"Jessie!" the man rasped, and his huge terrible hands seized at her.

She hammered down the parasol, jumping her whole might into it. She felt the shock along her arm as the cane whacked against flesh, and she gasped "Oh!" and struck him again.

The man staggered back, his hands falling off of her. He was a giant.

"Jessie, wait!" he whispered.

She got both hands on the parasol then, and she batted it at his head. She felt the shaft break across the forearm the man flung up. Then he had hold of her elbows, trapping them in a crush at her sides. His strength was fantastic, and she was in terror, and helpless.

"Oh," she sobbed, "oh, oh, oh!"

"Dammit, Jessie, shut up!" his voice grated.

"Let me go! Let me go, you . . . oh, you smelly tramp, let me go!" She screamed it, frantic, praying she might stir out the town. But at once it was over. The hands drew away and she needed no aid. Her outcry had won.

She stared up at the blackness of his face, and he groaned, weakly, as if even the agony of him was tired, and he swung away from her toward the light of the Two Bulls. In a stride he was tearing away, his tall man's feet beating thunder from the sidewalk boards.

"You . . . you lecher!" she screamed after him, and in an instant of yellow blaze she glimpsed his face, battered and swollen and hideous. Lord, how much only a fluffy umbrella had done!

Jessie shook, fearing she would fall, and she wanted to throw up. This again, she thought, this twice within the week. She began running, feeling a stinging wrath streaming down her cheeks. She cut for the street and into it, catty-cornering blindly toward her own gate, sobbing for breath, and damning the man and all men, running with the fright like a heavy ice in her legs. Then she stumbled on her skirts and was falling, and she cried out as she collided violently with someone soft.

"I seen it, dear, I seen it! I was coming, hard as I could run!" Mrs. Lavender, thank God!

Jessie dug deep into the massive arms, her head falling into a pillowy unfettered bosom that smelled of perspiration and warm bread, and she clung there, shivering.

"The brute!" Mrs. Lavender said, patting Jessie's shoulder too hard. "I seen it, poor child! That drunken brute!"

Jessie coughed before she could speak. "Quick, please get me home. Before . . . before they all come out here, and look at me."

"There, now, there," crooned the older woman, "I'll take you home, straightaway."

She reached down to pry Jessie's fingers from the broken parasol, and Jessie looked, pondering how it was she still held it.

"It's ruint, this pretty thing," Mrs. Lavender said, holding the tatter of silk and cane out from them. "Just ruint, child. But you dealt that one his misery, I'm satisfied of that!"

The big woman started Jessie walking, an arm over her shoulders.

"Did he hurt you, child?"

Jessie shook her head. "But he . . . he knew my name!"

Mrs. Lavender's bulging sleeveless arm steadied her, and she let the safe, puffing bake-woman guide her and unlatch the white picket gate for her, and steer her along the walk and into the house.

"Now, Jessie, we'll get in here and set down, and—"

"No, not the parlor," Jessie said. "Upstairs. My bedroom."

"Sure, child. Whereabouts is a lamp?"

"On the table, by the stairs."

A tepid staleness filled the big house, and as Mrs. Lavender made a light, Jessie saw first the red skin of dust lying over everything as though she'd not stayed up to all hours only two nights ago to clean and polish and scoop out. But if by some odd miracle there had been no dust, Jessie knew, the house would still have held its dead look.

It seemed she could see the house only that way any more, a lightless, silent, lonely place, a wasted collection of double-sized rooms and delicate nursery where children might have romped and slept and grown tall, a house equipped to no real end with such broad empty beds and soft unsat-on chairs, deep unspotted carpets, a generation's hoard of knick-knacks, a mighty kitchen range, gritty like the rest, all of it aging, like herself, without mellowness or fulfillment.

It confused her that while loving the house she could so dread it, and dread it even now after what had befallen her in the street. When she left it in the mornings, she hated having slept here, and in the evenings she hated returning. Yet she scurried and scratched to hold the place, and she knew she forever would.

Climbing the stairs she leaned on Mrs. Lavender. She whimpered out loud, and it seemed to have little to do with the attack of the tramp; more, it was because that under her feet not one stairstep so much as creaked.

"Poor child," Mrs. Lavender said.

She did love the house; she'd discovered it anew and with a trembling fervor only a short time ago. It was when she asked Brooks Durham why the bank permitted him to arrange new mortgages to cancel out the old ones. He had replied by leading her on a tour of her home, as if she did not know by heart each knob and cranny and dust trap.

"The directors agree with me that if we had to foreclose, this would make a first-rate bank building," he told her. "It'd be the damnedest bank in West Texas. Look, see what a lobby the parlor would make? Teller cages fixed in, about here, closing off the arch into the dining room. The kitchen, we could brick it up for the vault, and the upstairs would chop up into rent offices."

"Brooks!"

"Don't worry, Jessie, I'd never let the bank take it from you."

Despite the promise, she had an enraging vision of sheep buyers and lawyers, maybe even a dentist, using these rooms, bargaining here, conspiring with criminals, wrenching out rotted teeth in the chambers of her youth, the rooms where Uncle Henry, and lastly, Aunt Gussie, had their passings—and, yes, as she sometimes remembered, the rooms that knew the aura of her honeymoon.

"Can you see all right, child?" Mrs. Lavender said.

"Yes—yes. We're almost there."

The big woman led the way into the bedroom, her lamp bringing into view the rose-papered walls, the dark furniture, the frilly, high-posted bed. Jessie sat down on the satin coverlet while Mrs. Lavender, her breath working at a trot, lit more lamps and made a tumult of opening the windows.

Mrs. Lavender was a round fifty, or fifty-five, or in between, Jessie guessed, and she appeared to have grown a little every day of her life. As she pounded about, sweat ran off her rolls of neck, trickled down her front and into the fleshy white ditch of her bosom, inches of which showed in bland immodesty above her tight print dress and the dingy cook apron.

She stopped at the foot end of the bed. She said, "Now, child, I'll fix some tea. Make us feel better."

"I don't want any tea. I . . . well, after what happened down there, I need . . . honestly, I mean, tea of all things!" Jessie turned her head away, flushed at having spoken so badly.

"So?" Mrs. Lavender said.

"Well . . . nothing."

The big woman laughed. "All right, child. Where do you keep the stuff?"

Jessie gestured to the mahogany wardrobe cabinet, still not looking. "On the top shelf. Oh, Mrs. Lavender, that . . . that dirty rag of a man, he knew my name! And when he touched me, he smelled; actually, he smelled terrible!"

"God love you, child. His hands . . . did he—?"

"Mercy, no!"

Mrs. Lavender sighed. "Girl, you ain't the only woman as has got molested in this wolf hole. Why, me, I was, a few years back. I was in the john, if you'll pardon me saying, when a drunk cowboy flung his rope—"

"I know," Jessie said.

"You know? I never thought I mentioned it."

"I . . . I guess you did," Jessie lied, and she thought of a day well forgotten, of a big gray-eyed boy talking more than he meant, telling of the marvels he had seen, wanting to cut himself a notch with her.

Mrs. Lavender brought down the brandy bottle and as she crossed the room she hunched over it, studying the rich green label as if she might discover the recipe printed there. Then she cast her gaze around the room. "Where, Jessie?"

"Over there," Jessie pointed to the washstand. "The glasses are in the bottom."

The woman grunted at stooping, then waddled the things to the bed and crushed it down with her weight. She poured a half a glass and sniffed of it before handing it to Jessie. She watched Jessie, openly curious, and suddenly she chuckled.

"Child, it was a right-smart shock to me, too," she said, and hurriedly she poured a full glass for herself, as though she had brought the second tumbler to no purpose, until now.

"Mrs. Lavender, that was the second time. I was just coming home from the shop—"

"Oh, you ain't telling me, Coldiron ain't fit to live in, not since they brung in so many cows. You jumble a lot of crazy cowhands in amongst them goat-lovin' Mexicans, and every last jack of 'em gets into town nights, hounding and carousing, and us making do with a unorganized county. But I do hear, some of them cow people has been buying spots of grass around about, where they can might-near boss the rest, and they aim to git rid of them sheep, and herd them spics back down south where . . . say, let me tell you! Just last night, it was, I was setting the sponge for the next batch of bread when from that Two Bulls, clean across to my place, I heard some hussy woman whoop, and some man yelled at her, 'Dammit, Prue, get your bony pratt offen this table!' You could hear it all over town, loud, a word like 'pratt' hollered out that way. And then that fiddle-faddle council, they. . . ."

Mrs. Lavender paused for a slup of the brandy, and sat looking down at it, her face thoughtful on what she had said. "Jessie, they's no telling what was going on in that Two Bulls!"

Jessie smiled. "If the League—"

"That League!" Mrs. Lavender snorted. "It ain't bothered over business ladies like you and me. Them women, they don't have to get out on Crowder past sundown; no ma'am, they got husbands, and supper tables to set and snotty noses to wipe, and it don't worry them none what happens on the street. What you and me needs, hon, we need our own menfolks."

Jessie swallowed the last of her drink, and she held the glass between her two hands, rolling it, thinking almost in guilt that she should have remained far more disturbed by her ordeal than she was.

"Mrs. Lavender, yesterday Brooks Durham asked me to marry him."

"Well!"

The big woman beamed and dumped down the balance of her brandy. She quivered at conquering a belch, and said again, "Well, Jessie, well! What'd you tell him?"

"I said I was tired, and I'd talk to him tonight."

"Holy dern! You mean you ain't decided on him yet?"

Jessie knew Mrs. Lavender's thoughts; the whole town had watched them together—Brooks sitting near her in church, walking with her on Sunday afternoons to the cemetery, at times buying her gifts, carefully in order, out of her own store. It had been months now. Last Christmas time, she guessed, was the first that Brooks properly carried her out. She had wanted to go to the *pueblito* to see that pageant the Mexicans always put on; *Los Pastores,* they called it, and it was beautiful.

The brandy was needling along her spine, and she felt like talking, although she'd not meant to discuss it, certainly not with so newsy a woman as this one, anyway.

"I really was tired," she said. "We walked down to the creek to see if there'd be a sunset, and sat awhile, and walked back fast because Brooks had to meet some men and ride out somewhere. Anyway, we were standing out there at the gate. It didn't seem hardly the place."

"Child, you grab thet Brooks Durham. Any old place you can get him. Why, I had a hole in my roof you could of flang a dog through, and old Mister Lindy was so drunk he couldn't tell his hammer from his saw, and Brooks Durham sobered him up and fetched him anyway, since they was this cloud coming up. Now, was it me. . . ."

Jessie quit listening. The brandy thrill was feeding out into her arms and legs, putting in rest and strength, and she felt almost like relating the remainder, how when Brooks had suddenly kissed her there in broad daylight, practically, she'd had a quick shamed urge, the old kind she'd put aside—no, gotten rid of—when Julius left, and how she'd pushed back when he tried to kiss her a second time, though aware she didn't really want to push, and how she'd run to the house, leaving him standing, one thick hand resting on the gatepost, his eyes darkened with a hunger she didn't care to see.

"You going to marry him?" Mrs. Lavender said.

"I . . . I don't know."

"I'd judge you love the man."

"Oh, yes. Yes. Only . . . I'm afraid of him sometimes, the way he makes me feel."

"That's it!" the big woman roared. "That's straight from the book. You're stuck!"

"But . . . I've been married, already."

"Oh, him, that what's-his-name. Julius, weren't it? How long has he been dead?"

"Who knows that he is?" Jessie said.

Mrs. Lavender scowled at her. "Why, child, some drunkard shot him, up at Dodge, didn't they say?"

"I know, but—"

"But you ain't sure you believe it."

Jessie didn't respond; she wished she'd headed off the whole topic, and quickly, when the brandy glow first dredged it up.

"Don't matter, anyway," Mrs. Lavender said. "It's the law, ain't it? Your man stays gone and unheard of for seven years, then you're a widow woman. Free as water, you are. That one, he's been off ten years."

"Eleven."

"All right, eleven."

Mrs. Lavender changed her weight on the bed, and she looked down at the bottle on the floor, and grinned. "More of that tonic, girl?"

Jessie smiled. "You think we ought?"

"It strikes me, yes. Taking into account, of course, what us two just went through."

Jessie drew her feet up on the bed, scooted back, relaxed her shoulders against the glistening headboard. She watched Mrs. Lavender seriously considering the measure as she enlivened the glasses. The woman had threadbare gray hair, short, pinned straight back, and in the lamplight, the several switches she wore to thicken it stood out, shades off the true color, so that they looked slovenly and as false as they were.

Mrs. Lavender puckered toward her liquor. "Marry Brooks Durham, I say."

"If I could be sure about Julius. And there's that money owing between us—to keep this house, and put a fair stock in the store."

"That was the bank's money you borrowed."

"Yes, but Brooks lent it. If I married him now, people might say . . . they'd say. . . ."

Mrs. Lavender finished it, brusquely.

"The good ones, they'd say hooray for you, and hooray for Brooks Durham. The rest would say you sold yoreself off like a regular bitch, and what would you care?"

"I'd care, I think."

The big woman wrinkled her brow on the last of her drink, swallowed it with a temperate ruefulness in her eyes, and she said, again, "You marry that man." She took hold of the bedpost and pulled herself up. "Well!" she laughed, "if it don't seem I got a swimmin' in my head!"

"Don't leave."

"Got to get back; tomorrow's bread ought to be near ready to come out. You want me to find Brooks, and tell him about that tramp a-trying to—?"

Jessie replied at once. "No, please don't. Brooks will be coming for me after a bit. Besides, I . . . I couldn't point out the man if I saw him again, I don't think."

"Tell Brooks, anyways." Mrs. Lavender was at the door, balancing herself. "A man likes his woman to lean on him that way."

They said good night, and Jessie listened to the woman's thumping movement along the hall, down the stairs, slow and loud, stumbling once and chuckling over it as she left the house, and it occurred to Jessie that Coldiron's only other lady of business was a little bit drunk. She was sure of it when she heard Mrs. Lavender singing in the street, a silly song, sung loud: "Talk about your good times, talk about your glory, but when you get to Heaven, you'll all be hunky-dory!"

Jessie sipped, and looked across the room at the old shelf clock. It had been Aunt Gussie's fondest souvenir, for the shy way the face nestled back among carvings of fat angels and fat cupids and vine leaves. She read the time and started up; there was the barest moment to wash and dress before Brooks arrived, and she hoped a touch of the Maréchal Niel rose on her lips might hide her breath and its secret.

He'll be fresh shaved and gentle, she thought, and I love him—except damn that little mannerism of his, that endless bouncing and tossing and toying with the gold piece on his vest. It kept her guessing, when she didn't want to guess. Always guessing: heads, is it? Or tails?

"If I marry him," she told herself, "I'll see that he stops it." It could be no harder than . . . than conditioning a big farm boy to stamp off his feet.

She set her hair free, looking forward to brushing it, and got off the bed. It pleased her about her composure; she was settled and rested and unlike a woman recently mauled in the street. This calm, now. Perhaps it was the one good thing she'd won in so many years alone.

She glanced at the clock again, and began peeling off her clothes.

Chapter Seven

RUPP'S dirt-burred sleeve had come unbuttoned, and it bunched back to his elbow as he scruffed it across the drumming wet numbness the umbrella had poled from his ear, and he stilted wooden-leggedly into the Two Bulls and bellied himself to the near end of a bar breast-high to most men. He braced his hands on it, a bar built in the old style with its stick frame bound together with rawhide and with buffalo hides stretched over the whole of it and cured there, creating a yellow top as unyielding as any planking and a great deal smoother.

The place arranged itself around a tall brass stove, now coated with red summer dust and ignored. Along one side was the bar, and on the other, the monte tables, with the dancing space squared off at the back near the piano, over which was mounted a buffalo head. The customers were cowhands in overalls and gaiters, and a few Mexicans in moccasins and wide sombreros, wearing also some bright sashes and a cold fire in their black eyes. Underfoot dodged a dog or two, and above hung the big fearless flies. Between the dogs and the flies was liquor, sweat, and smoke, and the drone of two languages: the soft warm Spanish and the harsh loud Texan; humming over and under each other, unreconciled.

Rupp hardly saw or heard; he thought of Jessie, then of his

wounds and how, regardless of the pain, they seemed to be marks on somebody else.

A bearded barman swung about, came toward him, suddenly gaping, and Rupp saw the man's lips move, saying silently, "My God!"

"Whisky," Rupp said. "A bottle."

The barman reached under and set it out, his eyes holding to Rupp's face. Rupp thumbed the cork loose, pulled it with his teeth and spat it away. He hiked the bottle high and poured the rolling heat down his throat as though his stomach were full of rats to be drowned, and for all he knew, by damn, it was.

"Two dollars," the barman said.

The heat Rupp felt was not the night, or the liquor, or fever, nor was it only the way his wife had received him home. It was all of them, heaped into a thoughtless craving he'd not felt before, not even last night at the Little Dirty. He drank, and groped to put a name to it.

"That's two dollars," the bearded man said.

Rupp took the bottle down from his mouth, gripping it by the neck while he stirred through the motions of searching his pockets. He said, "I'll bring the money by, in a day or so."

The barman wiped his palms on his swab rag. "Here, it's cash money," he said.

Rupp lifted the whisky, holding it until the scald drew water to his eyes. Enough, and then some more, and he might squelch out the fire, might even kill off the buffalo stink, which now was what he'd brought Jessie.

"Look, you," the barman said, and pointed. "See that man yonder? That there is Mister Kratz; he keeps the deals right around here. You can hand over, else I call him."

Rupp grinned, oddly pleased, and he followed the barman's finger to a pale, wide-hatted man almost the size of himself. Mr. Kratz was walking a spiral out from the stove, dribbling water on the dirt floor from a jug to settle the dust, and around his middle hung a black belt cockled in silver the shape of hearts, diamonds, clubs, and spades, and it sagged at the sides from the weight of its pistols.

Rupp felt yet better, and he turned back and looked at the barman, seeing how the bearded man's eyes seemed to hunt a hole.

"You call your Mister Kratz," he said, "and we'll see if his rind is made of iron."

The barman glanced at the Colt in Rupp's waist. Then he spread his rag and went swabbing off along the bar. A while Rupp waited. Kratz did not come. Rupp drank again, and carried his bottle out into the street.

He looked at the night and spat at it, and it struck him as he walked what the heat feeling had been, and still was. The pain seemed to lift, a little, by the knowing. He needed, just, to kill somebody tonight.

Chapter Eight

JOHNSY Hood, who often got sick and tired of being low-rated to his face as "Johnsy Boy" and to his back as "Johnsy Hoodwink," wasn't the least despairing of himself this evening. In flourishes he snapped cameoed silver buttons into the wide cuffs of an immaculate, pleat-fronted white shirt, and at once his soul bloomed at the good clean crackle which meant that, at last, his Mexican washwoman had had enough of being cussed and was becoming less sparing with the cold starch.

Taking care, he packed the crisp wedged tail into his trousers and strolled closer to the big looking glass which, though mottled here and chipped there, was reserved proudly by the Rusk House for the senior of its resident guests. Johnsy craned around a mottle and smiled at himself.

It was a favoring smile, handsome, boyish, he thought, yet very damned virile. He'd found the smile useful to his business; he had proved, too, that it could fetch out the hidden, unwinding urge that lies deep in every woman—which matters, he mused now to the mirror, were practically the same thing.

He took a brightly flowered vest off a peg beside the glass, slipped his arms through it cautiously, so as not to crease it, and buttoned up with a series of small shrugs, finally tugging down the neat points until, stylishly, they hid the waist of his soft gray trousers. Johnsy turned next to the new red necktie, bowing it three fussy times before it knotted into the precise folds he wanted, thus looking—as he'd read in some book—"kept and careless at the one same time."

Satisfied, he drew out a drawer of the washstand and found the nozzled bottle of bergamot. He sprinkled a few amber drops of it into his palm. These he patted into the oiled black waves of his hair, and as he did so, he sniffed his appreciation of the sweet spicy fog which instantly crowned him. A few more drops he massaged into his lips, there to serve against his supper garlic.

A few times Johnsy had decided to give up garlic, at least, to cut down, no matter how well it helped the rough and flavorless food of this country. But in the end he'd come to a discernment, concluding that garlic might be the real breath of living as he enjoyed it, and therefore necessary to him: a staple, the way whisky became for some men. He thought of this presently as a joke while with light fingers he pumped up the waves of his hair, mashed down the slick black troughs between. He began a critical scrutiny of the result.

Men in these parts knew none of the niceties of good grooming, nor were they apt to learn, this season or the next. And this comforted Johnsy, for he himself had a mastery of such things. He understood, for instance, the considerable effect a man's scent might have on a woman, which was but one of the little detail things that assured him he'd make out, as indeed he had made out during the two years since he'd left St. Louis. Hadn't he, in Coldiron, an eminence in cards and women?—especially women? Unless, and now Johnsy frowned, unless you'd count that once, with that striped-haired storekeeper, Jessie Rupp, who shouldn't be counted, the God's truth being that he'd made no real, calculated try.

"Cur!" she had screamed, and flailed him with her fists. Blessedly, she'd not marked his face, and the night had been dark, and there had been a total emptiness of the street. Johnsy had not brooded. There were other women—less kittenishly pretty than Jessie Rupp, perhaps, but with more smolder underneath, and nowise so senseless to the gentler male graces.

For one, Bonnie Shelley.

He wet his finger from his tongue, and, leaning close to

the mirror, began rubbing down the even black lines of his eyebrows. Certainly, Bonnie Shelley. Her fattishness aside, hadn't she been attracted to him until she shivered at bearing it, and flamed in the face, even wept, while telling him so? And how she had loved his bergamot, from the first moment she saw him.

He had gone to the Stockman's Security to deposit a night's winnings and to lay out the poker bait once more for Brooks Durham. He'd had to line up and wait at the teller's booth, standing behind Brack Shelley, whom Johnsy knew only as a whiskered twist of a cowman, a brown and homely man constantly taut like a strained trace chain, and he'd noticed old Brack stuffing sheaves of new money into a sour-smelling money belt. Then he had felt the eyes cuddling up to his back, and turning, had surprised her.

Bonnie Shelley sat in one of the lattice-backed lobby chairs, waiting tamedly for her husband, looking tired and dog-plain in a homemade dress that came near to concealing the full swells of her body, and she had on a clumsy, silly hat decorated with wax berries. Her incongruous green eyes met Johnsy's briefly, approving him in the instant she smiled. Then her gaze fell, and she reddened while recrossing her ankles, and he saw her large harsh hands trying to dig a hole for themselves behind a knit handbag that trembled on her lap. Johnsy had nodded and thought nothing more of her, until a few days later when he heard about Brack Shelley and his crew starting a trail herd off to Kansas.

Winking at himself in the glass, Johnsy left the washstand. His full-tailed gray coat, St. Louis tailored, thanks to Klepstein's and the stage-line express service, lay ready on the bed. As he reached for it a thin yellow cat roused and snagged panicked claws on the lapel.

"Oh, damn you!" Johnsy groaned. He snatched the cat up and slung it hard against the room's farthest wall. His anger shot higher when the animal made no sound. He felt a rage, tingling and delicious, and he started to lunge after the pet he never fed. But suddenly the rage was all gone, and he was mostly afraid he'd broken the cat's back.

"Kitty, kitty!" he called softly, and he knelt. The animal crept away from him and under the bed, its diamond eyes watching and the belly almost dragging.

"All right," he muttered, "just stay the crying hell off my clothes!"

Johnsy was shaking when he straightened. It had been an unintended violence, taking hot command of him, tasting sweet and for a moment, terribly satisfying. Then he had regretted, which he hated. It was the old pattern, the same wild one of last night beside the Little Dirty when he had swung the pistol, when he rammed down with that branding iron.

He noticed how his sweat had begun soiling him, and quickly he set his thinking to other things. He picked the cat sheddings off the coat, and, back at the mirror, he drew it on, establishing the drape to match the sloppy perfection of the necktie. He fed a silk and lace handkerchief into the breast pocket, took the shiny two-barreled derringer from the washstand top and slipped it into a pocket of the vest. After a final, approving smile at the glass, he stooped and puffed out the lamp. His buggy and team waited in the alley beside the hotel, old Dub Stokes's nigger boy suspended sleepily from the bridles.

Getting clear of town, the tall, stockinged blood bays had to be scolded back to a walk, which pleased Johnsy; he liked owning the prettiest team in town; it was a part of gentlemanly outfitting. At the first lift of the trail he gave the horses their leave to trot, a way of praising them, and he sat back, loose and happy.

It was late. Late enough for the moon, and he let the cool gold light soak in to tinker as it chose with his mood. This moon, streaked across the waist by a thin gold-edged cloud, was as Johnsy preferred. Under such a glow and sky, he knew, women might melt of a sudden. It was a dreamer's light, wherein a lady could gorge her eyes on him at his best and turn sweet and wanton under the caress of his nighttime voice, as Bonnie Shelley so often did. Bonnie, he smiled, took precious little warming, any more, before her blushy, breasty melting set in.

Through the weeks since Old Brack trailed off for Dodge, Johnsy had grown familiar with all of Bonnie's stages: her early worried shyness, next the gradual open-mouthed thawing, then the wordless and fierce excitement storming her until you'd never know her for a tired, lonesome, old man's wife. She liked being hand-held, to have her lips touched only lightly at first; she liked being strolled on silent walks through the great cottonwoods that hemmed the Shelley place in a rustling horseshoe, making of themselves one hell of a natural fence. He could count on her saying how marvelous handsome he looked, and he could be fairly positive she'd wail a little when he got ready to leave.

But Johnsy intended more than this tonight. He would crowd her, again, for a decision. It was due time she came to one, for he was disliking the uncommon cash famine of these days, and if his shortage was but temporary, it remained none the more bearable.

The bay team had stretched stride, set and eager to gallop. Johnsy scanned his clothes, and quickly he talked the horses down; he must avoid what he could of the ruinous red dust.

The weeks given to Bonnie Shelley had been expensive for him. She had once lived East, before coming out to marry Brack, and from the East, Johnsy was sure, she had brought an eye for the custom and manner of gentlemen. He had sensed this despite the almost comic flaws in her own tastes, so pitiably displayed in the way she dressed herself, and he'd not have risked wearing the same suit night after night. But he did not condemn her eye for dress; he knew that he enjoyed pleasing it, however costly it became.

Besides the clothes, there had been other burdens. For Bonnie, he learned, there had to be memory gifts to mark each unimportant "anniversary" she so loved to prattle about—the day they first saw each other in the bank, the later day that they actually met, in a grocery store he followed her into. And another "date," one which Johnsy winced at now and which even Bonnie could speak of only in the dark. It was that first night she really heels-up forgot about Brack Shelley and remembered instead that she was a woman, and not quite old.

Johnsy spanked the bays with the reins, then pulled them in sharply as the dust rose, and he was annoyed that the thought of his money drought had driven much of the good moon humor out of him. It riled him, too, that he could not credit the entirety of his pinch to his courtship.

There had been, of late, an infuriating reluctance of Coldiron men to sit with him at cards, which threw a man back on his pride and at the same time starved his purse hollow. On neither count did Johnsy care for it. But, he decided now, this situation and the steep price on Bonnie would have mattered little, and he'd have been sound of condition still, in spite of them, had it not been for last night's chance discovery of the cow thief.

"Damn him," Johnsy said aloud.

He'd spent his best touches in baiting up a game with Mr. Durham sitting in, and he had managed it, counter to what people said of Durham around town. Coldiron believed its banker would have none of gambling. But to Johnsy, Brooks Durham's eyes suggested something else again. He had invited the banker to play, every time he saw him, and when at last Durham consented, Johnsy had taken it as a proof of his own shrewdness and, yes, charm.

"We'll have to get out of town to play," Durham had said.

"Aw, I've got a steady table over at Tate's," Johnsy answered. "It would be less trouble."

Durham shook his head. "If I played in town, people would get the notion every chip I threw came straight out of deposits. Find us a place to go, not too far out."

Johnsy had thought immediately of Elwood Coates. The foreman had a cabin to himself, out on the JC, and Johnsy knew the man would drink himself out of the game in short order. This was how Johnsy wanted it; he meant to have it head-to-head with Durham.

Johnsy frowned at the wind and sighed. The stakes would have been high. But they had happened onto that mangy thief.

The light Timken-spring buggy bottomed suddenly on a chasm in the trail, the jar of it painfully reminding Johnsy that his ribs would stay sensitive until fall. He shuddered. Damn that man! Whiskered, and barn big, and stinking—

In surprise he saw that the blood bays had completed the four miles. Close ahead lay the tall shadows of the cottonwoods, the trees themselves looking a cool orange and black under the moon, and beyond them he glimpsed a flickering light at the house.

The Shelley place was something of a botch, if you thought of the Rupp woman's mansion house in town, or the great, scattered, kept-up layout of Jerome Chester's JC, on farther north. But in any lesser comparison, Shelley's came off well. There was the grove of old trees, which in this grimy gale-peeled country could be envied of any owner, and centering these was the house, a piecemeal, tacked-onto confusion of planks and stone with a small show of glass—unplanned, but large, porched generously across the front, and zested up a trifle with a tall trellis built like a gentlewoman's fan. Past the house were the outbuildings, most of them painted in testimony to Old Brack's success with free range and wild longhorns freely gathered. The structures were not aligned, but seemed to have located at whims of their own like a handful of dice flung along a crap table.

Johnsy steered the team into a thicket of mesquite and creosote bush a quarter-mile short of the house. He filled a pair of feed bags from the buggy's grain box and slipped them over the twitching white noses; this was a reward the bays had come to depend on. Johnsy wiped his hands off on the seat upholstery before he started up the slight, moon-softened slope, keeping his eyes down, for stock grazed here. When he got into the cottonwoods, he saw her.

She leaned on a slim pillar of the veranda, one foot on the uppermost step, the other hooked on the edge of the porch floor, the whole pose absurdly girlish. As he stepped from the grove she turned toward him with a start. He decided the dress she filled, tightly, and its narrow neck ruffle that dipped until her breast beginnings showed, undershot her age by maybe ten years.

"Oh, Johnsy!" she cried, and she came from the porch at a run. He stopped to wait for her, but their meeting was nevertheless a bump that sent a twinge striking upward from his bruised ribs, angering him at her. She pulled him against her plump steaminess, and he held his tongue and reached his arms around her waist, feeling as he did a sob that was voiceless.

"Help me, Johnsy!"

He scowled; her tears were sopping into his lapel, and he checked himself, barely, before setting her straight that the coat was not to be wetted, it being still the same as brand new.

"What's wrong, Bonnie?"

Her face wiped itself up his front and lifted. He looked at the muss of yellow hair, the plainness, the paleness, the puffs about her eyes, and he saw she'd gotten hold of a shabby white rose, somewhere, and wore it over her ear like a bookkeeper's pencil.

"It's Brack!" she whispered.

He jerked back from her, and put her between him and the house. "Good God, is he home?"

"No, not yet," she said, and she fell toward him again. He caught her.

I could slap her, he thought, *slap her a-ringing.* Putting it that way, she had almost sent him running. "Well, tell me!"

"A letter came today; Brack found someone to write it for him, and he's coming home—he'll be here in three weeks!"

"I see."

A refreshing shock pumped through him; he did see, and he wanted to grin, even giggle, over the good luck after so much pissy bad. But her eyes were on him, damp and fearful, and he showed her a grave face while he gritted his white teeth for her and made his hands tremble on her arms.

"What can we do?" she said, smothering her voice against him once more.

At times it had seemed Old Brack might never come home, suspending Bonnie and Johnsy together, leaving it so she could go on and on putting him off. But the old man *was* returning. Either Bonnie would spit, now, or she would swallow, and glory be.

Johnsy stiffened himself against her weight, realizing that this particular moment was the crucial one. Roughly he bent and butted her head back with his and kissed her, not gently and until she stifled for breath and slid her head away to his shoulder.

"It's too damned bad," he said, seeing to it his lips brushed her ear. "Guess we'll have to cut loose and go now, poor sweet. Else let things finish, and forget about each other."

"Oh, don't say that!" she shuddered. "I'm all tore up, Johnsy, I don't know what, and I'm sick with thinking of it. If . . . if only we had a little more time."

He rubbed her cheek with his, aware that his own clean skin was, if anything, the closer to velvet.

"Why?" he said. "It wouldn't show up a speck different, not if we mulled it over a hundred years. That old fud, he'd still come home, and you'd still have to make up your mind."

She clung tighter as he spoke, and he found he wasn't suffering from the pain which danced up from his sore ribs and made his mind quick, and he smiled at her, feeling very clear and fine. He could easily have laughed over this whole stupid wonderful scene.

"Bonnie, you got to stop fretting over Brack. He's just a burnt-out old man, seventy years old."

"Sixty-two!"

"All right, sixty-two, and mean as hell and no use to you. He never was a husband to you, not even bull enough to try—"

"Oh, please Johnsy!"

"You told me that yourself. You, Bonnie, you need a man who can love you half to death."

"I know, I know! But—"

"But, nothing!" He hiked up his voice. "Brack didn't marry you for a wife anyway; works you like you was a tool, good God, that's the way he got you, too, just like ordering a plow or something."

"Not that way, Johnsy. Don't say it." Her words sifted through his shirt, feeling warm on his chest. "He wrote Papa back in Illinois, and they agreed, and I came out and married him. It wasn't exactly like . . . not like putting in an order; it was—respectable. I knew Brack when I was small, he was Papa's friend. I don't like it when you say—"

"All right." He shut her off. "But however you say it, it ain't him you belong to."

A long while she leaned on him. Once she raised her face, sniffled too late to keep her nose from dripping, and he panged at what surely must have happened to his coat. He had tired from her weight when she squared up and raised her head.

"It's you I love," she said.

Her breath was running deep, rocking her breasts, and the misty breadth of her eyes was shining at him. Something in her look put him on edge; it was a claiming look, as though he'd been bought and paid for, which as yet he hadn't. He shifted his feet and waited.

"I'm ready, Johnsy Hood," she said. "We'll go, whenever you want."

He kept himself in hand, looking down at her with a worship

and a pity spread for her to see, and to prop herself on if she cared to, letting her discover in him what was a treasure and soul food to her sex, the compassion in a man that Old Brack would never have an inkling she, or any woman, needed.

He was holding her again before he spoke. "I know, it's a trial for you, thinking how you do about sticking married. But we're doing right, Bonnie, and you won't be sorry, I swear it."

Bending slowly, he kissed her, remembering as he did a line he'd read, or perhaps heard, back East. He quoted it against her cheek as the kiss was finished. "God, if I had to, I'd crawl back from hell for that!"

She gripped him hard, and groaned, and she took his hand and led him across the sandy clearing, out of the moon and into the cottonwoods. They went to a tree they had sat under before, and she sat down, cross-legged, and pulled him after her.

"You're beautiful," he told her. "And myself, I'm not the ugliest man alive. Think what younguns we'll have!"

Johnsy was aggravated then; the younguns part had leaped itself out of him, uncalled for, the way things did with him sometimes. Always it was a commitment, one he couldn't call back. But he stopped caring about it as she drew him down to the grass, crying a little, but in a different way, and before he quit thinking altogether, he decided that nothing ever said to Bonnie Shelley before had made her feel so female, not in the whole drab forty years of her life.

They walked close, back toward the house.

"You'll have to do as I tell you, exactly."

"I will, Johnsy."

She sounded worn now, he thought, more tired than she ought, even if she'd handled the day's chores alone, as often she did when Brack was home, for Brack liked to say, "A man's wife is his helpmate." Brack counted hired men too costly to waste on feeding chickens and toting household water and grubbing in a vegetable patch.

"I'll pack the buggy tomorrow," Johnsy said. "Tomorrow night, I'll drive out for the money."

"About that, Johnsy—"

"He's got ten thousand, ain't he?"

"I . . . I guess so." She was looking down, holding her rumpled skirts clear of the ground. "More, I guess."

"That's it, then. I'll come out about the same time."

She moved a little away from him. "How could I get it, Johnsy? Someone would have to know what for. At the bank. I know they'd ask."

He was starting to ache from his ribs and from curbed temper; he was tired, too, of how she had to be nudged along from one minute to the next. She had never seen it, how it took money to be what he was, and that it would take a great lump more to be what he intended ahead.

"Now, Bonnie, you told me you could write checks on Brack."

"Yes, he lets me, for little things around the place when he's away. But—ten thousand dollars! They'd ask questions at the bank; I know Mr. Durham would. He'd say I ought to wait for Brack to get home and let him draw it out."

They were out of the tree shadows. Johnsy admitted, then, that the showering moon bettered her; in its wash she didn't seem so fat or so aging. She was more a simple and upset child, fumbling for evasive threads with clumsy child's fingers. Briefly he felt one of his regrets.

"It'll be fish in a barrel," he said. "Listen to me. You get to town tomorrow, late, say just before the bank closes up. If you have to explain to anybody, say that Brack's letter told you to get the money for a deal of his. That's all they is to it."

"Johnsy, I feel . . . well, I—"

"Look!" he said, speaking as the idea fastened on him. "Just see to it Brooks Durham waits on you. Tell him the money is for Brack, like I said, and wave your letter at him. If that don't suit him, send somebody to get me. Hear? It happens I know a thing or two our Mr. Durham wouldn't want told around, considering a ride he took with me and Elwood Coates last night!"

He had to slap his thigh; he felt gay. He was, since the branding, in a place to swap out with Brooks Durham if he had to, and he'd only now realized it.

"What'll you do?" Bonnie said.

"What I told you," he struggled for patience. "I'll take the money on to St. Louis, and straight away I'll get us a house. Then I'll go scouting around for us a investment, or something. You can come on after me, in a couple of weeks, before that old . . . before Brack gets home. Take the stage to Wichita, and catch the train there, and you can telegraph me, so I'll know which train to meet."

Her hand, hot and rough and overtight on his, quit its swinging, so that his knuckles stopped grazing her thigh as they walked, and she said, "Johnsy, it's . . . it's so much money. He can't afford so much. Don't you see, disgracing his name, that will hurt bad enough. Can't we leave off the money? I mean, just get up and go, you and me?"

She finished weakly, as if knowing his answer beforehand, yet bound to ask, wanting the question to pass her mind as a kind of liniment to herself. And Johnsy sighed, sure he had won. He turned her to him, and tasted the bergamot still fragrant on his lips and put his hands on her face and kissed her. When he straightened, he took the rose from her hair, kissed it also, and he said, "You must give this to me, Bonnie, to keep until—"

"Oh, my Johnsy!" she whispered, and she put her head against him. When he was ready to leave, she spoke his name again, and said, "Tomorrow night!"

He put her back on the veranda, allowing her to hold him there a moment longer and to murmur how he was a gentle lovely boy, and hers, and her breath and her life. Then he kissed her and started back to the buggy.

Once through the cottonwoods and covered by them, he began running. It was, he knew, partly to get away from her, and partly because of the booming, belly-down joy he always felt when he completed, with success, some long hard pull.

Driving back to town, Johnsy let the bright bays level their necks and he paid no heed as the wind unfixed, then tousled, his hair. Above the hoofs and rattle and wind, he whistled; a pretty tune of his own devising, one, he was sure, of the sort you might hear in some big city far from this sweltering dirty country, a city, say, such as San Francisco.

At Coldiron's north edge he slowed the horses, and though he ended his whistling, he went on hearing the tune in his mind. The night was much darker now, its moon almost done for, and he minded this, even though he'd had his full use of it. He thought of Bonnie, so starved for what he gave her, and so simple at receiving it, and he wished chance had offered him another way to the wealth he must have. Something quicker and not so tedious, and less taking of his time.

He turned the team into Dub Stokes's stable and flipped a half dollar to the black boy who would rub the bays and bed them. By the lantern light in the broad doorway he paused and brushed dry yellow grass off his clothing; he used his handkerchief to dob off his face before he moved south along Crowder Street, and across it, to the Rusk House.

Johnsy crossed the dim, empty lobby and climbed the stairs to the upper floor, passing his own room without a glance, coming up to the cracked and sloughing door next beyond. He bent and thumped more dust off his trousers, ran his fingers through his hair, and let himself in.

Maria was asleep, a brown ball in a huge frayed chair.

At his step she started up, blinked, dug her small fists into her eyes, smiled, shrieked happy Spanish, and came charging at him.

"At last, my Heart, you have come!"

Maria's voice sang, and as sleep fell away, her jet eyes shown with all the animal glow of a Monterrey queen, a thing inborn and instinctive, he guessed, for she had never been an hour distant from Coldiron. She looked half the size of Bonnie Shelley, yet flat nowhere; she was all coffee-skinned grace, young grace, in the burnt-pink kimono she wore.

Johnsy grinned at her. The kimono had come from a drummer's sample case, and he remembered breaking the buttons off it before giving it to her, a thoughtfulness Maria had never asked about, as if the buttons had never belonged.

"You are here!" she shrieked.

"What do you think?" he said shortly, and he pitched her the mashed white rose from his pocket. She bent to the floor for it, and stretched up, humbled, to kiss his cheek.

"By God, I'm glad that's over with," he said.

Worry like a blight snuffed the lights in Maria's black eyes. "What is this that is done with, my Johnsy?"

"We hit out tomorrow night," he said, and he let her see he had never doubted himself or the outcome. "About midnight, I expect. Suit you?"

She clapped her hands. "Oh, it will be as you promised, won't it be?"

He shed his coat and handed it to her. "Dammit, hang it up straight this time," he said.

Watching Maria's painful caution with the coat, breathing in the musk and vanilla-bean smells of her, he conceded he was close to jealous of her beauty. Her head was slow, yes, but lovely, like carved mahogany come alive. It might have been because of all Maria's praying and bead-counting and shrieks and bother that sometimes he forgot her prettiness, so much so that once in a while, coming in on her this way, he awoke to it like new and stared at it. He looked at the round tightening of the kimono across her hips as she tiptoed up to get the hanger onto a nail, and he thought how Maria might have been more, even, than Jessie Rupp, and would have been, and no chaff, had her mother borne her white.

He sank into the chair Maria had slept in, feeling her body warmth left there beneath him, and he kicked off his black patent-leather shoes, hoping that the recklessness of the wallow under the cottonwoods hadn't skinned and spoiled them.

"Yes," he answered her, "it'll be like I said. San Francisco, I've decided on. A real big city."

"Johnsy *mio*, it is not—"

"Hush fuming; we'll have over two weeks."

"Oh, my Heart, this is not possible! It is too short a time, two weeks!"

He laughed.

"But it is not time enough, to make our travel, and to hide us in a far-off place!" The slim brown hands fluttered to the swells of her voice. "The Señor Shelley, he is hard in the eyes; he is a Protestant man! He will hunt, and he will find us!"

Johnsy idled at getting the waves of his hair back into place.

"Oh, Johnsy, hear me, it is great trouble! I cannot pray of this, such a thing as we do! It will—"

"Shut up," he said.

She quieted, facing him, her mouth smalled with fright.

"Now then," he said. "There's nothing to go busting apart about. Bonnie will use up a week, maybe a couple, looking for me in St. Louis. And it'll be two weeks before she leaves. Hell, we'll be gone from here a month before she gets the idea I ain't in St. Louis feathering up a nest for her."

He darted a slim cigar from his vest, bit the end off, and

prodded with his forefinger to make positive no shred of tobacco had stuck to his teeth. He leaned to the match she held, catching how its flame trembled.

"You're a fidgety little bitch," he said, and pulled her to his lap. "Listen. How long you figure it'll take a woman like Bonnie Shelley to settle on traipsing back home to honest herself up to old Brack? How long, huh?"

"I do not know." Maria's voice was a mite of a thing, like her body, a miniature.

"Suppose you was a lady, Maria. Suppose you had you a high cheese of a husband, and suppose you took his money and lit out to meet another man. How long you think you'd be at trailing back home and telling your husband you got stood up? Quite a while, I'd say, if you ever got around to it at all."

"Oh," she said and leaned into his chest. Pain, this time not to be dawdled with, tore the shout out of him.

"Jesus, can't you watch it?" He bolted to his feet, spilling her to the floor. "My ribs, they're sore! Didn't I tell you forty times, a horse kicked me!"

She sat as she had fallen, against his feet, recoiling as if he would kick or backhand her, and wildly he thirsted to. Then he thought of the yellow cat, and the tramp, and he sickened a little as he eased himself back into the chair.

"Just watch it," he grumbled.

She was up at once, smiling as though he'd said he was sorry. "*¿Quantos dinero,* Johnsy *mio?*"

"Enough. And quit talking spic."

"Shall I have on my finger a ring with green lights deep inside?—a ring such as my mother told me, one such as the sun?"

Johnsy took the cigar from his mouth, took stock of the crumbly red coal on the end of it, and he drew Maria to him again, seeing the dark shine of her skin, the pulse bugging in her throat.

"You'll get it," he said. "Provided you quit pouring out my whisky every damned time I'm away from here!"

Chapter Nine

MIDNIGHT had shoved and hollered and staggered through the Two Bulls, and staggered out again, leaving behind the fagged and stagnant wee hours, and now the big echoing hall was disgorging itself, as if nauseated. Out in ones, pairs, and sets gushed card men and cowhands, a few reveled-out townsmen, and the handful of Mexican goatmen brassy enough to find their liquor where they pleased, the wag-tongued whites, *por Dios*, look out! The piano, much repainted and frontless, was suffering the tired blows of a bald man in a lake-blue shirt and orange sleeveholders, and the tune was "Old Dog Tray," or some offshoot from it. The last of the exhausted women were disappearing toward the rooms upstairs, and in a back corner a small knot of swearing men sweated over a magic lantern, trying to devil it into flashing its pictures on the wall, still failing when Julius Rupp came through the doors.

He walked to the bar, stopping at the near end where he'd stood earlier. He saw a man wearing an apron drop a glass, shake his head over it, then rear back to shout, "Drink 'em up, gents; closing 'er down in ten minutes!"

Rupp set his elbows in an unmopped puddle on the hide bar top, noticing in front of him a whitewashed wall, almost solidly fly-specked and decorated just below the roof beams by the faded painting of a rolly woman, reclining on a cloud, trying to smile a virgin's smile though she was stark raw naked. She was unreal and a mess, like the wound on his chest, like his meeting with Jessie, like the money he'd lost, like his temper and his thoughts; this virgin on a cloud, he could adopt her now as a part of his agony. He felt the brand pussing through the rag that covered it, and aside from it, the flames that had him afire. He grinned against the hurt. He still needed one good drink. He hadn't gotten it, and because of this, he built a rage for the Two Bulls.

He stared until the bearded barman looked over, and he signaled to him. The man came, but not eagerly, his eyes traveling about the room, as if this time he would let loose and halloo his Mr. Kratz.

"Goddam you," Rupp said. "Half that bottle was water. Lay me out some liquor this time."

The man met his eye, and his cheek whiskers quivered, and he reached under the bar and came up with a bottle. He set it in front of Rupp, keeping his hold on it.

"Cash money?" he said.

Rupp laid the long Colt on the bar. "Maybe," he said, "I better deal with your Mister Iron-ass."

The barman released the bottle. He backed away, until his head bumped a shelf. "Nothing like that," he said. "I ain't the boss, but . . . but you just pay when you're a mind."

A red-eyed cowman and a blocky man in a checkered suit and derby and then several others turned to look at Rupp. He glared back at them as he worked the handgun back into his belt, and he pondered what it was he saw like a scum in their faces. He was a sight to see; he'd not forgotten. God no! But he knew the looks on the men weren't because of his marks, or the gun he'd shown. It struck him they'd rocked back, as if ready to move away. They had glanced at him, and feared him.

Rupp had a drink, and considered this. Then—hell, it suited him.

Until he took up the bottle to leave, he didn't notice that movement in the Two Bulls had stopped, that the piano had died. He turned. Everyone watched him. The man Kratz leaned in the doorway, shoulder to the sill, thumbs hooked in the lavish silvered belt, his big body closing off the way, squint eyes watching.

Rupp thought he liked it. Then he was sure he did; it was a frame for the blood-letting he needed, and better than the liquor. He changed the bottle to his left hand and walked toward the man, taking no care against his limp. Close up, he stopped.

"It's your move," he said.

Kratz stared back at him a cold moment, before the eyes blinked and broadened and looked away. Slowly Kratz raised his hands, and he wiped one across his mouth.

"Sometimes," Kratz whispered, "we make a exception." He eased himself out of the door. Rupp walked out.

Across Crowder he went, back to the cramped little alley where the low-headed dun slept and waited, where he'd drunk the first bottle low, and smelled the buffalo stink on himself stronger than before, and decided full half of the whisky had been ladled up from the Little Dirty. He groaned at the T frying itself deeper into his chest, and he bottomed-up the new bottle, swallowing fiercely, until the whisky stung to his eyes.

Gathering the dun's reins he led it on north, toward the trail, drinking as he walked. But for the saloons, Coldiron was tucked in, and dark, and its houses quiet, except for one far east, where there was, perhaps, a weasel busy in a chicken pen. Rupp felt the mansion behind him; he need only to look over his shoulder to see it, and to see if it was dark, but he did not. He kept drinking, and above the bottle he saw the trim-wheeled buggy and white-legged team turn into Dub Stokes's.

Rupp was almost even with the stable doors when he noticed the man, hunched over just inside the barn and slapping his clothes clean. It was almost the way he'd seen the soft figure before, when it was bent over, and vomiting. Johnsy Boy Hood, the pretty pink bastard!

Bending, Rupp slid under the dun's neck, putting the drowsing animal between himself and the stable. He watched across the saddle seat as Johnsy Boy Hood walked south, cut across, and disappeared into the Rusk.

"Ain't he pretty?" Rupp said to the dun, and he put the bottle into his saddlebag, in the place where seventeen thousand dollars should have been. He mounted, but held the horse at a stand, and he combed his fingers through the ratty black mane as he gave thought to Johnsy. Then he got down and went to the stable.

There were meaner ways to live than the way he lived, Harris James was thinking. He tended to this and that for Mister Stokes, and for it got his keep, besides a dollar in hand every oncet in a while, and he pretty well liked most of the white younguns who came to look at him since he was the only nigger in town, particularly them that brought him tasties from their mammy's kitchens, and he laughed with them every time they said he had his name on backwards, no matter how often they said it.

Nowadays, Harris James liked to figure, Out West was a passel better than Down South. He had grain to scatter around, and thus could take a chicken, off and on, from which to make up a batch of perlue, and there was the big Mississippi house at the end of the street, to be looked at whenever he had the time to be lonesome for home. And if ever he got the heat for a wife, there were greaser girls nigh the color of himself, and should he choose one out, he was sure, the white folks wouldn't care.

He slapped the green stable flies away from his neck and bent to polishing one of the sweaty bay flanks. He tried whistling, which never came easy for him, but he stuck at it in case Mister Stokes was resting light up in the loft and maybe worrying whether he was tending to business.

"Easy, hoss," he crooned as the slick bay pawed, and he straightened and dug the half dollar out of his back pocket to admire it. It was an uncommon gift, and it reminded him he must not tarry over this handsome team. He got hustling busy. He did not see the tall towering man, not until the tall towering man was standing there and speaking down to him.

Harris snapped himself up and looked at the man's face. He felt quick beads of good darky sweat blister out on his forehead, and he swiped at them with his sleeve as the man spoke and waited.

"The gentleman as owns this team heah, you mean, suh?" Harris answered. "That's Mister Johnsy Boy Hood, I expect his name is."

Harris could not help it, he kept looking back and forth, from the ear with the notch in it to the ear that was fresh butchered and bloody, and if it was a bad sight, it seemed less a chore than watching the gray eyes; these, he thought, were fit to stick in you and run you to an altar.

"Yes suh," he answered the next question, "that's it. Mister Hoodwink, he's got him a room yonder in the Rusk House lodgin' place, and when he aims to use his team, he sends some li'l spic child to tell me, and I hitches 'em and takes 'em to him."

Harris beat at the flies and stood idle a good spell after the giant-man left, feeling guilty because the bays were cooling out a mite fast with Mister Johnsy's half dollar big as a wagon wheel in his pocket. But he could not put his head to the work, not right off.

He laid an apologizing palm on the silky red neck of the animal he called Smart-Alec Bill, and he looked the direction the big man had gone, seeing only the quiet street.

"Lawd, hoss," he said. "Lawd-ee!"

Chapter Ten

IT was evening, and noon-hot. Maria Alicia y Montesa Quintero sat before the mirror in her room, and she told herself, "I am grown a pretty one," and she fell to enumerating the coming days. This was a Friday, August's fifteenth day, and, as she counted it, there remained but twelve days more until she would become eighteen —or was it thirteen days more, this being the year of the Leap, with one day a surplus, and already behind?

In the search of such problems to an answer, Maria had never been wise of mind, even *un poco,* but this disturbed her little. She was happy to think of becoming eighteen, and a woman, and happy to consider that soon, in good advance of this birth date, she might in fact walk out of this Rusk House place and, looking neither to one side nor the other, and concerning her spirit with no one who watched, go to Pedro Street and follow it almost to Dirty Creek, and there pass through her own door again, paying a proper lady's call upon her Mama Quintero.

For this, now, she had only the smallest time to wait. If ever she would go to Pedro Street, it must be tonight, before the Big Travel: minutes, or an hour from this moment. She longed for a timepiece, so she might listen to the wait ticking itself away. But it would be soon, now, she knew; outside, it was dark. And she would go, she must believe it; she would. Johnsy had made it a pledge, and he would honor it so.

With the anticipations, Maria smiled and sped her hands and watched her black gloss of hair as it slid through the comb and wallowed into crackling, musk-scented hanks about her shoulders. She had used the day at packing, as Johnsy bid her use it, and already she was washed until she shined. She need only dress to be prepared for Mama Quintero, and after the visit, the Great Travel.

Maria dropped the comb and began the paint on her face, touching it on lightly as Johnsy had taught her, so as to look unlike the worn ones of the Two Bulls, and her heart frolicked. Returning home would be such a bell in the tower, ringing of her triumph.

In the grand dream of it she pictured how the meeting would be. She, Maria, holding out her hand to her mother, offering it with a pride, drawing the eyes of Mama Quintero to rest on a finger ring fiery with green lights.

"See, *madre mia?*" she might say, "I have done as you wished me to do, do you not agree? *Ándale,* you must make a welcome for me!"

Maria put down the rouge; she had no call for it, the manner in which her face burned already. Hungrily she imagined the look of relenting sweetness on Mama Quintero's crumpled old face, the quick wet kisses and the tears of her half sisters. Maria expected they would kiss her many times, for she'd not seen them in two years, though the Quintero's *jacal* stood where always it had, a short five squares away.

Ay, seguro que si, there would be a great many kisses.

She laughed and clapped her hands, watching the other hands in the glass clapping also. It will happen, she assured herself again, it will! Johnsy has given his promise.

His promise. Maria's thoughts slowed, and plodded, and she leaned her head to the side, and refused to make a frown. In truth, Johnsy had promised the ring, but it only. Yet had he not promised the fine ring for today, and would he not, then, spare her also one tiny piece of the clock before the start of the travel? To walk along Pedro Street would use only the smallest time. *Bien,* she would ask it. If Johnsy's head did not reason that she must go, then his heart would see the reason of it, all the same, and perhaps he would share in the visit and the delight. It would be a delight, despite the memories and those last heart-wounded words her stepmother had spoken to her.

"Daughter, did I not teach you should yield to none, save when his ring has been given you, a ring gold as the sun, perhaps with a stone, and green lights springing from it! I die of the shame! You, and this Hood one! Now, look upon yourself—Maria, a wanton! You do not live in this house!"

There had been more of it, wild and tearful, and finally, as she gathered her clothes into a roll, the sound of Mama Quintero's voice, weeping, saying to the others, "Children, at every sun we must pray for Maria!"

Maria had been rushing at sixteen then, alive and afrisk from the winey consciousness of being pretty, stirring to a heady awareness of the slim strong body in which the saps seemed to be rising. During these strange days of springtime the year around, she had liked the way the white men turned their suddenly lit eyes on her when they came with their soiled bundles for Mama Quintero's wash bench, and how some, when Mama was not alert, winked at her. But she had bravely shown her back to these men. Always, until Johnsy Hood came to Coldiron, and came to the Quintero's thatched picket house, bringing his beautiful shirts of linen and silk with the tiny JH embroidered on each of them. It was on his second arrival, while Mama Quintero searched for change money, that he whispered to Maria. That same night, she crept out of the *jacal* like a part of the oven smoke, and met him. It was morning when she returned.

Maria remembered, too easily, the white swish of the petticoat that Mama Quintero seized up from the washtub, the garment so leadened with water it seemed to break her bones. It whipped about her naked legs, across her back, once along her neck as she bent to escape, or to pray. But Maria thought she had forgiven this of Mama, almost as the welts lifted. For Mama Quintero had thought Johnsy Hood the first; Maria had not told her stepmother of the large boys from the gringo school who pinched whenever they might, and called her "pepper belly," and sometimes chased her into the Dirty Creek thickets and caught her there.

Now Maria shook her head, to rid it of these things which could so overrun her joy, and she turned away from her mirror, looking toward Johnsy's room. She hoped, hoped to the Blessed Mother, that he'd bring the ring in all haste. Then she realized that she meant to go along to Pedro Street, whether Johnsy permitted it or not. If he forbade her, she would slip away with her ring, for only a moment, while he was gone on his drive to the rich Señora Shelley's.

"It is a deception," she scolded herself, "and a sin." But she knew her heart could not change.

Beyond the wall the washstand creaked open, and closed, and she heard Johnsy's steps, and next a black oath, shouted, and taken upon Our Saviour. As she crossed herself, she heard the scream of the cat of yellow hair.

She shivered. She had only a hate for the cat; she feared it; she might have rejoiced in its punishment. But Johnsy punished so often, and the outcry, she thought, came like a nighttime anguish of her own. Quickly she took up a soiled puff and dusted starch powder on her face and neck, calming the paint, and becoming whiter of skin, as Johnsy wanted. When she heard his door open, she sprang up and got into the pink kimono. She was facing him when he came in.

He was dressed, oh, so very dressed. He was beautiful.

"My Heart!" she said, "how beautiful!"

"You packed up?"

"Yes, everything, as you said it must be."

He turned his dark head, glancing about at the disorder she had made. "All right," he said, "I'm on my way."

"Wait, my Heart!"

Johnsy turned at the door, feeling for his watch. "Well, what now?"

She put her hands behind her, so they might hold each other, and tremble out of view. "It's . . . please, my Johnsy, do you not remember the ring of green lights? May I not have it on my finger before we start the travel?"

He shouted at her. "Hell, quit your pestering me about that. You'll get the ring when we make San Francisco."

Maria could not believe. He had promised, and sworn it to her while in her arms!

"Oh, my Heart, it must be tonight! Please, as you said it would be! My mother, she must see this ring on my hand!"

"At Frisco, I said. You know I ain't got hold of that money yet.

Now, you get in there and put my clothes in the trunk, and be finished when I get back."

Johnsy jerked down his vest where it wanted to roll, and started out. The rage came on Maria then; she quaked with it. Her blood screamed of despair.

"You promised Maria!" she said wildly. "You promised, you promised, oh, you . . . you by-dam gringo!"

Quicker than her tears he was upon her, his hands on her shoulders, his fine long nails cutting like wolf's teeth, and he was shaking her. Her head snapped, and she bit her tongue and tasted the blood.

"You spic bitch . . . if you had . . . that ring . . . you'd tail off . . . down there . . . to Mex town . . . and squall out . . . everything! We ain't seeing anybody . . . before we leave here. Hear me? Damn you! Ain't leaving . . . a bunch of tracks . . . for Brack Shelley. And next time you yell at me. . . ."

The strength quit his hands and he stood panting, his neck a king's purple, and throbbing.

"Maria, act a pea brain!" he said. "Hell, if that old woman hollered about a ring, all right, but it wasn't a ring she was talking about."

He put fingers under her chin and raised her head, gently, while it beat and hurt and misted her sight, and he almost smiled at her. "Stop howling about it," he said, and he pinched her cheek, tenderly, and held on to it. Then, as if the feel of her flesh was a trouble to him, he pinched harder. Of a sudden it seemed he might tear the cheek away. She cried out and leaped back, sobbing.

He stared at her, his hand held up where it had been when she retreated, and he spoke hoarsely. "We're leaving here quick as I can get back, and see to it you're ready!"

When he was gone she faded onto the bed she'd not spread, sickening to anger and grief. But in it she could not hate him, poor Johnsy. She felt of the sting on her cheek, ran her touch over the bruises streaking her throat from an earlier time when she'd poured from the window all of the red and sour fool's water he kept in tall bottles on the sill. She turned onto her back, gazing upward. At thought of Mama Quintero, the glad anticipation of her birth date burned to an ash, and she begged for the child times that now she could only in small part recall.

She remembered childhood as a simple time: arising from her straw bed at the first lance of sun, sweeping out the *jacal* with a care to the corners, and picking up the shreds from the dry weed broom; milking the goat of soft eyes and boasting of its knowledge, for always it came inside and stood at the stool at the chosen hour; watering the fig trees planted at either side of the door, trees of beauty, if they never fruited; picking beans in the good seasons that they grew, parching coffee at the fire made on the clean dirt floor. On afternoons she had listened to the young men who believed the *pueblito* must yet gain its plaza, or watched them fight the cocks, or on days of rest, she clapped her hands as they laid their wagers and went charging about on horseback in the game of *El Gallo Corriendo*, where the finest rider mounted the fleetest horse and fled from the others, carrying a fat chicken decorated with ribbons and flowers and protecting it from capture. She had heard the old ones talk of the wisest sheep dogs, the greatest miracles, the coldest winters.

Sometimes she had known great secrets; once, she knew the hour that the *Casa de Las Lágrimas*, the house of tears spoken of as "pesthouse" by white men, would take ablaze and burn, and she had told it to no one.

But the loveliest had been when the padres came to visit, tall men, saintly and black, or small men, fat and bald and angelic, christening the children born since last they came, speaking requiem for the dead, bringing the mysteries of mass and confession to the creekside. Sometimes it was a Franciscan of San Antonio; more often they traveled from Anton Chico, in the strange land west. The kindest of the fathers she remembered rode a burro from Las Cruces, the city of the crosses, and it seemed this must be a heaven far away.

For the visits there were weddings, and parties, and wine to drink, and for the children slices of *panocha* and *cemita*, and until the padre blessed them and left, the children did not go about unclothed, not even the smallest ones. In all of this had been Maria, and her half sisters, and Mama Quintero.

Maria cried.

She got up and crossed to the mirror. She finished pinning her hair in back, and put in the shell combs above her ears. With the kimono sleeve she rubbed the streaked powder off her face, letting her skin shine as darkly as it would. A gust of the hot, gritty evening struck her as she passed the open window. She took down the rosary which hung on the iron bedpost, and she blew her nose on her underskirt before she knelt.

In the hallway Johnsy looked down at a fingernail Maria must have torn. He swore as he cut around a banister and onto the stairs. He thought of going back long enough to put straight that look he'd seen in those pit-black eyes in the instant when he'd meant only to caress her cheek. He knew the look and detested it. The damned little greaser, she pitied him!

He'd seen the pity in her other times; even often, since that stupid night when he'd drunk himself ragged and run off at the mouth while lying close to her. Oh, he'd been real drunk; he'd told her about Ohio, about the twin sister he had loved, about the Sunday his sister tripped and went into the pond, how he'd had to stand there unhelping, watching his sister drown because he wore a new blue felt suit with a creamy lace collar, too proud a suit to be plunged into a bog. He'd even told Maria how his father flogged him with a cane pole, and that somehow he had relished the pain.

Mostly, Johnsy had talked from his liquor, he knew, but Maria had goaded him on, and he'd been a fool. He was getting throat-full of that look in her eyes. A spic slut pitying him all the time, like she was God or somebody and forgiving him right and left.

He reached the Rusk House lobby and put aside the notion of returning. It was late, and he had Bonnie Shelley to think of, and the money.

He crossed to the street, feeling the clerk's nosiness on him as he stepped out into the night. He glanced at the moon, and at once things became agreeable. Accounting what waited ahead, he thought, the moon was more golden than any in his longest recollection.

Johnsy bent into the alley alongside the hotel and saw Dub Stokes's black boy there with the bay team, humming to them, holding one animal by the ear. The boy handed up the reins as Johnsy settled himself in the seat.

"Careful, Mister Hood. Them hosses is stompin' upset tonight."

"I can drive."

"Yes suh, you can do that, Mister Hood. What I aimed on saying was, they was a giant-man—"

"Well, why don't you get back out of the way!"

"Suh," the boy said, and he did not move," this man, he come into the barn last night, and he ast me—"

Johnsy snapped the reins. "Dammit, nigger, you want me to run you down!"

Harris James pulled back against the Rusk's warm wall, and the bays leaped into the street, trying to take charge of the bits as they danced away north. The boy sneezed on the dust, and moved to where he could watch the rig out of sight. "Yonder, that is a team of hosses," he said.

Johnsy steadied the animals to the trail, puttering them at a skittish jog until Coldiron was well behind. Then he gave in to their bow-necked energy and let them look a deal more sprightful. The horses would get all the work they could stomach before this night was out, and he warned them so, and laughed.

Propping his feet on the dashbar, he reared back. Excitement and the spicy feel of prosperity bolted around inside him like love's own lightning. Outside there was the scantiest of winds, at least, for this filthy country, and it seemed hardly enough to draft away the fresh lotion he wore for Bonnie Shelley this final time.

The road jarred a belch to his mouth; he tasted garlic and sighed, listening to the lively drum of the hoofs on loose trail dust. It was nearer than ever before, this richness he wanted, and he gave way to thick-carpeted, gas-lit imaginings of a ruffled and perfumed San Francisco.

There, people said, on an inlap of the ocean, stood a sure enough city. He'd heard it held out its best to those who would accept, and among the acceptors were handsome mannerly men with a humor for clothes and cleverness at cards and a style with the women. There they had women who bathed every week and carried picture-painted fans, gay women who glued tiny beauty spots to their chins and in the evening went gliding about with their men to the sound of whole big orchestras. In San Francisco, he never doubted, a man might live quite as fine as in the East. And in a place of such size he would meet little difficulty in getting shut of a spic wench, once he tired of her.

Johnsy recognized the hills about him; he was halfway to Shelley's already. He looked at the switching tails of the bays and smiled. Though he'd been minding them hardly any, here he was.

These were animals he could approve of; they'd learned where he chose to go, even to the Shelley turnoff that shuddered across a table of exposed gypsum rock as it left the trail.

He began whistling, listening to himself with a charity, so that what he heard was a genuine ballroom tune, stroked from a dozen violins. It occurred to him that whenever he was a distance from Maria, he was a cheerier man. Maybe it was her smallness, her beauty. Or was it her squealing, black-eyed dependency on him that barbed his spirit when he was with her? He wondered, then, if she need burden his trip to Frisco at all. As he considered it, he began to realize he was hearing too many hoofbeats, as if the bays laid down extra feet. He twisted to look behind. A horseman was cantering close to him.

Johnsy called "Hey!" and yanked the shocked bays to a pawing, squatting halt. The rider crowded up to the rig at Johnsy's right, his figure high and broad on a mount that looked aged and gaunt, even under the moon. Johnsy's mouth closed, and opened again. He was not mistaken; the glint he caught was off a gun.

"We'll change directions, Johnsy Boy," the figure said.

Johnsy's feet rattled against the dash from the tone of it, and he felt the horseman must hear, if not see, his fright.

"You, get back!" he said. "I got nervous horses!"

The rider nudged closer, bumping the bony shoulder of the mount against the buggy wheel.

"Watch out!" Johnsy shouted. "Hey, stop it; they'll run!"

The horseman laughed, and Johnsy fought against an urge to be away, to jump and go it hard afoot into the dark gash of the hills. His mind shoved the name at him—*Brack Shelley*. Oh, burning hell, what if Brack had turned in home ahead of time? What if a hired hand had told him! Brack was mean and old; he might have beaten it out of that tubby little wench herself!

He stared. It couldn't be Brack. This man was full twice old Shelley's size.

"What—do you want?"

"Coming in," the horseman said, and he set a foot on the wheel hub. In a casual motion he left the saddle and swung into the buggy, his boots tromping Johnsy's feet.

"Dammit. . . ."

"I'll drive," the man said.

"Get out; you can't climb into my rig! Give me them reins!"

"Scoot," the big man said, and the gun poked out, almost touching Johnsy's neck. His skin crept on him and strained itself too tight, and he scooted to his left, his fawn trousers, the most stylish he owned, whistling on the seat leather.

"What's it you're after?" Johnsy said.

The man did not speak, but flattened the seat springs with his weight, and he smelled of whisky and something foul and much worse. Then Johnsy glimpsed the eyes. Scalp dressing melted out of Johnsy's hair and went leaking down his forehead and made an oily drop at the end of his nose.

The man rested the long handgun across his knee. He jounced the lines in his left hand and grunted to the team. Of a sudden he looked at Johnsy and sniffed.

"Posy water," he said. "By God!"

"Look, you . . . wait, you're turning around!"

The bays fought the bits as the big man pulled and talked them about, and they sought to rear as sagebrush raked their bellies. The low voice seemed not quite strange. Johnsy frantically tried to place it. He felt his feet starting up again, and he doubled them back underneath the seat.

"What do you want?" Johnsy said. "I'm in a rush, I got a . . . an appointment to keep."

The man did not answer.

"You deaf?" Johnsy yelled. "I got someplace to go!"

"Yes, you sure as hell have."

Johnsy looked hard at the shadow of face, waiting for the moon to light it when the rig came the rest of the way around, and his body starched with fear that had to do with the voice, the size of the man, the fact that the bandit had called his name.

"You . . . I got a dab of cash on me, that's all," he said. "I'll give it to you, and you let me be."

The bays finished the turn, yet the gunman's face remained black and formless under the broad hat.

"Get!" the man said, and the bays put into a rapid trot, devouring the trail, back the way Johnsy had come.

"I . . . I guess I could swap you my rig for your horse," Johnsy said. What one devil of a night to be robbed, he thought.

He tried to consider he was in luck, that it would have been ten thousand dollars worse if he'd already seen Bonnie.

"Here," he said, "I'll get the money." He put his hand inside his coat, sliding the fingers along the silk of the vest, pausing it at the pocket which held the derringer. He closed his palm over the butt, yet he wasn't quite ready. There'd be risk, the little gun held but two shots.

The wind toppled the big man's hat back, and it hung by a string around his neck, flapping. Johnsy stared at the face, familiar like the voice, and his belly ducked in and pushed a little cry out of him.

"Just you rest easy, pretty thing," the man said, "else get blowed straight to glory."

Johnsy's hand fell out of his coat, empty. He stared at the big pistol, trained on his nose now, close up, and he saw the roll of the cylinder as the hammer went back.

"God, man, don't shoot me!"

The driver may have smiled. He laid the heavy pistol in his lap, dangerously cocked, and he reached, drawing out Johnsy's derringer. He held it a moment in his hand, looking at it with the disgust Johnsy knew all this country's savages had for pocket weapons. Then the giant muttered something and flicked the little pistol back over his shoulder as if discarding a dead cigaret.

"Where . . . where you taking me?"

The man veered the bays off the trail, jarring the buggy west over grass and rock. "Dirty Creek," he said. "Where they do the branding."

"Oh," Johnsy groaned. The branding! Water popped out on his face, and beneath his crisp linen, flooding down the valley of his back as though he were a sponge being wrung. He stared at the man's face. The beard was gone, the lips swollen, but it was the same face. The buffalo man.

"You . . . you got no use with me," Johnsy struck out, feeling the fear like a croup in his voice. "I ain't ever seen you before."

For an instant the dead-cold eyes were on him, and he flinched from them, seeing the shot-away ear before he cut his gaze down and away. The team was pulling fast, toward the moon-bleak hills, and he shook; the creek was so very near.

His mind raced. Jump and run? No, Lord no, not in a moonlight like this; he'd be shot. Then, talk. Talk to him! "Who are you, hey?" he rasped.

The big man gruffed at the horses, and the rig leaped on, falling over rock and brush so that pain bolted upward from Johnsy's ribs. He grabbed a damp hold of the seat, feeling the truth in the planed hardwood, the silky soft leather. This was real. Downright, terrible real.

"Who are you?" he shouted.

"Rupp," the man said. "Julius Rupp."

"You're all haywire, Mr. Rupp! Wrong man! I didn't have no say; it was that Elwood Coates, he's the one that decided on it. Me, I know where you can get hold of Coates, he's the one you're after."

Rupp slowed the bays.

"I swear it, by my mother!" Johnsy rushed on. "I only was going for poker, out at Coates's place, and I couldn't help myself; guess you can see that, can't you?"

Ahead rose the last red hill before the creek; they were on the first slant of it. Desperation knotted his body, scratched in his throat.

"Man, listen, it was all I could do to keep 'em from killing you; that's the truth! While you was laid out there . . . say, Brooks Durham was the other one, Durham, and I know where you could find him, too. They got to talking about hanging. Me, I told them, no sir, it wasn't right. Sure as life they'd have done it. Only I can prove it, I made 'em listen!"

The bays walked now, steering around a thrust of mesquite, then around the rim of a sinkhole and up the steepening bank of the hill.

"Hear me, now, it was an argument, I can tell you that. I said to Coates, 'You can't hang a fellow for taking a calf, not in these kind of times.' I told him, and I told Durham the same, I told them both we ought to turn you in to the rangers, or let you loose. I said I'd take a calf myself; I would, too, if I was hungry and one come by!"

The buffalo man was silent, not looking at him, and Johnsy trembled against the seat.

"It was a wrangle, oh, the worst damn kind," Johnsy said, and he found he was listening to himself, and shrieking like Maria. "I made them see it, though, we didn't need any hanging. Coates and that Durham, they thought up this thing about the . . . the iron. I was against that, too, but they'd have got a rope if I hadn't given in. I made out I wanted to use that iron myself, see; that's how come it wasn't on you a hair longer than it took for satisfying them two. Hell, Coates is a crazy man!"

Johnsy laughed, the sound of it surprising him, unlike any laugh he'd ever laughed in his life. "Don't get it wrong, Mr. Rupp, I'm not begging for any thanks; all I'm saying is, God, that man Coates would still have been burning you, that crazy drunk Coates, boy, he's crazy sometimes, Coates is!"

Johnsy panted, sucking in great swallows of dusty air, and he coughed on it.

Rupp stopped the buggy. "All right, Johnsy Boy."

Johnsy felt a drool on his chin, and he stared at the big hands fastening the reins through the seat arm. The man had not listened!

"No!" Johnsy screamed.

"We'll walk from here," Rupp said.

Johnsy wrenched his hands loose from the seat, then saw them waving in front of him, curiously uncontrolled. He could see the fireglow, winking a yellow edging around the shape of the hill, and he smelled wood smoke. He dizzied, and brushed at his chin.

"Lord, yes," he laughed, "that Coates is a mean one. Got spoiled, bossing the JC; takes a man mean as Coates to think of a thing like that hot iron, takes a mean crazy drunk."

He was being driven up the hill. His coat was missing and he couldn't recall taking it off. A hand gripped his galluses in back, and the knuckles bored hard against his spine. He stumbled and the fist jarred him up, stirring the hurt of his ribs.

"You're getting me all dirty!" he gasped.

He tried to begin all over, to think, to explain, to talk to the man—talk to him! Nothing came out.

At the hilltop he looked down on the fire, burning as if on the old coals, popping up red cinders that seemed to rush at him like insects out of hell, and he saw the steady orange lump of heat that was the iron.

"God's mercy!" he screamed, and his legs kicked and he fell. The galluses tore loose, and he tumbled down the slope. He bucked to his hands and knees on the flat, trying to run.

"My good clothes!" He choked.

Then the buffalo man had his collar and he was being dragged, being spun onto his back, and he lay blistering from the fire. The giant stood over him, slowly putting the long pistol back into his waist.

"You can't burn me! Oh, it was Coates and Durham; it was *them*, I told you! I couldn't help myself, they made me!"

A boot sat down on his stomach, its weight making him retch.

"Now, look at me, you fancy plaything," Rupp said. "Damn you, look at me!"

"Dirt. In my eyes. Please—"

"What went with my money, Johnsy Boy?"

"I don't know about any money, I swear to Christ!"

Rupp reached, spraddled, upset the fire, and came back with the iron in his hand.

"Give me a chance! You wouldn't—"

"Where's my money?"

"Oh, what money? I'd say if I knew! I never saw any money, that's God's truth, I didn't! Please, don't—"

"I ain't no cowman," Rupp said. "But I know that when you brand, it's usual to earmark 'em too." His free hand lifted and struck down, and a sheath knife buried its point in the ground beside Johnsy's cheek, the blade of it touching him as it quivered. "And they ain't any handier time to do the gelding."

Johnsy meant to laugh out at the joke; it was a joke, but he moaned, and threshed under the crushing boot, and his tongue babbled sounds that held no sense. He could not stop.

"Last time, Johnsy," Rupp said. "Where's my seventeen thousand?"

Johnsy hoped again to laugh, but the jibber streamed on, chanting itself into a single wailing refrain, sung over and over, as he used to chant as a child when darkness brought horror to his room and he had to hurry about lulling himself to sleep. His eyes were shut, but through the lids he saw the fiery head of the iron, suspended close above him.

He watched it, red and pulsing, big and small, big and small, like a star's twinkle, a star merest inches away. Then his mind clicked itself clear, becoming separate from himself, working quick and calm, so that to himself, he did laugh. He laughed at this mockery that was upon him, of the fortune which on Wednesday night had passed him by without his knowing, of the other one that waited with Bonnie, that tonight would elude him also. He opened his eyes to the iron, and the glare of it suddenly did not hurt; it was only a star.

He heard himself scream, and his hands snatched up and jerked his star down to his breast, and with it he was in an instant happy, happy!

A voice cursed and a terrible strength wrestled to pull the star away. Johnsy balled himself around it, clinging to his agony with all his being, fighting for this one thing he'd found. He shrieked at the power he felt, at how his arms and legs seemed jointed in many places.

"Good God, turn it aloose!" the voice shouted.

Johnsy fought, and hung on.

Chapter Eleven

AT the root end of each new day, even a teeming Saturday, Coldiron wasn't its common self. The sun would come up bully and bold, usually yellow, and on off times, red; but hardly anything around town began with it, so that the flat had a while of peculiar innocence. It was a time of quiet miracle, at least, for those sensitive to it, and Brooks Durham was one of these. He liked to rise early and to open his pores to these good moments during which the night's brief peaces hung on; he liked to be out on the street before anybody kicked a dog or got into a cuss fight or commenced swapping horses. The silence and calm order seemed to salve the whole singed flat, making the place into something better than a nasty blister on a tough, dry country. Such feeling, he confided to himself, might have sprung from the habit he was acquiring, that of thinking about Coldiron as a haven community of his own.

"Saturday," he yawned.

He had slept well, his dreams untroubled by the memory of that heathen thing at the creek. Actually, the incident had been submerged in his mind from the instant Jessie promised to marry him.

"Oh, yes, Brooks; yes!" she had said, and he'd never held a woman so tight.

That was on Thursday night and he'd been able to think of nothing else since.

He sighed, and stretched until he was too long for his bed, and looked forward to the day. By now, he calculated, there'd been time enough for word of his engagement to fly around.

He got up smiling at himself, and at the eagerness he had to tour Crowder Street and see as many people as were up and out. He would be embarrassed as they congratulated him, yet he savored the prospect of it. He was a lucky man; Jessie was beautiful, and she loved him.

A little haphazardly he dressed in yesterday's clothes, except for a fresh shirt. He finished by taking the thick Rockford watch, his railroad watch, off the dresser and installing it in the vest pocket it had sagged and stretched. He spun the kinks out of the chain which held the eight-sided California slug, and with this heavy fifty-dollar gold coin thumping against his middle, he went down the steep outdoor stairs which angled along the side of the bank building from his room to the street. He helped himself to the clean morning air and to the quiet as he walked the half block to the café.

So early, the street wasn't cluttered and those up and stirring were the hard-working kind, mostly the hopeful sort that didn't curse the land they lived in. Aside from his calls on Jessie, this was the most pleasant part of his day. Just getting his breakfast, a shave, having his boots blacked, yawning with the others, and trading lazy morning talk with them, reminded him comfortably of how far he'd come in so short a while.

He walked slowly, but, disappointingly, he met no one. When he stepped through the open door of the café, he saw only the lean, dough-faced German owner, looking up at him from a stool where he sat making noises over a crock mug of coffee.

"Morning, Mr. Durham," the man said, no differently from usual, and Durham felt slighted. He nodded and took the stool he always chose, liking to do so, it being the way of a settled man to have habits.

"How's for some buckwheats?" he said.

The German got up, fumbled himself into a dirty apron, splashed batter from a tin pitcher into a pan before he spoke again. "You hear about the thieving?"

Durham poured his own coffee. "What's that, Fritz?"

"Up at Sunderman's, must of been sometime early last night. Busted in the door."

"Well. Who'd want into a blacksmith's?"

"Dunno," Fritz said, "he didn't leave no note."

"Some liquored-up cowhand, or a Mex, maybe?"

"No siree," Fritz said, and he turned the wheat cakes too soon, splattering the batter. "It was someone as knowed what they was after. Knocked in that big old cross-braced back door, took a set of new branding irons. Sunderman says he only finished 'em yesterday, for the JC."

Durham grunted, ready to let it drop. He did not care to be reminded of the JC or its foreman. It was a shame, what he let Coates pull off there at the creek. But he had stopped them, he told himself; he had gotten hold of the tramp's rifle and he'd made them quit.

"Looks like cow thieves," Fritz said. "Nobody else'd be taking branding irons. Though I'm damned if I can see what good JC irons would do 'em."

Durham made free with the sirup and began eating, bored with his host, lacking zest for his food. Surely, Fritz must have heard about him and Jessie. A whole day and a night, it had been. Plenty of time, it seemed—unless Jessie hadn't mentioned it to anybody.

A dirty, fore-hunched man scraped inside, took the front stool, and stabbed his elbows into the counter and leaned on his hands, as Fritz mustered up a rag and went toward him.

"What'll it be?" Fritz said.

The man raised his head and began rubbing his hands together as if winter was upon them. "Guess I got to talk to you first," he said.

"All right, talk."

"You got any work I can do, for some coffee and pancakes, maybe?"

Durham glanced at the tramp. He was gray-whiskered, old, with dirt coating his neck and red sand in his ears and his eyebrows; between his shoe tops and his pants showed a pair of crusted bare ankles. Durham frowned; Coldiron held too many men without socks or soap. And it would keep them, until the merchants opened their ears to him and spilled a little out of their pocketbooks. He'd told them there was water if you doled out for it and drilled deep enough into this fiery ground, and there were close necks where Dirty Creek could be dammed up, and there was the talk of a Fort Worth-to-Denver railroad that might be built. Durham knew his share about how railroads get routed; if Coldiron would bunch itself together and holler in concert, the line might be sucked into a long swing southward—but Coldiron wasn't ready to bunch together. The town's scruffy ankles didn't have to stick out; trouble was, nobody minded looking at them.

He fell to his food, not much concerned with such matters today.

"I ain't got any work," Fritz said, "because I ain't got no business."

"I ain't a bum," the dirty man said. "I work; used to work hoodlum up north, for the Shoe Bar, and I been working for Mr. Wells, up at the pens. Excepting he laid off three of us; them goddam spics taken the jobs; they'll work for board, and they don't eat much. I ain't any bum; I'm just a mite pressed, that's all, an' I ain't et since Thursday noon. I can't do much nohow; the other day I got hit by a chair, over at the Two Bulls, and I ain't been very able since. Had to pay a dime just to sleep on a cot last night, and I didn't get much rest, neither."

"I'll fix you something," Fritz said.

The German cooked pancakes, half-size. The man seized them up, rolling them like tortillas and sopping them into the sirup. "I work," he said. "I ain't no bum."

When the man had gone, Fritz said, "Don't know what we'd lay things to, if we didn't have them greasers."

Durham finished eating and held out a dollar. Fritz grinned. "Don't pay," he said. "Looks like I'm givin' away vittles this mornin'."

"Here."

"Naw, keep your money. Call it a engagement gift."

Durham looked at the man, surprised, and Fritz laughed. "I wondered by Judas how long you could set there feeding your face and not mention it. Well, you outlasted me. Want to wish you the best; that's a fine strong woman, Jessie Rupp."

The morning was restored. "She is, thank you," Durham said.

Crossing Crowder, Durham felt good. He yawned, and the sun glinted at him off the two new windmill heads and rolls of barbwire on the walk in front of Sam Heidel's. His windmills and wire, maybe, for he'd argued old Sam into ordering these unheard-of new devices, and he'd practically pledged himself to buy them if no one else did. Windmills and wire: these might wake up this country, and would, if he had his way.

He headed across to the barbershop and climbed into the only chair, waiting at his ease while Dunce Moreno, the barber, completed his own shave.

"Hear about Sunderman's?" Dunce said. "Got robbed."

"Fritz just told me."

"Man a-livin', either a ox or a mule done it. Take one to kick that door down. That was oak, solid, a couple of inches thick. Whoever it was, he split the thing clean down the middle like it was a shingle."

So Dunce Moreno, the same as Fritz, wanted to pester him a while before mentioning Jessie. Durham was amused. He'd have to tell Jessie about these two; she knew and liked them both.

"Nice day," Durham said.

"For the time being, I guess it is. But it'll be up howlin' and blowin' dirt after a bit. This damned country, even the dirt keeps trying to get away. Don't think they's been a day this summer that it ain't blowed." The barber hacked and spat. "If a man had any lungs when he came—"

"It's a good country," Durham said through the lather Dunce was dobbing on. "It just keeps reminding you it's here, that's all."

"It does that. Rotten place to live in."

"I like it fine."

Moreno began stropping a razor. "I tell you, Brooks. You thinking like you do makes you the banker. Me thinking like I do, that makes me a half-assed barber."

Durham shut his eyes and listened to the crackle of the razor, which was, he thought, the cleanest sound he could name. Funny, how in the old days it was something he never listened to.

Dunce lifted the blade and nudged Durham's shoulder. "Hey, I heard it, about you and Mrs. Rupp. Tickled about it; everybody is."

"Well, thanks."

"Man, that Lavender woman across yonder, she's been announcin' it around as though she put the deal through her own self, the old flap-jaw!"

Durham laughed. "Dunce, you ought to marry Mrs. Lavender, the way you keep tabs on her."

"Maybe I ought to, at that. Leastways, I could count on fresh bread all the time."

Durham stretched in the chair, crossing his feet, considering the day's business. Six or eight rushed hours at the bank, and not bad hours, in view of a condition so good that not even the big Shelley withdrawal could worry him; then a trip back to Moreno's for a hot bath in the back room, and a quick supper before going, early, to pick up Jessie for choir practice. This was his week to bring off the Sunday morning special music, and he hoped that for once the hoarse old pedal organ wouldn't snort and choke to death and leave him to go it alone. He sang bad enough, even when the organ burped the dirt out of its flues and was loud.

He kept his eyes shut, and was amazed at himself. Brooks Durham running the bank, sitting at a desk in front of a whole town's stored-up wealth, marrying the prettiest woman, rising at church to sing "Standing On The Promises." At times he disbelieved what he'd become, as much as the old crowd would disbelieve it if they knew of it. But maybe it wasn't his climb he doubted so much as the wild, saddle-slick years behind. On some good days, such as this one, it seemed he'd never worn a gun, or used it.

Moreno kneed the chair accidentally, nicked Durham's chin, and said, "Hellfire, I'm sorry," but Durham hardly felt or heard. He was imagining that sometime he might buy the Union Church a real organ, one of those wall-sized ones with all the brass pipes, like back East. He could donate it in Jessie's name; she'd be pleased by that, and people would speak of it as the Jessie Durham Pipe Organ.

He grinned.

"Watch out!" Dunce bleated, "Want your nose lopped off?"

"No," he said, and sounded silly.

After choir he'd stay at the churchhouse for council meeting. They'd talk some more about street lamps needing to wait another five years, and about Mexicans staking their jackasses out to graze on grass they didn't own, and he'd make them another speech about how it was damn well time for a tax system to pay for a regular law force, and maybe a fire department as well. Then, after they said no, he'd lace them with his new notion, that the committee require every able-bodied man to work three days a month at road building, or else hire a hand to serve in his place, and they'd say it was a fine thought, and vote no.

Dunce swiped a towel over Durham's face and shoved the chair upright. The barber took the money Durham held out, dropped it in a drawer, and said, "Care to go out back and use my john?"

Durham blinked. "Well . . . no."

"Ought to go; I got me something new. I put in A. P. W. paper, keeping up with progress. Doctors, they have found out how printed paper, like almanacs and stuff, is what causes the piles. Drummer told me all about it, showed me them doctor reports. So I got me a big batch of this A. P. W."

"Well. . . ."

"Durham, I got the first big glass window on Crowder Street, didn't I? Ten feet by eight-six in one piece! Now, I got the healthiest damned privy house in town!"

"Some other time," Durham said and went out.

Durham was thirty-seven years old, but the lightness he felt now made a—what was it they called young buffalo bulls?—spike?—yes, spike—it made a spike of him, one almost snorting with love. He gave the gold piece a spin on its chain as he walked north, at leisure, smiling ahead at the early morning bunch who gathered regularly at Tate's.

Si Tate always unlocked his doors at dawn, chiefly for what he called his "downtown crowd." The men Durham liked best were often on hand; some had to drop in to get their eyes whiskied open; others relied on one unhurried, talkative drink to tame the seasoning of their breakfast sausage and to trigger the day off well. This morning Durham wouldn't have missed joining them. He'd let them hooraw him and pound his back about Jessie, and he'd pay for a round.

As he stepped inside, speaking to either side to his friends, some of the shine left him. Opposite the bar, sitting alone, was Elwood Coates. The foreman's pocked face puffed red and ugly; the green eyes were lit high already. Durham cut away from the green stare and walked toward the bar.

Even before the fracas at the creek, he'd had no use for Coates. The man was a gall to him; he disliked the things that mere sight of the JC foreman called to mind, like the notion he always had, that Coates was a man who needed killing. The very presence of the squat, bellowing fool seemed to push Durham back, toward other men like Coates, toward the shabby past days of violence and gun handling and clubbing people around and grabbing land for the railroad at seventy a month, when a good Colt and quick money was all of everything, and when he never once thought of a pipe organ.

Durham reached the bar, smiling at Si Tate. He wondered of a sudden if it might have been Coates that tried mauling Jessie in the street. A big man, Jessie said, and bad smelling. Durham ground his teeth; he wished to God he knew, and in the same moment he prayed his thanks that he didn't. For he'd come to understand one truth of himself, that violence had been born on him like a birthmark, and must be held against, always held against, if he were to remain what he had become.

"Whisky," Durham said. "For everybody."

Elwood Coates looked at Durham's back, and the heat rose to his face like a wind burn. Durham hadn't even nodded at him while he cronied up to all the others, and goddam him. The banker had the high and mighty stamp of all this Coldiron's bastards, and to hell with the lot of them. Wasn't a one that had been up the trail behind cows; not a one of them could claim he had. But Coates had been up, six times he had, and what was a heap more, he'd got back every time to tell about it.

So who was it thought who was so much? Coates hissed, and poured himself another drink.

The foreman had passed the night in town, drinking a spell at the Two Bulls before switching to his steady table at Tate's, where they didn't welcome him but knew better, by thunder, than say so. Then, very late, he'd bedded down in the cothouse near Crowder's south end, where of a night twenty men made do with a dozen bunks. But Coates cottoned to the place; it beat the hotel. Even if you did risk getting heaved on, at least them who slept at a dime a night would talk to you, and they didn't climb up on any high horses.

Coates took his drink up, said "To jolly old Jerome!" and swallowed it. He pictured Jerome Chester now, sitting up there in the big house in his red-seated wheel chair with the JC's spring tally sheets in his lap, grousing and pulling his spectacles on and off, making pencil scratches, gearing himself in general to go on another rip and tear about where all the stock got off to. Getting meaner every time, old Lordship was, dragging his questions a pinch closer.

Twisting in his chair, Coates looked at a tall-hatted man just settling down two tables away.

"Say," he called to the man, "why is it about Englishmen? How come they always got to have a writ-down figure on every last goddam steer, huh?"

The man reddened and looked away. Coates laughed at him.

"Come on, stud, what about that? Why can't a Englishman let a real cowman who's been up the trail run the cow business, huh, why can't he?"

The man gulped, and Coates answered himself. It was because, by God, the English always done so much stealing theirselves, so they figured everybody else waded in and stole too. A English boss in this country, he'd drive any good foreman to town and set him drinking. Hell, Coates hadn't meant to come in last night himself, much less to stay over. It was that bellering old knicker-britches, wanting his chair greased, or sitting on the porch reading out of books. One day, Coates knew, it might rankle until he came to town for good, and then they could just turn the JC over to the Mexican goats.

"Hey, stud!" he called to the high-hatted man, "You know what that old By Jove does of a evenin', huh? He rolls his chair out on the porch and he yells the hands up there and reads to us, that's what. Literature, he says, that's what us ignorant cowhands needs. Haw! Me, I know more about old Bloody Bill Shakespeare, or old Blind Johnnie—that there is Blind Johnnie Milton—as any sonofabitch west of London! Right, old stud?"

The stove-hatted man got up, gathering to move.

"Stick around, stick around!" Coates said. "Now, old By Jove, he tells us to be sure when we get the makin's that it's Bull Durham. Yessir, Bull Durham, on account of stuck to the bag is a piece of paper and you send it off and quick as the U. S. mule, here comes you back a book to read—Bloody Bill, or Blind Johnnie!"

He noticed that the man was gone, and that Durham had turned for a moment, and he realized it had been at the mention of Bull Durham tobacco, and it made him laugh. He'd not thought of it before; he guessed old Brooks ought to be called Bull.

Coates leaned back and poured his whisky and thought again about tallies. Never mind, never mind; Coldiron wasn't the sorriest place a man could be. He stared at the group at the bar; they thought they was making the town a sorry place for him, and he pretty near whooped. Right now, he knew, they were thinking he was drinking by himself, all neatly cut off. They thought he was talking to himself. They were always thinking that, and all the while he would be having one hellofa time with his friend, the Little Whisky Man.

Coates brought up his glass, looked at the deep amber in it. *I am pretty drunk,* he thought, and he shot the whisky into his mouth. He heard Si Tate, then Texas Wells, and old Sam Heidel, and some more making a fuss over Durham, and he listened.

So, Durham finally got that redheaded widow woman, had he? And that big house of hers to boot. So the big banker had got her, and got it, and what had he got, anyway? You could buy you a ticket for the same, at the first landing on the Two Bulls stairway, and there, you weren't put on to wag in any groceries.

He heard Durham inviting the house to step up. Coates didn't trouble himself; in the bottle before him, there was plenty and ample. Slowly he loosened in his chair; he felt sleepy, but he swore he would not doze off, in case his bosom friend—bosom friend, ain't that what they say?—showed up today.

Then his head jarred as Tate's doors split and whammed inward and the sweaty, gasping head of a horse rammed inside. The building shuddered, and over the horse's ears came Tod Wisdom, the young Shelley wrangler. The boy tumbled in with no hat on his cotton head and he hit the floor like a sack of shoe irons, bouncing, and his stringy body came up and beat for the bar, and he bleated, "I aim to get dog drunk!"

Twenty men looked at Tod's face, and made room, and kept on looking at him.

Chapter Twelve

"GET that hoss out of here!" Si Tate yelled, and somebody battered the beast's white-eyed head with a hat, and it whinnied and backed out, and it sounded to Coates as if the animal slipped from its shoes on the boardwalk, and maybe fell getting to the street.

"Damn you, boy," Si Tate said. "This ain't that Bulls place, and nobody rides his hoss into my place! Damn your damp ears!"

Si stopped, and with the others, he stared at Tod Wisdom. The boy hung to the bar as though it were something he had lost and been wild to find. He panted, and a black knot was rising on his forehead, and his whole willow-stick frame jumped and shook, Coates thought, as if he just might give birth. Tod's in-between voice squeaked, "Gimme whisky!"

Si Tate scowled and leaned close. "What's eatin' you, boy?" he said.

"I come to tell you!" the boy hollered. "Only I got to have whisky first!"

Si looked around at the others, and Coates yelled, "Give that boy a drink!", and Si paid it no mind, but he set out a glass.

"Just this one, sonny."

Coates grinned at how the boy hunkered there, working at the drink, working at being full-grown, and if you mentioned it,

Tod Wisdom had grown, for a fact. He'd stretched about a foot straight up, Coates decided, since he fired the kid off the JC last year. Now what was that for? It was hard to remember, but seemed like the boy had gotten on his nerves, being a kid that wasn't much for knowing but hell for finding out, or something like that.

The boy whistled air down beside his whisky, but his eyes stayed crazy and too big for his smooth face, and his skin looked too white to be alive. Men shuffled closer to him, and Si Tate refilled the glass without a word and put it in Tod's red-freckled hand.

"Dammit, quit getting up agin me!" the boy bleated. "Keep off me, and I'll tell it from the front. But I got to have breathing room, ain't I?"

"Calm down," Durham said.

"All right, all right! Only, I'm gonna tell it from the start, soon as I drink this up. Johnsy Hood—"

Tod gagged at the whisky, and wept from it while it drowned his voice—"but the first was, I turned in early last night, and I'd done fell off to sleep when I heard this hell-raisin' out in the yard. I figured I oughta go see; I'm sort of in charge while Mr. Shelley and the crew ain't here; Mrs. Shelley told me that herself. Sort of in charge around the place. When I got outside, here was this pretty team of bays, Johnsy Hood's, and I seen they was about to kick out of the harness, all tangled up, and scairt, and one of 'em turned almost hind end to fore. They was up right near the main house, one of them lamed, that was the one that got switched around, and hell, he might be ruint, I can't tell yet. I couldn't see nobody in the buggy right at first, so I ran acrost and grabbed the bridles. Then I heard him, groaning awful."

Tod drank, shuddered, and hoarsened.

"It was Johnsy hisself, down in the footboards. He had the reins wrapped around his arm, and he was all doubled up, the worst human sight I ever seen. The hide, it was hanging in strings off his hands, and I seen filth all over him. Looked like he'd et his own tongue half off, and he was burnt. I ain't making nothing up, and don't nobody say I am! He was burnt on his hands, and in his belly clean through his clothes, and I knowed it soon as I looked; somebody done it with a branding iron!"

Coates felt his whisky pitch inside him, except not like whisky; more as though a bucket of hot sour water had been dumped in his stomach, and his whole table trembled, and he knew it was because his knee crowded hard against a leg of it. He looked at Brooks Durham.

The banker, this Up and Important One, had braced a hand against the bar. He was pale and glaring at Tod Wisdom. A brush of his straw hair had come down on his forehead, and Coates saw the jaw muscles churning and straining as though they meant to break out.

"It'd of made you puke, just flat puke, to look at him," the boy said. "I didn't know what, so I hollered for Mrs. Shelley; she was in the house. Just her and me and Christie Jacobs on the whole place now, and well, she came out and looked into the buggy and screamed out and commenced bawling, but pretty quick she taken holt of herself. Her and me, we got Johnsy out on the ground, and I taken his feet and she got his head and we packed him into the house. Mrs. Shelley, she kept telling me to hurry, and hell, I was; and she said to me, 'We'll put him on my bed,' which was the first time I ever knowed her and Brack slept separate, but good Jesus, I guess they do."

Tod's head rolled, and he almost grinned; he was well along on his dog drunk now. "One thing I know," he said, "When Christie Jacobs had his old lady, he sure didn't sleep separate from her!"

Someone swore.

"Johnsy, he was running off at the mouth, sounding crazy, and hurtin'. Begged us not to burn him. Hell, I wasn't going to burn him. I was trying to help him out, and Mrs. Shelley was too, but he fought us. He kept on, up till we got him in on Mrs. Shelley's bed, and he was a mess to hold, in the dark, and I had to sit on that poor burnt belly while she went and lit up the lamps, and that's when we got us a good look.

"A sight, Johnsy was, like I said. Meat a-hangin' . . . you know how dandy-slick he always was. Well, he wasn't slick to look at last night, and anybody could tell he wasn't going to be slick, ever, anymore. Besides his tongue, he'd et his lip bad, and his hands all cooked and holes burnt through his vest and his britches was wet and red dirt sticking to him all over. He kept talking, mind you, and he had the idea he'd been cut—I mean, cut like you cut a hog or a steer. But he wasn't cut. An' Mrs. Shelley . . . I mean, I don't think she ought to of stayed there while I was finding out; I guess she was so set on she didn't know clear what she was doing either."

The boy waved his glass at Si Tate, just as a man—a newcomer named Rudo Horning, Coates thought it was—broke through the doors, grinning.

"Hey, Brooks, you old fox!" Rudo called, "Congratulations!" Then he said, "How's to buy me a redheaded drink?" He broke off, puzzling his eyes over the room. "What's all this?"

Tod Wisdom kept wagging his glass. "I want me a redhaired drink," he said.

"What the hell?" Rudo said.

"Shut up," Durham snapped. "Get on with it, Tod."

"When I get my drink. And I ain't scared of you, Brooks Durham! Or nobody else!"

Si Tate leaned and poured Tod's glass a scant half full. "Last one," he said. "What about Johnsy?"

The boy drank before he began again.

"Guess, well, I guess I told you, Mrs. Shelley went to screeching and hollering when she seen him. I never much thought of it before, but I reckon I know why that was, her acting that way. I ain't making nothing up, now. One night last week, I heard her and somebody talking out in the cottonwoods, and another time I seen them blood bays of Johnsy's—"

"Finish your drink," Si Tate said. Coates watched the boy bow up over the liquor, and he saw how the freckles had come out on Tod's neck like rushing new measles. He came aware of his own neck and felt its sweat soaking through his collar.

"Whew!" Tod said. "Oh, Johnsy simmered down a little, after a while he did, and he laid there on the bed, moaning and cussing. He mentioned some names, mostly it was about somebody by the name of Julius, and the best I could tell, whoever it was that cooked Johnsy's goose—hear that, cooked his goose?—whoever it was, he was hunting for a batch of money he claimed Johnsy stole off him, seventeen thousand dollars, it seemed like. But I couldn't tell nothing, Johnsy was talking about a lot of stuff, stars, and how his clothes was ruint, and he still thought he'd been cut."

Coates looked over at Durham, and their eyes held, Durham's despising, Coates's hot with a fierceness, until suddenly the boy was talking again.

"Mrs. Shelley, she got the basin and a towel and she bent over Johnsy and went to washing off his face. Guess it hurt him like sin when she come to his mouth. Johnsy reared up and batted her away. Swore at her, too; called her a fat old she-dog, only she-dog wasn't what he said. By Grab, I wouldn't of tolerated him talking to Mrs. Shelley that way, either, excepting he was so out of his head and messed up and all.

"But Mrs. Shelley, she took it up. Throwed a fit, and they had a hellofa row, right in front of me, like it didn't make a damn if I was there or not. He yelled a lot about going to San Francisco, and she yelled about St. Louis, and he hollered how he had him a girl that was young, name of Maria. I couldn't tell much about it, but Mrs. Shelley looked awful in her face. All of a sudden she run to that little dresser she has and grabbed a looking glass and stuck it up in front of Johnsy. She hollered at him, 'Look at yourself, pretty Johnsy!' She yelled it over and over.

"He looked, all right, and he screeched so loud I feared she'd upped and stabbed him; he bellered for some water, and when she didn't go for it, throwed his fist at her, and she fell backwards and dropped the mirror, and it broke. Scared me, a broke mirror."

Tod whirled on the crowd. "If you don't back off and give me air, I'm going to throw up on the whole pack of you!" He gulped, and wiped a hand across his mouth.

Then the words came again, as though he'd smeared them out.

"Well, him hitting Mrs. Shelley like that, in front of me, and me being sort of in charge, I stepped into it sure enough. But Johnsy, he came out with that old cap-ball pistol Brack leaves under Mrs. Shelley's pillow when he's gone from home, and he stood me back with it. The way he looked, I thought he'd kill me, sure. He got off the bed and walked like he was crazy drunk and went to Mrs. Shelley's big looking glass, the one that's fixed onto the wall. He just stood there wobbling and gawking at himself. He said 'oh God!' for a while, though it was hard to make out, his tongue chawed and swoll so bad. Then—I guess if I'd seen what he was up to, I could of stopped him, but it happened quick; it was done before I hardly knowed it.

"Johnsy just stuck that old gun into his stomach and blowed his guts out. Mrs. Shelley went wild, screaming and sort of laughing. She fell down and dug under the bed and came out with a carpetbag of hers. She got out a whole bundle of money and she kind of went jumpin' around the place and she didn't look noways right in her eyes. She went to throwing wads of money at Johnsy while he was dying and flopping around on the floor."

Si Tate forgot himself and handed the boy a full glass.

"A man's entrails," Tod said. "Know what they look like? Like a big ball of crawlin' blue snakes!"

"Drink, son."

"Me, I got out of there. Run into Christie Jacobs on the porch. That Christie, he slept through, right up to the shot; that's how old Christie sleeps. And you ought to of seen him, old Christie; he didn't have a stitch on him outside of his drawers and his boots. He'd cut through the tack room while he was hurrying up, and he had his shin knocked open; said he run over the saddle bench. I told Christie, and he hollered he'd light out for the law at Hudlow, and he did, quick as he got his pants on. I was willing; I can tell you, I wasn't feeling ready for any long ride. But I don't guess the law is gonna come over, not for the suicide part, anyways. And I guess that's all of it."

Si Tate said, "Boy, why'd you wait all night about it? If you'd of come straight to town—"

"Hell, how could I leave? When Christie went, they wasn't anybody but me, and Mrs. Shelley broke plumb to pieces. She was throwing things around in the house, smashing them up, and when I sort of spoke to her, she told me, 'This here is what they call busting up a home,' and a little later, she was going on about killing herself, and she kept going back in there where Johnsy was. She—"

"All right," Si Tate said.

"Mighty right, I stuck clost to her; I wouldn't of been here yet, if it weren't for Mrs. Ducky Ireland. Mrs. Ireland, she come by from a quilting and seen the lights and figured to stop off and borry some sweet milk. She stayed on with Mrs. Shelley, or I—"

"There's your drink," Si said.

Then, Tate's was quiet. Coates looked around at the faces. *Well damn me,* he thought, listen to all the big ones being stone quiet!

A few men began easing away from Tod. The boy flailed out his arms and said, "I want every buck of you to quit pushing in on me!" He sobbed, and sat down on the floor.

Coates splashed the table at charging up his glass. He pinched his eyes shut, tossed the drink down, and he felt the hair sticking out stiff on the back of his neck.

He needed his friend—needed the Little Whisky Man. Now, and bad. Where was he?

He saw Brooks Durham wheeling for the door and splitting through it, not looking back. Coates reached again for his bottle; he must rouse up his friend, and together they must think.

So the buffalo man had been riding with big money; so he had lost it; so he wanted it back.

To the Little Whisky Man, Coates whispered, "What do we do about this one, huh?" and he waited.

He was thinking, but the fear latched hold of him. Mother's son, he had been handed the short end of the stick! That night he had been drunk, and he couldn't make up what the tramp looked like. He struggled with his memory. Until he could recall, he could be got; he could bump into the man and not know it. Hell's hinges, what a fix for a man!

Coates gripped his hands in front of him. It was no time for loose figuring.

The way old By Jove Jerome had hawked him lately, the way the town was, the way good cowhorses had to wade through greaser sheep, these days—maybe it was time to move on.

"Yes," he said aloud.

He'd ride on—soon as he could lay hold of what this red-hot by-God country owed him!

Chapter Thirteen

AT the first feeble prod of daylight, Julius Rupp sat up on his blankets and looked at Dirty Creek piddling by in front of him, its water still black from the night. Around him the ground crept with stocky red ants packing sandburs on their backs, and the air, windless so early, buzzed with wasps and snake doctors and the green-shelled flies that darted without fear at the scum of blood fouling his ear. His belly growled; the fever baked him; and behind his eyes the sight of Johnsy Hood, balled and clinging to the iron like its impassioned lover, reperformed its hideousness. Rupp's flesh sucked inward, too tight.

What was it he had intended? To get back his money, Jessie's money, and maybe, to punish Johnsy Hood. But to punish the heathen way it had happened? No; heaven believe it, no. It seemed now he was sure, or almost sure, that he'd never have used the iron had Johnsy left it to his choice. Yet he'd been in a madness; and about the mad times how can a man say?

He waved away a hard-biting fly, and he realized he must think ahead, to the others. Coates and Durham: what did he mean for them? If ever he had known, he no longer knew. He wondered if there was, sunk deep beneath the T wound of his own, the craving to see his enemies as they had seen him and as he'd seen Johnsy: to hear them beg, to see them kicking and screaming and stuck to a shaft of fire. He shuddered. If this were so, he'd become an animal altogether. And he knew in the instant this might be it, hopelessly and entirely. But the sight of Johnsy Boy, hanging on, curling. . . .

Against the horror, Rupp shook himself again, hard, and he hacked out his throat and greeted the new sun, "Goddam!"

If he had slept, it had been with his eyes open and while he tumbled and wadded his bedding and suffered his fevers and soaked himself in sweat. Close by, in a dead chinaberry, remained the dwarf owl he had chunked rocks at a time or two during the night, and it whickered on like a witness accusing. Rupp scrubbed his hands over his eyes and down his face and began pulling the thorns that held his shirt closed.

The rag had crusted and stuck, welding its greasy coarseness to the wound. About it was an edge of dying flesh, strained into taut puffs and trenches. His skin crept as if beset by hide bugs, and the stink of rot was on him stronger, rising to his nostrils as a part of the torment. He groaned and reached for his boots and pulled them on, cursing silently as the motion uprooted his muscles and spurted a greater heat to his face. Being respectful of the pain, he worked himself to his feet and found Hanley's lard pail. Only a smear was left, not enough to grease afresh. He looked at his chest again. Mortification, Hanley had said, might set in in a hurry.

No help for it, then. He'd have to move to town.

He picked up the pistol and put it in his belt. He knelt and began rolling his soured blankets; bending was a stampede of pain. He quit the effort and flung the blankets into the stream, watching as they drifted and suddenly sank.

Rupp tromped across the cold ashes of his fire and along the Dirty's rocky flank to the stunted dogwoods where the dun stood picketed. Going it slow, grunting, he got the saddle up the third try. Before he mounted he washed his face in the creek's false cool, and drank what was left of the whisky.

Coldiron was sighing itself awake as he rode in. The stir loaded the flat with breakfast smells, the slam of doors; shrill child voices called in quarrels, and already a Mexican ass laden down with kindling was on the street. As Rupp halted at Crowder's top end, he saw the commotion in front of Tate's. Men had hold of a drunken, cotton-haired boy and wrestled to put him on a horse and keep him there. The boy swore at them, but no one hit him, or laughed. Other men walked away from Tate's, fast. Rupp shaded his eyes and looked at each of them. The two he sought weren't there.

He moved to where he could look directly into Stokes's stable and got off the horse. A few men lounged inside, as if they'd slept there. Rupp made and lit a cigaret. He kept watch on the stable's dogtrot, until he was satisfied Old Dub himself wasn't on hand to spot him. Then he led the framy old dun through the doors, toward three men who sat drinking coffee off a bale of half-ripe hay.

They argued.

"Now, I ain't lyin'; it was at one of them protracted meetin's, special called. Run all day with dinner on the ground and a little dancin' that night. July, it was, and powder dry, and Brother Aaron Halleck, he kept praying for rain till he was all played out. Then this feller I'm talking about, he taken over, and he says, 'Lord, give us puddles in the fields, and puddles in the gardens, and puddles on the graze, and puddles in the streets, and puddles in the back yard, and puddles in the front yard, and puddles in the hog lot, and puddles in the cow lot, and puddles in the horse lot. Only, right about there, sort of watch it, Lord, else You'll have 'er knee-deep in my cellar.' Well, it commenced next morning, and it rained three days solid!"

"You made it up."

"Well, I sure as hell didn't."

Rupp stopped the dun and walked around it. "Buying horses?" he said.

The men looked at him, then stared. A white-haired man in embroidered Mexican vest and skirt-sleeved silk shirt got up. Without speaking, he loafed to the dun and ran a hand along its neck, down the scarred forelegs.

"Crippled," he muttered.

"No. Loose shoe."

The man stooped again, lifting the hoof. "He ain't nothing but a passel of bones," he said.

A man in the hay laughed. Rupp turned and looked at him. He watched the lounger come awake, and shut up, and stare at him broad-eyed, his face at once like the faces Rupp had met in the Two Bulls. Rupp realized he relished the look. It set off a spark in him; it seemed to price him up in the market. Differently than he'd planned, of a certain, but he was priced up, all the same. It hit him that before this day was run out, he'd have the whole mess of them dodging, and the Mexicans would be whispering how his shadow was black.

"A man ought to feed a hoss," the white-haired trader said. "Even this kind."

"He's old," Rupp said.

The trader straightened. "Twenty dollars."

Rupp hesitated, then nodded. He had the quick thought that the old horse had seen and heard as he begged under the iron; it had looked on, also, while Johnsy Hood got his. Both times the animal had bucked and fled. But, Rupp knew, he wasn't merely settling that horses are more human than men; this he'd discovered half a lifetime before. Maybe he had to get shut of the creature because it had played spectator to his weakness; maybe it was this, more than any need for money.

"Saddle, too," he said.

"Forty dollars," the trader bid without looking.

Rupp turned and began unlacing his saddlebags. "Want the Winchester?"

The old trader glared up at him. "Hell, man," he grumbled, "I ain't no pawn shop." But he slid the rifle part way clear of the boot, took a slow look, and shoved it back down.

"You throwin' in the bridle?"

"I will."

"All right. A hundred for the lot."

Rupp signed the horse away, and kept an eye on the counting of the money. In his hand it looked like none. Three days back, seventeen thousand cash. Now, a scant hundred, and he was a man afoot.

The trader thumbed toward the horse. "What's his name?"

"Got none," Rupp said. "I never called him nothing."

"Weren't this hoss that buggered you up, was it?"

Rupp started out. Someone said, "Wonder what was all that stir up at Tate's?" and before Rupp got to the doors, they were arguing again, over who would walk down and see.

Squinting against the sun, Rupp crossed Crowder Street, getting to the east side, away from Jessie's shop. His limp seemed worse, and it rattled a sash weight inside his head and thumped it against his eyes. He moved along stiffly, peering into the store windows, reading the strange or forgotten names on the signs. Coldiron had become a foreign place; it was as if he'd not walked this street before—which was, he thought, just by-damn as well.

The stores were not open or busied up so early. But at a flat, tan adobe marked "Saddlery and General Goods," he looked in on a brown-maned young clerk putting money into a drawer. Rupp troubled the door. The clerk looked up, scowled, and fingered out his sleepy eye corners, and Rupp shook the door once more before he came.

"Ain't open," the youth said.

Rupp elbowed past him and inside. "Seems like it, to me," he said.

He bought two boxes of .45 shells, the old ones he had being corroded and untrusty. He bought two yards of raw muslin, a dime size of Sioux Wonder Ointment, tobacco, a razor, a hickory shirt, a tin of peaches he almost missed noticing, and he was done.

As Rupp paid, the clerk kept his eyes in a travel, switching them from Rupp's pistol to the strips of flypaper swung in gummy twists from the ceiling, and back to the Colt, and to the rack of horse collars, and again to the gun, across to a dirty candy counter, and once more to the pistol, and he was sullen and slow at making change.

"Don't open till eight," he muttered.

The Rusk House lobby was hot and vacant when Rupp entered. He crossed to a chest-high pine desk at the rear, and kicked on the foot of it until a half-fed man appeared. The man wore an open vest over his undershirt, and he was picking noisily at a yellow-corn row of teeth.

"Ain't but one room to choose of," the hotel man said.

Rupp wrote in the book, "Julius Brown, Dodge City."

"Wouldn't of been no room for you, if it weren't for what happened to one of the roomers last night," the clerk said, and his fingers clinked around in a cigar box of loose keys. "Johnsy Hood, his name was. Maybe you've heard of him; a real jim-dandy. Somebody hog-tied and burnt him."

Nobody hog-tied him, Rupp thought, and nobody burned him; he did it himself.

"That my key?" he said.

"Think it is. By God, caught old Johnsy Boy out somewheres, and branded him, square in the middle. Ain't seen his body, but Tod Wisdom says—"

Rupp chilled under his fever. "He dead?"

"You almighty right, he's dead! His team, that pretty pair, they taken him to Brack Shelley's, and Johnsy shot hisself, right in Mrs. Shelley's bedroom. And old Brack still off to Kansas! Blowed his own guts out."

"I'll take the key!"

"Me," the clerk said, "I just while ago taken Johnsy's stuff out of the room; don't know what to do with it. A lot of fancy clothes, and—"

Rupp reached and grabbed the key from the clerk's hand. The man drew back, looked full at him, and paled. "Number Seven," he said nervously.

As Rupp turned, the clerk called after him, "Case you want tending to, they's doctors in this town. I could send somebody."

Rupp got on up the stairs.

Johnsy Hood dead.

In the fever it was burning hell to think. Johnsy Hood dead. Here today, nowhere tomorrow, wasn't it? He asked himself if he'd expected anything else, after the devilish sight of it, of Johnsy Boy babbling and wallowing in the dirt, of Johnsy suddenly white-eyed and loco strong, grabbing the red head of the iron and hugging it to himself as if he died to kiss the fire, as a man not in agony, but in the tallest crest of his passions.

Grimly it crept to Rupp's mind that he'd been positive Johnsy knew nothing of the seventeen thousand dollars. And he'd been sure of it at the moment he threw down the knife. Yet he had got the iron and had raised it over the pretty boy, all the same. Coldly, and again, Rupp wondered if he'd have used it, if he'd have paid back in kind.

He cursed; he didn't know. Johnsy had skinned him out of the choice. Now it must be posed all over again.

Or could it be? He was now a man afoot. The others he must run down in town, and the irons were out there in the brush. Of a sudden he wondered if he was avoiding having to meet the choice again, if this was why he had sold the dun. The Winchester alone would have brought money enough. But he had sold the dun first, and impatiently, and as he traded, his head pounded with the memory of Johnsy, writhing and clinging and screaming.

Rupp shook his head. No, no, this wasn't the why of it. What, then? Maybe he hungered to trap himself in Coldiron; maybe he craved doing what was left to do with the whole town seeing and . . . and pricing him up, by God!

He found Number Seven and unlocked the door. Instantly the room confirmed it had belonged to Johnsy Hood. It had been scoured of Johnsy's do-dads, down to bareness, but a faint womanish scent lingered, a hint of crushed flowers not yet wiped away by the morning wind. Rupp spilled his packages on the bed and he thought how Johnsy's toilet water had outlasted Johnsy.

So the boy had shot himself. Strangely, Rupp regretted it. The least a man could ask of death, it seemed, was that death surprise him, and Johnsy Hood had been shorted of his surprise.

As he raised the window, he felt the rock chill in his shoulders, and he shrugged to be rid of it, as he must. He could recall how, at first, he'd felt out-of-stomach over the cold-blooded slaughter from ambush of the big, stupid buffalo. It was a thing that quickly passed.

Rupp rigged up at the washstand and shaved. He cut an X in the top of the peach can with his knife, pried up the corners, and between razor rinsings, stabbed the fruit into his mouth with flies fighting him for the sirup. When he finished he tossed the sticky tin out the window, seeing as he did a hollow-sided cat that crouched under the foot of the bed and watched him. He pursed his lips at it, and it disappeared.

Sitting on the dirty quilt, he shucked off his shirt. He pulled at one corner of the chest rag, and sweat squeezed from his face. Flesh was tugging off with the rag.

He sat looking and trembling until the pain petered itself out. Then he got the speckled crock pitcher from the stand and lay down on the floor. Awkwardly he lifted it and splashed water over his chest. A puddle spread underneath him, wetting the top of his trousers. Puddles in the back yard, puddles in the front yard, he thought. And puddles in Johnsy Hood's room. The water spread, but the bandage would not loosen. The filth of the cloth shed it off like oiled leather.

Rupp sat up. He breathed deep, shut his eyes, gritted, took hold and ripped the rag away in one crackling wrench. The sear was the branding repeated, and a groan hung in his throat, strangling there until his growl drove it out. He pulled himself up by the bedstead and unwrapped the muslin and folded it into a thick soft patch. He coated the face of it with a handful of the Sioux Wonder Ointment and pressed it over the wound. It felt camphorish and cool, and he breathed more slowly.

Getting into the new shirt, Rupp swore. The sleeves ended short, and they bound him about the armpits, and the front buttoned too snug over his chest. He wished he'd remembered to get a necktie. He went ahead and closed the collar without it, so the muslin wouldn't show at his throat. Still smarting of fever, he sat on the bed and loaded the bright new cartridges into the big Colt. In a moment the yellow cat sprang up beside him, curling, rubbing against his thigh. He put the gun back into his waist and was reaching to stroke the cat when he heard the woman.

She sobbed beyond the wall, and he listened.

Rupp had heard women cry: sober ones and not, slapped women, lonesome women, and women tired and painted and plain sad-sick of life, like the girls at Big Nose Kate's. But the cry he heard now seemed the most hopeless of all, and directed to him, as if meaning to roost in his own vacant soul. He felt the cat slide from beneath his hand. Quickly he stood, hooked his hat off the bedpost, and went out.

In the Rusk lobby he paused and cut back to the tall desk. The clerk straightened and flattened his hands on the slab top.

Rupp said, "Sounds like a woman sick, upstairs. You might see to it."

"Her, that's the spic girl." The clerk propped forward on his elbows. "Maria, girl friend of Johnsy Hood's. She ain't let up squallin' since she heard; me, I taken her the news myself. And I sort of hate moving her out just yet. Iffen it bothers you, though—"

"You puttin' her out?"

"Well, happens this is Saturday. Rent day, you understand, and Johnsy's been paying for her; she's a tart of hisn. Now, I ain't speaking evil of the dead, but Johnsy's been keeping that greaser a couple of years, right here, and he never much cared who knowed it, either."

Rupp bit out, "How much?"

"What, rent? For her, runs five a week. We don't cater much to spics, no kind of 'em, and it makes the price high. Fact is—"

The clerk stopped and looked at the money Rupp counted onto the desk, and a foul-winded, knowing grin swept his face. Rupp closed his fists. Such a splinter of a man, he thought, would snap across a knee like stove kindling.

He said, "Know anybody by the name of Coates, or Brooks Durham?"

"Sure," the clerk grinned, "you just named this town's sorriest and best, in one mouthful."

"Where abouts?" Rupp said.

"Well, Coates, you'd find him drinkin' at Tate's sooner or later; lives out on the JC. But if it's a job you're after, best see old Jerome Chester; he don't allow Coates the hirin' and firin' any more."

"Durham?"

"Him, I seen him this mornin'. Runs the Stockman's Security. I expect he's there and at it, right about now."

Rupp started out.

"If you got bank business," the clerk said, "maybe . . . well, I do a little dab on the side. Got a good safe, and people leave stuff with me."

Rupp crossed the lobby, and he heard the clerk mutter, "I ain't lost nobody's property yet!"

The wind and a little sand were up when Rupp stepped into the street, and heat blew with it. The sun's orange prongs struck his eyes down, and too late he saw his foot falling on a trail of sky-colored whipcord. He hauled himself back, glimpsing a wisp of tan lace as the skirt was pulled on and whipped angrily clear.

"Excuse me," he said.

"Watch where you're going!" the woman snapped. He looked up at Jessie.

Chapter Fourteen

JESSIE Rupp had overslept. But this rare lapse she accepted peacefully as she rolled her head on the thick down pillow, one of several such pillows that Aunt Gussie, rest her soul, had created through years of fussy effort with a flock of scrawny, shipped-in ducks, which, like some of the people, never for one minute belonged in this gusty red land. Now, as Jessie resettled her head, it seemed the down had a thunder in it, pulsing the ticking against her ear. Reluctantly she began to awaken. Someone was downstairs, and making the fact determinedly known, and pounding the good billy-hell out of the door.

The rumpus of it did not interest her.

Usually, with Jessie, to put aside sleep was a confusion and a fight, a resurrection wherein the responsible widow in her strove toward consciousness and bustle while the soft, she-animal part yanked back the other way. Most mornings while enduring this tug-of-war, she resented the widowhood because it would win. Yet today, like yesterday's leisurely rising, was different. The widowhood was not so powerful. She was going to be married.

"Jessie, Jessie!" Brooks had whispered as he held her. "You're all I want; you'll not be sorry!"

She wouldn't be, she knew it. He was big and calm and safe, and if he wanted her too badly—well, he was gentle in it.

Sun pricked her eyes open. She winked against it, then looked across to the clock clucking at her from its shelf on the wall. She stared, not believing it, and came up in a flurry of bedclothes. Her rule was to open the shop at nine, as always Aunt Gussie had. And it was ten past, already.

Again she heard the pounding down below. She walked across to the open window, forgetting the wrapper that might have made her modest, and leaned out over the upper gallery. "Who is it?" she called.

"Me, child. Mrs. Lavender!"

"All right," Jessie squeezed the words through a yawn, "come on up. That door lock is broken, all you need do is jiggle it."

She went weaving back to bed, fell in, and closed her eyes, the hour be blasted, and she sought her way backwards into the night's hundred dreams, letting the drowsy effort of it lift a sweet lazy mist off her heart. There'd been no nagging guilts or fears in the dreams; just Brooks Durham, looking strong and kind, and herself, acting free, and acting married.

Of a sudden Jessie blushed, and she wished she knew with an intimacy some woman who'd had two husbands. Did other twice-wed women keep matching off their men? Did they have to rest, even, on careful guard, lest the last be measured against the memory of the first?

She sighed and stretched the night's stale breath out of her chest, reaching until her hands bumped the headboard and her pointing toes touched the mahogany foot, and she listened to Mrs. Lavender huffing and banging her unholy bulk up the stairs, and she smiled, and in a whisper she tried on the name, "Jessie Durham, Mrs. Jessie Durham."

Mrs. Lavender rolled into the room, aproned and dripping and drinking air through her mouth.

"Child, I was scairt you'd fell sick! Seen the shop wasn't open, and they must be five or six ladies waiting on you to show up, peeking in and growling."

"Let them growl."

"You want me to tell 'em you're taking a holiday?"

"No, of course not."

"Then, as they say at the Bulls," Mrs. Lavender grinned,

"'get your little pink pratt' out of bed, and I'll eat some breakfast with you!"

Jessie yawned at Mrs. Lavender and frowned over what Brooks might be at, just now. Shaving, bowing his tie, eating? No, it was late; he'd be Saturday busy at the bank, speaking pleasantly, looking sure and serious at his desk, or maybe standing in the doorway making guesses as to why he'd not seen her pass on her walk to the emporium, and perhaps worrying himself over it.

"If you'll run down and make the tea," she said, "I'll get dressed."

"Child, about everybody's heard about you and Brooks Durham. My, it's the talk. Yesterday, I bet a dozen of my customers—"

"Mrs. Lavender, the tea!"

The big woman made a clatter, as if she somersaulted down the stairs, and she sent up a pell-mell sound from the kitchen. Jessie put her hands behind her head, and stretched again; the shoppers could wait, this once.

Most of them were idlesome people anyway, at least, as compared to herself, and some would appear only to comment about Brooks and herself, and a few would say with point, "Hon, you mean, actually, you never heard from your first man, not in eleven years?" Others would be concerned only that her new stock had arrived, and these would spend hours plundering through piece goods and millinery and ready-mades, sliding the silks along their cheeks, running their fingers through the laces, brushing hat plumes over their lips, pinching wax fruit that looked "so real, so real," and then they'd talk about how the hard times were supposed to be over, but in truth were not, and they'd buy a nickel corset string, or a card of pins, or nothing at all, and leave half the shelves to be straightened.

Jessie rolled her fist in her eyes and sat up. She put her feet into fluffy white slippers and, smiling at nothing particular, clumped to the wardrobe cabinet. She studied, then took down the blue whipcord dress and laid it on the bed before peeling away her gown. Regularly when she dressed, her mind ran to business, and spent no attention on her body. But business was far away this morning, and it struck her it was about time she possessed some estimation of herself. Wasn't she almost a bride?

She did not move to the mirror, but turned toward it where she stood, and drew in her stomach.

At twenty-eight, Jessie wasn't old, the best she could tell. She discovered a child freshness to her skin, a young turn to her breasts. If there was a trace more of waist, a broader, softer thigh, these caused her no harm. And the remainder. . . .

Jessie hadn't seen herself in a long while. Not as someone else might see her. Some man! She reddened to her ears, and ran at her clothes to hide. She hurried until the snapping up of the dress. Then more slowly, but without special care, she brushed and arranged the flaming folds of hair, so that the swath of gray looked less wide than it had become. She gathered up a blue bonnet and her handbag and the new parasol she'd brought home from the store and went downstairs.

"Purty dress, child," Mrs. Lavender said. "Did you tell Brooks about that drunk brute?"

"I told him."

"Well! When's the killin'?"

"Oh, there won't be any. He promised me."

"Huh," Mrs. Lavender said, and Jessie sat down to the kitchen table.

Mrs. Lavender poured tea, blew steam off a spoonful and drank it. "Never seen news spread quicker," she said. "About you and Brooks Durham, I mean."

Jessie smiled. "I imagine you saw to that."

The big woman tried to look guilty, and they laughed.

"That Dunce Moreno, that blabbering barber, he done his share. Never knowed a man as could talk so much; talk, talk, talk, that's him."

Jessie poured her tea.

"Girl, I think your groom is still celebratin'. They was some kind of a hullabaloo at Tate's place this mornin', real early, and I seen old Brooks come out. Just bet he set 'em up for the crowd, right at the crack of dawn!"

"Umm," Jessie said. She was annoyed with the tea; it hadn't been let steep. After a cup of it, she was hungry. "I wish we had some cakes," she said.

They rummaged out cold biscuits, ate them with more of the tea. Jessie remained hungry. She got up and made a breakfast of sausage and jam, and Mrs. Lavender steam-heated some of the biscuits. They sat eating as though competing, eating by the big mouthfuls, the way women never eat if a man is around, and well, Jessie thought, like a pair of bitch wolves.

She wondered about Brooks, whether he took tea for breakfast. No, he looked the coffee kind, and she frowned. Jessie seldom had coffee in the house, these years; for her it had become a stout drink best taken in bed.

"My Lord," Mrs. Lavender said, and she licked at grease on her chin, "Everyone wants to know when is the wedding? You didn't say, child."

"Why, in a week or so, I guess. I hadn't thought yet; I have to get a dress made, and after that, whatever suits . . . (she almost said Julius) . . . suits *Brooks.*"

The near slip frightened her; it was a flick of the guilt she could yet weep from, if she allowed it, and foolish, foolish. *He* had deserted *her,* hadn't he?

Mrs. Lavender let go a biscuit and threw out her arms. "Suits Brooks!" she shrieked. "You crazy? Good dern, girl, the man can't pick the wedding date! You have to get down your female calendar, and figure up."

"Yes, yes," she shut Mrs. Lavender off. She felt the embarrassment in her face, and she got up quickly from the table. "I've . . . I've got to get to the shop."

"Sure, child," Mrs. Lavender looked down at her plate. "Only . . . well, it's Saturday; it's gonna be a tryin' day for me, and—"

"Oh, go ahead and finish; eat all you like. Just shut the door when you leave."

Mrs. Lavender smiled, and dipped a piece of sausage in her tea. "Now, tell me, Jessie, how could any man pick the day? Unless, of course—"

"Bye," Jessie said. She escaped to the hall and out the door as Mrs. Lavender laughed and started to cook more meat.

At the front gate Jessie stopped and put on her bonnet, tying it fast under her chin against the wind and its dry rain of red dust. She walked on, slowly at first, and she counted in her head, then used her fingers for a second count, to make firmly sure. Two weeks from tomorrow, then. That would make it about right, and it could be a Sunday wedding.

A block from the house, the heat and stir of the street and

of the morning began to affect her, and she wished she'd roused out on time to open the shop. She began walking her limit, and in a moment she felt the blue dress moistening under the arms, and sticking to her back, chaffing up her temper so that she cried out, and harshly, at the big clumsy man who stumbled onto her skirts.

Julius Rupp teetered around on his heels, head ducked, his throat growling at his luck, his brain unhitched at the sight of her, so that his scramble back into the Rusk House didn't come off, or even begin, and he was caught before her in his fever and stink and ugliness.

"You!" her voice stormed, "You're the one who . . . you, the other night! Oh, you—"

"Stinking damned tramp," he said.

She stared up at him, her brown eyes hard, and he hated the look as it raked his wounds.

"Oh . . . oh!" she gasped. He saw recognition whiten her face, and sicken it, like a slap.

"I just rose up from hell with my hair on fire," he shot at her.

"Julius! My God, Julius, it's you!"

"Don't yell," he said.

Her body, wrenched aside in one of those colt-gawky poses he remembered, rocked back and forth as though she might fall, and he offered his hand. Jessie whipped straight, staring yet, her feet seeming pointed the wrong way, and he saw she carried another umbrella she might hammer him with. Her lips parted.

"Dammit, don't yell," he said.

"You—came back!"

She said it in a whisper, and he watched her eyes, of a sudden praying them to soften along with her voice. But in the brownness he saw only the hellion image of himself, hideous like sin in a new shirt, the reflection just as before, just as Dirty Creek had mirrored it.

Jessie's hands fumbled themselves up her dress front, coming to her throat, and she looked beautiful, more comely than his closest memory of her. Rupp licked his lips; the scheme he'd ridden six hundred miles with jostled at him, urging, reminding him he was to have grinned and shown her he was the same man, unchanged, that he was to pass the filled saddlebags to her hands, and quick, and crowd into his speech.

But if he'd forgotten, her eyes retold him. These were things gone, no easier to recall than his toes, or the hide cooked from his chest, and he stood silent, exposing to his wife the blown-away ear, the salt-cure texture of him, the scarred empty hands that had no tender gesture left to them.

"You're hurt," she said. "My parasol. Did I—?"

"No."

He recollected now to lift off his hat, and he freed his gaze to drag slowly over her, along the whole handsome mold she was and up to the streak of gray hair which now filled and rose, then fell and flattened with the wind, the eternal dirty bellows that spelled the character of this country and which, said some, would at last weed out the weak ones. He tried to smile at her, and he stooped for the small black parasol she'd dropped. In a caution not to touch her, he put it in her hand.

"Oh, Julius! Why, for God's sakes, why?"

"I didn't aim scaring you; thought you'd know me, day or night."

"I don't mean the other night. I mean why . . . why did you come back?"

He thought of charity cakes beside the creek, and boy's work, and *to who laid the chunk,* and seventeen thousand dollars, and he had no answer.

"You have a gun!"

He put on his hat. "Good-by, Jessie."

"Wait."

Rupp turned down the walk.

"Wait, damn you!" she gasped, and he stopped and looked at her, and walked back and took off his hat.

"We . . . we have to talk," she said hoarsely. "Not here. Come on, to the shop. Quick!"

"No reason to talk, Jessie."

"Come on!"

He followed a stride behind, willing himself not to limp, yet limping. They stepped into Crowder Street and hurried catawampous across, toward a blown cluster of women waiting at the emporium and one-handedly holding down their bonnets and staring. Rupp set his eyes on Jessie's back, a small proud back, poker straight, and she led him, along a path the women yielded, up to the shop's German-pink door.

"Lord, Jessie, it's ten o'clock," a woman said.

"I won't open yet a while," Jessie said, and she put in the key. "Not till . . . not till eleven."

"Well, Great Hannah," the woman said, and Rupp felt eyes bearing up at him and whispers around him. He looked down and found he was stomping the dust from his boots on the walk boards.

Jessie made the way inside, up an aisle laid by tables of buttons and thread and lace, past shelves choked with bolt goods, around a cluttered rack of dress patterns. She led him into a smothering coop of a room shantied onto the rear, where, he recalled sluggishly, Coldiron's ladies used to fit things and where once, a short bit after Miss Gussie opened the place as part of her "civilizing," he and Turner Wallace had tried very hard to peek in. The room had one small window, its glass painted green, and a single cane chair, and nails and hangers on the wall, and papers spread on the floor to cover the dust.

Rupp stood at the door, barely inside. He watched her place the parasol on the chair and strain at hoisting the misfitted window, and he saw the back of her dress had sweated wet.

"Shut the door," she said.

A spoke of daylight leaked in on her, and it struck him he'd been off center, if only a little; Jessie had someway changed. He could make out the tiny arroyos threading out from her eye corners, the forked blue veins that raised under the tight white skin of her hands. She was beautiful—oh damn, she was that—but not seventeen.

"Jessie, I didn't mean to see you."

"I . . . I thought you were dead. There was a story, they said someone at Dodge—"

"Clay Allison. He had poor ammunition."

"Oh," she said. She was standing beside the paint-blinded window, her face green-tinged from it, yet pale, and becoming damp.

"Jessie, I'm going."

"No. We have to decide . . . let me think a minute."

She watched his ears, he thought, the scabbed one, the opposite one notched. He trembled to get hold and pull her so close she could look at neither wound, and it seemed he hungered, also, to roughen and fight her. His nostrils spread to the faint smell of her lily-of-the-valley perfume, drafting off the bronze hair like a pure, pure whiteness, making his buffalo rot the blacker.

"You sorry?" he heard himself say.

"Sorry of what?"

"That Clay Allison didn't kill me."

"Oh, Jesus!"

It lay on his hearing like an ache. His wife had learned to swear. "You look pretty," he said.

"You . . . you look butchered!"

"Hell!" he shouted, "I didn't choose it!"

The flame surged to her eyes, but her voice evened, and she said, "After eleven years, Julius. You come back—like this!"

Rupp moved toward her. She shrank against the wall, small and blue and bronze and white, and he dropped his hands and stopped.

"All right," he said, "I ain't staying long."

"Oh, why did you come at all? You don't know what you've done."

Something shivered her; his look, it appeared like, and he wondered. Would it have dealt itself out the same, even if he made it home of a piece, the big cash money in his hand?

"You said out there you wanted to talk, Jessie."

"I've enough to say," she fired at him. "I . . . oh, you deserted me, Julius. Left me like a . . . like a whore you got tired of. Now, what do you think we ought to do? You think we ought to yell and brawl over it, and start out all over brand new? You think I ought to . . . to kiss your filthy sores and holler 'welcome home, dear husband!'? Oh, I don't think so! I think different; I think I have a right to tell you what to do, and have you do it!"

"Jessie, I was coming back. To make it up, and I had money. I wasn't like this."

"Oh, money!"

"I'm sorry, Jessie," he said. He reached for the door.

"I'm not finished," she shouted. "Wouldn't you care to hear how it's been for me? How I've lived while you were off with your guns and your stinking buffalo? Oh, Lord yes, I'd have gone with you that day, except for Aunt Gussie; I told you that! But you were so thick sure she wasn't sick at all, weren't you? —so almighty positive she just stunted all the time! Well, let me tell you, Julius, she never got out of her bed from the day you left, and I never got to tell her I lied, that I wasn't carrying your child, that nothing . . . nothing wrong happened at the creek! I hated you the day she died, Julius! Hated you! Oh, yes, yes, yes, I'd have followed you, even after that! I would have, but where was I to find you? Where? You never wrote, remember? Not one measly line in eleven years!"

"I'm sorry, Jessie," he said.

"Stop saying you're sorry! Eleven years, and look at you—yes, and look at me—and you're sorry! Where were you when everyone got after me? Aunt Gussie owed everybody, you didn't know that, did you? She even borrowed the money she spent on the wedding, that's how stingy she was! Oh, you don't know how I've scratched to keep the house, and keep the shop, do you? Oh, damn you, you don't know anything; you weren't here!"

"This ain't getting anywheres."

"I fought it all by myself, Julius. For all you knew, I might have ended up in . . . in some dance hall! If I hadn't found me one friend—"

"Jessie!"

"You listen! I used to think what I'd say to you if you ever came back, and you're here, and I'm going to say it, and I don't care a good damn how it sounds!" She was crying, and her fists pumped up and down at her sides.

"You turned me into a . . . a married widow, Julius Rupp! All the trouble of a widow woman, and none of the hope, that's what you did! You could come back the way you went, any old day or time! A married widow, that's it, all the years I ought to have been having my children!"

She wheeled and began pacing, and he thought if she didn't quieten and stop, he'd grab her, and hurt her.

"Oh, I loved you; I loved you! Don't say I didn't, or I'll scratch your eyes out! Enough to break Aunt Gussie's heart for you, only, you and your tight skin, your damned dugout pride, you couldn't see that! All you could think of was shotgun wedding; you never tried to look at the other side of it! You didn't see Aunt Gussie laying there dying, thinking the last of her kin was a slut! You didn't see me, either, trying to tell her the truth and choking on it because she'd never have believed me! You spoiled everything, leaving me, and now you'll spoil it all again, coming back! I hate you for both, Julius; I hate you!"

"Aunt Gussie," he said softly. "You ain't mentioned her notion about the pesthouse."

"Oh, shut up; she's dead!"

The little room was quickly silent. Jessie stood again at the green window, shaking, panting, linen pale. Rupp squeezed the roll of his hat and put it on.

"I'm leavin' now," he said.

"Oh, go ahead. Go . . . go murder your buffalo; that's what I want you to do! Go away, stay away! I don't want anyone to see you. I've got someone now!"

It spun him around to look at her, and he saw that she whirled also, as if in terror of him.

"Tell me, Jessie," he rasped.

"Oh, please, get out. Leave me alone!"

"Tell me," he said.

Her voice fell small. "I've . . . I've got a right," she said. "I'm getting married in two weeks."

He lost his hold on the doorknob, and he was cold, and moving toward her.

"Please, Julius. It's my right!"

He lunged and hauled her to him, clamping her to the pain of his chest, and while she fought, he yanked her head back by the hair, and he knew he could break her neck over his arm, but he kissed her mouth, bruisingly. She tried to bite him, then loosened, and for a terrible moment she kissed him back, her tears smearing onto his face.

He let her tear free, and she smashed her fist to his cheek.

"You . . . you . . . I'll tell Brooks!"

His chest throbbed, fever shot to his forehead; it did seem now his hair was high afire, and he stared at her.

"Who, Jessie?"

"Brooks Durham! He's decent and steady and clean, and I'm going to marry him!"

Rupp crashed the door back, got through it. His thigh jabbed on a table corner in the shop. He spilled the table up, and cut around it, charging for the street.

"Leave him alone!" Jessie shouted. "Oh, I wish the pesthouse hadn't burned down! Let him alone! I love him, hear me? I love him!"

He hit through the women at the door, into the street, lining straight for the bank. Johnsy Hood did not matter, the weeping spic woman did not matter. Crowder Street was looking at him, damn them all, and hooray.

Then someone caught his sleeve, and turned him.

It was Kratz.

Chapter Fifteen

THE man from the Two Bulls let go of Rupp's sleeve and stepped back. He stood tall and spraddle-legged in the street, his eyes black and lizard-cold, his chin toughened forward, slick-shaven and gray. Kratz wore the silver-cockled belt, not at his waist, but low about his groin, and his hand rested on one of the black-rubber gun butts—except the fingers didn't rest at all.

"Maybe you got 'em joshing about me," Kratz said, his tone braked under, almost to no hearing, "And we can't abide that. You owe the Two Bulls, two dollars in money, and you pay up. Now."

Hey, hey. Welcome, old Iron Rind!

Rupp hit him bull-square in the face, the sound splitting out unlike flesh, but as of a dropped melon breaking; and Kratz fell whole-lengthed, the furred white sombrero still aslant of his head. Rupp went quick and down to the man, and he heard himself grunting and swearing as he beat him, one fist in the way of the other at the batting out of their fury: here, one for Jessie's hate, another for her kiss, a fist for Brooks Goddam Durham, a lick now like seventeen thousand dollars and a T-burn mortifying, a lick for old Jay Gould and marriage up a ladder, and for *who laid the chunk*, and for watered whisky and barrel staves and mansions and pest barns, and after that just a lick, and a lick, and a lick. He hammered the face until its wet splatted to the breast of his new shirt and gummed like a thick hot paste to his knuckles, until his breath screamed shy and sore in his lights, and ran out of him rasping; and of a sudden he was sober ashamed.

A moment he sat, his ribs stretching, then caving. Then slowly he got up, his feet yet astride of the man, and he looked around him at Coldiron.

No one had moved toward him; they stood as the first blow had caught them—on the walks, in the street's red-dirt middle, hand-propped on hitch rails and water barrels, some half in and half out of stores. They stared, silent to a man, and only a ragged Mexican sheep guard seemed not to care, for he crossed himself only lazily. Rupp looked into the closest eyes. In one moment of wind and sun blast, he saw Coldiron crouching against him.

The man Kratz stirred between his feet, and Rupp stepped over and away from him. On the ground he saw merely a gun-keen prodder for a cheap saloon, nothing of the like of Brooks Durham. And if he'd half killed this man, Rupp could not dwell on it or even think of it with unease. Underneath his top mind, it seemed, there hummed no consciousness able, any more, to regret. Even the shred of shame he'd felt at the last blow was gone.

Once more he scanned around at Crowder Street's stony faces, and in the swing of his head, he saw the bank sign. But he did not stride for it. Away to his left, a man stood in the shade of the sidewalk awning, watching him intently. Small and trod upon, he looked, but he wasn't; he was Texas Wells, who used to could slap a boy's strings loose, who presently posed a shotgun across his forearm.

Rupp glanced again at the bank, and the shotgun. He felt the street's people packing together, for bravery or in their fears, which was it?—and he knew if he began it just now, he'd not get quite through. He would wait. Soon enough would be tonight.

He wiped his hands on his thighs and bent for his hat. He shook the dirt off it, straightened, and opened his mouth to the burning front of the wind, inhaling it deep, and he walked very slowly toward the Rusk House.

Chapter Sixteen

THE drunken wrangler, Tod Wisdom, still sat on Tate's good board floor, his spine against the bar, his long legs sprawled slackly toward a brass spittoon upset on its yellow cork doily, when Brooks Durham elbowed clear of the crowd and pushed through the fast fanning doors into the street. Coldiron's morning miracle had been uprooted, abruptly as usual, but by no measure in the ordinary way. The Johnsy Hood tale was running Crowder Street like a fire in October grass, and Durham felt the town's sudden aura of excitement as surely as he felt the sun and grainy red wind. Yet the tense and buzzy hustle of it reached him with meager impact, next to the chill core of fear he felt knotting in himself.

He headed straightaway across Crowder's blowing ruts, toward the high board-and-batten front of the Stockman's Security, and although he walked, he was fleeing, and he knew it, and for the moment, not even his most deliberate thought upon Jessie or her promise could slow him.

At the hot obscenity of a man's shout, Durham jumped back, barely saving himself from the wheels of a buckboard. He heard himself swearing at the driver in a language belonging nowise to a choir singer, the words remembered from the uncaring years behind. Quickly he shut it off.

Johnsy Hood burnt, and dead, and hideously.

Durham shuddered. He'd not weathered Tod's account of it without shock, but the event itself concerned him little when laid next to its meaning, the plain fact that he was, himself, hunted by a cow thief turned mad. And, God witness, he'd done it to himself! He'd left open a window of his sturdy new house, through which the old times looked in on him and might take hold and suck him back.

As he walked he thought how impossible it was, that a Saturday that had gotten off so ripely content might become the day of his helpless falling back. But it wasn't impossible. Oh hell, he accused himself, maybe he had faced himself around already, the other night when he'd lied to Jessie to get away early in order to ride out for poker, this last a kind of lie to his town; or maybe when he'd agreed to the company of a blood-sucking fop and a drunken, bellering saddle-bum.

He had found the reasons, then, to pardon himself; that Coldiron mustn't see its banker gamble, and more honestly, that no one need see how he played with a yearning to lose, and to lose a great deal, so that while the money went he might laugh, and laugh each time with a truer heartiness, and from the sound of it know still more certainly that he wasn't the actual same man he used to be.

But however he reasoned, the dangerous fact stood close to him now. He was hunted, and the threat was almost due him; he had been "out to see the elephant," and stirrup-to-stirrup with a pair whose very looks offended him.

For this lapse Durham muttered a merciless judgment on himself. If he'd learned a whit from his new life, it was that nothing damns a man so quick as to offend himself, for this offends, also, the small splinter of God each man carries in his chest.

Splinter of God—he'd heard that at Union Church.

Of a sudden he wondered if the rustler had heard when he took his stand, when he prevented the hanging; if the big man knew he had gotten the rifle and made them stop the burning, if too late. Hell, of course not—not a man kicked so hard in the head.

He hit the plank walk in a fierce high stride and came to the bank's double doors. Like the windows, they remained shaded and locked, and he used his key and went inside.

"Morning, Mr. Durham," said Emmitt McLowery.

The consumptive, wedge-faced old teller arrived first, by habit, to serve as janitor before he became the teller, and he stood now in front of his cage, hauling up his sleeveholders and surveying the lobby dust through steel-rimmed spectacles which enlarged his eyes and appeared to bring them forth on stems.

Durham nodded to him.

"You're some tardy," Emmitt said, and he drew a dust rag out through the bars of his paying window.

"Yes."

"You got a letter; Sam Heidel sent it over while ago."

"Where?"

"There, on your desk. Say, congratulations. About Jessie Rupp, I mean. Not that I'm much surprised, but you didn't mention it yesterday. If that Mrs. Lavender hadn't come in—"

"Thanks," Durham said. "Let's get busy."

He thudded his heels across the raw gumwood floor he meant to carpet sometime, making for his desk. The desk had begun as a table, until he ordered drawers built into it, and was placed at the rear, so he might face the street with his back to the limestone vault and yet keep in ready view the teller's stall off to the right. He got into his swivel chair, the only one he knew of in Coldiron, and sat mopping the extraordinary sweat from his face, watching until Emmitt McLowery went reluctantly at the dusting. Then Durham slid out a lower drawer.

On top lay the sealed brown envelope, where he had put it two days before, and in it Jessie's notes, twenty-eight hundred dollars' worth, now stamped "paid." The debts had begun with Jessie's Aunt Gussie, and had grown so old, with only the interest paid each year, that they put Durham tight in the middle at each meeting of directors. He'd not thought of buying the notes himself until the night he proposed and encountered the owed money as a fence Jessie kept strung between them. He would give her the envelope soon, he hoped, but not until the giving carried no suggestion as to how he had won her.

He brushed the envelope aside now, and with it other papers, coming to the worn, soap-needy gun belt underneath. He looked at the walnut butt of the heavy Remington revolver, curving up from a cutaway holster. The gun seemed to speak of safety, and at once, of the old way as well, and he raked his lower lip with his teeth, and he thought, one way or another, it is lying, damn it all.

"You heard about Johnsy Hood?" McLowery called to him.

"Yes, all I care to."

The teller started, and shrugged, and turned away to bend in a far corner and curse over signs of the rats he eternally battled with. Not rising, Durham took up the gun belt and strapped it about his waist, fearing the feel of it, submitting to a sudden gloom that came as the weight settled to his hip in a way more natural than strange.

He drew his coat over the weapon.

"Well," McLowery said, "guess it'll be another of them Saturdays."

"I expect," Durham growled. "You can open the doors when you're ready."

The teller yawned and turned to it. "Ain't you going to read your letter? From Mexia, I noticed the mark; that's back East Texas, ain't it? Blackland country?"

Mexia, yes. Blackland, yes. And his mother's labored hand. He peeled it open.

August 2nd, 1884
Mexia, Texas, Route 1

Dere Sonny:

I am filled with Happiness to receive by The Post of today your treasured Lettere after these many years. I have been very sad of the Prospect, dere one, and resigned during this Great While to passing on to my Long Home without a Knowledge of Your Fate. Since your lettere arrived, I have churned, but I have Otherwise only prayed on my knees in happy Thanksgiving to our Kinde and Gracious Lord for saving My Son from his wild & sinful ways. Now I hunger to see you & hear from your own lips the whole detailes and adventures of your Great Experience and Pledge to the Right Way, as it would add to my Sweete Joys. I wish also that Papa might partake of the Happiness, but in sadness I must announce to you, dere Sonny, that he was Called to his Rest last Spring. Do not Grieve deeply, My Son, but be Proude to know the Foul smell of Likker had not lain upon his Breathe for very nigh four months when his Summons came in the Nite. Tho the Dark Path you have trod laid heavy upon his heart, dere boy, he loved you to the Last, & I have heard him discuss with Mr. Kelso how straight a Pistole you fired.

Dere Sonny, how much I would pleasure to tell all of Mexia of You, and show them your Lettere, tho I will Refrain as you Ask, until your consent comes. It is Enough that my Fond Prayers have been answered from The Throne and Blessed Altar, & to know of Your whereabouts at last, & that You have Won the Victory & found an Honourable place for yourself, however Far away. Yet I shall not be able to keep this Good News of You a secret entire, as the Joy is on my face, I know, & I must confide your Fine Lettere to the reading of your Gentle Sister and to Brother John, for they have Suffered in the Worry and Prayers beside me, & must be shown this Miracle of God and His Wonders also.

I do sincerely thank you for the One Hundred Dollars, dere Sonny, & as it is without Taint, it will be laid to Godly Purposes, for as You might Suppose the yeare of Your Father's Departure to his Glory has been taxed most Severely & his Final crop on this Earth was short as the Devil sent the Bole Weevils in Great Hosts.

Will ever You travel back to visit, dere sonny? It would Cheer my Heart, & I can think of No Persons in Mexia towne who suffered injury & robbery at the Greedy Hands of the Railroad, & whatever is spoke of you here, it is of no Personal Offense & Malice, and I am sure You would meet no great Dangers. How can I begin to write all The News of since you left, for it is yeares, but I expect you would Choose to know the goode sorrel horse You left that last time died of age some thirty months past.

Your Lettere being so short, Dere Sonny, I am left to imagine Only how it was brought about that you Quit the Way of Guns & Riding in Employ of the Greedy Railroad, tho The Miracle of His Mercy is not strange to me, but of His Workings I never tire, & I would be obliged when again You write to learn how You Achieved your New & Fresh start.

If You were here Tonight, dere One, You could Carry Me to Camp Meeting, which is a Fine meeting out of doors by the Brother Selman St. James, who is a Marvelous Man of God that Preaches the Word with Vigor and with a Pen of three Hogs beside His Pulpit. Brother St. James owns a Great Gift, & in this Joyous Week he has healed a goode many of the sick & burdened & infirm, such as Mrs. Grover Shankleton, whome You will well remember from the strawberry jam & johnnie cake. Brother St. James took a grippe on her Neck, where the seed growth hung, & he shook it to a fright, & prayed very Loud & strong & he shouted "Loose this Woman, thou Demon of the Goiter, I command thee in the Name of the Lord," and already this Unsightly growth has become smaller. The Demon was cast into the hogs, which are very large and Vicious animals indeed, & I am told the largest hog has a small growth Appearing on his neck. Mrs. Shankleton is very Happy, but no Happier than I, since Your Lettere.

I wonder, dere sonny, how it was your Own Demons of Money & Guns were cast out, and I hope truly you will state it the next time you write to me, for this Blessed Information would raise yet further My Joys in Your Victory.

Now I will close, goode son, & I trust you will Post a reply, & yes, you may send yet another draft if it pleases you, for Your Brother has small Energy when he looks to the land.

I love you, & I love the Lord, and I Praise Him for your Sweete Salvation.

Lovingly,
Mother

Durham wadded the letter in his fist. He had looked forward to hearing again from home, to the thought that sometime, when Jessie knew about him, he might send for his mother and make her a good life in Coldiron. But today the letter came all wrong. He'd buckled on his gun, and he was sitting here afraid and asweat, and nearer the old violences than he'd been in five resolute years. Durham knew, then, that if he replied to his mother at all, he'd not answer her questions.

How could a man say what reversed and reharnessed him, or when it happened? Was it in El Paso, when the widow came out of the inquest and screamed to his face, "Were you paid well, God Durham? God Durham is right, ain't it? It must be, because you're only one man standing where four men ought to stand—or is it five, Murderer!" Or was it at Vegas, when he saw a man rammed through with a stove poker? Durham had watched the man crawl under a hazard table with the hook of the poker showing red from his back, and had heard the whisper, "I wish, I wish . . ." before the man died, leaving untold what it was he had wished for so bloodily and so lately. Or, Durham wondered, had he simply gotten puke full of bullying through land purchases for the almighty railroad, to the end that the company might own what was destined to become townsites along its route, thus profiting heavily, and rewarding him with bonuses?

Whatever, he could never write of it to his mother; it was well lost behind him, or had been, until the branding—until Johnsy Hood, and today.

"Anything the matter?" Emmitt McLowery said.

"I don't know of it," Durham said, and he glared at the teller before he set to work.

"Mr. Durham," McLowery called from the front window at midmorning, "maybe you'd like to come up here a second. They's a hellofa fight out in the street."

"It's a Saturday," Durham said, but he looked up. Instead of the brawl, he saw the woman coming in. Carpetbags hung in each of her hands, pulling her towards the floor, and her yellow head bent, neither bonneted nor brushed.

"Mrs. Shelley," he said.

She raised swollen, stark-green eyes and came toward the desk, the bags rustling against a wilted skirt. At sight of her, then, Durham knew what must be in one of the bags, and he was rattled. Tod's tale must have addled him more than he realized; until this moment he'd not connected the thousands he'd let Bonnie Shelley withdraw with the money that had mocked Johnsy's ugly dying. If he'd thought of money at all, he'd thought of the great damp wad behind him, locked in the vault and souring the vault's air with the smell of horse sweat.

He kept standing while she plumped into the armless chair opposite him. In the out-of-form gray dress, trailing by some years the fashion, and too woolly-thick for the season's sun, she looked, he thought, like a heap of unsorted charity clothes. She was breathing hard, looking at him with a dull defiance. One red, man-sized hand, its nails nibbled short, stroked back a string of the untidy hair.

"Can I help you?" he said softly.

She leaned her heavy bosom to her knees, grunted, reached, and straightened back with the smaller bag in her lap. She worked the clasp open, spread the wood-frame mouth, and bottomed up the bag over his desk. Soiled fists of currency spilled out.

"Brack's," she said. "It's hisn; put it back."

Durham glanced down, unproud of the small relief he felt. He had let her trick him of the money, and he realized now that Brack would have called about that, spitting fire, and holding him to account.

"We'll . . . we'll count up," he said, "and I'll make you a receipt."

"You'll see it's shy," she said evenly. "I kept out two hundred dollars."

He began separating the broken money wrappers from the pile, and he noticed thin lines of red trail dirt sunk into the fleshy white creases circling her throat. Her fair round face and the mouth which, with color, might have been pretty, looked tired and sloven and wretched and old. A pity for Bonnie Shelley surged in him. He was not prepared for it, yet quickly he nourished it, and he hoped to treat her kindly. Of a sudden it was important, like an offered way of pushing back against the steel weight on his hip.

"Everyone knows, don't they?" she said in a whisper.

"Well, Mrs. Shelley—"

"Don't they all know? Don't they!"

He rested his hands and looked at her. "Ma'am, I can't name a man in this town who'd tell it to Brack. Maybe if I made a few calls. . . ."

She shook her head. "I'd tell him myself, Mr. Durham, if I was staying."

"You're going away?"

She watched her hands now, in her lap, one picking thoughtlessly at a torn yellow callus in the palm of the other.

"On today's stage," she said.

She should be crying, he thought, in this woman's worst moment—running from a husband whose least right was to flog or throttle her, her name alive on Coldiron's tongues.

"You could wait till Brack gets home," he said. "I mean, if I seen him first, before he heard anything—"

"No. Only—you can tell him I'm taking the two hundred dollars. You can tell Brack I . . . tell him them's dirt-cheap wages for fifteen years toting his water and hoeing his bean patch and shaving his neck for him Sunday mornings and squeezing out his blackheads for him and . . . Mr. Durham, you tell him two hundred is fair hire."

He gazed at the cherry bruise beneath her left eye, one that would expand and blacken as time went.

"You'll tell him?" she said.

"I can try. But Brack . . . listen, Mrs. Shelley, suppose we both talked to him, told him how it was?"

"Nobody knows how it was. Not me, leastways."

She had stripped up a dry shred of the callus, and she raised it to her mouth and bit it off like sewing thread and popped it off the point of her tongue toward the floor.

He said, "If you'll say where you're headed, then? You know, in case?"

"I'll decide when I get to the railroad."

"Back to Illinois, maybe?"

"No."

"Bonnie, for God's sake—"

"Oh, for God's sakes yourself!" she sobbed at him. "Take care of the money, and quit talking about it!"

The puffed eyes were not truly angry, or truly alive, or truly anything else, and he thought he smelled a trace of hard liquor about her. He began flattening the mussed bank notes into stacks of a thousand.

She waited silently.

"Comes to me," he said after a time, "that we could just put this money back, and tear up the check you gave me yesterday, and you could draw another one for the two hundred you want, so's Brack wouldn't need to know about the money part at all."

"That would go easier on him, wouldn't it; a man like my husband?"

"I think it might."

Then she laughed, so coldly that he knew she'd had a drink. "Don't do it, then," she said.

Durham ran through his second count, leaving the bills in ten wrinkled stacks in front of him. "Ninety-eight hundred, correct," he said. "I'll make you a deposit slip."

"Keep it for Mr. Shelley. And tell him about the fair wages, and tell him I didn't take no clothes, outside of what's on my back."

She got out of the chair and bent for her bag. "This here," she said, "it's a few jars of stuff I put up."

She turned, swayed, stumbled on her skirt, recovering as Durham came to his feet, and she moved away toward the doors, one arm frozen straight outward, shoulder high, to balance off the bag's weight, and she looked fat, he thought, and plain, and deathly, and old.

When she made the street, he crossed the lobby and watched her out the front window. She angled through the hot Saturday din, her burdened side warping steadily lower and the opposite arm rising higher, her hair flagging where the wind found it unpinned.

It seemed of a sudden that Bonnie Shelley had given him less to fear. For it had occurred to him how handily he might pocket the ninety-eight hundred, allowing Brack Shelley to believe the money had fled with the wife, with no one the wiser, depending on how much Emmitt McLowery may have heard. But the fact was he hadn't really considered it, and this seemed a confirmation, like losses at cards, of—what was it his mother had called it?—his Sweete Salvation. Yes, his Sweete Salvation.

As Durham turned from the window, Emmitt McLowery set to hiccuping, choking a little each time, and the teller's weak wet gaze met Durham's, and Durham resented him. Except for the teller's ears, Durham knew, he would have asked Bonnie Shelley the questions, all of them, about the madman who did for Johnsy Hood.

He moved back to his desk, spinning the watch-chain gold piece in his hand as he went. The coin had a calming, thoughtful way with him now, when before, he guessed, it had been to flaunt and to show. It wasn't the first fifty dollars he had earned, but it was the first fifty he'd ever had to spare, which was another, more confident thing. It rode his front, proving him, as the bank vault proved him as it stood at his back.

Emmitt McLowery quit choking, cursed the blowing dirt, and began to wipe and grin.

"Hard to think of, huh, Mr. Durham?" he said. "Solemn little woman like that one, ups and—"

"Damn you, Emmitt!" Durham bit him off. "You spread any part of whatever you heard, and I'll stomp that snort out of you!"

At the desk he sat down and leaned back, and felt less afraid.

Let's see, he thought, that rustler had been whiskered, and big, with one notched ear, in clothes most men wouldn't even mop with, and he had power—enough to smash in Sunderman's solid oak door.

Chapter Seventeen

JESSIE to marry Brooks Durham: it ate at Rupp's linings like a draught of hot lye, yet he limped on, away from the Stockman's Security to the Rusk House, holding to his "calculated withdrawal" and dreading the hours of the wait, as he must wait, until Coldiron turned its enraged eyes off him and its alertness cooled. Stuck before his sight was the look of Jessie as she screamed at him, and the picture of the man Kratz battered into the dirt, and the gilt-lettered sign on the bank glass, reading "Capital Stock, $25,000," as if taunting him that he had been, briefly, almost as rich as this whole moss-horned town, and reading also, farther down, "Directorships, Jerome Chester, Samuel Heidel, Lacy J. Tate, Cass F. Bellew, Dodson E. Kesterling," and at the end, "Brooks Durham, Pres. & Mgr."

Brooks Durham, in successful gold paint. The name Jessie wanted.

The reedy clerk backed rapidly away from the lobby door, and away from Rupp as he came in, and he said as though needing grease, "My God, Mister Brown, what was it old Kratz done to you?"

Rupp cut aside from him and toward the stairs, feeling scared eyes and the sun's fire tracking him.

"You sure done him up crisp," the clerk said. "Was it somethin' he sassed to you?"

Rupp went into Johnsy Boy Hood's room, now hell-hot and bleak-looking, like any room newly orphaned, and he dumped his ache and fever onto the bed and rolled over on his back. He lay staring up at the bald, cobwebbed ceiling. He was breathing too much from the stairs and the misput wrath of his fists. He had begun to feel the brand again.

What a mile-long day it was. Oh, damn, the very longest and slowest, and with most of it yet ahead, to be waited out; and it seemed that whether he swore or mourned, nighttime got no nearer. Jessie and Brooks Durham. Jessie's unintended kiss, wet and panicked on his lips, Jessie yelling her love for Brooks Durham. Of a sudden he thought of Jessie a new way. Not in blue whipcord, but in black crepe, with funeral eyes and a veil. Jessie as she would be, after he killed Durham.

He pained, and was tired. He hiked up one foot to rest on the iron bedstead. Abruptly he smelled the hog-lardy odor of the Sioux Wonder Ointment, waving from his chest and from the jar he'd left uncapped. The salve's scent had chased down and killed off the last ladyish hint of Johnsy's bergamot. The noticing of it made it seem Johnsy Hood had only this minute died.

Jessie and Brooks Durham.

He needed a cooler brow, and sleep.

The yellow cat sprang from no place to the bed and writhed, purring, against Rupp's thigh, its thin back arching to meet his hand. The street's sunglare was fading from his eyes, and he saw the furnishings more clearly: the washstand gray under its shell of dried soap; the brass lamp crowding the chipped washbowl; the joint-sprung bureau that strained away from the window's wind gusts, leaving empty drawers pouched half open; the low-boy heating stove shoved into a corner to rest up for winter; Johnsy's stuff.

Beyond the wall the spic woman was crying again. Rupp shut his eyes, and while being sure he couldn't, he sank towards sleep. At once, it seemed, the voices stirred him. First the clerk's, out in the hallway, pitched high, and laying her out.

"See here, Pepper Head, this carrying on ain't fixing anything, and you got the tenants hollering at me, like I don't have plenty to bother over already, with that damned centipede running Mister Hoagland out of the john, and the town all roiled up and hissin'! You got to hush up; they're complainin'!"

The woman's reply was low, spending itself short of Rupp's hearing.

"Well," the clerk's voice said, "just shut up, that's all I'm askin'."

"Please, in his room," the woman said, her voice suddenly ranged farther in its pleading, "was there not something there, for me? A ring, he promised it, one for Mama to see. Please, if I might myself look there, I would find it. If. . . ."

"Hell, wasn't no ring in there, no cash neither. And the room, it's took. But your rent now, it's paid, the way I told you. Only, shut up; I can boost you out of here, rent or not, if you keep up that bawlin'!"

Again the woman spoke, below Rupp's hearing. Then the clerk laughed, nervous and brittle, and he said, "Look, gal, if it's a man you're missin', let me in. I'm one as ain't so old as he looks!"

A door clapped shut as Rupp sat up angry. He listened to the clerk's step as it lagged past his own door and down the stairs. When the sound died he unfolded his fists and felt for his tobacco. The sleep he hurt for was lost to him.

He wondered why he'd been so riled at the hotelman, and twice now, over Johnsy's spic woman. It was a folly of the sort he'd seen in drunks who could, at times and in seriousness, toast the chastity of some saloon-room frump. The nearness of this girl—it seemed to hinder him, as had the thing with Johnsy Boy. But, since seeing Jessie, since hearing her, he needn't lapse toward softness. Jessie with Durham!

He spat on the floor and fired his cigaret, watching the smoke, and he tried to recall Jessie's kiss, if kiss him she had; and now, so soon after, he couldn't swear it. If he thought to taste the linger of her on his lips, as though she were a sweet berry wine, then he thought insanely. The moment itself had been unreal, and its memory quickly false like a bucket without bottom. He'd made the kiss no lovers' reunion; it had been, instead, a rage and a punishment on her, and he'd given it as an executioner, and after it began, he'd felt only the unparticular bull-hunger a man gets for a woman, any woman at all, and for this last he was sorry.

Jessie. And Brooks Durham.

They sliced into his mind, then, the put-off suggestions: of Jessie sharing the big house with Durham, setting for him a table to his likes, pouring his coffee, combing the bronze hair the style Durham might choose it, climbing Aunt Gussie's stairs on his arm. Yes, Jessie up in the corner room, and in her bare nothing for Brooks Durham!

Rupp bolted up from the bed.

He swung to the window and looked out, hating the forenoon light that showed him the hurried Saturday affairs of the street, the people who'd watch him, and too close, if he were out there. To hell with them. He drew the long Colt from his waist, inspected the shiny new loads, grabbed up the hat he'd wallowed flat on the bed, and punched out the crown and put it on. But he paused; he must wait these day hours out. He swore and sat down, and considered how he might buy whisky and drink and be drunk through the waiting.

Then he heard the running, light-footed, in the hall. He listened, and heard nothing more. Stepping quiet, he crossed to the door and looked out.

The girl was soot-haired, childish in a dingy pink kimono the hue of a sandstorm sky, the sum of her no bigger than the half-minute he used in looking at her. She stood at the wide hall window, her back to him, intent on something down in the street. She rustled and her small hands lifted. In them he saw a rusty-barreled pistol. She laid the muzzle across the window sill and made a team of her tiny brown thumbs so they might cock the hammer. The girl withdrew her head to align the sights, and in the instant, Rupp moved and clamped his arms around her.

"*Cristo mio!*" she shrieked.

He grunted "whoa," and saw that she had come up off the floor, a flailing bundle in his grasp. He broke the gun from her hands and spun her small body away from the window.

"I pray your gringo soul to Hell!" she gasped. Her black eyes burnt as if to fasten on the curse, and he thought she would spit at him. Instead, she reached. Rupp felt her nails trenching his scabbed ear. He dropped the pistol and snatched hold of her arms.

She struggled and whimpered, and he kept his hold of her. He turned his head to glance into the street, seeing there a thick and yellow-haired woman who angled away from them, toward Tate's or the adobe stage office next door, her back slumped from a flower-printed satchel and the off arm balanced far out.

Rupp looked again at the girl. Johnsy's girl, Maria.

"You aimed to shoot that woman," he said.

She cursed him in billowing Mex, her furious eyes interpreting and making it thorough. Then the starch milked out of her, and he dropped his hands. She sagged back against the wall, her face lowered, and she was crying without sound.

He watched her. His head ached; the scuffle had aroused also the bone-deep soreness of his body. He found no cause for having troubled himself, yet no regret that he had. After a moment he took the girl's arm and steered her along the hall, to his room, and inside.

"This's the room you wanted to see into, ain't it?" he said.

Maria backed from him, almost the room's depth away. She stared at him, and he watched her brown cheeks darken, coloring deeper the black bruise on one of them, and he saw a long welt, like a rope burn, on her neck. Johnsy Hood, Rupp thought: his mark.

"Would you of shot her?" he said.

The girl's hands bunched together the pink collar at the joining of brown throat and brown breast.

"*Si!*" she said. "*Por Dios,* I would have splashed the street with her brains!"

"Who is she?"

"Big one, you need not have set hands on me! It is not given you to choose."

"That woman, what's her name?"

Maria's eyes were hot. "*Ay,* the hair of gold," she said. "The Señora Shelley!"

Rupp smiled. "Sounds like you'd butcher her for hide and tallow."

The girl (a kept spic girl, he prodded himself) shook her head, and shuddered, and went mincing to the bed; one, it struck Rupp, that she must know each lump and vermin of, and she scrubbed a hand over her forehead as in her gloom she sat down.

"Why?" he said.

"It is not of your account."

"No," he said, and he saw that she would tell him.

"It . . . it is this fat ancient that has killed my Johnsy, in the fine house of hers. Oh, you will say to me, 'it was not the Señora Shelley,' but it was, it was. He was sick with a fire, and for a comfort she gave him a wound to his soul, so that he must die of it! Oh, this bitch of bright hair, my Heart's blood is on her!"

Maria twisted so that her eyes, also, pleaded to him. "Please, I must go! She takes a case and walks toward the coaches. Soon she will leave!"

Johnsy's blood, he thought. She'd placed it wrong.

The girl rose off the bed, and he thought she would charge him. Then in a quick black flicker, her eyes gave it up and she crumbled back to the ragged quilt, looking small and sorrowful and like a weary pink doll.

Rupp crossed to the washstand and looked in the glass at his ear, trying it lightly with his fingers.

"I . . . I have wounded you," she said, her voice at once rid of its tough dry shuck.

"No."

"But I am not blind."

"I done had it," he said.

"It . . . it bleeds."

"Not now."

In the glass he saw her eyes moving over him, studying, hunting his stripe, with their smolder almost gone. "You are tall," she said suddenly. "Yes, I think it is you!"

Rupp tautened; he wondered if she could know, if Johnsy had told a good deal, if, then, all of Coldiron saw him as the man with the iron.

"It's me what?" he said.

"You are the Señor Brown who has paid the rent of my room!"

His breath spewed out, and he turned.

"Why was this, that you paid?" she said.

She was standing now, and disorderedly pretty, her skin young and shiny, a crescent of a comb ready to fall from where it shoved back the dense bendless hair, and in the room's close air he smelled an unfresh mist of vanilla bean. At once he thought of the perfume of kissing Jessie and of his waiting rage. He stared at Maria while he wondered about rage, whether it might fan itself into heat for a woman, the way woman-heat, sometimes, could flame into wrath.

Under his stare a tired anger clouded the girl's face.

"*Ay, comprendo!*" she speared at him, "I am the hotel woman, you think? I must pay!"

Her hands seized the kimono waist and slung the front of it apart. A latch pin hit the floor, hard enough to click. Underneath, Maria was clothed in nothing.

"*Aqui!*" she shrieked.

Rupp started ahead, stopped, stung still that she had discovered him even while he struggled, lucklessly, at discovering himself. He gawked. Not at her daylit femaleness, but at the hopeless, bitter pinch of the brown face, looking suddenly as he felt, like the whole unhappy countenance of this useless soapweedy country.

"Fix your dress!" he rasped.

She did not move. "It is the pay you thought for, is it not?"

Rupp heeled about, facing away from her, his fever raw and doubled. "Button up, goddamit!"

"Come, you might say when you boast of me to the others, 'I was repaid most well by Maria.'"

"Shut it up!"

It was quiet, and then her motion and the vanilla air quivered his nostrils, and he heard the bed creak as she sat down.

"In eleven days," she said, "I will be of age eighteen."

"I thought you craved a look at this room," he said. "If you ain't going to look, you'd better get out."

She snuffed, as he'd heard her snuff through the wall, and she whispered, "Please, if I may remain a little time? The *hombre del hotel,* the small clerk man, he bids to . . . visit in my room."

Rupp picked up the water pitcher and drank from the thick warm lip of it, as though it were whisky, letting the water spill off his chin and trail along his throat toward the muslin stuck tight to his chest.

"He won't come," he said.

She rustled out of the kimono a flattened Mexican corn-shuck cigaret, holding it to her mouth, looking at him until he pitched her a match. She sat holding the cigaret between thumb and forefinger, drawing the smoke no deeper than her mouth, whistling it out hard.

"You spoke, I think, as my Johnsy might have spoken to me," she said.

"You smoke," Rupp said.

"Oh, such a least little. When I am hungry."

"When have you et?"

"I had goat's milk from the street, yesterday, and *panocha.*" She looked up, the crippled cigaret held high and away from her, as Johnsy Boy had held his gun, and her eyes lit proud. "I have received much to eat, before. Always, my Johnsy brought much."

"All right," he said, "you can eat with me."

She shook her head. "No, when it is day, I do not go out of this place."

"I can fetch up something, I guess," he said, and was surprised.

He got to the door, and turned. "Get your clothes on," he said. "You got another gun?"

Her teeth were an even white. "There is no other," she said. "I think I would not . . . I think I could not kill the Señora Shelley now. I have thought, and it would be too much to pray of."

Rupp started out.

"Please, a moment," she called. "I . . . this that I offered in your sight. I have not done so before."

"Don't tell me."

"It is true, by the Holy Mother I vow it! From the time I have grown big, my Johnsy only!"

"Hell," he said, "what you like to eat?"

Maria smiled, then of a sudden shrieked and bolted her naked feet up onto the bed and sat on them, and she wailed, "*Ay,* Señor Brown, the cat! He is beneath the bed muttering!"

Rupp went downstairs.

Chapter Eighteen

ELWOOD Coates rested himself in a loose, leathery pile at his table, drinking, and eying, and hating this smugged-up breakfast-liquor crowd so kowtowed and catered to by Si Tate. Coates had long had his craw full of these, the town men who got themselves up in white collars and churchy-looking clothes, even on Saturdays, and who teased so damned temperately at their whisky while they parleyed of Coldiron doings in which he, as the JC foreman, ought to have at least some little say. But this morning it nigh delighted him to watch them, these self-set bulls-of-the-lick; not a man jack of them could say he'd once rode drag up the trail.

The drunker Coates got, the funnier they looked. Men who followed Brooks Durham's lead like mules stringing after a bell mare. And Brooks Durham, he was gone, and likely holed up to do his shaking and praying, haw!

As he watched, he turned up his glass, sweeting up "the sweet poison of misused wine," which was something Old Blind Johnnie writ into one of old By Jove Jerome's books, and he saw several of them come dallying back through Tate's doors from the street, looking stretched, and their clubby hum almost hushed. A minute before, they'd got Tod Wisdom laced into his saddle, and they'd yelled and hatted the sweaty horse into a hell-bending gallop back toward Shelley's.

While the crowd lined itself again at the bar, Coates grinned at them openly. The Johnsy Hood business: it hung around them like a thunderhead, and he thought, "Now, when I lay holt of seventeen thousand dollars, or a half-slice of it, they'll talk to me; it's money counts, that's what brings 'em to their milk!"

He listened to some of their choked-down guesses about Johnsy, that Old Brack had slipped back unbeknown to anybody, that maybe somebody Johnsy Boy had skinned at cards had paid him back, that maybe, even, Johnsy being sort of odd, he'd done the whole thing his own self. Coates kept grinning; damn them, this high-muckity few, and damn them every one and each. It felt pretty good, that this once they stood on the outside of something with the gate up and barred. Among them, now, only he knew why Johnsy Hood was dead.

Coates felt the sun looking in on him through a dirty, unshaded front window, cooling him by sucking the yellow whisky sweat out through his shirt, yet of a sudden, he wasn't cool. Though he'd taken his pleasure from the situation, he knew he was only piddling, putting off sure-enough thinking until he was ready for it.

He grabbed up the brimful drink he'd just poured and buried it at one motion. His throat scarcely sensed the heat, and he took pride in that. Coates was a big man for his height, big as skillet bread and sowbelly ever made a man, and whether Coldiron shined to him or didn't, he was the goddam ramrod of the goddam Chester, and one real buster at it, and when he put down his drinking whisky, it was down to stay, which was a deal more than most of these priss-pants boys could claim. Measuring their backs at the bar, Coates thought, "Saw off my right arm, and I could still lick any pair of 'em!"

This was a notion that lit on him often, and commonly, it was satisfying. But today the idea ran shallow, and right behind it he thought of the scorched tramp, surely out to burn him, or maybe kill him, and he must plan—soon as he found the Little Whisky Man. This wise friend, he'd turn up after a bit. A few drinks more.

Now Coates noticed how two of the mighty-high had turned from the bar and looked at him, as though they'd laid bets on how long he could sit up with his load, and he glared back and poured and swallowed another drink. The liquor fell to his innards like a dropped log, numbing him, and he shut his eyes and tried one last duel with his memory.

What could he recall to mind? The tramp had been bearded and stud-muscled, a barn-wide man with the buffler stink heavy on him, brownheaded—or was it red?—and past this, Coates couldn't remember. The by-God fact of it was, he'd not know the man, not if he came wading into Tate's this minute with the head of a branding iron sticking up out of his hip pocket!

Coates's jaw clamped shut. You'd reckon a scalded dog would yelp like hell, and run. But this one hadn't.

He puddled more whisky into his glass, jacked it to his mouth, and he rinsed the venom of it through his teeth before he rolled it on down. His fist chilled around the glass, gripping hard, and he saw his nails flush up with the pressure. Then a sound gurgled in the back acreage of his mind, like a bubble switching places in a man's guts, and with it was a sunburst of pain that went quick.

"That you, Little Whisky Man?" he said.

Now Coates felt good; Tate's and the world moved back from him, so he could see them hard and clear. He sighed to welcome his friend.

Showing late, that was the Little Whisky Man's habit. He'd never stir himself until Coates's chair was a chore to hold down, or until sleep nagged and begged and sulked for him like a hot spic hussy; yet Coates forgave this. The Little Whisky Man was a smart head to talk to, and a private one, and whenever they commenced, Coates didn't need anybody else, and no one could horn in. A time or two, Coates had thought to give his friend a better name, and sometime, when he wasn't so busy for old damned By Jove, he'd think of a fitting one, and do it. But not now. Right now he was busy as hell's front gate with this affair of his own.

"You took your by-damn time," he said to his friend. "And me in a bind!"

Coates shut his eyes to wait for the Little Whisky Man's answer; he liked the smooth deep voice of his friend, for it ran as his own voice might well have, if it weren't for the rifle ball he'd gotten through the throat at Chickamauga, so that afterwards he must either beller and yell, else only whisper, which wasn't a foreman's sound at all.

The Little Whisky Man said, "We'll figure something."

"Figure, like thunder," Coates said. "They's a time to bow up and stand, and a time to pack and ride, ain't that what they say? Well, I'm at my ridin' time, looks like."

"Maybe," the Little Whisky Man answered, his voice good-bottomed and felty and seeming to vibrate in Coates's head as though his skull was a rain barrel being shouted into, and it ached a little. "But maybe you ought to just roust up a posse. Tell old Jolly Jerome you burnt you a rustler, and that the rustler got back at Johnsy Boy. He'll tell you to take the hands, and you can ride them hills out flat, till you catch up with him and leave him swinging."

Coates shook his head. "I done told old By Jove about that brandin'; hell, that was the idea. Sort of thought that burning would match off them figures of hisn on the stock, and maybe get that goddam English beak out of them tally sheets. Except, hellfire, that old knicker-britches, he just cussed and bounced them chair wheels up and down under his ass, and that's all."

"Well," the Little Whisky Man seemed to sigh, "it's sure as hell a wide country. To move, you'll need movin' money."

"I can get it," Coates said.

He cracked his knuckles on the table, tilting it as he helped himself to his feet, and he legged it for the bar, aiming himself at Si Tate's unpeaceful face and pointing his finger at a bottle.

"Elwood," Si said, "ain't you had a plenty for one settin'?"

"Si, you know when aplenty is? Plenty is when I say!"

The saloonkeeper flapped his arms around and brought the fresh bottle, bumping it down, and different than he'd bump it for one of his petted "respectables," more as he'd pass cheap mescal to a Mex, and to hell with him. Coates closed his fist around the humped brown neck of glass, stumped a chair out of the way with his toe and got back to his table. For a time he sat batting his eyes against their smart and bloodshot and the hot light that shimmered around him.

"That buffler man, he toted big money," he told the Little Whisky Man, "and it was cabbaged onto."

The voice at the back of his gray matter was silent, and in a rush, Coates threw down some of the new whisky, not bothering to use the glass, and he whispered, "Hey, little stud, you there?"

"I'm here," said the Little Whisky Man. "Who got the money?"

Coates frowned. "That there, that's the nut of it, as they say."

The money. Johnsy Boy, was it? That yelping, blood-licking little sweetbread, he had his taste for money; that much, Coates could reckon, Johnsy had been a normal cut of a man. Money heat stuck out from Johnsy Hood, much as stout as the smell of flower water, and Coates had seen the lust of it on him those drunk nights when he passed across his own foreman's pay, and some extra besides, to honor up Johnsy's cards. But Coates couldn't decide that Johnsy had wolfed off with the tramp's thousands. Judas and be damned, old Johnsy Boy was a man too pretty, and too shy of belly, and he'd have coughed up the cash, and quick, when hog-tied under a spittin' iron.

"So," said the Little Whisky Man, "Brooks Durham."

"That stud, he don't sound right," Coates said, and he pitched off another drink.

The big-muck banker paid money its deserving due, Coates knew, but Durham was, all the same, a man who held to rules. Durham always wore the look of a chicken thief on his face when, once in a seldom while, he rode out somewhere for poker; and on Sundays Coates had seen him heading for the church-house with a prickly-pear bloom pinned to his coat and that red widow on his arm and a big amen look turning down his mouth. Whatever Brooks Durham was—no, Bull Durham, haw!—he was mainly in the law-and-curfew crowd of this town. Besides, Durham wouldn't let them hang the buffler man, and he'd stepped in with a rifle, even, when the branding went maybe a little far.

"Ain't Durham," Coates told the Little Whisky Man. "Had my eye on him while that Wisdom boy was talkin'."

The smooth voice of his friend mused. "Maybe they wasn't any seventeen thousand. Maybe Tod made it up."

"Tod wasn't lyin'."

Coates leaned back and reamed an ear with his forefinger, and he studied until his scalp seemed to swell from it. Then like a whip it hit him, and he bellowed out a laugh and slapped the table.

The whisky glass frogged to the floor, and Tate's edgy crowd spun around from the habañero it was pouring in memorial to Johnsy Boy Hood, and stared at him. Coates grinned and glared them back, and took himself a long drink from the bottle while they watched. Let them look and let them whisper; they'd be saying he was mumbling to himself, they always thought that when he was in conference—conference, that's what old By Jove hisself might say. Let them talk; they'd creep up to his boots when he was rich, their tongues hung out and all foamed up for licking, by God!

Coates wiped his mouth. "Lil' Whisky Man," he said softly, "I know where that money went, and I can lay hands on it."

He had one more drink, for topping, and to feel at his best, and he got up and brushed to the bar. He sold back the leavings of his bottle. In no hurry, he made for the street, happy that he walked a shade ahead of his legs, and that his mind was clear, and the Little Whisky Man with him. He turned north, past the stage office, past Jessie Rupp's shop, where a flock of fussy women waited for it to open, and past the Union Church and on into Dub Stokes's.

"Hey, black stud!" he yelled to Dub's nigger, "run me out a good hoss, and them spurs I see yonder!"

Coates had driven the JC supply wagon to town, and no wagon he knew of really fit a cowman's seat when he meant some sure enough riding.

Coates mounted, slicker than most men sober, and he put the critter to a lope, northward into the whistling hot dustdevils leaping up from the trail.

It would take only a little spell, he knew, to get to Lee Hanley's.

Then Coates slowed the rented horse and swore.

"Sit still, Lil' Whisky Man," he said. "You make a hellofa knocking in my head!"

Whatever Coldiron took from Elwood Coates, it granted him this one due, and he knew it, that he was a man that could sit up there and ride, and to a fair. Bellering drunk, or sober as the Reverend Brother Gossett, or mean and ugly in that lonesome in-between, his yoked-in legs swallowed the barrel of a mount like a set of extra ribs, and his shape made plush whichever saddle it sat, and what was more, he owned weight, letting a horse feel that a man was on top, and up there to ride, and to ride straight to hell, if to hell it interested him to go. Though he'd lived forty-six years, age was no hurt to Coates; it was as he told the Little Whisky Man, the years were just by-damn handy, priming him up with the strength and the whisky room of two green-boned younguns of twenty-three, haw!

The rented sorrel he sat now was jelly-withered, bloated at the flanks from ease in a stall and a stable's ignorant overfeeding, and it shied sideways, looping its long neck to see back toward Cold-iron. Coates kicked in with the spurs, hacked the bits as though cording wood, and the animal settled, sheep-meek, to the trail. The foreman grinned, fully appreciating, and to the Little Whisky Man he said, "Lee Hanley; now, old Lee Stud, he won't be ex-pectin' us."

He'd met Hanley, who yet swore and bedamned he'd et roast Injun, during the drought-ruint summer before, when, like any range boss good for his salt, Coates had treated himself to a little howl, down in the south country. That was between the time Vic Berner cussed the Mex sheep and sold out his spread, and fired Coates, though Vic most ways was a white man, and the time His Old Book-Reading Lordship took over and hired Coates back.

But, Coates swore, he'd not have hired back if he'd known it would be a part of the job to sit in on the porch while old By Jove Chester rested in his rolling chair and read out loud the stuff of Bloody Bill, and so damned often, *The Pair of Dice Lost* by Blind Johnnie, and likely read none of it right, since he hardly ever even looked down at his book, for fear some fagged-out hand might slip away to bed.

Anyway, Coates had got together with Lee Hanley down south.

They had paired to skin the beans out of a game at Piedras Negras, which was a spic stinkhole across the Rio Bravo, itself no more than a boggy smear of red mud, and afterwards they had drunk, and got their sampling of the chili wenches; and together, somehow, they shot a soldier of the governor, so that when Coates headed to Laredo, then home, Hanley rode along, and it was natural.

Hanley used up all the tales he had about whores during the ride, and after that they set their plans: Coates, as the goddam foreman, to see to it JC cows scattered into quiet roughlands gullies, Hanley to gather them up, in one-man bunches, and point them for the border.

Stealing, old Jolly Jerome would have called it, if he knew, which it wasn't, not at all. Real cowmen, those that were Texans and not hard-skull English, figured on the hands branding a few for themselves during branding time; it was the way they themselves got their start. Well, damn the English.

Considering it now, Coates vouched they'd done pretty well. Hanley had learnt to fix over the JC brand into a clean double-O, and lately, he'd come to handling a dozen head at the bunch. By creaming off half, Coates could, most times, show ample liquor money and spare some, besides, for poker.

A few times they'd talked of putting on a hand or two, holding the cattle instead of selling, so as to broaden out. But each of them seemed to stand it down. Hanley, as he said, because old By Jove hawked the tallies so close, and because he liked best to eat in small bites, unless something turned up that could be gulped down quick and ridden off with. For Coates, the hitch was Lee Hanley himself. The little gray-hair worked too careless for anything sizable. Hell, proof of it was in the fire Hanley had built, too nigh the trail, the other night.

The thought of it, of the trouble that branding fire had started, chapped Coates. Of a sudden he could blame Hanley for the whole of it, for the big burnt tramp who craved killing him, for the knocking in his head, even for the dirt now caking into his sweat, making him hotter.

"Best shake a leg," said the Little Whisky Man. "If Hanley's got rich, he might head off somewheres."

Coates roweled the fat sorrel out of its trot and whacked at the neck with the reins until he got a lope.

Coates grinned. Since that thunderclap in his head, back at Tate's, he'd been sure how it happened. Hanley lying out in the brush, watching them feed iron to the buffler man, Hanley easing in later, so as to collect his running iron and coffeepot, and then, little stud Hanley picking through the tramp's pack, at his own easy time—and latching onto seventeen thousand dollars.

"That mop-headed sonofabitch!" Coates agreed with his friend. "He might be a hunnert miles gone!"

He cut the horse left from the trail, beating the animal up a rump of red hill, over the top, down it, across the blowing ash of the branding fire, into Dirty Creek's stirrup-deep water and out of it, up and over a woolly rise, across grass grubbed short and spoiled by Mexican sheep, into the breaks, pounding up a red wake of dust and sending fat grasshoppers bouncing into the air. Mescal, mesquite thorns, grabbed at his leg leather; the wind came at him in a singe like dry steam. Shortly the horse winded itself, and he had to stop and sit swearing while it heaved and blew. He made up a smoke while he waited, and looked around at the yellow graze sprinkled with sheep sign, and he thought that, by damn, here was a sight of the one thing old By Jove was right about, that one day soon the spic herdsmen would have to be mounted against and driven back south.

But it was no chore of his; he was getting rich, and pulling out. He spurred the horse. Then he came in view of Hanley's house.

It stood at the far end of a grassy flat that was shared also by prairie dogs and their mounds and nearly locked in by red hills that pointed their gullies toward it. It was square, a sod house up to the waist and a plank shack above, then again sodded a foot deep on the roof, except for shingles topping the front awning. Through the small windows shaded by tow sacks, Coates saw nothing, and no smoke lifted from the new stovepipe that reared through the roof.

He plunged the coughing sorrel at the house. "Hey, Hanley!" he yelled. "You there?"

The little man came out. He was tousled, his sweat-wet gray hair touching his shoulders, and he looked sleepy. Hanley siestaed like a Mexican, only more, for he gave himself a forenoon nap to boot, and when he stepped through the low door he held a rifle loose-handedly in front of him.

"Damn it!" he shouted, "don't come rippin' across there! I got me some turnips planted!"

Coates yanked in the horse, letting its last motion swing him to the ground. Hanley leaned his rifle against the house, stretched, threw back the long hair, and as he came to meet him, his hands worked themselves down into tight back pockets.

"You raise one hellofa fuss," Hanley said.

"I'm in a hellofa hurry, by God."

Lee Hanley idled his gaze over the lathered sorrel, frowning. "You could kill a pony, that way. Ain't you noticed the heat?"

Coates belched, tasting hot liquor jarred loose by the ride, and he thought, the man is a jackass, he ought to be scairt of me. Fools with me, and I could grab onto that handle of hair and wring his skinny neck, same as a pullet in the back yard, Mother's Son!

"Never you mind," he said. "You got any cows penned?"

"Few, I guess. Seven head."

"Shoo 'em loose."

"What?"

"Turn 'em out!" Coates bellered, "We're quittin'. Old Jolly Jerome, he's nosing into them tally counts agin. Worse'n before, since I told him about that doin's on the crick."

The gray man dangled himself backwards, as though he hung on a string, into the wind shelter of the house, and he poured tobacco into a brown paper and began rolling. "Coates, you run a fat hoss half to death to come tell me I'm out of business?"

"Naw," Coates said, and he moved after Hanley, wishing there was a shade, wishing the Little Whisky Man would hold steady between his ears. "I rid out for my money."

"Come agin?"

"The money, goddammit! My half of that seventeen thousand!"

Lee Hanley's dirty-snow eyebrows bucked upward, and he mused over Coates a moment before he set his cigaret afire. "You're drunk, Elwood."

"Sufferin' hell, yes, and I'm ready for my slice of that money!"

The little man shook his head, rustling the long hair outward, and he said, "Won't be none, till I sell them cows. You know that."

Coates swore, silently, to the Little Whisky Man; he might of known it. If old Hanley meant to share, he'd have ridden in with the cash, already. Coates stirred up a grin, and spread it on. "Partners, ain't we, old stud? Reckon half what you taken off that big buffler-stink is mine, huh?"

Hanley pinched the cigaret down from his wrinkled-in mouth, licked the barrel of it where it was drying apart, and he spat brown and scowled.

"Skunk drunk on Wednesday night, too, wasn't you? You all, you sure did for that poor devil, didn't you?"

"What about that money?"

Hanley's long mule jaw pointed a trifle aside; he was gazing past Coates, toward the baking pink hills, as though, out there, he'd lost something he put a value on, like his younger years, or maybe the sheaf of naked Mex pictures he pleased to carry around, and he stared hard, as if under the sunglare he might lay eyes on it, this whatever he was missing.

"Elwood," he said slowly, "I didn't take to what you done to that man. I laid up in the brush; I seen it. Hell, you knowed whose iron that was."

"Oughta been you!" Coates shouted. "Damn you, making a fire in sight of the trail; you're the one as caused it, the whole guttin' mess!"

Hanley spoke soft. "You know, me, I could of shot you down, the three of you, easy, I could of. Fact is, I studied about it, you stickin' my iron to a human man that way."

Coates hurt to hit him. His liquor was boiling, yet he held off, listening instead to the Little Whisky Man, and his friend cautioned him, "First, man, the money."

"Near kilt him," Hanley said. "I seen him afterwards, and I wouldn't care to stand in your boots. He's the kind . . . if I was you, Elwood, I'd get damned seldom, in a hurry."

Coates felt good; he'd mulled it out right. Old Hanley, he *had* come back after the branding.

"Hurryin', that's what I'm doing," he said. "Where's the money?"

Hanley kept looking at the hills. "I reckon that was what the big feller was huntin'."

Coates squared up, cutting into Hanley's gaze-away, shoving close enough to bite, mad, and he roared, "I'm sick of twiddlin' around! Where'd you put it?"

"Myself," said Hanley, "I didn't get no money," and he backed to, and sat down on a sun-curled wood bench under the sod shanty's front window. "Guess I said it before, the Lord sure done queer when He put bad temper into big men."

Coates choked; this shaggy nickel's worth not minded to fear him, and the wind burning, his whisky growling, and he was getting no place while the Little Whisky Man waited and watched.

He let Hanley see that he'd hooked a thumb into his gun belt.

"Lee, 'spose I take me a look through the house?"

"Now, why do that, Elwood?"

"The money, damn you!"

"Ain't in there."

"You won't mind if I look, anyways, will you?"

Hanley got to his feet, unrushed, like a bull nettle unsticking itself from wallowed mud, and he said, "Guess I do mind. Unless you put it some better way."

"Haw! You got it hid in yonder!"

Hanley looked again at the hills, and he spoke it cold. "You drunk sonofabitch, get out of here. And keep the hell off my turnip patch!"

Coates stood spraddled in front of the sod house, staring down. It seemed that a heap of time had gone, but he knew to heaven it hadn't. There was yet no shadow from the building, and in the white sun blast he saw Lee Hanley's body do its last dance where it strung out on the ground. The ropy limbs spidered out from him; the gray eyes gaped up, broad now, with a dampening clod of red clay resting on one of the pupils, unblinked at, and someway the little man's body looked not so skimpy as before.

The ditch in Hanley's skull, straight like the crease in a kicked milk bucket, was commencing to ooze color into the blowing, smoky hair.

"Death on his pale horse," Coates thought. Old Blind Johnnie, he writ that.

Coates shuddered, trying to roust out his senses, and he heard Hanley's well-made blue roan pawing at the fence rails out back, whinnying, as though it pained where its owner, seemed certain, had not.

"You played hell," the Little Whisky Man said.

Coates groaned. "You think I aimed it, huh? It . . . hell, it just happened, that's all. But he had it comin', didn't he? Just happened; but Judas, he was aimin' to clean me out of my share!"

It was true and so; he *knew* it; he hadn't thought. He'd drawn his revolver and hammered down with it in one motion. The blow had cocked and let fly itself, the immediate way a man will gasp if he's doused with cold water, and that was all.

Coates hated it. Hanley was one that talked to him. But damn the little thief, it was his soreheaded kind that could make you think with your belly, as though your brains were there.

Of a sudden Hanley's shoulders jerked and the long jaw fell

open, exposing tough naked gums that seemed indecent to look at, and Coates shivered.

Good God, he was sorry. Since the Rebs in the War, he'd not killed, nobody outside of Comanches and a greaser or two. But Hanley lay dead, and it was done.

"Stud, you had your hand in it," he told the Little Whisky Man. And he reminded himself that, for a minute, old Lee had raised himself into Coldiron's muckity few, bleating at him the same way of those who talked to Elwood Coates only when they meant to lay him out, and, by damn, hadn't he promised himself a lick at these?

He wiped away sweat that tried to sneak into his eyes. Hell, a man on the run couldn't sit around arguing until his hind end got bloodshot; he had to be moving.

Then, in a breath, Hanley didn't matter. Seventeen thousand was a pile, even if cut up between two men, and when it rested in the hands of one, it was a goddam fortune, and it would knock the big ones to their fancy knees, wherever he went, and if a killing had got mixed in—well, it was better to ramrod in hell than to serve in heaven. And didn't old Blind Johnnie hisself say that?

"Haw!" Coates brassed aloud to the Little Whisky Man, "Don't he look natural, ain't that what they say?"

But right off, he couldn't really laugh. He was hot, his stomach bidding to spill up, and he cursed himself for not keeping the bottle he'd sold back to Si Tate.

Crouching, Coates wiped off his gun on the collar of Hanley's hickory shirt, and when it was clean, he walked around the house. The roan horse looked at him and shied off, and Coates hooted and flapped his arms at the animal. They'd had their troubles before, he and the horse, a week ago when he bought him at Dub Stokes's and rode him out to Hanley after Lee's own stunted black mare grazed on ragweed and died, and the worst of it had gone to the roan. But now, Coates paid the critter no mind.

Against the rear sod wall, he found a sack of cracked corn, a two-bitted mattock, a coil of new barbwire that Hanley, or no one else, had any business with, an empty keg, and the iron tire off a wheel, all of it heaped onto a pile of scrap planking that maybe the wind blew off the house, or maybe was collected for patching it. But there was no shovel. He leaned against the wall, sleeving off his forehead, deciding he wasn't disappointed. For gravedigging, the day was too scalding goddam hot, anyway.

The roan neighed. Coates looked at the whitened wild eyes, the withers jumping against the flies. "Shut up," he said.

Then he knew what to do, like the snap of his fingers, and he slapped his leg and told the Little Whisky Man, "Me, old stud, I'm better drunk than most of 'em sober!"

He dragged Lee Hanley's heavy double-cinched roping saddle out of the house and into the corral. Twice he cursed the roan into a back corner but lost him. At last he had to rope him and snub him to a post. When he got the saddle up, he led the animal around front. At sight of the dead man, the horse went hauling, rooting Coates's heels through Hanley's soft ground and turnips before the bits hacked in and bled him and stopped him.

Running sweat, swearing, Coates worked the horse back to the body. He tried not to look at the dusty, open eyes, the gaped toothless mouth. But he did. He'd seen Hanley sleep before, here at the shanty, at Piedras Negras, at Laredo, but never, never had Hanley slept so sound.

"Hell," he said.

He threw his weight down on the reins, pulling the roan head low, and he stretched and got hold of one of Hanley's gaiters and picked up the thin, rag-limber leg. He poked the run-over work shoe through the stirrup, hanging on with his whole strength as the roan pitched and stomped, long enough to make positive the heel and toe caught through. Coates was too winded to shout when he let go and jumped back and threw the reins at the animal's head.

The horse spun, kicked at the body, then screamed in its break across the flat. The body trailed alongside, bouncing, slewing up a wake of red dirt, suddenly twisting and rolling face down as the ankle broke; towing then with a flopping neck, with the shirttail out and snagging at bear grass, blood streaking suddenly from the naked ribs, the free foot abruptly switching over to drag beside the head.

Coates gagged dry.

Jesus, he hadn't aimed killing him—which wasn't the same as meaning to, was it?

As the roan plunged into the breaks and out of sight, Coates lagged back against the wall, still panting. For a moment he watched the dust lifting from an arroyo. Then he bent and blew his nose on the ground, one nostril at a time.

It had been two-three years, he guessed, since anybody around Coldiron got throwed and dragged to death by a horse.

After a while Coates turned and went inside.

He commenced with Hanley's bed, a tick sack of corn shucks spread flat on dirt floor. He looked under it, then ripped the rotted ticking apart with his hands, scattering the powdered shucks and a thousand gray-backed bugs. There was a pole table he squatted to look under, a Mexican oven made of mud and rock and fitted with an iron door that he opened and probed his hand into. He went into Hanley's grub box, stirring out a chunk of salt pork, dried beans, coffee, a Sharps powder tin half-full of sugar. He lifted a keg of flour, pouring it slowly empty, his eye caught only by the weevils that fled out of the white heap on the floor.

Nothing, by God!

Breathing loud, he kicked the rubble around on the floor, exposing every foot of the hardened orange dirt. He hit on no sign of recent digging. He cursed Lee Hanley, that skinny mop-head, and he longed again for the whisky he might have fetched along, and he drank from a pail of stale lukewarm water that still tasted of turtles and Dirty Creek moss. At once a heavy sweat began leaking.

"All right," he said to the Little Whisky Man, "it ain't in the shack. Whereabouts, you reckon?"

His friend didn't answer. Coates paused, sickening, fearing he'd sweated the little stud weak, then drowned him with the water, and maybe now was alone.

He ran outside. The sun pained his eyes now, setting off a hopping ache behind them. He ducked his head and started walking a spiral around the sod house, widening it six feet at each turn, staring down at burnt grass and the cracked red earth. At each clump and rock he got down on one knee and prodded with his hands. A hundred yards from the house, his shirt was fit for wringing, and he'd sunned himself sober, and he was tired. But he knew it wasn't these things that stopped him.

He'd been wrong.

He turned back to the shanty and flooded some of the bad water down his collar.

So Hanley, who was dead, hadn't lied.

Coates's body began to shake, maybe from the water, he thought, and in a hustle he recalled to himself how, anyway, old Hanley had it due him; hell, he'd only burnt that buffler man to cover for Hanley, and Lee hadn't thanked him.

But what of the money?

He butted out the door, carrying the water pail, squinting over the heat-wobbly flat for the rented sorrel.

Brooks Durham. It had to be.

The horse had wandered far, dragging the reins as no honest cowhorse would ever drag them, and Coates tempered up and strode toward him through the sun. As he went, he tried to make it out, about old Durham that night. The memory of it was a hard birthing; he'd been good drunk, but it seemed like, as he stewed at it, that it'd been Durham, and not himself, that booted the big tramp in the head, and Durham that chased the horses into the dark when Johnsy and his iron and his commotion flighted them.

"Haw!" Coates blew off. That was it. The tramp's horse, toting its saddlebags, had skitted off with the rest. And Durham had gone after them, and he'd stayed away a good spell, and when he got back, he'd stopped them with the iron, and he'd done it with the buffler man's rifle.

Coates laughed into the heat. Old simon-pure Durham, bossing his goddam bank and sparking his damned widder woman, and caterwauling in the churchhouse, and hiking off with seventeen thousand dollars!

Hey, high stud, smell yourself again; you ain't such a posy!

Though he hurt for a little whisky, Coates was grinning when he came up to the sorrel. He held the water to its nose, and when it had drunk, he dropped the bucket and climbed up. He headed back for the trail.

Old Bull Brooks Durham.

In the first mile he kept out his eye for the runaway roan. Here and yonder he saw crippled sage, and hunks of dead grass sledded out by its stringy dead roots, and at one place, a little piece of leavings caught on a mesquite thorn.

About Hanley, he thought, it was bad. Only, that woman-haired old crud, he hadn't amounted to much, and what there was of him, God knew, had been disrespectful and sassy. Maybe it still was a killing, but hell, some rise by sin, and some by virtue fall, and old By Jove had read that out loud, and Bloody Bill hisself writ it.

Coates looked behind him and spurred the lazy sorrel, coming awake that out here in the open he needed to watch sharp for that big stink who packed a hot JC iron in his tail pocket. But it was easier to eye ahead, to Brooks Durham and seventeen thousand dollars, to how he'd raise himself a little with some sinning. And what was sinning, anyways? It was nothing except whatever the high-mucks decided to say it was.

Seventeen thousand dollars. Hell's bells!

Chapter Nineteen

THE haunt of wrath and the chest fire had reclaimed Julius Rupp at the squeak of the door he shut on Maria, and at once his mind upended. Hell, he was almost mothering the girl. He mistrusted this, and mistrusted, also, how the brown face, bruised like his own, so readily had gentled his tortured waiting. He'd paid Maria's rent, and wrestled her clear of a killing, and presently, without aiming to, he'd made himself a mission of a meal for her—and none of it from the simple cause of her tears, Rupp was positive; instead, he seemed compelled.

He delayed at the foot of the stairs, then, over the notion it was Johnsy Hood that compelled him—Johnsy, for whom the spic girl wept, and he did not like it.

"Through *and* dead, Johnsy is," Rupp told himself, "and I didn't kill him."

It struck him that if Maria wanted charity cake, she'd not said so. But Rupp didn't turn back. He hurt for whisky to kindle him against his body's weaknesses and to speed off the time until nightfall, and he would get it and let the girl's food come second, if handy.

The Rusk's simmering lobby was empty as he crossed it, deserted to its paper walls of faded jaybirds and unlikely flowers, its iron chandelier and the dirty furniture worn bare like the thin clerk who now glanced up, his unease showing through. The gun butt chaffed the tail end of the brand as Rupp walked, and the midday sun thrust at his eyes and jumped a painful beat to his temples.

Crowder Street pushed and crawled. On a Saturday, he remembered, they all made town: Mexican sheepmen in creaky, plaited sandals without socks, their bellies belted in narrow by broad silk or dyed goatskin, their stiff hair clotted and overhanging greasy collars, their eyes sullen as black knife-points; the cowhands, leather-legged and slick-shaven, hallooing pomp at each other; the cautious, harried townspeople and the tuck-tailed dogs underfoot, but mostly, the big-handed, denimed dirt farmers who yet believed that good corn could climb tall out of blowing red clay, and starved lean with their error. These had unhitched on the peeled grounds above Texas Wells's pens, and threatened the children against wandering from the wagon shade and quilt pallets, and with their silent womenfolk they walked the street, buying slowly, hushedly, with the slim dab of cash a hard country had consented to their use.

Rupp paused on the walk. Coldiron seemed not to pay immediate mind to him; a Mexican gamecock was loose and running a yelping hound, and it faced them away from him. He went to a sign that said "Drugs & Sundries" but where the window showed only liquors, and bought his bottle. As he came out, he speculated across the street, to the bank, and he read the café sign just beyond it, realizing that despite the hour, he was considering between them.

Then Dub Stokes stood in front of him.

The old man peered up, his head cocked aside, and he said, "Holy damn, Jessie was right."

Rupp glared down at the excited old-man eyes, at the red flesh exposed like moons of raw meat where the bottom eyelids had aged themselves inside out.

"Julius," Old Dub said.

"What do you want?"

"To talk to you, son; been watchin' the hotel, sort of waitin' for you."

"I'd as soon not."

Dub said, "Maybe I got a bone to gnaw with you."

Rupp shook his head and moved away. "I'm bound to eat."

"Starved, myself," the old man said, and he stirred his high-topped shoes as though to follow.

Rupp stopped. "Jessie was right about what?"

"You, son. That it's you, come back."

Rupp stepped into the street and back across it, leaving the old man atrail, and he passed the Rusk House, then the Stockman's Security glass without letting himself look inside, on south, with the feel of many eyes on him, and to the place marked "Fritz's," where the noon trade seemed to be noising in, and he strode past the counter stools, to the table and cane chairs farthest back, and sat down. In a moment Dub Stokes blustered in, and he puffed, foul-breathed with snuff, as he dropped into a chair at Rupp's table.

"Damn you," Old Dub panted, "still stubborn as Berends's gray mule."

"What do you want?"

The old man appeared rounder, and his hands aged surprisingly close to feebleness, and he stared at Rupp's face as though his sight had turned poorly. "Boy," he said, "you look like the wolves about et you."

"And you strike me as the same whoring old Dutchman I remember."

It flashed out of him unintended, and at once not a thing he could call back, or fix, and it struck him that if he'd never taken a shine to his foster father, leastways he'd never really hated him. The words were on the old man as his fists had been on Kratz, and it had little to do with either of them.

"Now, hell, now, hold on!" Dub hoarsened. "I ain't come to cuss nothing out with you, or to anoint you with no homecomin' oils, neither. Quick as I've talked, it'll suit me to get out."

The old man swiped dust off the table top, hailed a split-rail cook he called Fritz, and growled, "What's to eat?"

"Stew, corned beef, buffalo tongue," the man said. "Ain't another place in town you can get buffalo tongue. And three kinds of pie, as I tell it—cross-bar, open-faced, and covered—all made of dried apricots. And puddin' with calf slobbers."

"Stew," Dub said.

Rupp said, "Tongue," and he called for a plate to take out.

Fritz wagged his head. "Don't do that," he said, "nobody ever gets back with my dishes."

"I'll buy 'em," Rupp snapped.

The cook started around, and met Rupp's eyes, and hurried around the counter and behind it.

"Got them hoppin' scairt, ain't you, son?" Dub said. "All except me. When a man gets old, he's done been scared by everything, at least one time, and they's nothing left that can do it agin, exceptin' the sight of that long black coach." He laughed.

"What do you want?"

"Jessie. She come tearing up to see me this mornin', telling she'd seen you. I didn't swaller it, not right off; thought you was dead."

"I ain't."

"She's in a uproar, son, says she told you something she hadn't ought to, and she thinks you'll do something about it."

The plates came and Old Dub began at once, wadding a thick cut of bread, making noise, and sending little red rivers of stew juice down the creases in his chin.

Rupp watched, raising no real anger for the man, but beginning now to blame him coolly for every crooked corn row he had spent his boyhood over, and for the undug grubs, the unsnug dugout, the licks with the barrel stave, and damn the old bastard, for his clumsy wenching so soon after Helena had the service spoken over her, and even for the wedding-gift shoes that had galled up sore bubbles on his feet.

"Hell," Rupp said.

"Now, hold on, son!"

"Don't call me 'son'!"

The flash, once more—sounding different than he meant, not saying, as he wanted, that "son" was too close to "boy," or that such had driven him from Coldiron.

A spoon of the red-seasoned grease had stopped short of Dub's mouth, shaking there, and Dub was glaring across it. After a moment the old man took and swallowed it, and he said, "All right, boy. What I'm after is, how come you back here?"

Boy. Rupp let it go. He started to get up.

"Least is, you can let me say my piece," the old man said.

Rupp looked at the age and wear on him, and slowly, he sat down.

"Jessie's afeared of what you mean doing. They's a good man courtin' her, he's due to carry her to the churchhouse tonight, choir meeting I reckon, and she'll have to tell him about you."

"Don't matter," Rupp said.

"It ain't only Jessie I'm talking for. You got this town jiggling in its boots, stalking around here with that gun in your belt, and them marks fresh on you. I guess me and Jessie is the only ones as knows who you are, but we dead certain ain't the onliest ones watchin' you. That whisky stunt down at the Two Bulls, and what you done to Kratz—hell, I hear his nose is busted, and maybe his jaw is. And they's Sunderman's gettin' knocked in, and that Johnsy Hood mess on top of it. Me, I'm sticking two and two together. When a couple of men is buggered up, and one of them is dead like Johnsy Hood, then you naturally figure the man that's up and walking might know what happened to the dead one."

Rupp commenced eating, scowling low over his plate at the pain of his jaw, swallowing chunks of meat unchewed. Under his ears the unwilling bones popped and echoed. He'd not been listening well.

The spic girl, he thought. She's hungry, and waiting. For me, he thought, as though I'm somebody come, or coming.

"Two and two together," Dub went on. "Now, I guess it'd take a man about your build to bust into Sunderman's, the way he built his door, and I'd say it was likely one of them stolen irons as was used on Johnsy Hood, though brandin' irons wouldn't be stole just for that. Stolen iron, that means cow thieving, and stealing beef ain't good."

Rupp looked up at him, almost amused. Old Dub had missed out, right when he seemed to be calculating things so nearly straight.

"There's worse things done to food than just stealing it," Rupp said, and he nodded at the juice drying stiff on the old man's chin. In the instant, he hoped the old man would laugh.

Dub glowered, and grunted, and wiped with a sleeve.

"Boy, what I'm saying, we ain't wanting any trouble around here. We get a . . . a killing, or something, and sure as God's green apples, that council of Durham's, it'll slap on taxes to hire us a law force. And they's a heap of us ain't geared to taxes."

"You're telling me to clear out."

The old man spread his hands. "Seems like you ought to pay

your Christian respects to them graves of your folks; and my Helena, she's out there. And then, leave out of here."

"So my wife can marry the banker," Rupp said.

"Partly that."

"Or you'll bunch 'em up to chase me out."

Dub shrugged. "Boy, if you'd of got back—different, I'd of took you into the stable. I'd of—"

"Part time, maybe? Say, eight dollars a month?"

"Aw, hell," Dub said. "I hear you're afoot; ain't you afoot? Well, I'll give you a horse. Find you one today, and my nigger'll bring him to you, first thing in the morning."

Rupp sat back, badly fed, hot-skinned, struck that he'd been thinking of a brown child with her kimono gapped apart, and of Jessie and Jessie's soft mouth, her fist in his face. He stared above Dub's head, at a printed poster for Baker's Bitters, "the oldest and best stomach bitters, fine also as a cordial," and at the filthy calendar pages below it, and he said, "You might owe me a horse, at that."

"That's sense," Dub said. "He'll be in the alley alongside the Rusk—that's where you're at, ain't it—early in the mornin'. Be the only critter there; ain't no hitching, so nobody hardly uses it."

Rupp looked toward the counter. "Where's the traveling plate?" he said. The cook dipped into his kettles, and Rupp took up his whisky and got up.

"The horse will be there," Dub said.

Flies tagged at the covered plate as he balanced it on his hand and at his ear scab as he finished the stairs. Maria's door hung open. He went past his own and looked in. Her bed was plowed up, and a trunk sat near it, the lid cocked up with musky clothes bulging out. Maria wasn't there.

He turned, recalling that he'd dropped her pistol and forgotten it. The weapon was gone from the hallway. Rupp swore; damn her, he'd believed her, and she'd lied. Then his own room opened, and the girl stood small in the doorframe, still in the kimono, and barefoot.

"The pistol, Tall One?" she smiled. "It is here."

"Told you to dress," he said, and he followed her inside. She came close to take the plate, and he waited for her to shrink from the look and the buffalo smell of him, but if she caught it, she did not cringe, and not even her eyes gave the sign.

"Oh!" she said.

She took the newspaper cover from the plate, as if it must be spirited off with a reverence, and gave a little squeal, and while he held it, clapped her hands. She fled to the bed to eat, sitting, holding the plate on her knees, and using her fingers and often licking them, and she said to him, "Good!" and he wished he did not watch.

Rupp heard himself say, "If you had you a man, and he come home busted and half-butchered, would you . . . what would you do?"

"*¡Que lástima!*" she said.

"I got no Mex."

"I think," she said, and she frowned. "I would kiss him, I think. I would have no money to give . . . yes, I would kiss him many times, because he was home. Señor, is it—?"

Abruptly the cat came out, and Maria's eyes widened and brightened.

"Evil one!" she whispered, as though the animal knew her tongue, and mustn't hear. "Once, the cat would have smothered my face in the night!"

Rupp took off his hat, opened the bottle, and drank from it. The sudden flush ran outward from his stomach, driving back his weariness, and the pain, and he drank again.

It was noon.

He crossed to the bed and sat down beside Maria, seeing how insatiably she ate. He picked a string of fat beef off the plate, and while he fed the yellow cat from his hand, he thought of Jessie, to be married. Jessie, in her nothing for Brooks Durham.

Chapter Twenty

THE tremor and recklessness remained in Jessie's hands; she saw it now as she tore open, fiercely, a carton of the emporium's new merchandise; and she saw, also, the swelling middle knuckle of her right hand, reddened and turning black where it had smashed against Julius's face. Twice she had seen him, she thought, and twice she'd struck him, and the last time, it had been as if she had struck as much at herself, as if, indeed, she blamed herself for the butchered look of him, the deathliness of his eyes, the animal rage he radiated like a hideous light when he battered Mr. Kratz down in the street.

It smothered her like a guilt. But *he* had deserted *her*, hadn't he? Oh, he hadn't the right to come back, or even to let her know he was alive!

From the carton she began putting away a dozen of the new Common Sense Nursing Bottles, these of glass and jug-shaped with a nipple attached at the end of a long rubber hose; and, no matter how Eastern, or how modern, they would be doubtful sellers at best among Coldiron's breasty women, and she should never have ordered them. She got the bottles onto a shelf, dropping one that did not break, then went to the door to look out into Crowder.

Dub Stokes wasn't in sight. He'd promised it would not take

long. "Girl, iffen it *is* Julius, sure enough, I'll catch him and talk to him, and I'll let you know directly."

The morning had crept by, and now the afternoon went, a minute at a time, each passing slowly like the drizzle from a leaky pump, and still Old Dub hadn't come. But he couldn't have forgotten, she knew, and if he'd passed her by and headed back toward the livery barn, she would have seen him, for she'd kept a constant watch on the front.

She wondered what she wanted the old man to tell her when, at last, he did come.

Between flights to the door and the annoyance of customers, she worked hard at shelving away the new stock, hard as she could without giving it thought. Her face beaded and her clothes grew sticky, and she wished she'd left off one of the petticoats, and that the talky women would stop coming in.

There were many of them, and they fingered, crumpled, disarranged, tried on, dirtied the new ready-mades, and, as she'd known they would, bought cheap buttons, or thread, or nothing at all. She flushed whenever one looked at her too pointedly, and from anger when several probed at her openly about the wild-eyed giant who'd delayed the shop's business and had that awful fight. They asked sweetly, but still in that holy-mouthed, lawful, and temperate Ladies'-League fashion that meant they cared to know about the man, and counted on being told.

Jessie hedged them off, and she spoke almost sharply to a few who would die trying, if they must. To one woman, even, she sold a ten-cent card of snaps for a quarter, this as much a punishment for the customer as a confusion of her own.

"It's . . . just someone I used to know," she said.

Someone who had kissed her, she might have told them, and showed her where to find wild honey in the bluffs of the Dirty, and brought her coffee in bed, who bought her a sidesaddle she had never thanked him for, or even touched.

Jessie wanted to scream. What is expected of a woman who is in love and engaged, when her dead husband comes alive? She'd talk to these curious ones, all of them, if they'd answer her that.

The trade dribbled off, then died in midafternoon's sun fury, and Jessie climbed up on her tall bookkeeper's stool behind the counter, exhausted, and she folded her skirts up to her knees, and a little higher, for air. She sat watching the door for Dub Stokes, her hand idling with a bottle of Maréchal Niel rose that, among the new things, she'd ordered for herself.

Maybe she shouldn't have trusted the old man in this; he was a snuffy somebody she'd always disliked, even before she first met him. Once when she was a child she'd said to Julius, "Is Mr. Stokes your godfather?" and he'd responded, "No, he's just my goddam father, I guess you might say," and Jessie had remembered it every time she saw Dub for a long, long while.

But who else was there? She'd thought only briefly of going to Brooks instead. Lord, she could not, and the why of it she didn't know. It was just that now, she couldn't tell Brooks; she dasn't even warn him of what she'd seen in Julius's eyes, for whatever that was, she seemed herself to have put it there.

No, that was wrong.

Almost, Jessie prayed. If only Julius would go away, she could forget him again, even to the kiss she'd been bruised by and hadn't fully fought, and after a time everything would lie as before, and she'd have nothing to decide.

She stared at the cut-glass perfume bottle, and her nails had begun shredding away the label when a shadow fell across the front.

"Mr. Stokes!" she called, and looked up. It was Mrs. Lavender, and her only, beaming and apronless, sweaty and huge in the doorway.

"My God, child," the big woman panted, "Do I look that peaked old?"

"Oh, of course not," Jessie said.

Mrs. Lavender heavied on inside. "Whew!" she huffed, "they ain't been a hotter one or a noisier one, not in my time! Town's creepin' with them Mexican goaters and cowboys, and a heap of others that'd go on home if they wasn't so much to talk about. It's like everybody's waitin' around to see what'll happen next. It's a sight, a woman can't get her work done . . . hey, child, you sick?"

"No. No, I'm fine."

"Your time, maybe? That'd make it a snap, figurin' up your wedding day."

"Heaven's name, do you have to talk about that!"

Mrs. Lavender ruddied to the jowls, and quickly she plowed from her bosom a great handkerchief meant to be a man's and scrubbed her face with it. She said, gently, "I was only joshing, Jessie. I'm sorry."

Jessie hated her for coming; she wanted now to see Dub Stokes, and no one else—not Mrs. Lavender, not even Brooks. If Brooks walked in this instant, flipping that gold piece of his, she'd scream at him and run.

She dropped her eyes from Mrs. Lavender. "I didn't mean to yell," she said. "It's been such a day."

"Land of Goshen, it has that!" the big woman forgave her at once. "A bit ago, I heard some more about Johnsy Boy. Dunce Moreno, he says that Tod Wisdom told somebody Johnsy was drivin' out to Shelley's three-four times a week, ever since Brack went to Kansas. The way folks talk, I bet if Johnsy wasn't dead already. . . . Say! Say, Jessie, they got Johnsy's remains in over at Belmeade's, while ago, and a bunch is goin' over to see him. Me, I don't specially care to look at dead people, but I thought maybe, if you felt like it, we could—"

"Oh, please!"

"Hon, I didn't say I was goin' myself!"

Mrs. Lavender moved slowly around the shop, feeling of the goods, and she said over her shoulder, "What I really come about, I thought I'd get that red dress, the one you fixed for Bonnie Shelley. It'll let out to fit me, wouldn't you figure?"

Jessie gasped; what was happening to everyone?

"I . . . I couldn't do that," she said tightly. "Mrs. Shelley had me order the material, and I sent it to Quanah to be made the way she wanted. It's hers, when she calls for it."

Mrs. Lavender turned from a table, a ball of green yarn in her hand.

"Child, you ain't heard yet, have you? Mrs. Shelley won't come for that dress; she taken the stage this morning. Gettin' out before old Brack comes home. God pity her, she's gone for good."

Jessie wanted to cry, at once for Bonnie Shelley and herself. She looked at the red dress hanging on the far wall, a brown wrapper folded over the shoulders to fend off the dust. It was of velvet, lace-topped, ribboned softly at the cuffs, the style young, and from the start it had seemed to her like a party costume gotten up in haste for some immense and ill-gifted child.

"It . . . it was for an occasion," she said. "An anniversary, she told me."

"That Johnsy Boy, he must of liked velvet," Mrs. Lavender said, and she crossed and caught up the skirt and stroked it with her round fingertips. "This here, this is material!"

"Twelve dollars' worth," Jessie heard herself say, and she stared at her. What was happening? Julius had come home, and to the town, it was as if . . . as if Satan himself had ridden in naked.

"Lordy, I'll pay it; cheap at the price!" Mrs. Lavender said. "This here's one piece of goods even a barber can notice. 'Course, Dunce Moreno best know one thing—I ain't a woman that lets herself be meddled with, not like Bonnie."

"Oh, take the dress!"

The big woman turned to look at her. "Child, you sure you feel all right?"

"Take it," Jessie said. *Oh, take it! Wear it down to Belmeade's to view the remains!*

Mrs. Lavender stretched up, grunting, and she took down the hanger. She held the red velvet up in front of her, wrinkling her face with thought.

"Might wear it to choir tonight," she said. "Leastways, I'll bust it on them at church in the mornin'. If it'll let out. I don't know, hon, them seams, they've been pinked off kind of close."

Once more alone in the store, Jessie considered locking up, walking—no, running—home to the big house she loved yet dreaded today as always, but she could not. Old Dub had promised he would come. She urged her hands back to their chores, so that when, at last, he did come, she was at the shelves, wrenching items around, feeling the touch of the things as a kind of grip on what was familiar and real. She did not hear the old man's slow step in his soft oiled shoes, and it started her around with a gasp when the snuff and warm beer smell of him reached her.

"Oh!" she said.

Old Dub grinned.

"Mr. Stokes, you . . . you found him?"

"He's up at the Rusk House. I et my dinner with him."

"That's been hours! You said you'd come straight here!"

The stable keeper shrugged, crept a hand inside his shirt, rubbed roughly at his shoulder, as though it would comfort him to bark it, and he said, "Well, I had people to see. Stopped off at Si's. . . ."

"What did Julius say? Is he leaving?"

The old man roved his gaze around the store and wiped his mouth corners before he spoke. "Girl, I flat don't know."

"But he told you something?"

"No, he didn't tell me nothin'. Set there swallering his vittles, looking like he'd eat horseshoe nails if they served 'em; big Colt's pistol sticking in his belt and a little loose blood on his ear—never seen a boy worse chawed up. But it's him, all right, the way you said."

"Didn't you tell him I—?"

"I told him; I told him how things is. Fact is, I said I'd shag him up a hoss and send it to him, free gift, if he'd get."

"He'll go, then. Won't he, Mr. Stokes?"

"Holy damn, girl, I told you, I didn't learn nothin'. Guess it rests on what he come for. If he come for you, he's liable to stay a spell. If he just aimed to steal a few cows, I expect he'll give that up, me laying it to him like I done." Dub clawed at himself with his fingers, the vulgar way old men take as their right, and he mused, "Did appear he took to the notion of gettin' a hoss for free."

"He won't go," Jessie said.

"I'm bettin' he will."

She backed against the counter, propping herself. She knew what Julius came home for, what her parasol and fist had beaten him away from.

"Mr. Stokes, I'll . . . I'll have to tell Brooks tonight," she said.

"If it was me, I wouldn't go mixing Durham in," the old man said.

He went to the door and spit out of it, and came soft-pedaling back, and he bent his worn-out eyes near to her. "Far as the law goes, that boy is dead. Far as the town goes, too, he is. Besides you and me, ain't nobody else picked him out. I hear he put his name down as Brown. Look, girl, can you keep Brooks Durham away from that council meetin' tonight?"

"Keep him away?"

"That's what I said. I been collectin' a few; they're coming to the meetin'. Got a hard one or two; that Kratz at the Two Bulls, he's comin' if he's able, and I left word for Elwood Coates. You keep Durham away, and we'll get us up a committee, and if Julius don't use that hoss in the mornin'. . . ."

"A committee!"
"Now, don't take the wrong notion."
"Committees—they hang people!"
"Has happened, I guess," the old man grinned. "But I reckon we'd just ride him out a ways, sort of a escort, that's all, if he's reasonable."
"Oh, damn you!" she heard herself shouting. "You! Stirring up a mob!"
"If they's been any stirrin', Julius done it hisself!"
She stared at him, and it seemed he had an excitement beneath his calm, like a poorly hidden lust he meant to nourish, and she was suddenly afraid of him. "You! He's . . . he's the same as your own son!"
"No son of mine," the old man said. "He told me that."
Her fists closed; she shook to hit him. "Oh, what did he ever do to you?" she said, strangling. "He never . . . oh, I've heard about you, Mr. Stokes! You always blamed him for what happened to your wife."
"You're out of your head!"
She turned from him. Lord, how had she thought he might help her? She should have gone to Brooks, or gone home—or anything.
She whirled back. "You aren't going to hurt him!"
Old Dub spat snuff on her floor. "Lookee here, you, don't go bracin' up at me. I ain't rememberin' my good woman, or them grubs. It was you brung me in on this, and I know a mad dog when I see one. We'll get shut of him, before he kills somebody else, like he done Johnsy Hood."
"He . . . he said he did that?"
"He damn well didn't deny it."
Jessie was crying. "A dog, you called him!"
The old man looked down at his feet, one palm cupped around the back of his neck. "Well," he said, and his voice sounded tamed, "that was what happened to come to mind. I was thinking of that spotted hound, down on Pedro Street; belongs to some spic woman, and when I'm passin' that way, this dog hangs out his cutters and stands up his neck hair like a currycomb and goes to nudging at my legs. I commence walkin' a mite faster, and that dog goes to trottin' a mite closer, till pretty soon I'm runnin' and he's chasin'. Then this Mex

woman, she'll yell out, 'do not run, my Chico will not bite you.' But it's too goddam late for me to slow down, and too late for the dog to slow down, and what it amounts to is, if that dog don't bite me, it's only on account of he ain't goin' to catch me. Now, I tell you, girl, that's how she lies, betwixt Julius and this town. I aim stoppin' it."

Jessie said, "You won't hurt him?"

"Well, it don't look like they's much you could do to one like him. It's all been done before."

"Where . . . where is he? Right now, I mean."

"Hotel, I reckon." Old Dub looked at her sharply. "You ain't thinkin' to go see him?"

"No," Jessie said, "I won't see him."

"How about Durham? And the meetin', I mean?"

"All right. I'll keep him away, if I can."

Then again she was afraid, at how Old Dub grinned and nodded before he turned and padded out the door. She felt he had lied to her, that the old man meant to blunt his memory of Helena, and blunt it on Julius. Oh, that vulgar old man, he craved to see Julius dead!

She shuddered. Lord, wasn't that about what she wanted herself? She wondered what had happened to everyone, and to her; she worried about the evening, sure that tonight Brooks Durham, however big and fine he looked, would fail, like the house, to make her feel safe.

Then a woman came in for lace, and Jessie received her as she would the plague, and after that came others, for the sun was past its peak. Then came Mrs. Lavender, wanting thread to match Bonnie Shelley's dress, telling of a furor at Crowder's north end that turned out to be some stranger dragged to death by a horse; letting mention she'd been into Belmeade's, since everyone else was going, but only for a little peek, and how heathen folks acted about it, since by the time she got there, not a button was left on Johnsy's clothes, and some had done worse, even, like that crazy Dunce Moreno, who helped himself to a twig of Johnsy's hair, saying "Hell, I was his barber, wasn't I?" And it was said Johnsy had carried a good watch, but if he had, it wasn't on him now, meaning maybe Mr. Belmeade was a thief, and likely he was, because, "Know what, child, he's tryin' to take collection from us visitors, to pay for the buryin', he says!"

Mrs. Lavender huffed and sweated and tumbled-up a rack of thread, until she found the nearest shade, and she went on talking, of how she'd decided to quit baking on Saturday afternoons, at least for the balance of the summer, the heat making it a job for the Old Nick himself, and "Listen to me, child, you sure don't look good in the face. Is it your time?"

"Please go," Jessie said.

"What?"

"Get out! Oh, get out, you . . . just go away, won't you!"

The big woman stared, becoming red, then gray, and her mouth opened and shut before she threw down a handful of spools and charged to the street.

The Ladies' League, Jessie thought; by sundown, they'll know about the brandy; and she realized she couldn't abide their knowing. But she did not run after Mrs. Lavender.

It was closing time when Jessie penciled out the note the third time and folded it and sealed it in an envelope and took it outside, to where the small boy was playing at the alley's littered mouth and, as he played, crooned in soft Spanish to himself.

Jessie put the envelope and a dime in his hand.

"You must take this to Mr. Brown at the Rusk House," she said. "Understand me, Mr. Brown, no one else. Can you find him?"

The boy stood up, and she saw he wore a flour-sack cutout that made a sort of square dress with nothing at all underneath. His black eyes lit, and he spread his bare arms, showing her the hugeness of Mr. Brown, as a tree is huge, and he said, "*Si, señora, el tigre!*"

"The . . . tiger?"

The boy broke from her hold, fleeing through the red-dirt air, and toward the hotel, a Mason jar of pebbles bouncing behind him at the end of a wire.

Tiger, the Mexicans had named Julius. Oh, damn him, that's what he is, she thought. It's maybe what I made him! She shook her head. No, no, Julius had deserted *her,* hadn't he?

Quickly Jessie put her hands to work, closing the place in a routine Aunt Gussie had first set and which now seemed to carry out itself, free will, and when she was in the street, walking, she kept her gaze on the mansion at the far end. The house looked bleak, and terrible, as if she need not have clung to it. The rooms waiting her would be dusty and empty, the air stuffy as a spinster woman's soul, and when she got there, she knew, and started up for her drink, not a stairstep would be concerned enough to creak.

Chapter Twenty-One

"NO," Rupp said. "Leave me be."

Maria stood at his back, but he saw her in the washstand mirror he faced, and from it he glared at her, until she let fall the small hands she'd raised toward him.

Maria Alicia y Montesa Quintero. Wasn't that what she'd told him, and a damned wallowing tongueful of a name, he considered it, for such a speck of brown woman and black hair and burning spic eyes.

She frowned, seeming to fit it to the streaks of powder and paint on her face, then smiled, and her voice pouted. "Tall One, you do not like Maria!"

"I like you fine," he said. "Just quit messin'."

The girl turned from him, but only part way, so that he saw the full dark mold of her. She spoke softly. "It is not meant as before."

"What ain't?"

"Now, it is not . . . not to pay you that I think of; it is perhaps. . . ."

She stopped.

"Well?"

"Perhaps I wish you for myself!"

Rupp faced around, and it swung him nearer to her. He looked coldly down at the smallness and turn of her, his head at once light from the lift of her musk. Should have sent her flying, he thought—right off, even before feeding her. But watching her as she ate—he hadn't liked it, yet someway it had the peculiar feel of pricing him upwards, as though for once, maybe, it had been himself that came to the creek carrying a basket!

"You forget Johnsy in a hurry, don't you?"

"No," she said. "It is that my Johnsy . . . I can not call him to me; he is dead, he has no need of me, but only of my prayers. Señor Brown, I have thought, and I think it was for my ring I wept. I think I wept only for myself!"

"I got no need for you," he said shortly. "And no ring!"

Her eyes brightened, too sudden for his understanding, and she said, "*¿Quién sabe?* With you, I think, it is of no matter!"

"It matters," he growled. "Stick to your own damned kind!"

"*Oye,* I see you, Tall One, and I say, 'here, this one, he is of my kind!' "

Rupp swore, and he looked about for his whisky. "You can get back to your room," he said. "You seen that ring ain't in here."

"But, the man of the hotel?"

"He won't show."

"I . . . I do not wish to go!" She threw out her hands, and brought them together at her front, and her eyes forced him to watch her. "Please, how is this you cannot talk? I have told you of me, and of Mama Quintero and my sisters, and even I spoke of the white boys who named me 'Pepper Belly,' yet of yourself you say only that you have been a killer of the buffalo, and all the buffalo are dead!"

"They are dead!"

"Then, what is this you seek, with your eyes, and the great pistol?"

"Go on, this ain't Johnsy's room now; you ain't got the free run."

"This free run," she smiled. "I would like it." She reached up suddenly, putting her hands on his shoulders.

This is not Jessie, he thought—not Jessie. But the girl stood close, with eyes that were seeing him, and a nose too fine not to smell, yet still she reached her hands to him.

Of a sudden he pulled her against the chest pain that came and went like an inconstant drizzle of hot candle grease, and he swore in a rough and troubled whisper, "That goddam clerk, I ought to throw you downstairs to him!"

Chapter Twenty-Two

AT his desk, sticking with a will to his unique swivel chair, Brooks Durham looked up from his work and ran his hands over the piled straw of his hair, feeling it wet from the heat and strained nerve, and he longed to shuck his coat. All day he'd worn it, fastened and hiding the gun he wore like a sore. He had before him the huge, blue-lined Stockman's Security ledgers, halved open and waiting his posting of this Saturday's pell-mell of business. Commonly, the pen-and-ink task was a pleasure; there was a satisfaction and a confirmation in the neat setting down of the figures, each a clean little sign of what a man could make of himself.

But today it was a tedious job, and his hand was smudging the pages, and wandering so that queer little crooks showed in the numbers. At the next meeting of directors, he supposed, Mr. Kesterling would ask what had happened to his handwriting, but it couldn't be helped. His breakfast pancakes had worn thin, for one thing, and he'd been too cautious to go out for a noon meal, or even for the jarring and steadying drink he would have liked at Tate's.

Durham drew the heavy railroad watch from his vest, hearing its loud heartbeat and the thump of the big coin fob swinging against the desk.

"Five past three," he said to Emmitt McLowery. "You can lock the doors, if you care to."

The teller nodded, and sighed. "Another bitch, wasn't it?" he said. "My back, it's killin' me."

McLowery went slowly to the front, propped his spine with one hand and reached with the other to draw the door shades. He stopped, staring out, and he whistled.

"My God, Mister Durham!"

"Now what?"

"Somebody hurt, or dead. Up at Stokes's!"

Durham broke from his chair and to the door as, in the street, someone shouted. A few men ran past, and others stood where they were, looking north. Then Durham saw the horse, a tall blue roan. It limped toward the stable, staggering as though hoof-split, its good legs cut and soaked with blood, a hideous bundle dragging from one side.

"A bitch!" Emmitt McLowery whispered.

The roan threw its head, snorted out a pink foam, wheeled away from hands that grasped at the bridle, kicked without force at its burden, and dropped in the street with a groan.

"Stay put!" Durham said to McLowery, and he struck out, running with the others through the windy heat of this town that right now, he knew, he could curse if he paused to.

The Remington beat the holster against his hip as he went, and he was aware that in those used-to times, when he'd kept the leather slick and oiled and tied down, the pistol would have jumped out into the dust had he run. He sped faster, feeling that someway the fallen roan concerned him, and all at once he was hoping the dead man would be big, and bearded, a man with a T brand fresh on his chest.

He came up to Texas Wells at the crowd's outside fringe. "Who is it, Tex?"

Texas was panting, his lips drawn and purpled. "Don't know. Just . . . got here, myself. Oh, damn me, Durham! I oughta knowed better than run! I ain't preserved for it!"

Durham shoved past him and on through. He saw old Dub Stokes down on his hands and knees, his cheek laid to the ground. The stableman was peering at the dirt-caked tatter underneath the horse, a dead horse now, if not at the moment it dropped. "Can't tell," Dub called up. "Jesus, they ain't hardly no face left!"

A bareheaded Mexican knelt and looked under, crossed himself and broke running, toward the *pueblito,* to be the first to report it to his kind. Around Durham voices spoke low, toned as if in church, except for one that said, "When it rains, it sure as hell pours!"

Dub Stokes's black boy brought a mule team out of the barn, harnessed quickly and without britching. Old Dub took the lines, backed the team around, and bossed while men tied the tug chains through the roan's saddle cinches. Then the old man shouted and blasphemed at the mules, and the dead horse rolled over.

The man's body came up, crushed and torn, one foot still hung through a stirrup.

It was suddenly quiet.

Durham looked, and looked again, and he saw the wrong of it. He sprang to speak, then did not.

The crowd squeezed in, as though not caring to, but forced, and they took their short glances at death, then backed off in hushed twos and threes, eying at a distance, agreeing, calmly now, that it was a sight to make you sick, what a scared horse might do to a man. Durham turned from the body. For a minute he watched them. So, only he had noticed. To the others, it was a runaway.

"Nobody know him?" Dub Stokes said. No one answered.

"Well," the old man said, "I know that hoss. Sold him myself, to Elwood Coates, a short while back. Hell no, this here ain't Coates, but I'd reckon if somebody'll find old Elwood, he can say who he swapped this roan to."

Then Willie Belmeade arrived, trailing one end of his stretcher in the dirt and complaining how this, likely, was one more free case he couldn't afford, the same as Johnsy Hood; how rent and coffin lumber, you could damn well bet, didn't come free, and that he ought to have stayed a cabinet maker, which was what his old daddy told him, anyway.

Durham watched until they'd parted the foot from the stirrup. Then he started slowly back to the bank—his bank, wasn't it, in his town?—and he gazed at the great mansion at Crowder's south end, spearing its slim lightning rods up into the sky as though to mark where he would live with Jessie—that is, if he lived at all. Something of his new way had lined off and left him; he felt it, and he knew it as he walked. His hand clamped harder on the California slug, until the eight gold corners of it bit like barbs in his palm.

Emmitt McLowery stood in the door. "Who was it?"

"They can't tell," Durham said.

"Like I said, Mister Durham—"

"I know, it's a bitch of a day. Why don't you go on home?"

The teller bobbed his head as if he'd counted on it, rubbed the curve of his back and put on the blocked hairy hat he called a "New Orleans beaver." His throat hacked mildly at the beginning sounds of a consumptive fit as Durham closed and locked the doors behind him.

Before he drew the shades, Durham looked again toward the stable and at the news having its lick at the street. Directly across, he saw Elwood Coates. The squat JC foreman tied a fat lathered horse to a hitch ring and went into Tate's. Durham swore.

The sight of this man, one not worth the cost of his killing, even with shells cheaper than water, at once enraged him. It spun his wheels, sent him back to passing judgments on himself.

He shook his head. He *had* prevented the hanging, hadn't he? And as for the burning of the man, good Lord, how could he hold himself to what he'd become if he stood against the punishment of a cow thief, if he couldn't, at least, allow it, regardless of what crimes he might recall of his own?

It was just the going out with those two. He'd been a mush-headed fool.

He moved to the windows and hauled down their "open" signs, and at once shed his coat. For an instant, his sodden shirt made the brimstone air seem almost cool. He got back to his desk and took up a pen; his mind suddenly nudged him that he had letters to write, if truly he intended writing them. Then he put himself quickly at the postings, instead.

The work merely lagged from him; he scratched crudely onto the ledgers between thoughts that wouldn't remain fixed on Jessie. Damn today's wildness! Each time he logged the date, he had to look again at the curled Black Draught calendar on the wall, seeing it was still August 16. Once it occurred to him it was the date he might lose his life, either the new one, or the old one, or both, and with them this thing his mother had called his Sweete Salvation.

An hour went. His fingers cramped, and he was thirsty and far from finished when the front doors rattled.

Durham started up taut, feeling quickly for his gun, hating the gesture as he made it.

"Hey!" someone yelled, and shook the door again.

Durham stared at the front, waiting. Then knuckles beat on the glass.

"Just a minute," Durham said. He got into the hot coat and crossed the lobby, walking as lightly as he could, despite himself. He drew the shade aside. Elwood Coates grinned in on him.

"Bank's closed," Durham said. "What do you want?"

"Money, old stud!" the cowman bellered. "What else you come to a bank for, huh?"

"You got no bank account," Durham said.

Coates kept grinning, his green eyes whisky-bright, and shot with cobwebs of raw red. "Maybe I'll borry," he said.

Durham thought of the dead man and unlocked the door.

"Coates, they were hunting you. About the man the horse dragged in."

"Hell, they found me."

"You know him?"

The Chester foreman reeked inside, and reeked across the lobby to the back. He grunted down into what Emmitt McLowery had named "the bad news chair," opposite Durham's desk, and he said, "Haw, death on his damn pale hoss!"

"I said, did you know him?"

Coates belched. "Sure, I knowed him; sold him that roan horse. A bad onion, I guess. Lee Hanley."

Durham thought of the mules turning the roan's carcass, the stirrup coming up with the foot stuck through it.

"Don't know any Hanley," he said carefully.

"That stud, he sot off up in the hills, west of the crick," Coates thundered. "Never got to town much. Now me, Bull Durham . . . haw . . . I could make do with some cash."

"You got no money here. You're drunk."

"That I am, I sure as hell am!" Coates yelled, and his neck bulged like a lizard's. "But I ain't needin' you to tell me, hell no.

I can feel my liquor, and I don't have to be told about it by any of you up-and-mighty bastards of this town, by God I don't! I get sick of the bunch of you tellin' me!"

"That's a plenty."

Durham narrowed down at the cowman, grateful he'd remained standing; and he did not move his hands from the desk, but only shrugged to make certain his coat was unbuttoned. This could be it, he thought, the violent moment, the time he'd feared, that of his terrible turning back. He glared at Coates, this man who sat there needing killing, looking as sin-ugly as his own mistakes, and for the instant, Durham didn't care.

But Coates only loosened and eased back in the chair. "Hell, stud, don't get your hocks hot," he said. "I come on business."

Durham waited, and the JC boss watched him, grinning, then leaning forward.

"Stud, when you plan on gettin' out?" he said.

"Say what you mean."

"Trailing, that's what I by-God mean. You ain't waitin' around till that big buffler-stink catches you up like he done Johnsy Boy, are you? Hell, me, I ain't, not by no gutful. Which is how come me here for my money."

Durham let down into his chair, putting his back to the open vault, putting his gun between Coates and wealth. "Talk sense," he said. "You quitting the Chester?"

"Stud, I done have, only old By Jove, he don't know it yet. I've seen the wall's handwritin', ain't that what they say, handwritin'? Nothin' holdin' me, outside of my travelin' money."

"You came to the wrong place."

The foreman laughed. "Haw, now, I ain't a man to go twiddlin' around. You want 'er spelt out, I don't mind; I just want my piece of that seventeen thousand you taken off that dun hoss."

"Damn you. . . ."

"Hold on, stud. I been figurin'. Old Johnsy Boy, he didn't get it, and me, I didn't, and old Hanley, it weren't him neither, so—"

"Hanley?" Durham said quickly, "what's he got to do with it?"

Coates grinned, but he wiped at his face, and Durham could see him turning to, to make up his thoughts as if spreading a mussed bed.

"You've seen Hanley since this morning," Durham pushed him. "Maybe you killed him."

"Hell, hoss throwed him; everybody seen that!"

Durham's hand crawled the rest of the way to the butt of the Remington, and he watched the drunken eyes, seeing behind them and picking the whiskied brains with the same knack he had boot-strapped himself up with in this town and this bank, and he felt better. What he could see, he could handle.

"I went up there, Coates," he said quietly. "The foot was still hooked in the stirrup. That was the right foot in the left-hand stirrup, seems to me."

Coates's sledge fists took grips on the chair arms, and his face sullened and darkened, his ox mind appearing to go plundering backwards, sorting over the crime for the error.

Durham said, "Right foot, left stirrup. I can't think anybody goes riding around this country sitting backwards."

Abruptly Coates grinned.

"Well," he said. "Us two, stud, now we got no secrets, huh?"

"You killed him."

"Hell, I didn't exactly aim to."

"I could see you hung."

"Aw, is that all the friendly you can be? Me and you, we're kind of clost now, ain't we? No secrets; hell, we got that pile betwixt us. Now, a half of seventeen thousand, I figure, comes out—"

"Hanley," Durham cut him off. "Was he out on the creek that night?"

"Sure, he was in the brush somewheres. That was his fire, you see."

"What!"

"About that cash, Durham. We—"

"Damn you, tell me about Hanley!"

Coates did not stir, but he had thought away his grin, and he said, "Hell, don't get your high-muck bowels in a uproar! I told you, it was Hanley's fire. Me and him, we been gatherin' a few head off old knicker-britches on the side, so I didn't have no choice much, exceptin' to hop onto that buffler-stink."

Durham shook. "You . . . you knew that man wasn't a cow thief!"

"I told you, weren't no choice. Besides, you and me, we wasn't partners then, was we? Had to make me a little showin', and I figured you a good witness. I couldn't tell that stinkin' tramp would come ahellin' after us."

Durham gritted on his rage; he'd let this stupid saddle scum make use of him, as much as he'd used that twist in Johnsy Hood.

"Don't matter none," Coates said. "We got us seventeen thousand damned dollars, ain't we?"

Durham brought the revolver off his hip, training it on Coates's belly.

"My gun's on you, Coates," he whispered. "Under this table, and I'm thinking of killing you!"

The cowman's breath sucked in short, then blew out slowly, sour with whisky. "Ain't no cause for that," he said. "Hell, whyn't you get out our money, and we'll git, right now?"

"You'll go, damn you."

"What about the money, stud? I got to—"

"Get on your feet."

The foreman rose with a slow push of his hands, his eyes cutting down on the desk top, as though they might bore peepholes through to the gun.

"You aim to thieve it from me."

"Get out!"

"All right, big stud! Only don't get no by-God notion that big buffler-stink is goin' to leave town chasin' me! He'll stick for his crack at you, hell, yes. It ain't me as got his money or is messin' with that redheaded woman."

Durham beefed up from his chair, bringing his gun into sight. "Keep Jessie off your goddam tongue!"

Coates stared up at him a moment, hard, and of a sudden his grin was back. "Well, I'm damned!" he said. "You ain't onto who that big stink is, are you?"

"You tell me."

"Haw, you don't! You don't know."

"Tell me," Durham said, and he cocked the pistol.

"If you shoot me, I won't be sayin' much of nothin'." The foreman stepped back, his leather hands held wide, away from his thick body.

"I been doin' some drinkin' and listenin', since I come in from Lee's. Happens everybody is all goosed up about this big man that's in at the Rusk. Well, that's him."

"Who, damn you?"

"Feller is marked up, bad, and he bought hisself some burn salve this mornin', and he whipped the taters out of old Kratz; everybody seen it. Besides that, they's some saying he had a yow-yow with Jessie Rupp at her place, real early, and they's some recollectin' that woman oncet had a man the name of Julius. And if you'd ask, you'd find out this big feller at the Rusk writ his name down 'Julius Brown.' "

Jessie's husband!

"Get out!" he whispered.

Coates backed toward the door, holding his hands far out, and he said, "Half that money, by rights, it's mine."

Then, as the cowman opened the door and dodged quickly outside, Durham knew he should have killed the man. He knew it from the liquored eyes, that if he'd been hunted before, now he was stalked twice over.

A long while Durham sat at the desk, the Remington uncocked and put down on top of the soiled ledger still waiting its postings.

Jessie's husband, alive, and home. It chopped the legs from under him. Her husband back, and she'd not come to tell him.

He groaned, letting his fingers goad through his hair, and he swore his worst and best to the walls of his bank and his town. He was all dirtied up, and he was seeing Jessie tonight, and how would he tell her of it?

Jessie, I had to go out for poker, you understand, I have to lose some once in a while, to make sure I'm not what I used to be; and Jessie, I kicked your husband in the head when he said something about money, but it was only because I couldn't trust those other two to hear, you understand, and Jessie, I thought he was a thief, I really did, and I let them brand him, and when the horses ran, I caught them, and out there in the dark, I found the money on his horse, and I stuffed it under my saddle, and filled his saddlebags with grass, but just so the others wouldn't notice, don't you see? And Jessie, I wasn't stealing it; I thought your husband was a thief, I thought his money must be stolen money, and I brought it to the bank and figured to write about it to the Rangers. No, Jessie, I haven't written yet; I guess I only wanted to hold it a while, you understand about that, don't you? It's like my Papa, when he wasn't drinking he kept some whisky in the kitchen pantry, and he took it out to look at sometimes, so he could say to Mother, "See, I've quit; it don't bother me!" You understand that, Jessie, about the money? And Jessie, listen to me, I did keep them from hanging him, that's the truth. And when I got back with the horses, I made them take that iron off of him.

God witness it, it was so. And it sounded rotten.

He pulled out the desk drawer and got the brown envelope filled with Jessie's notes and put it in his pocket. He'd need what weapons he had.

Then he stopped and took out the envelope and looked at it again. The twenty-eight hundred to pay the notes. He'd taken the money out of the seventeen thousand—as though, all along, he'd thought of the cash as his!

And how could he fit this in for Jessie? He knew no way to explain it to himself, even—no way at all.

He licked his lips and put the envelope back into his coat. He rammed the pistol into its holster, took up the ledgers and jammed them into the vault, shouldered the iron door shut and spun the dials and went to the front. It was then he knew he hadn't quit. Before he stepped out, he looked both ways of the street: south, toward the Two Bulls, the cothouse, and mansion, the direction Coates had gone; north, toward the Rusk and Julius Rupp; then he looked across, toward Tate's, where either of them might wait.

Rapidly he locked the doors, and he only glanced toward Dunce Moreno's barbershop where on another day he would have gone for his bath, which had become a part of his settled-man's habit, and he strode off the other way, around the bank corner, and he tore at the outdoors stairway, two steps at a reach, and he sweated at how long his back was exposed to the street.

He drove into his room and shut the door, standing against it while he whistled for air, his face cold but dripping.

He sat down on the bed, and he swore. Then, for the first time, he knew he wasn't the same man he used to be, and he knew it for sure. Because he'd met enemies before; he'd locked eyes with death and stared it down. But this time, God help him, he was afraid!

Chapter Twenty-Three

JULIUS Rupp sat on the floor, cross-legged, looking out the Rusk House window into the street, his Colt on the sill before him, and he kept guessing at the time. This long, long day; it seemed at last to be burning itself out, and pretty soon now, a gritty evening gray would rise like a smoke and fill Crowder up to its sagged ridgepoles, and the waiting would be finished. Except now, he hadn't such a beating hunger for the dark.

As he watched, people left the street, bent for supper and their rest in that lull before the nighttime saloon howl, and he mistrusted how the town's sudden calming seemed to aim at including himself and his thoughts. And, it struck him, he did think now, whereas before he had merely calculated, which was different, even to the words by which it explained itself to his mind.

He got up, catering to the soreness of his limbs, and slowly he tromped the floor, five paces from the window, then again, five paces in return. At each window stop, he saw Coldiron and the street, and when he wheeled at the far side, he brought to view in the hot dimness the small shape of the spic girl, curled on the bed and half-covered and moist, sleeping deeply with each breath of her drawing only the least thimbleful of air.

She was a woman, and here. But not Jessie.

He reached the window again and paused, stooping, resting his hands on the sill where splinters were shedding. He could see Jessie's shop, closed, and dark behind the glass, as it had become in some moment when he didn't watch but instead played at love, or played the hound dog with Maria, whichever it came to. Once more he had the notion that kept lancing at him, that a rage might warp itself into the craving for a woman, and when spent, take its easy time rebuilding.

But if he was budding into some kind of wise man, then the budding was too late, by eleven stinking damned years. To hell with it, and Maria, and them all.

If Old Dub told it straight, Brooks Durham would be setting out for Jessie's right soon.

Rupp went to the washstand and struck a sweat-soddened match on the butt of Maria's big pistol. He lit and trimmed the lamp low, and idly looked at the old gun. The barrel was pied with rust, the frame grimed and pitted, the five cartridges aged almost black. He doubted it would fire, and he was oddly sorry of it; it meant that maybe he'd not saved Maria from her killing, or Bonnie Shelley from her dying, that likely the girl could never have brought it off at all.

He poured water into the washbowl and rinsed off his face, and as he stuffed in his shirttail, the yellow cat came from under the bed, stretched itself two feet long, and padded along the floor to Maria's plate and began lapping at the edges of it as if, already, it hadn't been slicked clean.

"Scat," Rupp said, and the girl awoke and looked at him.

"*Hola,* Tall One," she said. "How I have rested!"

He grunted and closed his belt, leaving space for the pistol.

Maria batted drowsy eyes at him, then quickly sat up, drawing the pink kimono up to her chin. "You go?"

"You too," he said. "Back to your own room."

"Oh, I have not pleased you!"

He crossed to the sill and picked up the long Colt and put it in his waist, flattening his belly inward so the butt might stand clear and away from the fester of the brand.

"What is this, of the gun?" Maria said.

Rupp stared at her; she was a child, soak full of a child's questions—and Mexican, he reminded himself. He took his gaze away, glancing about for his bottle.

"What went with that liquor?"

Maria got off the bed, the pink kimono properly about her now, and she said, "You will be angry."

"Where is it?"

"The fool's water, señor—in that small while you slept, I threw it from the window."

"Goddam!"

"This is as I cared for my Johnsy," she said quickly. "One day he laughed of it himself, for there was someone down below, and we heard this one shout, '*Cristo,* it is raining red whisky, and I have me no cup!' "

"Ought to choke you," Rupp said.

She came at once to stand small and brown in front of him, as though to offer her throat to his hands. "You," she said softly, "you find no way to laugh."

"Get back to your room."

He swept her muskiness aside, getting to where his hat had tumbled from the bed, and he felt it as she followed him.

"Do not go, I beg you."

He did not answer.

"What is this upon you? Is this the shadow of the dead buffalo only, so black you must run from it? This wound that is covered, that you hurt of?"

"Dammit, do like I say!" He turned, and she was there, close in front of him.

"To kill, it is a thirst in you. Is this what I see, Tall One?" She spoke low, and suddenly she strained up high, and she kissed the underside of his chin.

He scowled at her. This little spic, alone among them all, she cared nothing for the buffalo smell, or the marks. He took hold of her, cursing her for a wench, putting her cheek against his.

"How you swear!" she whispered. "Even as you sleep!"

"Can't you hush up?"

The girl's lips moved at his ear. "*Ay,* we must have no light from the lamp!"

He set her down, head set against her, but he swung toward the lamp and reached for it.

There was a knock at the door.

Rupp drew the pistol, lagging it easy in his hand, at his side, and turned the knob.

A boy stood there, Mexican and dirty, holding out a letter in his hand. "*El Tigre,*" the boy said, sweeping black eyes from Rupp's boots to his ears, and he dropped the letter and ran barefoot for the stairs.

Rupp looked after him, then put the gun away and picked up the envelope and tore it open. The note was woman-written, in broad grease pencil. He held it to the lamp to read.

JULIUS. YOU MUST LEAVE COLDIRON. TONIGHT THERE WILL BE FORMED A COMMITTEE. IF YOU WILL COME TO THE HOUSE PAST DARK THERE WILL BE PREPARED A KIT OF FOOD TO STAY YOU ON THE TRIP.

He read it again, and hope like a shout echoed through him. Jessie cautioned him; she wanted him safe.

He raised the paper to his nose, and it was there, the scent he hunted, the frail lily-of-the-valley scent he'd once breathed strong, when she brought coffee, when alone with him she tumbled down her hair. Then he read her words again, and cursed himself. She wanted him away, away to stay dead, to bequeath her to Brooks Durham. For that she would hand him a piece of charity, out the mansion's back door.

He ground the paper into a ball between his palms and spun for his hat. Maria held it, two-handedly against her front, her eyes big on him and afraid.

"Give it to me," he said.

"Oh, this letter. It puts a wrath on you!"

"My hat!"

"You will kill, I know it!"

He took his hat from her, and as he pushed the crown out, he wished he'd not drunk of her this afternoon.

"What would you do to whoever burnt Johnsy?" he said.

"The golden one, this morning I would have killed her! But tonight, Señor Brown, I could pass her by and not look at her!"

"The one as stuck the iron to him, I mean."

She spit out her answer. "That one I would cut the heart from, as God is my life!"

He nodded. "Then you got no fuss with what I'm doin'."

He put on his hat and went out.

Chapter Twenty-Four

RUPP stepped out onto the sidewalk, and he tightened his eyes against a wind growing lazier, as if tired out from the day, and he thought of Brooks Durham. But he had to notice the town, and he did. Under the evening dark it seemed larger and unlike the shabby carpet of shacks beneath a mansion, as he had seen it in the sunlight.

He halted in a shaft of blue dark and put together a cigaret. This was, for a fact, a slut of a country. It fooled you with red sunsets which could color up the dry flats like leaves of a Sperry catalogue and made the barrenness almost pretty, and, as now, it popped at you a pumpkin moon which spread the hot ugliness with a peaceful feel of blue and orange, and a light that was gentle, and a liar. But if the evening almost lulled you, there was the wind and red dirt to wake you up. These were the truth of the land, Rupp thought. They didn't fool you, for they never lay down to rest, and it was correct as people said, this was a Jumping-off country with tricks of its own for culling out, or killing out, the weak ones—which, come to think of it, was hardly different from what others said of Indian Territory, or of Kansas. It might be, indeed, the main truth about the whole damned world.

He held a damp match to the wind, to dry it before he lit his cigaret. The smoke tasted good, and with it he recalled the tale of Birch Soderfeldt, a Kansas sodbuster who stuck when his wife and younguns passed on from spoiled meat, and stuck when the splenic took his milking cows, and even when a spinning black wind carried off his house, but who cursed and pulled out one pretty fair day when he bent to wash in a stream and his last sack of tobacco fell out into the water.

Rupp felt of a sudden stronger than the country. It whittled out the weak ones, but tonight when he did his own weeding, it would be of the strong.

He stood a moment more before the Rusk House looking at Crowder Street. Northward, and across, lights burned in the Union Church and in front was a buggy, an iron-wheeled buckboard, and two hipshot cow horses: the early comers, he guessed, for choir, or the committee Jessie mentioned. A committee and a rope to replace the pesthouse.

To the south was the high stand of Aunt Gussie's house—no, Jessie's house—and in between, almost nothing that showed through the dark. The time he'd picked seemed as good as Coldiron could offer.

Smoking deep, Rupp wanted with it a drink, a whisky to scratch him raw and maybe unlimber the blood that seemed now reflective, that Maria in her wild seventeen tenderness might the least bit have cooled.

He idled off the walk into the moon blaze and slanted across to Tate's. But he kept out of the light which spurted from the doors, forsaking the drink he couldn't get without being seen, and he leaned his shoulder against a barked cedar pole that held up Tate's wide awning. He looked back across the street at the Stockman's Security Bank.

In the room upstairs a lamp burned, sifting an unsteady yellow glow through a paper shade. Durham would be sprucing up for Jessie. That was all right. There could be more dignity for a man if he was clean and looked nice when he died.

Rupp glanced again at the mansion, now to his right. High there another lamp flickered, lifting and waning like the glow from the bank. Rupp's teeth set. The lamps winked of a vile togetherness, of Jessie lying to wife for Brooks Durham.

The suggestion beat whisky. Rupp was ready.

He spat into a scummed water barrel, one of the fire guards

Coldiron kept forgetting to fill, and it occurred to him he'd made no plan for Elwood Coates, nor had he thought much of the money. It had come down to Durham, only Durham, and Jessie.

A creaking, piled-up wagon, tarped over and double-teamed, rattled into the street, moving slow toward the south and the freight station. The teamster was muttering dull threats against mules named Mag and Mandy. Rupp watched the big Murphy until it passed, as he'd watched such rigs as a boy. For a moment, Crowder Street might have been unchanged by the eleven years, and again almost a good street, pleasurable to walk along in the evening, as it had been when he was nineteen and scrubbed up, and headed to sit up a while with Jessie.

He turned his eyes back to the bank.

The stairway was not in sight, quite, but he could see the mouth of it, plain and moonlit where Durham would reach the walk. He waited for the lamp to go out, hungry to get on with it now. He counted slowly up to ten, betting himself that Durham would darken the room and show before the count was done. When he lost, he counted again. His mouth dried cottony, but he smoked, and smoked again, and he breathed without depth so the too-snug shirt would lie a little looser across the burn.

"Eight, nine, ten," he said, and the lamp went out.

Rupp straightened away from the post. Brooks Durham came down the stairs.

At the walk the banker stopped, turning his head both ways, taking stock of the street, as though he had an inkling. It suited Rupp, and suited him when the big bareheaded man brushed back his coat and reset the gun on his hip. But it made no difference, Rupp realized. If Durham had come out unarmed, he could have killed him anyway, cold, and slept off the rest of the night just as sound, goddam him.

Durham struck out along the walk, keeping to the far side and close against the buildings, hurrying toward Jessie's. Rupp watched him melt under an awning, covered by a blueness like smoke, then burst out, showing himself clear once more in the moonwash gushing from an alley. Rupp grunted, the night's light was good enough.

He felt of the Colt in his waist, chunked his cigaret at the water barrel, and strolled slowly off along his own walk. He lagged himself a short ways behind, and he made his steps match Durham's, so that the whomp of their heels sounded on the boards like one pair only.

Ahead, down the street, the first trial chords rang from a piano, at the Two Bulls, it seemed, and Rupp heard behind it, somewhere off toward Dirty Creek, the shrills and chatter and strings of a Mexican wake or wedding fixing to begin. He passed a white bitch sniffing at a doorpost and looking motherly, or poisoned, with the pups she carried. Otherwise, the street belonged to Durham and himself.

He shortened his stride, to hold the big blond man on a line between himself and the moon, and he felt no urgency. Any moment of his choosing, he could step out into Crowder's dust, yell as he needed to yell at this whole pricing-down town, and gun the man down. It struck Rupp, then, that he should take a little time, as the three of them had when they gabbed and drank coffee before, at their damned easy leisure, they paid him the iron.

That night, they'd seen him beg—as Durham begged now and didn't know it.

Rupp leaped across an alley and one block was gone. The mansion stood broader and higher up ahead, and he saw it had gone completely dark. It bothered him, until suddenly a new light flared downstairs in the parlor. Hell, yes, Jessie would wait her banker in that frilled and brassy place that Aunt Gussie had herded a farm boy out of. Gussie, who was dead, *to who laid the chunk.*

Again he tamed down his stride to keep the distance from Durham what his hunter's sense wanted, and with the slowing came less outcry from his muscles. He caught himself thinking, not calculating—thinking that someplace in this affair someone else deserved a free shot. The spic girl, he guessed, she was due some blood, much as himself, and he needn't have robbed her of it.

Rupp tripped, catching himself against a mud wall.

"Watch what you're about, tanglefoot!" an old voice yelped at his knee. The man sitting on the walk with a sign hung from his neck was legless, and he swore as though his stumps remained touchy. "Hell fire, man!"

"Didn't see you," Rupp said, and he flattened back against the wall, watching Durham. The banker had turned to the sound. He hesitated, then struck out south again, next to running.

Rupp stepped around the cripple, unable now to tune his steps to Durham's. His limp got in his way as he passed the Two Bulls, passed the barber's, and a feed store. He saw Durham trot through the shadow thrown west from a tent-roofed cothouse. Then the planks ran out, and Rupp stepped down into a packed red pathway. He glanced toward the big house. Its whitewashed picket gate, unlatched and wagging, wasn't a hundred feet away.

It was time.

He cursed himself; he had dallied. But instantly he knew why: he'd meant for Jessie to see, or hear it.

Rupp's hand set around the pistol butt and he sprang out into the street's moon, his feet stomping down wide as they hit. He sucked in the dirty wind, but before he could hail, it all went wrong.

A shout shotgunned the street, from a squat rider who whooped a fat horse into the open, breaking from the freight-station dark, cornering off of Pedro Street and hard on to Crowder. The horse snorted and skidded, and the rider dug with his heels, shouting again, and he fired a pistol blast across the pony's neck.

"Here comes yourn, old stud!" the rider yelled, and he bore the horse at Brooks Durham, firing again as he came.

Coates. Rupp swore.

He saw Durham break running, cutting toward the middle of the intersection, stretching for the mansion.

He'll never make it, Rupp thought, never in this hot world, and he saw Durham bumped by the horse and going down. The animal was over Durham then, rearing and screaming. The banker rolled, kicking to fight away the hoofs. Coates sawed the bits, twisting in the saddle to line his gun on Durham, and he yelled, "Hold still, goddam you!" maybe to Durham or maybe to the horse.

Rupp stared. These two, they hadn't his leave!

Coates fired again, and a gray-white smoke thickened around the tumble of horse and men.

Rupp drew the long Colt and held it level. He watched the

bloom of smoke that hid Coates and most of the horse. When from the cloud the next flame spurted, he stepped ahead and yelled, "Lookee here, Coates!" and squeezed the trigger.

He saw the horse jump sideways and dive to its foreknees. Coates slewed forward, then bounced back to hold his seat; he battered the animal's neck with his gun and yanked the wounded mount to its feet. He looked at Rupp as the pony struggled to run.

"Haw, three-handed game, ain't that what they say?" Coates bellered, and he sang a bullet past Rupp's head as the animal broke north, clumsily, down the center of the street, the sound of blood bubbling in its throat.

Rupp only looked, suddenly hating to know that he'd maimed a horse. He felt nothing of what a man is supposed to feel when he is shooting and being shot at. Yet he could hear, and there was a scurry among the buildings, and there wasn't much time.

He turned to look at Durham. The banker sat on the ground, his gun at last drawn, but unpointed. He shook his shoulders and pushed himself up, brushing dust from his vest front, and he squared himself up with his pistol at his side.

"You're Julius Rupp," he said.

Rupp did not answer.

"That drunk bastard," Durham said, "he'd of killed me."

Rupp loosened. He let the Colt swing down alongside his thigh, muzzle toward the ground, which made it even, as if he'd meant it to be, and he hadn't. The banker was gasping for air, but he stood there solid.

Rupp walked toward him. "You get hit?"

"No."

Rupp walked closer. "All right. You got a gun. Commence when you're a mind."

"Wait, man—"

"We don't need no talk."

"Not now," Durham said, "damn it all! Jessie—she's on the porch!"

Rupp did not believe it and he did not look. If she was there, he'd know it; a man would know when his own wife was somewhere about.

"Make your move," he said.

"She's seeing this," Durham said.

Rupp stopped, barely shy of reach.

"Your gun's in your right hand," he said.

Durham did not move. "First, you ought to know I thought you were a cow thief; that's no lie. I didn't find out Coates rigged it, not till today. Listen—"

"You aim to fight?"

The banker sounded older, and tired. "I guess, if you make me. Any man hates to die."

Rupp raised his gun. Still Durham did not move.

"Jessie's on the porch," he said.

Rupp cocked the revolver, feeling the iron weight of it like the power of God in his hand, the power to fold Brooks Durham into Coldiron's red dust and leave him in it with the sandy drafts blowing among his bowels—paying in full, and buying back eleven haunted years and seventeen thousand dollars—exploding Jessie back into her widowhood, and to an aloneness of her own up there in the big house. Quickly, Rupp tried to think of her, of the sound as she shouted, "I love Brooks Durham!" but he heard only a girl's voice instead, a slow spic voice saying, "It would be too much to pray of."

That was all.

Rupp stepped aside, his gun lowering, and in the instant he saw Durham's pistol flash and jump, spewing only its smoke on him, and he heard the tumbling clatter of glass shattering in a window behind him.

The banker did not fire again. He stared at Rupp. "Now, *you* fight," Durham said. "I don't mean to murder you."

"Go to hell," Rupp said, and he turned and walked, unhurriedly, north along Crowder.

He thought of his rage, but it was not there to be felt. It was gone, much as the whisky a spic girl poured out a window.

In a moment Rupp's chest again drew and gnawed and his legs ached, and he thought of the drink he could relish right down to the dregs. A hundred lights seemed to have been lit to either side, their flush almost reaching him out in the street, and the moon was pitching long shadows of men and a few women who stood near the walks and watched. Ahead he could see Coates's horse, abandoned and down and floundering short of Tate's. He went toward it, a mercy bullet ready. He walked in an odd still in which nothing else moved.

Far up Crowder he saw people bunched in front of Union Church, and nearer, others who stood back in doorways, or packed themselves together before Tate's and the Two Bulls and Harlan Swift's, silent except for small hisses of tense Spanish. The pumping breath of the horse was loudest, groaning like a giant croup as he reached it, and he recocked the Colt. Then he tightened at how no one called out or ran, as though it wasn't yet done, and he remembered Elwood Coates.

He looked up as the first flash licked at him from behind Tate's water barrel, and a clod spurred up short of his feet. The shot echoed, and a girl screamed.

"Kill him, Señor Coates!" she shrieked. "Kill him down, for my Johnsy!"

Rupp stood fixed, though the second shot came and dropped nearer, and he searched the shadows until he saw her. She stood far off, under Tate's awning with the crowd there, her child's head shawled black, her hands held in front of her as if she must be ready to clap them when he fell.

He shot the horse.

Maria knew about him. He was sorry.

"Kill him, Señor Coates! Somebody!" she screamed, and a tall man looped his arm over her and dragged her back while she cursed and fought him.

Rupp walked at the fire barrel, a sickness of new despair like a bile in his throat. Maria, also, wanted him dead.

He came into range of Coates's gun now but he did not crouch or run. He walked straight up, as you go when you stalk buffalo, since crossways draws their eyes, and you shoot for the lights, not the heart, else you'll need to go chasing after your meat, and where was it he first learned that?

He could not see Coates, and he wondered how it was the cowman didn't again let fly. He raised the Colt and centered on the barrel. Then the foreman's tub shape blurred out in the open street, a pistol in each hand.

"Hey stud, look at me!" Coates yelled, and his guns blazed together.

Rupp laid thorough aim and nudged his shot away. Then he touched off another.

The Chester foreman grunted. He jerked back, catching himself on pitiful slow feet. He groaned and turned a full circle, then away from Rupp like any man who's had his sudden fill, and he weaved off toward Tate's, driving a crowd back inside ahead of him.

This is a man I'm shooting, Rupp thought, and it's real, though so damned unreal. Nobody's in a hurry. Nobody complaining.

He saw Coates pause with an arm shored against Tate's door. The cowman looked over his shoulder at Rupp, his mouth open, the green eyes glinting like a cat's as he faced the moon.

"Oh, God!" He coughed. "You've sure as hell kilt me!" He split on into the saloon.

Rupp stepped up on the walk, reloading as he went. He crossed the awning shadow and followed into Tate's, and it felt the same as if he went after his drink and it only. Coates leaned against the bar, head low, his squat body shortened down until it was square. One fist still held its gun, and he was trying to drink back the blood in his mouth.

"Kilt me," he whispered. "And the Little Whisky Man too!" He snapped up the gun.

Rupp shot him twice.

Powder smoke mixed and tumbled with the heat, its smell stout and sour. Rupp sneezed on it and wiped his nose on his sleeve. The crowd held itself where it had packed back against Tate's rear wall, and in front he saw Maria, panting and yet writhing against a man's arm that held her. Her shawl was gone, and her black hair had got loose, and her eyes cursed him with their hate. All at once Rupp was tired to his toes.

He started the long Colt back into his belt, cringing and drawing it again when the barrel heat burned him. He looked again at Maria; he'd not seen her dressed before. And he hated what he saw. A trollop kind of red, low-necked and too ruffled, this dress. God, he hated it.

He dropped the pistol to the floor and put his toe to it. He sent it skidding to Maria's feet.

"It ain't a bad gun," he said. "It'll swap for a ring."

He turned and went out, leaving them the smoke and heat of this whole peculiar country, and it was as he reached his room that sleep fell over him like a pitch-dark sack.

Chapter Twenty-Five

SUCH a Sunday morning Coldiron had never seen. Even the sun had aroused early, with an early seriousness for its work. For the first time since Aunt Gussie made them build the Union Church, Crowder Street's saloons had run all night, and run hard, and two were running yet, supplying the appetites of those who had awakened early, and helping to ease the tired eyes and tiring tongues of the greater crowd that hadn't gotten to bed at all. Nothing seemed to be in order.

The Reverend Gossett himself was on the street, solemn and bony in his black pulpit frock, and he dashed about condemning Demon Whisky, and the drinkers, and calling upon God to assert Himself that this was the Lord's Day, and if necessary, to cave in the roofs of the Two Bulls and Tate's, sparing Harlan Swift's, perhaps, because if Harlan was a liquor monger, he at least feared Heaven and had shut his doors at the first show of daylight.

A few women came to aid the Reverend, and as he led them in charges against the whisky haunts and the idlers on the street, it was remarked the minister might well use a small shot himself, considering how frayed he looked as he shouted, "We must fight! The Sabbath is in the hands of the Philistines!"

In the wake of the Reverend was Willie Belmeade, asking a

collection: there was Elwood Coates now, added to the other two, and coffin lumber cost a good deal, even if you didn't count in the freight. Willie kept at it, even after old By Jove Chester himself came in, driving a white team to a buggy and carrying his wheeled chair in back and pledging the JC to pay expenses on its foreman. "Rent ain't exactly free," Willie Belmeade said.

Dub Stokes, who of common slept until noon on Sunday, was out, drinking at Tate's and going now and then to the alley beside the Rusk to look in and see whether his black boy had brought Rupp's gift horse, as directed. And Mrs. Lavender was up and everywhere.

The big bake-woman walked up one side of Crowder and down the other, talking to whomever she caught, putting in the League's licks for street lamps and a law force at this time so plainly opportune. Many stopped a while with her, not so much to hear her views as to gaze at the fine red velvet dress she wore and was sweating through, and which sacked her up so tightly that there was a good chance she'd bust out. Some noticed, and laughed, at how Dunce Moreno kept Mrs. Lavender in sight, as though he was done with joking about her and considering, maybe, that she might bring more to a man than mere fresh-baked bread.

Farmers trickled in, as if Saturday had been held over, and cowhands arrived as word spread that the saloons were marvelously open. Among them came Tod Wisdom, arguing, ready to tell again all he knew, and declaring his right to get drunk all over again. Children appeared as if sprouting from the ground, some dressed for church, but looking and listening and milling as though intent on escaping. Two boys set up a stand on the walk in front of Tate's, hawking cider in frog voices, and holding to it, unwilting, despite Si Tate's threats.

People fussed over the order and details of the shooting, shaking their heads over how an old trail hand like Elwood Coates could do so poorly with his guns, and yet, how stubborn strong he died; about Durham, maybe wise, or maybe rabbit-hearted, or a bit of both, and about the frightened spic woman, the one that bore a whopping big son on the ground, not a hundred feet from the gunplay.

The calmer men stood along the street in groups, close

bunched, but scattering to re-form elsewhere when the Reverend Gossett charged at them with his frock blowing and his holy frown on tight. Each time these reassembled where they could watch the Rusk House.

In the hum and turmoil was one curiosity not mentioned, if noticed: the Mexicans. None was on hand. The Mexicans were in the *pueblito,* at Pedro Street's Dirty Creek end, grouped together, and at mass.

In the mansion from which it all spoked outward, Jessie Rupp stood at the parlor window, looking out, holding one hand to a dusty old drape that still showed the spots where Aunt Gussie had sprinkled it with water to make bearable the hottest days; and she thought of Julius at the Rusk House, a brand on his chest. She wondered how such a wound would look: like meat forgotten on the stove and cooked black, or would it be as a kitchen burn, only red? How great, she wondered, was his agony?

She shuddered, sick from her imaginings and her weariness. Brooks had paced and talked most of the night away in this room, pleading his case, as he put it; but to her it had seemed a begging, as Julius would never beg, or never had, not even on the day he rode away and left her.

Or had he left her? Maybe she'd left him; all night, it had seemed very near the truth.

Her legs trembled. She was weak, she told herself, because she'd not gone to bed; at least, she'd not undressed, but only lain as still as she could with her fear and memory and indecision. It was all with her yet, and she wished for her brandy, but cared not to climb the stairs for it. She turned from the window and sank down on the settee.

"Please God," she whispered, but the guilt still descended on her, as if whatever crime had been was her own, as if she herself had put the burn on Julius's chest.

She looked around at the house and hated it. But she had kept it, fought for it, and why? For the same cause that kept her in it eleven years ago? Because it was big and strong, and yes, safe?

Again she told herself she had lied for Julius, had broken Aunt Gussie's heart for him. And again it seemed a wrong thought, that she'd not lied for him, but for herself in order to have him; and that to lie for a man wasn't enough.

Her head ached, and suddenly she wished for coffee. Coffee

after all these years—coffee, brought to her in bed. She shook her head; she wanted now to think, not to feel. Then she heard the step on the gallery.

"Oh, damn," she said. She knew it was Brooks Durham.

"Jessie," he said, when she opened the door. His straw hair was unbrushed, his eyes haggard, and he seemed, too, to have rested in his clothes.

She turned from him and he followed her into the parlor.

"What is it?" she said.

"Well Lord, Jessie! You said you'd . . . think about it. About us."

"I'm tired."

He sat down on the settee, leaning forward with his elbows on his knees, looking huge, but huge only.

"I've decided to stay in Coldiron," he said. "I won't run out like a thief."

"How very brave of you!" she said.

"Jessie, for God's sake, I didn't know he wasn't a thief! I didn't know I was stealing from him! I told you, if you could sort of understand about me and the money."

"What's to understand?" she said from the window.

Durham groaned. "Please, Jessie. Help me!"

The anger of last night, when he had told her the whole of it, hurt her throat. "I'll help you," she said. "If you know a way to take that hideous T off his chest!"

"You're acting wild," Durham said. "Oh, listen to me, honey, I told you, I didn't have anything to do with that; I stopped them."

"After you had his money!"

Durham came to his feet. "Jessie . . . don't you love me?"

"Don't ask me that now."

She looked out at the street's boil, at the same moment hearing the terrible quiet of the house, even to the thin chuckling of Aunt Gussie's cupid clock, far upstairs.

"I'm sorry," she said. "I need time to think."

He came to her, forcing her to look at him. He held a piece of paper in his hand.

"This is a draft for his money," he said. "I'll . . . I'll have to take your notes back, but we can send him his money. He's getting ready to leave."

"He's leaving?"

"The hotel clerk. He says Rupp means to go right away. Don't you see, when he's gone, it'll be like before. I . . . I may have to leave the bank, but I'll get into something. We don't have to put off the wedding."

"I have to see Julius," she said.

Durham put his hands on her shoulders, turning her to him, roughly. His face was white, his eyes red and suddenly lit with temper. "Don't be such a redheaded fool! You're wrought up, that's all."

"Do you realize I've seen my husband twice since he . . . since he came home, and both times I've hit him?"

Durham stepped back from her. "You can't want him back! Eleven damned years . . . you're just mixed up!"

"I am mixed up," she said. "Do you know what I'm thinking? I'm thinking you don't even know me, no better than I know you! I'm thinking Julius was right about me, and always was. That this house and being a Larkin, that's what I really cared about. Oh, in Heaven's name, Brooks, stop bouncing that damned gold piece!"

She might have spit on him or lashed his face with a coach whip. He stepped farther back from her, and she saw he had put the bank draft in her hand.

"All right," he said. "Give that to him."

She saw on Durham, then, a look she had missed in all their courtship, a flush and shadow and pain that meant he deeply cared for her, that he could spend his life for her, make her safe. Safe? No, Lord no! She started for the door.

"Wait a minute, Jessie!" Brooks said.

She turned.

"What'll you say to him?"

"I . . . I don't know."

"You can't just go up there and . . . oh, nothing."

"I can give him his money," she said.

Durham rubbed his eyes, his forehead, the top of his head. "All right," he said. "If you don't mind none, I'll wait here, till you get back."

Jessie was out on the porch before it struck her that getting to the Rusk would be an ordeal. The street swarmed; the very glimpse of her would stir it more, and besides, she'd not gotten a bonnet, or her parasol, and it was Sunday morning.

She strode quickly down the walk and out the gate, and she set her eyes on the Rusk House signboard and held them there. Voices grumbled down and shut off as she passed, taking up again behind her, and the town's peering eyes rang a heat to her face. She got to the bank with the Rusk just ahead when someone snatched hold of her arm and stopped her with a jolt.

"Jessie, child, you oughtn't to be out!" Mrs. Lavender said.

Jessie glared at her, suddenly and finally disliking the woman, and as quickly not caring what this town thought of the widow woman in the mansion. She jerked her arm free.

"I . . . I don't care who knows I drink brandy," she said, "and no, it's not my period; and . . . and Mrs. Lavender, you look like a fat brood sow in Bonnie Shelley's dress!" She turned and ran to the hotel.

She raced through a crowd in the lobby, directly at the stairs. The clerk beat her, but barely. He spread his arms, blocking her way.

"Now, ma'am—"

"Which room is it?"

"Listen, Mrs. Rupp, that's—"

"Oh, damn you!" Jessie shouted, feeling tears at last creeping free, "Where is he?"

"Well, Number Seven."

Jessie went past him and up, into the dirty hallway, and she stopped at the door, panting, pushing recklessly at her hair, wishing for a bonnet, wiping at her eyes, wondering how to knock.

"Who's out there?" Julius said through the door.

Jessie turned the knob and went in.

If the night had seemed to smell to its roots of dead buffalo and gunpowder, Rupp had rested, nevertheless, and the peace of it had run him late, so that when Jessie appeared, it was first as though his sleep still hung on.

"Well," he said.

"Oh, Julius!"

She came deeper into the room, and he had the thought he could take her in his arms if he tried. He turned to the washstand.

"You oughtn't be here," he said.

"I . . . I've brought you something."

"That handout from your kitchen, maybe?"

"Oh, please. You . . . aren't helping me. Everyone saw me come. I . . . oh, wait a minute, I'm out of breath."

He rinsed his face in warm stale water, scrubbed it dry with his hands, and wiped his palms on the back of his pants. He began gathering his razor, the Sioux Wonder Ointment, the coins that lay beside them.

"What are you doing?" she said.

"Packin', seems like."

"Brooks said . . . they said you were leaving. That's why I came. I . . . oh, can't you hold still while I'm talking to you!"

He turned, the razor in his hand, and looked at her. She had not dressed for church, it was plain; she was mussed and red-eyed, with the trenches at her eye corners drawing deeper, as though she grimaced back tears while trying to smile.

"Can't you see?" she said softly. "I'm . . . here."

"It ain't doing your name much good."

"I don't care. I . . . I don't want you to leave, Julius. I mean, wait a while. So much has happened, I have to think. Anybody would have to think."

"All done with, now," he said.

She came a step nearer. "Oh, Julius, I was on the porch last night. It was awful. I thought you were going to shoot Brooks, and I thought he'd shoot you. I . . . oh, he told me. You have to see the doctor, about the burn."

Something of this caught his thoughts and held them—this about Jessie being on the porch.

"You better leave," he said.

"You'll wait a few days?"

"No."

"Oh, do you have to make it so hard? And don't keep looking at me like . . . like I came up here to jump in bed with you!" She shook her head, so that a strand of hair fell loose. "It's just that, well, Brooks made a draft for your money. I brought it. This is it in my hand. Your money, Julius. Oh, don't look at me like you never saw me before!"

"You ought to go, Jessie."

She came toward him, and he turned to the bed where his

things were piled up and he began tying them into a bundle.

"Julius," she said, suddenly hoarse, "you have to show it to me."

"Do what?"

"The . . . that brand, Julius. I have to see about dressing it . . . oh, listen, you don't know how I feel! You have to tell me. Did Brooks do it? I mean, he says it was Coates and Johnsy Hood; he says. . . ."

She stopped, confused and flushed, looking to Rupp like a woman he might like to know.

"You best talk to Durham," he said gently.

"Oh, damn, what's the matter with you!" she shouted. "You act like . . . oh, don't you even remember me?"

Rupp straightened, the bundle in his hand, and he reached for and got his hat.

"I don't seem to remember much, Jessie," he said. "I guess I got my gorge of rememberin'."

"Oh, no, you have to wait! A few days, till we can talk."

"Good-by, Jessie."

She turned quickly, flaring her wide skirt wider, and ran ahead of him to the door and pressed her back against it.

"I haven't given you the money!" she said.

Rupp nodded, not at her or her words, but for himself. He had hold of it now: the truth. Last night he had disbelieved Jessie was on the porch watching; yet she had been. And he knew that what he'd already stated to himself was so, that a man will know, and for sure, whenever his own wife is about.

So there it lay. He had no wife. Nor could he have had her again, ever—with money, or without it.

"It's gettin' late," he said. "Let me out."

"Oh, please stay, please—a few days. I have to think! Brooks—the money has . . . it's destroyed him! So much money, Julius, can't you see? A fortune! It wouldn't be like before!"

"Keep it, Jessie. A inheritance, from your dead husband."

"Oh, no, no! I don't want it. Can't you listen, Julius? It'd be like . . . like my house. I hate my house, Julius! I hate it!"

"I'm sorry," he said, and he put a hand on her shoulder, and, being easy, as though she might break, he put her aside. Then he glimpsed the yellow cat beneath the bed, and sitting to watch them, its tail licking slowly from side to side.

He turned back and picked up the animal. It limbered itself

at once, hanging over his hand like a fresh-killed pelt, purring, maybe returning to sleep.

"Good-by," he said, and went on out, hearing her hard breath, scenting faintly her lily-of-the-valley, regretting how she cried. Then he was in the same moment remembering her, and beginning to forget.

He stepped down to the lobby, seeing a crowd of men who drew back to watch, men who appeared to have waited up the night for fear of missing a bit of it and thus having less to relate to their wives, and he went through them to the desk and paid for his room, then put down four dollars more. "The Two Bulls, for some whisky," he said. "See they get it."

Someone whispered about the cat as Rupp walked to the door, and he didn't mind it. Without interest he speculated that sometime it might be told that Julius Rupp left the Rusk House one Sunday, carrying a dead tiger by the neck scruff. He walked on through the heat and dirty air to the alley.

Dub Stokes's gift horse was there, standing alone and dozing, and Rupp had to grin; Old Dub hadn't strained himself. It was the same old ribby coyote dun he'd sold yesterday, wearing the same saddle.

"Well, damn you," Rupp said to the horse, and he tied his bundle on behind the cantle. He walked around and lifted the right forefoot, and grunted. At least the loose shoe had been replaced, and he grinned again at the thought that when he got to Dodge, he'd take no more joking about this old bone-bag. He'd tell them, by damn, that he sat on a mighty expensive horse.

Rupp reached up and draped the cat across the saddle and swung up, careful of his soreness, and as he prodded his toe at the off stirrup he saw the girl.

She came into the alley at the back, as if she'd watched for him. She was rumpled and small and dark, still in last night's poor cheap dress and black shawl. She held her hands in front of her, and in them he saw his gun.

"Maria," he said her name, and he thought of kicking the old dun to bolt past her, but did not. He sat back and rubbed the cat as she came up to his side and lifted the long Colt. The muzzle pointed at his chest. But she wasn't aiming. She was offering.

"Keep it," he said.

"No, Señor . . . Señor Brown. It is yours."

He bent for the pistol and put it in his belt and gathered the reins.

"No," Maria said again, "you must take me also."

He stared down at her child's face, the eyes that blazed up to him. He did not move.

"Help me," she said, and she strained to hike up a foot and set it on his instep. She put a hand on the dun's rump and struggled to come up, and fell back.

"*Oye*, your hand!" she said, "Or I shall say no prayers for you!"

In the gawdy dress, the slipping shawl, she seemed, then, someways bleak and someways blessed. Slowly he put down his hand.

"Hell," he said.

She smiled, and he emptied the stirrup for her. She came climbing his arm, panting of musk and vanilla bean, and he heard the starch breaking in her red ruffles as she floundered and grunted and sputtered her way around him and sat herself sideways on the dun's craggy rump. Never, he thought, had he seen anyone mount so gracelessly, and he shrugged. She wasn't enough weight to hurt.

The old horse walked to the back end of the alley, crossed over the litter behind Crowder's buildings, cut back through the next alley to the street, and carried them on north, past Belmeade's, past the white spire of Coldiron Union Church, and Dub Stokes's and up the first rise of the red trail. And the town was out to watch them go, and afterwards, to recall it.

If it was told different ways and argued about, then there was Mrs. Ducky Ireland for the last word, for she had watched them go past her place, a few miles out, and they were fighting, she said, as a white man and Mexican girl were bounden to—only, not really fighting, but arguing as they rode, with Rupp speaking too quiet to be heard, and Maria going at it with waving hands and shrieks, fussing that if a cat meant to go to Kansas, it ought to get down and walk, being the Devil's own beast and no more. The sun stood well up and the heat had fired high, but there wasn't much of a Sunday wind, for it blew steady and not very hard, like what used to be spoken of by buffalo men as a hunter's wind, and thus there was less red dirt astir, and the day was turning out to be a notch more decent than was, in this man's country, expected and usual.

ABOUT THE AUTHOR

Al Dewlen was born in Memphis, Texas, thirty-five years ago and now makes his home in Amarillo. His background includes forty-five months in the Marine Corps, after which he settled down as a newspaperman on several Texas papers while unsuccessfully trying his hand at short stories and articles on the side. He finally quit the newspaper business, as he says, "to lash out at writing, make or bust." He took his wife and son with him to the University of Oklahoma and enrolled in the writing school there. *The Night of the Tiger* is the result and bears eloquent testimony to the wisdom of his decision. The novel is, among other things, a reflection of his deep-rooted interest in Texas, its past, and its people.